The Plantagenet Vendetta

John Paul Davis

The Plantagenet Vendetta
Second Edition

First paperback edition: © John Paul Davis 2016
Original ebook edition published: 2013
ISBN: 978-1537016474

Praise for The Templar Agenda

Can't wait for the new one . . .
Richard Doetsch, international bestselling author of *The Thieves of Heaven*

John Paul Davis clearly owns the genre of historical thrillers.
Steven Sora, author of The Lost Colony of the Templars

A well-researched, original and fascinating work – a real page-turner
Graham Phillips, international bestselling non-fiction author

Books by John Paul Davis

Fiction

The Templar Agenda
The Larmenius Inheritance
The Plantagenet Vendetta
The Cromwell Deception
The Bordeaux Connection
The Cortés Trilogy

Non-Fiction

Robin Hood: The Unknown Templar (Peter Owen Publishers)
Pity For The Guy – a Biography of Guy Fawkes (Peter Owen Publishers)
The Gothic King – a Biography of Henry III (Peter Owen Publishers)

For more information please visit www.johnpauldavisauthor.com
And
www.theunknowntemplar.com

Bloody thou art,
Bloody will be thy end
William Shakespeare, Richard III

Prologue

The Tower of London, 11 p.m., 3 September 1483

"The king is dead; long live the king."

So went the cries in the streets.

Even six months later, the prince remembered it well. Despite his father's death, it had seemed a more positive time back then. Though England remained at war, there were signs that thirty years of conflict was nearing a conclusion. A golden age lay ahead. In future they would refer to the chaos as the Wars of the Roses.

To him, it would forever be known as the cousins' war.

As memories of his father dissipated, thoughts returned to the present. The young boy looked up at the duke, his eyes wide open, his body quivering. Although the man in front of him was small in stature, his reputation was legendary. Even before the young boy's incarceration in the Tower, he had heard rumours of the duke's potential. According to hearsay, he coveted power above all things and had already murdered one monarch.

But the boy did not believe such rumours. There was kindness in the duke's eyes.

The young boy looked to his left and saw movement. A rowing boat had appeared by the water gate, barely visible beneath the light of two fiery torches. The boat was small, occupied by two adults, one of whom he recognised. He saw his mother smile at him through a mask of tears as the burly man alongside her helped his brother and cousin aboard. Fever had gripped his brother's fragile twelve-year-old body, already ravaged by tuberculosis.

It was the curse of his family.

The prince didn't need to consult a physician to know that his brother was dying.

He returned his gaze to the duke. "What happens now?"

"That is not your concern anymore," the duke replied, tears in his eyes. "For you, there will be no more war."

The young boy struggled to keep himself together. Seeing his brother that way made him want to die himself. For several months he had been his constant companion, his only playmate in the confines of the Tower. It had become his home – his one guarantee of safety from his enemies.

The duke moved closer. "I need you to be brave, for both of us. Someday you shall return. And should anything happen to my own son, it will be you, and one day your descendants, who will rule England."

The boy remained silent. On hearing the words he felt his resolve strengthen, as if the life force that had once guided his father had now entered him.

His concentration was now unbreakable.

Close to the water gate, the small boat was ready to cast off, its oars vibrating against the rowlocks as they bounced against the waves.

The duke placed his hand to the boy's face and kissed him on the forehead.

Seconds later, the boy got into the boat and silently sailed away.

Corsica, 1994

The sniper watched through the telescopic sight as the white Mercedes accelerated up the hill.

The Merc had been on the road for almost an hour. It had started the day at the usual place, a lavish but discreet villa twenty miles north of Nonza with fine views west across the Med. He knew from the records that the property belonged to the family, and had done for over a decade.

The car had stayed there till 5 p.m. An hour later he followed it to the car park of a luxury resort about thirty-five miles away. The casino was one of their favourite hotspots; he guessed more so for the wife than the husband. Either way, he didn't seem to object.

Even if he lost, he had plenty more where that came from.

The driver of the Mercedes changed gear as he increased speed. He savoured the moment as the 450-BHP engine provided the familiar rush. The roar was as good as the feeling. To him it was almost sexual; to his wife, even more so.

He looked over at her and smiled, taking delight in every aspect of her appearance. The blonde hair, the white complexion slightly bronzed from eleven days on the island, the fine jewellery . . .

She was as beautiful as she had always been.

The perfect white rose.

He accepted the cigarette that she placed delicately between his lips and leaned forward for the light. She lit his before her own and exhaled gracefully, the smoke leaving the car through the open sunroof.

As the driver removed the cigarette from his mouth to take a breath of fresh air, he became aware of the passing mountainside. It was slowly getting dark. The white rock reflected the fading sun, creating a unique yellowy-orange colour as the light hit it. The road was lonely, a famous part of the mountain pass used for the local rally circuit. Its use by others was not uncommon.

But tonight they had it all to themselves.

The sniper watched as the Merc slowed its pace to negotiate a series of minor turns before accelerating again as the road straightened. He knew from experience that the D80 was arguably the best road on the north-west side of the island, both the least populated and most unspoiled.

A driver's paradise, some had dubbed it.

The scenery was stunning. In the daytime, rugged mountains, nestled in between mile upon mile of natural woodland, were visible in every direction, masking the countryside in an intense green shade. At dusk, the landscape took on a different type of beauty. Though the sun was yet to set completely, the moon was out in full, its hazy gaze affected only by the relative earliness of the hour. As the mountains began to merge with the skyline, small lights sparkled in the distance, lighting up the countryside like small fireflies. As the ocean disappeared, the sounds became louder. In between the squawks of the nocturnal bird life, the soft swaying of the sea against the jagged coastline offered a calm, soothing effect.

Almost hypnotic.

The sniper followed the car through the crosshairs of the telescopic lens. Even from a distance, it wasn't the hardest of jobs. The high-powered lens included infrared, perfect for surveillance of this sort.

Even though he had left the forces, working for his present employers, he wasn't deprived of the best technology.

He had set up his base on a corner of D433, some five hundred metres above D80. The position held great strategic importance. Aside from its loneliness, he knew from experience that a large hairpin preceded the next stretch, forcing the driver to slow down. It was also there where D80 came nearest to the sea.

Exposed to the elements.

The driver of the Merc looked up to his right, suddenly confused. He saw light, not electronic, but something smaller. Instinct told him it was a reflection, light on glass.

His wife picked up on his change in mood. "Richard, what is it?"

The fair-haired husband didn't respond. He had no proof that anything was wrong, but his intuition was bothering him.

The events of three weeks earlier were still fresh in his memory.

His wife was becoming concerned. "Richard?"

"It's nothing."

The sniper detected a change of pace from the Merc, surprising given that a turn was imminent. The driver braked late as he took the bend, much too fast. The area to his right was forested, whereas the landscape to his left was more open. A large railing flanked the road, the only obstacle between the road and oblivion.

The sniper steadied the long-distance rifle and followed the Merc in the crosshairs. No sooner had the driver taken the bend than he picked up further speed.

The sniper fired.

The driver felt a bump on the right side of the car, then another. He heard a noise, a dull clattering sound. He saw sparks lighting up the car momentarily before disappearing as soon as they had arrived. He looked in the rear-view mirror and saw nothing.

Whatever had happened had come from above.

"Richard . . ."

He floored the accelerator, despite another upcoming bend. As he did, he felt a further thump, this time on the bonnet.

Then he heard glass breaking.

The sniper cursed under his breath. His inaccuracy had forced him to reload, losing him valuable seconds. He quickly loaded four new bullets into his rifle and sought to compose himself.

He took a breath, in then out. He aimed just forward of the front right tyre, his mind doing the maths to allow for speed. He estimated 110mph, far too much for the road.

He squeezed the trigger.

Five hundred metres below, the Merc started to zigzag. There was movement beneath the car, outside the driver's control. A tyre had gone, perhaps two. As the car veered left, it became locked on a course for the cliff edge.

Going over was unavoidable.

1

Westminster, Present day

From high above, the blond man watched the procession as it made its way through the streets.

Everything about the occasion was gloomy. In the distance, heavy rain battered down from Greenwich to Tower Hamlets, its water causing ripples as it landed on the Thames. The sky above the city, clear blue as the sun rose that morning, was now covered by heavy cloud, threatening anything from a prolonged shower to thunder. If the forecast was correct, the thunder was still to come.

The wind had also picked up, at times practically a gale. Being situated atop a large building, he was susceptible to the full effects. The flagpole behind him moved from side to side, the flag blowing wildly before becoming wrapped around the pole.

Like every flag in the city, today it flew at half-mast.

On the streets below, the event was in keeping with the weather. Though the rain was imminent, thousands upon thousands lined the streets, watching the hearse as it made its way towards Westminster Abbey.

Even from a distance he could sense the silence. Aided by his high-powered binoculars, he could make out the faces of the bystanders. Not a single mouth was open. He liked the way the passers-by seemed to lower their heads as the coffin approached. Some threw flowers into the road, landing before the horse, softening the sound of its feet.

For the first time he wished he was nearer. Through his binoculars, he could see but not hear crying from among the bystanders, some cuddling up to the person next to them. He wanted to witness the sounds, hear every personal remark.

He turned his observation to the man walking behind the hearse, the deceased's eldest son. As usual for such an occasion, he was dressed in military regalia. The watcher at the top of the tower was quietly impressed. The man chose to walk, exposed to the elements, as opposed to being driven in the comfort of the Roller, like the rest of his family. Like most among the procession, his expression was sombre, but more natural than the rest. Had the circumstances been different, he might have found it possible to find sympathy for the man.

The blond man changed his position as the procession reached the abbey. For the first time the silence gave way to applause, evolving into loud cheers as the body of the late king approached.

Soon the deceased would enter the abbey, his coffin resting temporarily at the side of the main altar. Soon he would be laid to rest in the grand company of the kings and queens of old.

And a new king would emerge.

2

The North York Moors, 10 a.m., one week later

The sandy-haired woman pulled up about midway along the high street and stopped to take in the sights.

Visually, the village of Wootton-on-the-Moor was just like many others in the North York Moors. Like most, it was located in the middle of nowhere and offered breathtaking views of the rugged landscape. In the height of the tourist season, the medieval high street was a famed haven for ramblers, tourists and nature lovers enjoying a summer's day frequenting its quaint boutiques, teashops, and art galleries or a walk or horse ride on the designated pathways and bridleways.

But these days the village had another claim to fame. A year earlier it rose from isolation to infamy in the blink of an eye. The woman remembered it well – it was impossible not to. A young girl went missing.

A year later her whereabouts remained a mystery.

Jennifer Farrelly had been less than two years out of university when the story broke, though back then she worked elsewhere. Like most researchers in the TV productions industry, she was technically self-employed and in less than three years had already worked on everything from soaps to documentaries, BBC to Discovery and news broadcasts to shower commercials. Officially this was her first job for the current company, but it felt more or less the same. She knew the people, and more importantly she knew what to expect. It was the same for every researcher in the industry.

Do everything for as little pay possible.

She made her way across the deserted high street and headed along a narrow side alley up the hill, in between two shops. The alleyway led her to a small forecourt, surrounded by over twenty houses, all bathed in sunlight.

One in particular caught her eye: a small Elizabethan-style house painted in the usual black and white and leaning forward slightly above the ground, one of seven in a terrace.

She recognised it immediately. Even though this was her first visit to the village, the house was as famous as the story. Its exposure to the news channels was almost unrivalled.

She crossed the forecourt and stopped in front of the house. A small sign was located on the side of the door, displaying the number 4 and the name of the house, Swallow's Nest.

She rang the bell, and seconds later a woman answered, blonde, green-eyed, probably in her early forties. Again, she recognised her – though she didn't know her personally.

"Mrs Harrison?"

The woman's expression was unwelcoming. "Come in."

The mother of Debra Harrison was an unwilling celebrity: a self-opinionated fireball who loved too much and fought too quickly. She had developed a reputation as being a loose talker . . .

Some claimed loose other things as well.

Today they were alone. Mr Harrison was at work overseas, while little Marcus and David were both at school. It was obvious to Jennifer that the last thing Mrs Harrison wanted was to expose the boys to a second media circus.

At least being mid-July, school still had a week to run.

Gillian Harrison smoked like a chimney; that much was obvious from the smell alone. Other things were also giveaways. The numerous ashtrays, marks on the furniture, the yellowing of her teeth . . .

But mostly it was the way she breathed. The woman had a permanent cough; Jennifer had become aware of that from watching the news footage a year earlier. Barely a minute passed before she needed to clear her throat.

Jennifer surveyed the living room as she followed Mrs Harrison inside. The room suited the persona of a maverick. The large wooden beams were heavily decorated, their ornamentation ranging from photographs to gimmicks to souvenirs from far and wide, mostly Asia. A large mirror covered much of the main wall above the fireplace, a traditional feature that was now just for show. Several crosses, crucifixes and other small religious artefacts adorned the mantelpiece, while others were scattered around the room, apparently at random. Several photographs accompanied them, all of the same person:

Her daughter.

At the woman's invitation, Jennifer sat down in a large leather armchair. The first thing she noticed was how quiet it was, the uneasy silence disturbed by the regular ticking of a pre-war brown-cased clock with Roman numerals, located above the mantelpiece.

She crossed her legs, her posture replicating that of her hostess.

"I appreciate you taking the time to speak to me, Mrs Harrison. My producer is something of a stickler when it comes to preparation."

Lighting up a cigarette, Harrison shrugged, but otherwise did not respond. She glanced at the researcher, her eyes saying 'get to the point'.

"Tell me about the last year."

Gillian Harrison took a long drag on her cigarette and exhaled. "And where exactly would you like me to start?"

Jennifer placed her hand to her hair, brushing it behind her ear. "How about everything that has happened since 18 July?"

The woman looked back penetratingly. "You mean the day the cameras left Wootton?"

She meant the day of the memorial. Nevertheless, she nodded.

Gillian blew smoke. "I take it you weren't part of the original circus when my daughter went missing."

"No. Back then I worked for a different company. I only know what I saw on the news and read in the papers."

Harrison puffed again on her cigarette, clearly in a gesture of disgust. It was evident from her time on air a year earlier that the woman hated the media.

"They stayed for a week, eight days if you include the packing up. Sky had been the first to arrive, then BBC." She flicked ash into the nearest ashtray. "They all left the day of the service."

Jennifer noticed emphasis on the word 'service'. "I appreciate that there has been a lot of conjecture in the media over the last year. Can I confirm that your daughter has never been found?"

Gillian made prolonged eye contact for the first time, her eyes striking in the light. "At least not by me."

The answer made Jennifer feel uncomfortable, though appreciated in the same situation she might have reacted in a similar way.

"How have the police fared in their investigations?"

"Since the 18th?"

Jennifer nodded.

Gillian paused before answering. "They continued to search for three days after the service, apparently it continued as far away as Berwick and Harrogate." She hesitated slightly. "On the 23rd they told my husband they'd ended it . . . I was out at the time."

Jennifer watched her. "But you continue to search?"

The woman stared, now more fiercely. "I continue to believe."

For several seconds nothing was said.

The ringing of Jennifer's mobile phone interrupted the silence. She removed it from her handbag and looked at the screen.

She cursed herself for not turning it off.

"Aren't you going to get that?"

"It's my producer." Jennifer frowned apologetically. She answered. "David, hi, I'm just at the . . ."

"Slight change of plan, Jen." The voice replied. "The team have had a bit of a delay. The shooting will have to wait until Friday."

Four days.

Jen was horrified. She looked up at Gillian Harrison, trying to conceal her concerns. The woman seemed to possess a talent for looking at everything and anything at once.

Jen lowered her voice. "That's ridiculous; I'm speaking with Mrs Harrison right now."

"Sorry, Jen, can't be helped. Two of the crew are still in Iceland."

She tried to control her frustration. "And just what am I supposed to do until Friday?" she asked, her tone a whisper.

"I don't know, try research, book yourself a hotel. Use your initiative."

"David . . ."

"I'll be in touch again later today. Cheerio."

Moving the phone from her ear, she looked at the screen; the display had returned to normal. She locked the keypad and looked up at an empty chair.

Harrison had moved into the kitchen.

Jen left her seat and ventured through the open doorway, espying a traditional period layout with white walls, a large fridge-freezer and lots of cutlery in the dish rack. As Jen entered, the sound of washing up got louder, ironic since the woman had offered no tea or coffee.

"That was the producer; I'm afraid the team have had a delay."

Harrison didn't acknowledge her. Instead, her blank expression focused on the window that overlooked the garden.

"See that," she said, pointing somewhere towards the shed. "That used to be her swing."

Jen looked outside, noticing the unoccupied swing set. It could have belonged to any child in the world, including her own niece. The fact that it belonged to the missing girl affected her more than she would have expected.

"Mrs Harrison, I can come back in a few days. There's very little we can do without the production team."

The woman didn't respond, which made Jen nervous.

"Mrs Harrison . . ."

The woman turned, grabbing Jen's wrist. For several seconds she just looked into her eyes, her stare blank.

"Oh," Harrison said, her tone noticeably weak. "I'm sorry . . . for a second I just . . ."

The woman looked away, placing her hand to her face.

The atmosphere was now horrendous.

"Mrs Harrison, I'll see myself out."

Jen hurried out of the kitchen and stopped halfway across the lounge.

"Are there any hotels in Wootton?"

A delay preceded the reply. "Try the White Boar."

3

The disappearance of Debra Harrison had occurred on the evening of 10 July in the previous year, sometime between eight and ten. She had last been seen walking to a friend's house: a girl named Stephanie Stanley, who lived in a 16th-century period mansion on the east side of the village. Both girls were sixteen and had recently finished their GCSEs. According to the news, Debra had only finished her last exam three days earlier.

Sad, Jen thought.

She never even had a chance to enjoy the freedom.

According to the locals who had been interviewed at the time, Debra Harrison was known to everyone in the village, and evidently well liked. Her parents had been raised within three hundred metres of one another, and the family were seen as part of the furniture.

No one in the family had any known enemies.

Everyone in the village knew the killer, assuming she was actually dead. According to hearsay, the culprit was a boy of eighteen named Luke Rankin, an awkward boy, possibly autistic.

The lad was dead; that much was confirmed. He'd been found hanged from a nearby bridge within a week of the disappearance.

It didn't take long for people to start putting two and two together and make something that resembled an equal number.

Debra was the eldest of the three Harrison kids. She was tall, brunette and, based on the photographs, developed for her age. Her aspiration had been to be a journalist, and her GCSE grades reflected her talent. Her strongest grades, four A*s, were in English and the humanities, and even her weakest grades in science and maths were still B.

The girl was bright; that much seemed evident from the photos. There was not a person in the developed world that hadn't seen at least one. There wasn't a broadsheet, tabloid or news channel that hadn't shown it.

The face confirmed the facts. The brightness of the eyes, the genuine smile, the playful persona . . .

Yes, Jen thought.

The poor girl was a typical target for rape.

Jen walked back along the high street and returned to her Kia Picanto. According to the clock on the dashboard, it was now 10:20 a.m.

It seemed incredible the interview had lasted only ten minutes.

She booted up the Satnav and typed in the name of the hotel. The White Boar, she thought to herself.

Sounded quaint.

The Satnav confirmed the hotel was only 0.4 of a mile away, convenient, all things considered. She guessed it would be too early to check in, but she figured it was worth a try.

She started the car and drove slowly along the high street, taking in the sights as she passed. A small gathering of tourists frequented the ice cream shop on the corner of one of the side streets, while others checked out the boutiques. Outside the newsagent's, a group of young adults, perhaps hikers, sat drinking at an outside bench, clearly enjoying the sunshine.

The village had apparently been something of a minor tourist hotspot, at least prior to the last year. Tudor, Jacobean and Georgian architecture abounded, the black and white exteriors reflecting the warm sun as it blazed down. Most of the shops were small, privately owned and open – impressive considering the financial climate. She liked the way the street was devoid of household names and big chains.

Visually, she guessed not much had changed in a hundred years.

She followed the Satnav's instructions and turned left along a side street and immediately crossed over a bridge.

The setting left her speechless. The river flowed at speed, passing rocks and pebbles as it accelerated downstream. A large medieval church was located just up the road, surrounded by a well-maintained churchyard. Further afield, mile upon mile of rolling hillside soaked up the sunlight, the grass a radiant shade of untainted green.

She smiled to herself.

The North York Moors at their finest.

The White Boar Inn was located on the left side of the road, almost immediately after the bridge. Like most buildings in the village, it was black and white, and obviously historic. The inn's logo hung from a freestanding post: a white pig with a slightly comical expression and dating the inn's establishment to 1471.

Jen locked her car and entered the inn through the main doors, carrying her suitcase. She was used to staying in a campervan from her time at Discovery, so potentially this was a step up.

The inn was quiet, if not deserted. She explored the area near the entrance before heading along the nearest corridor. Somewhere nearby she heard the sound of quiet chatter and furniture being moved.

She continued along the corridor, taking in her surroundings. The interior was in keeping with the outside. The walls were white, decorated by artwork, prints and memorabilia, most of which dated from the previous two centuries. As usual in such places, the main theme was history.

Which as a history graduate, she liked.

The bar was located at the end of the corridor: a two-sectioned layout with lots of ale on tap, plenty of wooden tables and chairs, and an original fireplace. A list of specials was written on the chalkboard, including everything from scampi to pies, priced at anything between £4.25 and £13.99.

The bar gave off a relaxed, airy feel and was deserted apart from a large burly man with a strong forehead and lots of dark hair. She placed him in his late forties.

The man smiled. "Ey up."

Jen smiled back. "Hi, are you the manager?"

"You're not the 'ealth inspector, are you?"

She shook her head, confused.

"In that case, yes, I'm the manager."

Jen laughed, annoyed with herself for not getting the joke.

"Harvey Mitchell. Owner and proprietor. How can I help?"

"Well, I was hoping you might have a room. I appreciate it's early."

"Not at all, I've got a nice room overlooking the river, or another overlooking the church."

The river appealed, but her love of history swayed her. "The church sounds perfect. I just love old churches."

"In that case I'll see right to it. Tara."

Almost immediately a young woman came in, aged somewhere around the mid-twenties. She was brunette and very attractive, despite wearing little make-up. She smiled warmly at Jen.

"Take Miss . . ." He turned. "Sorry, didn't catch your name."

"It's Jennifer, Jennifer Farrelly."

"How do, Miss Farrelly." The man offered his hand. "Tara'll show you to the blue room."

"Follow me, Miss Farrelly."

Tara Simpson was as pleasant as she appeared, and naturally chatty. Unlike the Harrison mother, it was obvious to Jen that Tara and Harvey had not been traumatised by the events of a year ago. If the press were to be believed, life in Wootton would never be the same again.

In reality, Jen guessed not much had changed.

She followed the barmaid up two flights of stairs and along the corridor to the penultimate room on the right. Tara opened the door with the key, and showed Jen inside.

The room surpassed her expectations. The walls were an appealing mixture of white plaster and wood, illuminated by natural light that entered through two large windows. Most of the furniture was antique, including the bed, a four-poster but without the accompanying railing and curtains.

Jen pressed her hand down on the mattress as she passed. "It's perfect."

Tara smiled. "I'm glad you like it. If you need anything, just give us a bell."

"Thank you."

Tara closed the door behind her, leaving Jen to examine her surroundings in peace.

The room suited her mood and personality. As in the bar area, a varied selection of local and historical pictures and artwork was displayed on the walls. A 19th-century print of what appeared to be religious ruins, either an abbey or a priory, included a signature, while a similar scene depicted a castle, not quite a motte-and-bailey, but not full-scale Norman either.

The third picture of note was a large manor house, apparently named Wootton Court, evidently a house of some prestige.

She walked across the room, stopping on reaching the windows. The manager was as good as his word. The view was stunning. A large house was situated about two hundred metres away from the church, separated from the churchyard by a red wall.

She guessed it was the presbytery or rectory.

She looked across the churchyard, her attention briefly on the graves. She assumed the church was the same one where Debra Harrison's memorial service had taken place. She'd heard a rumour that something had been placed there to honour her.

Even if Debra Harrison wasn't buried there, she guessed it was the perfect place to start her investigation.

4

Royal College of Physicians, London

The results had come in earlier that morning. Though he was still to check them himself, he knew from his colleague that the outcome was not what they had hoped for.

Unexpected was the term he had used.

The experienced physician double-clicked on the mouse and read the email for the first time. The content was brief; the body of the text itself told him nothing new. Attached was a large pdf, which he scanned quickly.

His colleague was not lying.

The result was unexpected.

The Royal College of Physicians was one of the oldest societies of its type. Originally named the College of Physicians, it was granted a royal charter by Henry VIII in 1518, affirmed by an Act of Parliament five years later.

Its purpose was straightforward: it had been established to grant licences to qualified professionals.

And to punish those who practiced unqualified.

Ten minutes later the physician opened the door of a large room, airy and ornate, one of the finest at the institution. Four large windows overlooked Regent's Park, while the other walls were decorated with original works of art, mostly concerned with the society's past. Even those that weren't were of the same era.

In the centre of the room, four people, all men of prestige, were seated around a large antique table.

The physician entered quickly. "Sorry to have kept you, gentlemen."

The first man rose to his feet. He wore a dark suit, his expression befitting the occasion.

He was the Home Secretary.

"Time is of the essence, Dr Grant," he said, pointing to his watch. "I'm sure I don't need to remind you."

The man next to him was less impressed with the Home Secretary than the physician. He was in his late fifties and had brown hair with hints of grey and a handsome face.

"Come now," he said, looking reassuringly at the physician. "We all appreciate your time, Maurice. Particularly at such short notice."

The physician smiled, almost a frown. He knew the man well, in his position it was impossible not to.

The man he addressed was the Duke of York.

And he, the Royal Physician.

The physician carried a printout of the pdf attachment. "I have the results."

The final two present were yet to speak, but their concern was evident from their expressions. One was noticeably younger than the other three. He was thirty-one, lean, with a full head of wavy dark hair that on this occasion appeared slightly rugged.

The second man was of similar features, but thirty years older and dressed far more smartly. A clean-shaven face revealed strong cheekbones and an uncanny resemblance to the young man next to him. He wore a kind expression, but his eyes were piercing and alert. His once brown hair, slowly thinning and partially grey, was neatly combed to a side parting.

His demeanour was royal in every sense of the word.

He was the King of England, Stephen II. Alongside him was another Stephen. Prince Stephen Winchester, now Duke of Cornwall.

Eldest son of the king and future Prince of Wales.

The King leaned forward. "Well, Maurice, let's hear the worst."

The physician removed his glasses from his top pocket and immediately began reading the printout. "In accordance with Your Majesty's orders, the post-mortem was carried out in two stages–"

"Get on with it, man," the Home Secretary said.

"Don't interrupt, Heston," said York.

The Duke of Cornwall smiled at the physician. "What killed him, Dr Grant?"

The physician removed his glasses. "It is still too early to ascertain the exact cause of death, Your Grace," he replied, this time more tentatively. "However, the autopsy did confirm one thing. The King's death was not of natural causes."

A heavy silence descended on the room, almost as if a gun had gone off, leaving all present partially numbed.

The Duke of York was the first to break the silence. "You believe it was poison?"

"At this stage, Your Grace, it would be impossible to say with any certainty–"

"You mean you don't know?" Heston interrupted.

"Shhh." The King raised his hand, ordering calm. He leaned forward, his eyes fixed on Grant. "Go on, Maurice."

"The tests we have conducted so far confirm only what areas of the body were affected. The King's death," the physician felt breathless on saying those words, "was a direct result of failure of the heart and lungs. The initial misdiagnosis of heart failure was consistent at least with the reported symptoms."

All four waited in anticipation.

"Well–" Heston began.

"Minister, please, I'm sick of the sound of your voice," York shouted.

Heston breathed out deeply and frowned. He swept his grey hair to one side and shuffled for comfort in his seat.

York looked up at Grant. "Well now, old friend, what's the official verdict?"

The physician resumed, "The results confirm beyond any reasonable doubt that His Majesty died due to failure of the heart and lungs. The damage to the lung tissues is itself confirmation of contamination." He took a deep breath. "It is the view of all who have studied the results that the King died of an allergic reaction."

Silence followed. Again York was the first to respond. "You are quite sure?"

"It is the professional opinion of my colleagues–"

"And what do you think?" asked the son of the king.

The physician paused before answering. "Sadly, I feel sure that their assessments and conclusions are correct."

The three royals looked at one another.

"Who else has seen this?" the son of the king asked.

"Only us present and two of my colleagues."

The King nodded. "Make sure it stays that way."

The black limousine pulled up outside the rear entrance of the college. Unlike the famous Rolls, this one was more discreet and unlikely to be recognised. The glass was cleverly tinted, allowing no observation from the outside.

Seconds later the limousine set off, heading towards the palace.

*

In the second car, the Home Secretary opened the rear left door and got inside. Immediately the driver set off, heading towards Westminster.

A man with light blond hair was sitting in the seat next to him. "Everything all right, Minister?"

Heston was noticeably rattled. "Get me the Director General of MI5, will you? Find out everything you can about the bugger arrested in Clapham."

5

The original Church of St Michael's was once the oldest building in Wootton. According to its official history, it was built on the site of a much older church around 1060 and developed into a Dominican priory. Jen had learned from a free leaflet in the foyer of the inn that the priory had been destroyed in 1490, apparently on the orders of Henry Tudor.

That had surprised her. She knew only too well that most of the religious houses in England and Wales had fallen victim to Henry VIII's Dissolution of the Monasteries some forty years later. Assuming the leaflet was correct, the church had been rebuilt in the early 1500s but survived further upheaval following its purchase by a local knight in 1538.

The church was Catholic, which was also a surprise. Jen knew enough about the history of England that most from that age became Protestant. She knew Harrison was Catholic from her research, but the crosses in the family house were an equal giveaway.

One question remained.

Where was the girl?

Jen left the inn through the main door and walked along the road to the churchyard. The lichgate was shut but unlocked, covered by the usual sloping roof that joined at its centre. A large notice had been put up on the inside right wall, listing Mass times and confirming visitors were welcome.

Jen continued across the grass, pausing to investigate the tombstones. Three years studying history at Nottingham University had taught her the basics of reading old lettering, but these were nearly impossible. The stones were evidently not of this century.

Obviously of no connection to Debra Harrison.

In truth, Jen didn't have a clue what she was looking for. She had learned from her notes, more or less confirmed by Debra Harrison's mother, that a service had been held in her 'memory' in a nearby

Catholic church. According to some reports, a coffin had been buried, but its purpose was merely symbolic. Another had claimed there had been no burial, which she guessed was more likely, as officially the service was not a funeral. As a rule, hearsay was something to be avoided. She knew from her research that rumours circulating the Internet were numerous, including that a body had been found and buried in secret, whereas alleged 'sightings' of the poor girl had been documented from France to Fiji.

She sighed to herself.

No wonder the mother was so depressed.

Jen walked from grave to grave, noticing nothing of relevance to Debra Harrison. The names had a pattern, Catesby, Ratcliffe, Lovell, Stanley and a few others appearing consistently. She was aware that the village was small and close knit, so evidence of similar names was hardly a shock. The absence of modern graves was more noticeable.

As best she could tell, no one had been buried there for over twenty years.

"Are you lost?"

She looked up, her eyes on the lichgate. A man had appeared, walking towards her through the graves, his accent unquestionably northern. He had a neatly cut beard, dark hair, impressive for his age – she guessed sixty – and a strong physique. She assumed from his appearance, he was probably a farmer.

Accompanying him was a large Alsatian.

She knelt down to stroke it.

The man laughed. "I'm guessing you're not from around here."

Jen smiled awkwardly.

"Thought as much; we don't get too many visitors round these parts anymore."

She assumed that was a reference to the disappearance. "I was looking for the grave of the Harrison girl."

The man disguised his surprise. "You knew Debra?"

"No," she replied, rising to her feet. "I was told she might be buried around here."

The man delayed his response, his eyes never leaving her. "There was no burial as far as I'm aware."

"Mrs Harrison said there'd been a service."

"You know Gillian?"

Jen nodded.

The man changed his tune. "There's a small memorial inside the church by the choir. She didn't want to leave a grave. She still harbours hope her daughter will return."

Another nod. "Thank you, Mr . . ."

"Catesby."

She shook his hand. "I'm guessing these are your ancestors."

He laughed quietly. "Yes, we do go back a long way, my lot. Many of my forebears used to be friars over there." He pointed over the wall towards the presbytery.

"Wow."

"If you ever have any questions about Wootton . . ."

"Thank you, Mr Catesby."

The man began to walk away and stopped. "I didn't catch your name."

She paused before answering. "Jennifer."

"Nice to meet you, Jennifer."

Jen watched as Catesby made his way through the graveyard and along a narrow footpath, heading away from the high street. There were houses in that direction, evidently large, but their exteriors were hidden by dense woodland.

She'd heard a rumour there was significant wealth in the village.

She examined the church for the first time. The grey stone appearance was like any other church in England, but she could tell from the exterior it was bigger than most. She recognised the architecture as Perpendicular Gothic, which made sense given what she'd read in the leaflet. Flying buttresses supported the church on every side, most prominent around the nave. There was a large clock on the bell tower, a more recent addition.

The church was open. She pulled the door to as she entered and took in the view before her. Her personal tutor at Nottingham had once told her the first thing one must do on entering a church or cathedral is to look up.

She followed his advice and was immediately inspired. Two lines of circular pillars, with numerous arches, led up to a vaulted ceiling, its appearance reminiscent of a cathedral. There were stained-glass windows in the usual places, the most impressive of which were found at either end, all depicting scenes from the New Testament. Over thirty pews were spaced equally on either side of the main aisle that continued all the way to the altar.

Less surprising, the number of visitors.

Her.

Catesby mentioned that a memorial was located in the choir area. Technically, there were two choir areas: one at the top of the church, up a narrow wooden staircase at the back; the other, the original choir, situated in front of the main altar.

Jen guessed he meant the latter.

She walked along the side aisle, doing her best to minimise the constant echo as her high heels made contact with the floor. As expected, several plaques of various descriptions marked the walls, mostly listing the names of soldiers lost in war. Accompanying them were references to former residents of the village, some of whom had been interred below the floor.

Again, she recognised names: Catesby and Ratcliffe being the most prevalent. Less than an hour in Wootton and she could already tell what families had been most prominent in the village's history.

She stopped on reaching the altar and genuflected tentatively, suddenly feeling guilty she had not been to Mass since leaving home. She moved slowly towards the choir area on the right side and began reading the various wall markings.

The plaques were all in remembrance of something or someone, but none were obviously relevant to Debra Harrison.

She heard a door opening nearby. Turning, she saw a woman appear from the Lady chapel.

The woman smiled as she passed. "Sorry, luvvy, didn't mean to disturb you."

The woman was a redhead, probably late forties, and had a kind smile that suited her face. Jen noticed she was wearing an apron, partially covering a slightly overweight stomach.

"You need any help?"

Jen shook her head and smiled. "I'm just passing," she said, returning her gaze to the wall markings. She continued her search for the stone, only now more circumspect. After examining everything on the right side of the altar, she moved on to the left.

The woman made it as far as the first pew, her hands full with polish and a cloth. "I've never seen you in the village before, luvvy. You just passing through?"

Jen smiled and nodded.

The woman delayed making a start on her cleaning, choosing instead to pay closer attention to the newcomer. She watched as Jen began to read the nearest selection of wall plaques.

"I think you'll find what you're looking for over there."

Jen looked towards the pews and saw the woman pointing to the left side of the choir. She hesitated before walking slowly in that direction. There was another window behind the lectern, this one depicting one of the archangels surrounded by a heavenly glow.

The woman approached, stopping beside Jen. There was a stone lying atop a wooden stand and below a white tablecloth. The stone was white: chalk or perhaps limestone.

"She didn't want anything too elaborate," the woman said, "at least not while they continued the search."

Jen looked at the stone. It was small, no more than three inches by six. Indeed, there was no name, nor anything that resembled concrete information.

Instead, there was only a quote.

While he was still speaking, there came from the ruler's house some who said, "Your daughter is dead. Why trouble the Teacher any further?" But overhearing what they said, Jesus said to the ruler of the Synagogue, "Do not fear, only believe."

"It's a verse from the Gospel of Mark," the stranger said. "I'll never forget the day she disappeared. I mean, you don't, do you? After all, it isn't every day you lose one of your own."

Jen placed her hand to her heart. "I'm so sorry. Were you related?"

"Distantly," she replied. "But some things matter more than blood; ask anyone and they'll tell you. Everyone belongs to everyone – that's always been the way in Wootton."

Jen nodded, her eyes fixed on the stone. She read the passage twice, silently troubled by the clinical wording.

"Did you know her?"

Jen shook her head. "No."

The woman continued to watch her, now with greater scrutiny. "You see her on the telly?"

Jen chose her words carefully. "I'm here to research a documentary. A year ago, the company I work for filmed a documentary on the disappearance. The family hoped it might renew interest."

The woman nodded. She removed a tissue from her pocket and blew her nose.

"If only all companies were so considerate."

Jen didn't miss the irony.

"They never did find her," the woman resumed. "They continued to search, at least for a while. After that . . ." She ended the sentence with a shrug.

Jen nodded, still distracted by the wording on the stone. There was no closure about the marking, nor any recognition. Had the woman not pointed it out, she would never have guessed it was what she was looking for.

"Do you remember when you last saw her?" Jen asked.

"The day before. She was friends with my daughter, Anthea Brown: she works with me in the hairdresser's. I'm Martha."

Jen accepted the woman's outstretched hand. "Jen."

The woman smiled.

"I don't suppose you'd know who was the last person to see her?"

"That'd be Stephanie."

"Stanley?"

Martha nodded. "Aye. They were all friends; all had been at school together."

An idea was forming in Jen's mind. "Would your daughter speak to me about her?"

"Aye. You come pay us a visit; we'll be in the hairdresser's."

Jen smiled. "How about Stephanie?"

The woman became more evasive. "Nay, you best leave that poor soul alone. She hasn't been the same since."

Jen detected extra seriousness in the last sentence – not quite a warning but close enough. According to reports, Stephanie Stanley took the news of her best friend's disappearance badly, choosing to shun the cameras when they arrived. Jen had learned from her colleagues the girl had declined the opportunity to be interviewed.

The woman smiled. "Well, I best be continuing with this; we don't want Father Martin to think I've been slacking."

Jen watched as Martha Brown headed towards the rear of the church. As she disappeared from sight, Jen heard the sound of a door opening and closing.

Now alone, her mind returned to the matter at hand. She examined the stone a final time before taking in more of the church itself. Through the nearby archway, a small Lady chapel was richly decorated in the usual style and included a large altar at the far end. She poked her head inside before heading towards the nearest closed door.

Jen stopped, surprised. Instead of an exit, the door led to what remained of the cloisters, part of which was surprisingly intact and abundant in glass.

26

The stonework was impressive. Countless ceiling bosses occupied the gaps between the windows, their sightless eyes staring down from above. The windows, though clearly more modern, were all intact and complete with the original carvings in their stone surrounds. While Jen understood the remainder of the former priory buildings had been dismantled centuries earlier, the cloisters were complete along two sides, and continued all the way to the wall that surrounded the modern-day presbytery.

She looked at the windows. Unlike the images of the New Testament inside the church, these depicted nobility from 1100–1300s. Again, she recognised names. The Catesby, Lovell and Ratcliffe families all featured prominently, only now there were faces and bodies accompanying the names.

She turned the corner to her left, navigating the final part of the cloisters. This section had further windows, these depicting members of the Royal Family from the Middle Ages. Starting with William the Conqueror, the chronology of kings continued to Edward III and Richard II. Following on from Richard II, she recognised Edward the Black Prince, father of Richard II, and John of Gaunt, uncle of that king.

Had she not studied history, the scene that followed might have baffled her, but she immediately understood the significance. The House of Lancaster had no mention. She smiled to herself, not missing the irony of being in Yorkshire. The next selection depicted Edward IV, crowned, glowing, magnificent, sitting in his coronation chair. Unlike the typical history book, the window made no mention of his briefly forced abdication for the return of Henry VI.

Next on was Edward V, one of the Princes in the Tower. Like his father, the boy was sitting in splendour, a crown atop his head. That surprised her; she knew the 'Prince in the Tower' had never been crowned, despite being later recognised as king.

She heard footsteps to her left, followed by a voice.

"Can I be of any assistance?"

A man had appeared at the top of a staircase that led somewhere beneath the church. He was well built, perhaps over six feet in height, and dressed in black. The dog collar confirmed the man's occupation.

"I was just admiring the windows."

"Ah, yes," the priest said. "The work of my great-great-uncle, no less."

"Wow," Jen said, not knowing what else to say. She looked again at the images on the windows, attempting to make sense of them. Although the style was typical of the cloisters of an average cathedral or abbey, the subject matter was unique.

"You must be the priest."

The man smiled. "I'm Father Martin Fisher, priest of the parish."

"Jen."

He smiled warmly at her. "I'm pleased to meet you, Jen. I take it just a flying visit."

She hesitated and revealed her purpose.

"What a fascinating career," the priest replied.

She smiled. "Thanks. I was thinking just now how great it would be to do some filming here. The memorial stone is obviously relevant . . . who would I need to ask for permission?"

"Me." He smiled.

She laughed awkwardly. "Would it be possible, perhaps Friday?"

"I would have no objection whatsoever."

She smiled again, this time less forced. Almost immediately they heard a voice from nearby, evidently the woman Jen had just been talking to.

"Please excuse me."

"Sure. Thank you, Father."

Jen watched the priest depart, heading towards the interior of the church. Jen, meanwhile, returned her gaze to the window. A metre to her right the cloister came to an end as it joined with the wall that surrounded the presbytery.

She turned away, heading towards the door from where the priest had come. She could tell from the doorway the passageway led to an underground vault.

As she considered entering, her phone rang.

6

Buckingham Palace

Buckingham Palace was a place that needed no introduction. Situated at the end of the Mall, the half-mile-long road at the heart of the City of Westminster, it was famous for one thing.

Being the home of the British Royal Family.

Originally constructed in 1705 as a home for the Duke of Buckingham, it was bought by George III in 1761 as a present for his wife, Queen Charlotte, and renamed from Buckingham House to The Queen's House. After its enlargement in the 19th century, the expanded palace became the primary residence of Queen Victoria and has been the home of the Royal Family ever since.

Escorted by an armed guard, three men made their way along the main corridor of the third floor of the palace and through an elaborate set of double doors.

Inside, the room matched all prior expectation. Red carpet and drapery decorated the floor and large windows, perfectly complementing a further three strong walls, painted bright yellow and decorated by priceless works of art. A large Belgian chandelier hung from the centre of the ceiling, an exquisite shade of white that matched the original fireplace. A number of Victorian busts and small statues were located at various points around the perimeter. Unlike most of the offices or conference rooms that the three men were used to, the chairs in the reception room were also one hundred years out of date and monetarily priceless. All were vacant bar one, the room's owner.

The King of England.

The King rose quickly to his feet. Unlike his appearance of several hours earlier, he now wore his trademark military regalia.

The dark navy blue uniform of an Admiral of the Fleet in the Royal Navy.

"Let's keep this brief, shall we, chaps? As I'm sure you are all aware,

I have one or two rather pressing engagements to follow."

The Home Secretary looked on uncomfortably. "Sir, may I introduce my right honourable friend, Mr Dominic West, one of my ministers at the Home Office, and our Tory MP for somewhere up in the north, no joke intended, West."

The man with fair hair smiled nervously. Unlike the Home Secretary and the other man present, this was his first trip to the palace.

The Home Secretary resumed. "You, of course, already know Bridges, Director General of MI5."

The man from MI5 smiled weakly as he placed his glasses to the corner of his mouth. Like the Home Secretary, his once dark hair was now largely grey.

The King eyed each man in turn, ending with Bridges. "I trust Tim has given you the brief, Colin?"

The man from MI5 glanced at the Home Secretary and nodded. "Yes, sir, he did."

The King began to pace. "Now then, gentlemen, what in heaven's name are we dealing with?"

None of the three were willing to speak.

"Colin, let's start with you."

"The man's name, Majesty, is Andrew Simon Morris. Born 15 August, 1979, in the city of Leeds; baptised six months later and raised Catholic; left school with practically no qualifications; eventually he found work with the merchant navy and later the royal before leaving to apparently become a Dominican friar."

The King nodded, taking it all in. "I suppose the most important question I could ask is, is this man telling us the truth?"

The DG of MI5 was unconvinced. "The man is clinically insane, sir."

"Is that an opinion or a diagnosis?" the King asked.

"It is the firm opinion of three independent psychiatrists, sir. I trust their opinion."

"Insane or not," West began, "everything that the friar has told us so far that has been possible to verify has indeed been verified. Like it or not, two of my colleagues have recently been found dead. Had it not been for this man, the death of my boss would have been wrongly written off as accidental."

The King accepted the point. "Have you made any progress regarding what caused the explosion?"

Bridges nodded. "Yes, sir."

"And?"

The man from MI5 hesitated, slightly uncharacteristically. "Tests on the car suggest evidence of tampering."

West was not surprised. "Well, there you have it," he said, buoyed. "Majesty, surely this proves it."

The King remained unmoved. "Has this friar fellow been interrogated since?"

"Sir, the man has been interrogated on several occasions," Bridges began, "and every time the result has been the same. As I say, the man has been proven insane."

"Just because one is insane, does not mean one is a liar," said West.

"How exactly were they killed?" asked Heston.

"Some form of remotely controlled explosive device," West interrupted. "I've read the report. As I'm sure you're aware, following the death of the Secretary of State for Justice, the responsibilities of the office now lie solely with me. And frankly, it is sadly my opinion that the JIC seems to be dragging its heels somewhat."

The King looked on, now slightly worried. He knew from his meeting with Dr Grant that the exact method of his father's death was still to be proven.

Despite confirmation of foul play.

"How exactly were they murdered, Colin?"

"From initial examination, it seems that some form of manually detonated explosive is the most plausible explanation."

The King nodded. "And you agree that this friar was the man responsible?"

"There is no concrete evidence for that, sir."

"No evidence," West said, dumbstruck. "The man has already confessed."

"We have the man's word," Bridges replied. "The word of a madman alone is not proof, nor is the word alone of a sane man."

"That's quite true." The King nodded, still pacing slowly across the carpet. Today, no one was sitting. "What else ties the killings to him?"

"Only conjecture," Bridges said.

"Majesty, the case against Morris is watertight," West said.

"The case against Morris is strong," Heston corrected.

"Has he provided us with any further explanation as to why he carried out the killings?" the King asked.

Bridges shook his head. "No, sir."

"How about his employers?"

"He merely repeats the same words: Beware the Sons of York."

The King nodded.

Nothing new.

"What of his more recent history?"

Bridges answered, "Morris left the merchant navy at the age of twenty-one and signed up with the RN until he was kicked out at age twenty-seven–"

"On what grounds?" the King interrupted.

"Dishonourable discharge."

"For hitting a superior," West added.

Bridges was unimpressed.

"How about since then?" the King asked.

"Nothing concrete. His navy record confirms his age is now thirty-four. He hasn't given any details of his present life."

"What of his order?"

"His personal keepsakes suggest he's a Dominican. Initial inquiries into his mother house have come up fruitless."

The King nodded. "And what of his present location?"

"The usual place."

"Which is?" asked West.

"Sorry, Minister, I am not at liberty to say," Bridges replied.

The King turned his back on the three visitors and headed towards the window. Outside, a large number of tourists had gathered as they always did around the gate or the statues while others made their way towards St James's Park.

"Keep trying," Heston said to Bridges. "Soften him up a bit. Perhaps he might feel like talking."

"I've already put five of my best men on him, Minister."

The King continued to look out across the grounds.

"As, gentlemen, shall I."

7

Jen returned to her room after leaving the church. She had started the day in London before six and felt the worse for wear because of it.

She lay on the bed, her eyes on the window. In the distance she could just about see the sun sinking slowly behind the distant hill. For several minutes she focused on it. The brightness of the sun shining on the perfect scenery somehow created the illusion of timelessness.

It seemed impossible the village was the scene of such a heinous crime.

She had spoken to her producer on returning to the room. She assumed the worst from their conversation earlier that day, and sure enough, that was now confirmed. The documentary would be delayed for at least three days, perhaps longer.

Ideally she wanted to return to London, but her producer suggested otherwise. Put the time to good use, 'make sure every angle gets covered', her boss's exact words. Had the documentary been for something else, the setting might well have been enjoyable, but the situation was disturbing. She remembered from watching the news a year earlier that the locals could be protective of their privacy. Even today, she had detected as much. Ideally she wanted to question some of the locals.

But she knew she must do so with tact.

By 7:20 she was feeling lonely, and, more importantly, she hadn't eaten for over eight hours. After changing her clothes and checking her appearance in the mirror, she made her way down to the bar area.

The White Boar Inn was the heart of the village, and even on a Monday it was not deserted. Known locally as the Hog, it was the kind of place where a local could come along for a few pints with the regulars or for a couple to enjoy a quiet meal.

In the main dining area, at least four tables were in use, its wooden chairs frequented by local families. In the bar area, most kept themselves to themselves, the odd curious gaze in Jen's direction reminding her she was on unknown ground. Two rugged locals were propping up the bar, their attention alternating between each other and their pints. One was fat, one was thin; one had grey hair, the other brown. Directly opposite them, the owner stood silently, his hands busy wiping a dirty glass.

The thin man with brown hair eyed Jen inquisitively as she passed.

"Ey up," the man said. "Who do we have here?"

"That there is Miss Farrelly," the owner of the White Boar, Harvey Mitchell said, still drying a glass. "She's the one with the Picanto."

"A Picanto?" the man said. "What's a Picanto?"

"You don't know what a Picanto is?"

The man looked back with a blank expression.

"I know what a Picanto is," said the fatter man sitting alongside him.

The thinner man looked at him. "Well, go on then, smarty-pants."

"A Picanto is a piece of art by Picanto."

Mitchell's expression was one of disbelief. "That's Picasso, you great twit, not Picanto."

The thinner man turned around, now looking at Jen. "It isn't a type of dog, is it?"

Jen looked at them both, then Mitchell, for now unable to respond.

"Ey, I know," the thinner man said. "Maybe a Picanto is simply . . . a Picanto."

For several seconds no one spoke.

"By gum, I think he's cracked it this time," Harvey Mitchell said, as the three locals burst into laughter. Standing alongside them, Jen smiled.

Silently she was dumbstruck.

"So what exactly is a Picanto, Miss Farrelly?" the thinner man asked.

"A Picanto's a car, you great Jessie," Mitchell said. "Pay no attention to these barnpots, love; they've never been quite right in the head."

Leaning against the bar, Jen struggled to keep a straight face.

"Oh, right," the thinner man said. "I'd like to see your Picanto if you don't mind, Miss Farrelly."

"Well, it's just outside, so be my guest."

"Well, thanks very much, I think I might just do that," he said, laughing.

"Miss Farrelly is just with us for the week," Mitchell said. "She's researching a documentary on the disappearance."

"Is that right, Miss Farrelly? Are you here to research a documentary?"

Jen looked inquisitively at the landlord. "I never told you I was here to research a documentary."

"That's right, you didn't. I was told by that one who cleans the church."

"Cleans the church," the thinner of the two barflies said. "You haven't been speaking to Martha Brown, have you?"

The fatter barfly laughed. "Gossip central, she is. Pound to a penny it'll be all over Wootton by closing time."

Jen smiled half-heartedly. She knew that the disappearance was a sensitive issue, but at least these three seemed undisturbed by the memory of it all.

"Ey, pay no attention to our Gavin," the thinner man said. "His mouth has always been larger than his forehead. Here, let me buy you a drink, Miss Farrelly."

"I was actually hoping to get some food," Jen said, looking at Mitchell.

"Restaurant is open until nine, or if you prefer, you can get bar food here – that way you can continue to talk to these two idiots."

Jen laughed, not knowing what else to do. "Do you have a menu for the bar?"

Mitchell passed Jen a menu. She scanned it quickly and settled for the cheeseburger with chips.

"Anything to drink?" Mitchell asked.

"Just a Coke, please."

"Here, let me buy this," the thinner man offered.

"Thanks," Jen said, placing her hair behind her right ear, "Mr . . ."

"Hancock. Brian Hancock."

The man offered his hand, and Jen accepted. "Thank you, Mr Hancock."

"Think nothing of it, Miss Farrelly, please call me Brian."

Jen smiled, this time more warmly, half amused, half not wanting to offend. She looked around the bar area, taking in the sights. No matter where she looked, she saw thick wooden beams crossing the large beige-coloured ceiling, reflecting the yellow of the wall lights. Although the inn was far from empty, many of the tables and booths were vacant.

It was cosy, but she guessed it wasn't a place that was regularly frequented by outsiders.

"So you work in telly? I always fancied myself as a bit of a film star, me." Hancock laughed as he reached for his pint. "You weren't down here before, were you? I mean a year ago?"

"No, I was working on something else then."

"Ah, I thought I didn't remember seeing your face. Never forget a face."

"Just everything else," Mitchell said, as he passed Jen her Coke. "That'll be £7.49, then, please, Mr Hancock."

Hancock smirked as he passed over the change. "Don't forget to take one for yourself, Harvey."

"Did you know her well?" Jen asked.

"What? Debra?" Hancock asked. "Not a person in the whole village who didn't."

She expected nothing less. "How about the boy?"

So far no one had spoken of the alleged culprit.

"Again, they were both local, you see. It's a small village here, Wootton. Everyone knows everything about everyone in these parts."

Jen sipped her Coke as she listened. The thought intrigued her. In London, she was used to the opposite. Though she was reluctant to take gossip on face value, she knew that local knowledge could be a reputable source.

And often an easy one to tap.

"What was he like, the lad?"

"I never liked him," the man named Gavin said, beating Hancock to a response. Until now he had seemed less interested in Jen.

Jen was intrigued. "Any particular reason?"

"Mainly his personality."

Jen smiled. "Was he selfish? Unpleasant? Arrogant?"

"No. He was one of those."

"One of what, sorry?"

"He wasn't quite right in the head."

Hancock shook his head. "Poor lad was autistic."

"You're certain?" Although Jen was aware of the rumours, she had yet to hear any firm confirmation.

"Well, that might not be the technical name for it."

Jen nodded, unwilling to push the issue. "You didn't know him well?"

Hancock shrugged. "Didn't really see him that much, to be fair. He didn't appear that much in public."

"Any idea where he went to school?"

"St Joseph's secondary, that's the Catholic school."

"No," Gavin interrupted. "He didn't go to St Joseph's; he went to that special school."

"Oh, that's right." Hancock remembered. "He used to go to St Joseph's. Then his mother took him to another school."

For the first time Jen was learning something new. Right or wrong, she knew it would be easy enough to check.

"Why did he leave St Joseph's?"

"Ah, well, it's quite sad, really. The poor lad was being bullied."

"Was he an awkward child?"

"Definitely," Gavin said.

"No, no, no," Brian said. "Now, be fair, Gavin. He wasn't awkward exactly. I think, really, he just needed a friend."

"You think he was isolated?"

Hancock nodded, sipping his pint.

Jen looked behind the bar. Mitchell had returned with a large plate in his hand. He placed it on the counter in front of her. The smell of chips, burger and bun immediately increased the feeling of hunger that had been escalating since leaving her room.

She picked up a chip, her eyes on the two barflies.

"Can I buy you two another drink?"

The DG of MI5 was speechless. Leaving the subterranean prison cell after seeking to question the occupant, he walked quickly alongside the smartly dressed officer, doing his best to ignore the unsettling sound of manic laughter coming from behind the bars.

"That tears it," the DG said, keeping his eyes in front of him at all times. "Let the King have his wish."

Standing in the windswept grounds of the palace, the young man felt a tap on his shoulder.

"Father."

The older man smiled. Like his son, he was dressed for the occasion.

"Come inside. When you're ready, your uncle would rather like a word."

8

Twenty minutes later, Jen had established a reasonably solid body of information about the late, and largely unlamented, Luke Rankin, and the supposedly late, and widely mourned, Debra Harrison. She had spent over a tenner and lost almost half of her chips, but the result was worth it.

From what she had gathered, Debra Harrison had been something of an outgoing sort: a smiling child and a smiling teenager, a friend to all and enemy to none. As a cute little girl with pigtails, she had been something of a darling among the villagers, particularly the elderly. As her breasts got larger, so did her male fan base, according to the barflies, including a few who really shouldn't have been. Her initial aim had been to work in fashion – *don't they all at that age*, Jen thought – whereas, according to Gavin, the new craze was to be a photographer and journalist.

At least that agreed with the official stance, the words of her mother a year earlier.

The word on Rankin was more interesting. The boy died just shy of eighteen, his death purported to be suicide. Unlike Harrison, Rankin had been something of a lonely child, who had endured an unhappy childhood – particularly at St Joseph's. His father had died when he was eleven. According to Gavin, he was a man of similar tendencies to his son, whereas, according to Brian, he had been well regarded in the local community. Though Jen had decided to keep an open mind about Gavin's claim that the father had committed suicide, she had come to the conclusion that Hancock was the more open-minded of the two.

Despite Rankin's difficulties, it appeared the boy was more than competent. If Hancock was correct, Rankin was even set for university. Harrison, being two years younger, would have been staying on at St Joseph's to do her A-levels.

Jen looked through her notes, finished her Coke, and ordered another from Mitchell. She rewarded her witnesses with two more pints of Abbot Ale, and each man a bag of pork scratchings.

Jen fiddled with her hair. "Okay, so let me get this straight: Debra and Rankin were not good friends."

Hancock tasted his latest pint and wiped white froth from his upper lip. "They knew each other; like I say, everyone in Wootton knows each other, but they definitely weren't friends."

Hancock seemed pretty certain.

"What makes you so sure?"

"Well, for a start, Rankin were two year older. For the most part, they were at separate schools."

"Were they ever at the same school?"

Hancock shrugged. "You'd have to ask the teachers."

She intended to. "How well did they know each other?"

"I'd guess hardly at all. People like Luke Rankin don't hang about with people like Debra Harrison."

She detected snobbery in his tone. "You mean because Debra was pretty?"

"Aye, she were definitely that, but not just that: Debra were popular, even the girls went crazy for her."

"Did Debra have a boyfriend?" Jen had never heard one mentioned before.

"Not that I'm aware. Not that she lacked admirers, mind."

"Any casuals? Dates? Anything like that?"

Hancock shrugged. "Well, now that you mention it, there was this one fella. Wasn't really a boyfriend as such."

"Go on."

"She were quite good friends with the Rat's nephew."

"The Rat?"

"Aye, see that's what we call him: Richard Ratcliffe, or Lord Richard, I should say. He's something of a bigwig round these parts."

Ratcliffe, Ratcliffe: she had seen the name a few times already. The church and the graveyard had been full of Ratcliffes.

Ratcliffes and Catesbys.

"So who is this Lord Ratcliffe?"

"He lives in one of those big mansions," Hancock said, gesturing with his hands. "You know that footpath what heads off down by the church?"

She guessed he was referring to the same one she had seen Catesby heading towards earlier.

She nodded.

"Follow that, and you come to a lane. He lives down one of those. Lived there for years, his family has."

Jen allowed the information a moment to sink in. "Tell me about his nephew."

"Nothing to tell, really. I haven't seen him for yonks."

"Yonks? What happened to him?"

"He went away," Gavin said, his first comment for a while. Almost immediately he returned to his pint.

"Where?"

Brian delayed his answer, distracted as the outside door opened. "Ey up, you can ask him yourself."

Jen turned, her eyes on the door. A smartly dressed gentleman had entered. He wore a black overcoat that matched the colour of his hair, a white scarf, and shoes so well polished that they practically sparkled. A vibrant smile shone from between his shaven chin and bushy moustache.

"Evening, Lord Richard," a bald man said from his position by a booth near the door.

"Ah, how do, young Michael. How's that trouble and strife?"

The man named Michael raised his beer as a salute.

"Good evening, Mr Ratcliffe, sir," the next man on said.

"Ey up, Billy lad. Ey, I just saw your missus; she was just finishing with the butcher – or maybe it was his assistant."

The man laughed at his own joke, as did the others. Watching from the bar, the first thing that Jen noticed was how the man attracted attention, as if a switch had been flicked.

He headed straight for the counter, less than a couple of metres from Jen, and removed his scarf, placing it on the bar by the till.

"How do, Lord Richard?" Hancock asked.

"Ah, how do, Brian lad? Good result for City, wasn't it? I mean they only lost six-nil."

Jen laughed, failing to control herself. The man's charisma was contagious.

"I say, who's this pretty young thing sitting next to you?"

"This is Miss Farrelly," Brian said.

"She's the one with the Picanto," Gavin said.

"A Picanto?"

"Don't start," Mitchell said, appearing behind the bar. "We'll be here till bleeding Christmas."

Jen smiled, silently relieved.

"It's a car," she said.

"Is it really?" Ratcliffe replied. "Well, in that case, I'll have a pint of the best Abbot's for moi, two pints of your second-best Abbot's for Brian and Gavin, something stifling for Sir William, and a sticker for the Picanto," the man said, laughing. "Oh, and, of course, whatever Miss Farrelly's drinking?"

Jen smiled. "Just a Coke, thank you."

"Just a Coke, thank you," Ratcliffe said.

"Can I take one for myself?" Mitchell asked.

"Cor, it never bloody rains, does it? All right then, Harvey, if you must."

"Ta very much."

Ratcliffe searched his pockets for change and began to count it in his hand. "Never seen you around these parts before, Miss Farrelly."

"I'm just here for a few days on business."

"Oh, I see; what kind of business are you in?"

Jen hesitated. "I work in television."

"Oh, super."

"Jen is here to film a documentary," Hancock said.

"Is that right? What you here to film? A wildlife show?"

"It's a documentary on the disappearance," Gavin said.

Jen grimaced. She felt as if she could have throttled him.

Ratcliffe was confused. Then his expression changed. "The disappearance. Oh, yes, I'm with you. Poor Debra Harrison. Oh, why do such things happen to the young?"

Mitchell reappeared with three pints of Abbot Ale and the Coke. "Anything else?"

"Just the usual for William."

Mitchell picked up a glass before turning his attention to the brandies that occupied three shelves behind the bar. "I didn't realise he was in tonight."

"I just got off the blower to him; he's on his way down now."

Mitchell poured a single brandy and placed it down on the bar. No sooner had he collected the money, the door opened.

"Ey up, speak of the devil."

Jen watched the door as the newest arrival made his way inside. As expected, it was the same man she had met earlier that day in the graveyard.

"Ey up, it's the Cat," Hancock said.

Catesby smiled wryly. "That's Sir William to you, Mr Hancock."

"You're quite right," Brian replied. "Let me buy you a drink, Sir William."

41

"Oh, I wish you'd have volunteered a minute ago; that way, I need not have bothered," Ratcliffe said.

Catesby approached the bar and picked up his brandy. He downed it in one and replaced the glass on the counter.

"Ahhh."

Two seats along, Hancock's enthusiasm had faded. "Same again, please, Harvey lad."

Mitchell raised his eyebrows before turning to refill the glass.

Brian fidgeted for change. "We don't often see gentlemen of your status down here in the common part of the moors."

"Tell you the truth, there was nothing good on the telly," said Ratcliffe. "Every single channel was nothing but politics – there's nothing I hate more than bleeding politics."

The comment made Jen laugh. As soon as he had said it, she recognised him.

"Hang on a minute. Now I know who you are. You used to be chancellor!"

She couldn't believe it was the same man.

Former Chancellor of the Exchequer and Democrat Party MP, Richard, now Lord, Ratcliffe.

"Oh yeah, back in the boom years – and a Democrat government." He looked at Catesby. "This is Miss Farrelly."

Catesby nodded. "Ah, yes, the girl from the graveyard."

Jen forced a smile.

Not the one with the Picanto.

"Did you find what you were looking for?"

"Yes, thank you. I really liked your dog."

"That's the one unique thing about Wootton, Miss Farrelly," Hancock said. "It must be the only place in England where you see a Cat walking a dog."

Hancock's joke got a grin from Jen and a boisterous laugh from Ratcliffe. Catesby remained purposely firm.

"I'm guessing that's your Picanto parked outside."

"Did you see it?" Hancock asked earnestly. "What did it look like?"

"Now that you mention it, it looks just like a Picanto," Catesby said.

"You're kidding?" Ratcliffe said. "A Picanto that looks like a Picanto. By gum."

Jen smiled, shaking her head. Six years had passed since leaving Nottinghamshire. She'd forgotten how much she missed the northern banter.

Catesby sipped his second brandy. "Come on then, Richard. Let's find ourselves a nice table, away from all the riffraff."

Ratcliffe picked up his pint. "Aye, I think we've been pleasant long enough. Good evening to you, Miss Farrelly."

Jen shook Ratcliffe's hand as the former Chancellor of the Exchequer made his way through a large archway, heading into the heart of the bar area.

"He's much more down-to-earth in real life," Jen said. "Why do you call him the Rat?"

"It's short for Ratcliffe," Mitchell said.

"It's all to do with history," Brian added. "The village goes back a long way; most of them from the old side of the village can trace their ancestors back to the Middle Ages."

"The old side?"

"Aye. Everything this side of the river is the old side. Or the posh side as we call it."

The comment intrigued her. As a history student, Jen was aware that a William Catesby, Richard Ratcliffe and Francis Lovell had been prominent statesmen during the reign of Richard III. She thought back to earlier that day, particularly the cloisters of the church. Many of the windows were concerned with that period of history.

She knew that Yorkshiremen were always proud of their history.

Her mind began to wander. Ratcliffe's nephew had been a friend of Debra Harrison; perhaps they had been even more than friends. The Ratcliffes were clearly a family of prominence in these parts, the head of the current generation particularly high profile. She wondered what had happened to the nephew. Ideally she wanted to interview him, see if he could shed any light on Debra Harrison's last days – assuming, of course, she was dead.

Should that fail, an interview with the man's uncle could surely do no harm.

Had the last election gone the other way, the man could well have been the current Prime Minister.

9

Buckingham Palace

The young man strode purposefully up the stairs and turned left on reaching the second-floor corridor. After twenty-eight years, he knew every inch of the building, and the various artworks, mostly portraits of his family and ancestors, appeared as little more than dots on the landscape.

He knew the stories of most, and of the remainder he had at least a passing knowledge. As a Winchester, his education had included detailed study of the family's history from an early age, but, unlike some of his relatives, for him, it had continued into adulthood. As usual for members of his family, his life up until now had largely been mapped out for him. His education had included five years of boarding at Winchester College, followed by a degree at Oxford. Keeping to the strengths of his youth, he chose history.

It had been both a blessing and a curse.

The young man followed the corridor towards one of the far doors and stopped as he passed a mirror.

He looked himself over. His brown hair was slightly askew, the inevitable result of over an hour standing in the windy grounds. He hated the formal occasions, particularly when they were televised.

At least this one was over.

Satisfied he appeared presentable, he continued to the far door and knocked.

Immediately he was welcomed.

Like most rooms in the palace, the setting was lavish and the furniture predominantly Victorian. A brown French carpet from the 18th century covered the wooden floor, surrounded by an antique chest and several side tables decorated with photographs of the present family. Two large portraits of his grandparents hung from the bright cyan-coloured walls, accompanied by masterpieces by Canaletto,

Gainsborough and Monet, and a gilt mirror that reflected the evening sunlight as it entered through the large windows overlooking the grounds.

Standing by the windows was his uncle, better known to most as His Majesty King Stephen II. He had reigned less than a month and was still to be crowned.

The King smiled at his nephew. "Take off your jacket, Thomas – there's a good chap."

The prince obeyed, taking care to fold the fine material before placing it down on the back of the nearest chair. Beneath it, he wore the black regimental uniform of an army captain.

Standing opposite, the King was also dressed in military uniform, in his case an Admiral of the Fleet, a courtesy for the sovereign, but only a small exaggeration of his real-life service, peaking at the rank of commodore.

"Father says you wished to see me, M-Majesty," the young man stuttered on the final word.

The King smiled at him. "You know you don't have to call me that, Thomas. Least not when we are alone."

The young man felt slightly foolish. "Yes, Uncle."

The King looked again through the window, his eyes on the forecourt. Though the recent ceremony had passed without a hitch, his mind was troubled.

"I'm afraid, Thomas, that once again I must ask too much of you."

The King turned towards his nephew.

"I assume your father has already given you the gist," the King said. "You are aware, Thomas, of our friend's claim regarding the two politicians?"

The young man stood rigidly with his hands down by his sides. "I know only of the claim; I d-didn't realise the findings have been c-confirmed."

"Well, Thomas, I'm afraid they have; Bridges gave me the news not two hours ago. Frankly, I think he seemed a little reluctant to give it."

Again the prince hesitated. "Well, he always did have your b-best interests at h-heart."

The King smiled again. "So he keeps telling me."

The young man watched as the King slowly began to pace around his desk. His outward appearance was as smart as ever, but today Thomas noticed a certain remoteness in him. As an Englishman, he knew the man's past, but as a relative, he knew the man himself. He had encountered sorrow, and not just recently. He had lost his wife, the would-be queen, within a year of losing his mother. The young man had never seen him show much emotion.

Today was no exception.

"How about the m-motive?"

The King walked slowly around the desk. "Thomas, before the funeral I asked Dr Grant to use his contacts in the profession to carry out various tests on the condition of my father at the time of his death. It was not until today that he received the results."

Thomas wondered where this was going. As a minor royal he was used to being on the fringe of the ins and outs of royal protocol, but since graduating from Sandhurst, his role had changed beyond recognition.

To the outside world, he was a captain in the army. On the inside, his role had no formal job description.

He was, in the words of his father, the protector.

"Despite our strongest hopes and prayers, the tests proved conclusive," the King began. "Your grandfather, Tom, was murdered."

Thomas swallowed, an unavoidable reflex. It took him several seconds to muster a response. "What happened?"

"We don't know, at least not entirely," the King said. "According to our only suspect, he was working on behalf of something called the Sons of York."

The name meant nothing to Thomas.

"Prior to my father's death, he received this." He showed Thomas a piece of paper. "Sadly, Father didn't tell me about it at the time. Unfortunately we have been unable to establish either when or from where it was sent."

Thomas accepted the paper and scanned the text. It was an A4 sheet and typewritten.

Now is the winter of our discontent
Made glorious summer by these Sons of York

"Shakespeare," he said. "It's been changed. These Sons, instead of this s-sun."

"Exactly."

The young man was confused. "Who are they?"

The King laughed, only without humour. "Legend has it, letters of this kind have been sent to members of our family throughout history. This is the first I've seen."

The King turned towards the desk.

"Until recently I had no knowledge of the matter whatsoever. In truth, I had believed the stories to be nothing more than a myth. Hard evidence, sadly, is minimal. I discussed the matter a few days ago with your father. Apparently this is the best we have."

The King picked up two books from his desk and showed them to Thomas. Neither of them was modern.

"According to this," the King opened the first book to around the midpoint, "published by a local historian in 1712, the writer talks about the existence of the Sons of York as far back as the 1600s. This man, apparently, was their most famous member."

"Monmouth," Thomas said, recognising the facsimile of a famous portrait. The man was James Scott, 1st Duke of Monmouth. Illegitimate son of Charles II. As a history graduate, Thomas knew the man had been the chief instigator of the failed Monmouth Rebellion in 1685 against James II.

"Again, your knowledge serves you well. If the writer of the work is to be believed, he had access to rare sources, including those once owned by Monmouth himself. Sadly we are unsure which."

"Th-they c-could be forgeries."

"Perhaps, perhaps not. From what your father tells me, the originals might have been destroyed in the 1800s. No official reason given. However, according to this second book, apparently one of the Pitts personally saw a copy and found the revelations 'compromising'."

The King paused. "A few days ago we received another message." He picked up a second document from the desk. "I'm sure you're familiar with the rhyme."

The King cleared his throat.

"Sing a song of sixpence, a pocket full of rye,

"Four and twenty blackbirds baked in a pie,

"When the pie was opened, the birds began to sing,

"Wasn't that a dangerous dish to set before a king?"

"Dangerous?" the prince interrupted, noticing the obvious change.

"It goes on." The King passed him the sheet.

Thomas read the content quickly.

The King was in his counting house, counting out his money,
The queens were in the parlour, eating bread and honey,
The princess was in the garden, nattering on her phone,
When down came a blackbird and pecked off her nose.

They sent for the duke's doctor,
Who sewed it on again;
He sewed it on so neatly,
The seam was never seen.

"The ending is new."

"No," the King corrected. "Just less common."

"The duke's doctor."

"Right. That has changed."

The prince read it again. "Here. The maid was in the garden."

"Yes. That has also changed."

Thomas read it through several times. Suddenly it struck him.

"Queens," he said. "Not one queen. Two."

The King took a deep breath. "I think it's referring to my wife and mother."

Thomas was speechless. The king's wife had died three years ago, within a year of the king's mother.

"Eating bread and honey?"

The King closed his eyes, an extended pause. "Mother was found in the pantry. Matilda in the lounge. The official diagnosis for both was food poisoning."

Thomas nodded, trying his best to remain calm. As a royal, he remembered the deaths of his aunt and grandmother well. The official verdict on their deaths was illness, but he knew the true cause remained unsolved.

"Which king?" Thomas asked.

"What?"

"The king in the c-counting house. Which k-king?"

"In the original rhyme I believe it might have been Henry VII. Famed administrator."

The King looked again at his desk. "Which reminds me. According to your father, the two books have one thing in common. Apparently both make reference to the same source."

The King opened the second book and showed Thomas the line of relevance. "According to the book, the source in question was something called the Ravensfield Chronicle. Does this mean anything to you?"

Thomas read the page in its entirety before responding. "No. But I have heard of this." He pointed to another part of the page. "The

Croyland Chronicle. Written in 1486. B-banned by order of Henry VII."

The King let out a rare smile. "Once again, you never cease to amaze me with your knowledge."

"You ask of me only to be a historian?"

The King delayed his response. "If only it were that simple."

He picked out two more papers of relevance from the pile on his desk and immediately set about organising them.

"Since the 1700s, many people have been intrigued, apparently, with the legend of the Sons of York. In recent years it has apparently become something of an obsession for the revisionist historian."

The King showed him the two newest papers. Both were Internet printouts.

"According to your father, the two books I've just shown you could well be the only two in existence that offer anything remotely interesting on the Sons of York. Interestingly, both books were published posthumously and were incomplete at the time their authors died. Even more bizarre, the authors died in peculiar circumstances. Furthermore, both were historians living in the north of England."

Thomas accepted the printouts and read them quickly. Both were *Dictionary of National Biography* overviews of the authors' lives.

Both had apparently been murdered.

"According to Bridges, the possibility of a connection between the two politicians and my father cannot be ruled out. If our friar friend is telling the truth, we must also consider the possibility that there is a connection between these as well."

Thomas was practically speechless. "These go back centuries."

"As I say, Thomas, all we have is speculation," the King said. "But I must confess this is not totally new. I remember a number of years ago I brought up the subject with my uncle Albert. Apparently my grandfather believed in their historicity . . . according to Uncle Albert, they were none too pleased with his controversial marriage."

The young man was captivated. "You b-believe they exist? And have done throughout h-history?"

The King's expression was grave. "All I know to be true, Tom, is that two politicians have been murdered, and the only evidence we have is from the ravings of a Dominican friar who, according to Bridges, is madder than the Mad Mahdi."

It was clear that the King's joke was not intended to be humorous. "You believe him to be genuine?"

"Ever since my father died, I've had people telling me one thing, and others telling me something else. Two months ago, in all honesty, I would most probably have ignored the lot of them. Yet that was before I became king."

The young man bit his lip. "I suppose s-satisfactory diplomacy leads one to sometimes forego the opinion of one's own gut."

The King laughed to himself. "Yes, it certainly feels that way."

The prince looked again at the printouts, then at the King. "Wh-what exactly did my father say?"

"Frankly, he seemed equally disturbed by the matter. Disturbed, or at least, perplexed. Without question, something relating to the Sons of York is factual. What are less clear are the identities of the people behind them."

The King looked at his nephew, this time more seriously. "In truth, I was hoping these tests might have put the matter to bed."

The young man understood the significance. "You believe that the p-politicians were killed by a man who b-believes himself to be a m-member?"

"Our friend is currently being held in our most secure location. If he is as mad as they say he is, then surely you won't learn much from him.

"But even if our friend does decide to keep mum, it is here," the King said, pointing to the pile of papers and books on his desk, "where the trail seems to be at its warmest.

"What I must ask of you, is to find out just how warm it is."

Thomas left the study and headed through the grounds of the palace.

"Thomas!"

He heard someone shout his name as he headed for the car. An elderly man was waiting for him by the gate, his entry denied by the palace guards.

Thomas swore under his breath. "For crying out loud."

"Unhand me," the old man said to the well-presented guard currently depriving him of entry. "I am the Earl of Somerset."

Thomas took a deep breath and gestured towards the guard. "It's okay. He's allowed in the grounds."

The old man pushed aside the guard and headed along the pathway towards the prince. He wore a monocle over his right eye, partially obscuring the larger of his deep blue eyes, which was scarred beneath the lid. His white hair had almost completely thinned on top, the rest flanking a round head that had seen over eighty winters.

"The Sons of York are one of the most dangerous societies known to man," the old man said, struggling to keep pace. "Their influence spans far and wide; you underestimate them at your peril."

Thomas shook his head, doing his best to ignore him. He knew the man well, and had done his entire life. To the wider world he was James Gardiner. Earl of Somerset and brother of the late queen.

Also former tutor to the prince.

"Not now, Jim," Thomas said, heading towards the car.

"So you keep saying . . . Tom, you must listen."

"You know you're not supposed to be here. My uncle won't be pleased if he finds you."

The old man was getting het up. "You never change, you know. You're always the same, always incapable of looking beyond the end of your own nose."

"Later, Jim."

Gardiner shook his head while he muttered under his breath.

Not for the first time, the boy refused to listen.

10

Jen waited until closing time before leaving her seat at the bar. She said goodnight to Brian and Gavin, tentatively agreeing that she would see them again the following evening.

In truth, she had enjoyed the evening. Without question, the harmless banter of the locals made a refreshing change from interviewing relations of victims and hunting for memorial stones. She knew that their accounts of people and events could be subject to inaccuracy – both of them were pissed come closing time – but she was satisfied their stories were worth following up.

Even if they were wrong, during the final hour she had learned of some useful contacts. Helen Cartwright, supposedly Debra Harrison's favourite teacher. Francis Lovell, full name Francis Lovell the 23rd, another man of long ancestry and with another bizarre nickname, the Dog. Apparently he was something of a character, until four years ago headmaster of St Joseph's, now retired.

Thanks to Hancock, she had also obtained an address for Rankin's mother, Susan Rankin, an emotionally drained widow still coming to terms with the loss of her only son. She knew from her producer that Rankin had declined the opportunity to be interviewed as part of the documentary; hardly surprising given her son was the chief suspect – the only suspect – regarding Debra Harrison's disappearance. Jen knew that following up that lead would be a risk, but she decided it was worth it.

After all, she reminded herself, her job was to document the facts, not to take sides.

She walked up the stairs and continued along the landing. The hallway was quiet, with no obvious signs of life from inside any of the rooms. According to Tara, there were four guests in total.

For all she knew, she was the only one.

She entered her room and closed the door behind her. The lateness of the hour and the effects of a long day's work were finally catching up with her.

She was asleep as soon as her head hit the pillow.

*

Outside the Hog, the young brown-haired girl watched as the light came on in one of the upstairs rooms. She'd heard rumours that day of a newcomer in the village, following in the footsteps of a year ago. Though she was still to see the woman herself, the facts didn't seem out of place. It was just like a year earlier.

History repeats itself.

She waited until the light went out again before making her way down the footpath towards the old part of the village.

11

Less than an hour after leaving the palace, Thomas had reached his destination. Though the King had been unspecific in telling him where the prisoner was being held, he knew from experience there was only one such place.

It was the same place where traitors to the Crown had always been held.

He breathed in deeply, attempting to rid himself of the feeling of claustrophobia as he waited for the lift to reach its destination. As the doors opened, he saw before him a lengthy silver corridor, its appearance uncannily reminiscent of a top-secret nuclear facility.

Two burly men had been placed on the doors, standing rigidly to attention. Like their colleagues above the surface, they were dressed in the typical undress uniform of a Yeoman Warder: dark blue with red trimmings, including the symbol of the Crown and the letters SIIR, denoting the reign of the present monarch, Stephen II. Like all Yeomen Warders, they were NCOs and had previously served over twenty-two years in the British Army.

But unlike their colleagues above ground, both men carried L85A2 automatic weapons.

The standard weaponry of the British Army.

Both Beefeaters turned to face the prince and immediately saluted. Without further word, the Beefeater on the left escorted Thomas to the end of the corridor and inserted an eight-digit pin into the keypad on reaching a metal door.

This was the most exclusive part of the Tower of London: a secure facility known as the Cromwell Tower, named in honour of its creator. Unlike the building above, the facility did not appear on the itinerary of any guided tour. Indeed, its existence was known only to a select few.

He was among the select.

Thomas waited for the door to open, and was immediately greeted by a man of imposing features, measuring six feet three with red hair and a matching goatee. His appearance was impeccable, typical of an officer. Thomas knew the man well, and had done for years.

He was the Constable of the Tower of London, a position of rare privilege. He was Sir Thomas Edmondes, Chief Yeoman Warder.

The man saluted. "Good evening, Captain."

The prince returned the salute. "Before I joined the army, I would never have believed such a p-place to be p-possible."

Edmondes led the way along the next corridor, its appearance in keeping with the one before. "The less public exposure a man like Morris receives, the better," the Constable of the Tower began. "I've tried interrogating him myself several times; the man seems to be a complete lunatic."

The statement matched the rumours. "What of his background?"

"Prior to recent days, practically nothing. He's former military, almost certainly a professional assassin. It isn't every day you find someone who's taken monastic orders who has the ability to administer explosives to a government vehicle and detonate it."

"Any progress on determining the s-substance?"

"Tests are ongoing."

"He's said nothing of his background or training?"

Edmondes shook his head. "No. But madman or not, his expertise is far ranging. And if correctly driven, most profitable."

"You believe him to be a h-hired assassin?"

"In truth, we don't know. His answers have been peculiarly ambiguous – quite obviously rehearsed. At this stage, nothing can be taken for granted."

They reached another metal door, which Edmondes opened using a code. This was the quietest part of the facility. Another smaller corridor followed: its walls painted grey, with the lack of light adding to the gloom. Even from the doorway, Thomas could sense the depression. It was as if something lingered in the air.

The cumulative result of the building's history.

Edmondes led Thomas to the second door on the left, visually a large sheet of reinforced steel. The door opened electronically as Edmondes placed his palm into the scanner, revealing a small desolate room, partitioned into two by metal railings.

What Thomas saw left him speechless. It was as if the prison cells of the past, like those of the building above, had been established again in this modern-day facility, over fifty metres below the surface.

"Here he is," Edmondes said, pointing.

For several seconds Thomas looked at what appeared to be an

empty cell. Then, he saw movement on the floor. Something was there, definitely alive. He could see blond hair, probably bleached, and crew cut.

The man sat with his back to the newcomers, stripped to the waist and with his hands joined together. From Thomas's position, the man appeared to be meditating.

Thomas placed his head to the bars, the cold metal bracing against his forehead. The air was heavy and musty, the smell, he guessed, a depressing combination of steel, a recently painted wall and the man's natural odour.

The prince looked at Edmondes. "I need not detain you any longer, sir. You may go about your business."

The request made Edmondes uneasy. Metal railings or not, he didn't feel safe leaving the prince alone.

"Capt–"

"I said that will be all, sir."

Edmondes nodded and reluctantly left the room, the automatic door closing swiftly behind him.

Now alone, Thomas concentrated on the cell. A basic single bed had been placed in the corner where two walls met. The paint was fresh, explaining the smell. All of the walls were painted a monotonous grey. The toilet aside, the only other furniture was a small desk in the opposite corner.

There were no windows, no televisions, no reading material.

To the prince, looking at the grey walls and panelled lights on the ceiling was like looking into a pit of despair.

Thomas stood with his arms folded, his eyes on the prisoner.

"Who are you?"

He received no response; instead the man continued to sit perfectly still with his back to the railings and his hands joined together.

"Show yourself!"

Again there was no sign of acknowledgment. The prince walked to one side of the bars and then back to the other. He stopped again, his head leaning against the railing.

Even topless the prisoner looked like a monk. Looking him over completely, the humble barefoot appearance and grey trousers – approximately half of the standard uniform of the prison inmates – suited a man of piety. The man carried himself with a certain radiance, even purpose.

Inwardly, Thomas admired the man's concentration.

"Who are you?"

Again nothing.

Just complete and utter stillness.

Thomas stood still for at least another minute. Looking at the man's back, it was impossible to see whether he was even awake.

He pretended to leave.

"I have been waiting a long time for you, Captain. It saddens me that you should give up so quickly."

The prince stopped and looked again at the man in the cell.

Apart from his mouth, the man had still not moved.

"Didn't they teach you in the navy that you must stand to face a superior?"

The prince waited for a reaction, but again none was forthcoming. He swallowed, composing himself.

"Enough playing games. On your feet. Stand!"

He shouted the final word, which echoed around the cell. Although the prisoner remained initially unmoved, Thomas noticed a slight turn of his head.

The figure turned further, revealing other parts of his body. For the first time Thomas could make out facial features. The man appeared younger than he had expected, looking no more than thirty. He was white, slim but well built, and, judging from his accent, a native of the north of England.

Morris looked at the prince for the first time, his eyes on the uniform. He made lengthy eye contact before looking up at the silver panels on the ceiling.

"They can see us, you know."

Thomas remained unmoved. "Who can?"

The man rose to his feet and walked towards the bars. "For over five hundred years your ancestors have sat on the throne of England. Even to this day your family refuses to give up what has never been rightfully yours."

Thomas folded his arms, confused. "And what might that be?"

The friar laughed, his smile immediately fading. "Soon the rightful inheritors will at last be restored. Accept it, and you may yet live . . ."

The man gripped the bars.

"Or perhaps you would prefer a different fate."

Again Thomas was rendered speechless. He looked the prisoner directly in the eye, the window to the soul. Out of keeping with his hair, the man's eyes were a deep shade of caramel, broken by red veins, perhaps evidence of an infection. In the light, one eye seemed slightly darker than the other, be it a trick or the use of a contact lens, the prince, in truth, was unsure.

"Enough games. Who are you working for?"

"They can see us. Even now. They're watching us."

Thomas maintained eye contact as the friar tightened his grip on the bars. He considered speaking but for now decided against it. The man's concentration was resolute and unblinking.

Almost as though he was looking at a statue.

Morris moved. "Boo!"

The prince jumped, only slightly but enough to excite the prisoner.

"I must say I expected better of you, Captain. A prince of the realm. You are unworthy to be classed in the category of the princes of old."

"So you know who I am?"

"I know many things."

Thomas folded his arms, his attention on the man's torso. There was a tattoo below the left side of his collarbone. It looked like a flower.

"How long have you had that?"

No response, just eye contact.

"Wh-who are you working for?"

The friar moved closer, his body touching the bars.

He spat in Thomas's face.

The prince remained unmoved. He kept his eyes shut, a reflex from the spit. He removed a handkerchief from his pocket and wiped away the saliva.

The prisoner placed his head to the bars a second time. "Enjoy yourself, son of Clarence. Soon the rightful inheritors shall return. And my work will just be beginning."

Thomas moved closer to the bars, his face almost touching them. He held the prisoner's gaze.

The expression in the man's eyes confirmed his initial suspicions.

Thomas's reactions were too fast. The prince placed his hands through the bars, grabbing the prisoner's upper body.

The friar was struggling. The strength of his arms caused Morris to leave the floor. With one swift movement, he turned, his back now to the bars.

"Right, time to drop the charade."

All Morris could feel was a hand to his neck and another to his upper body.

"Who put you up to this?"

58

Morris wriggled uncomfortably. Despite the choking sensation, the friar was able to laugh scornfully.

Thomas held him tightly, his hand restricting his air passages. "Tell me, who are you working for?"

The prisoner continued to struggle. He laughed, managing little more than a gagging sound against the prince's firm hand.

"Tell me who you are working for, and I shall release you."

"I do not crave release. Nor do I fear death."

Thomas pounded him against the bars, causing red marks to appear on the friar's back. "You really believe it to be a secret worth dying for?"

The man struggled to breathe. He fought the feeling of gravity, kicking against the bars. All the while Thomas's grip remained strong.

Morris choked. "Talbot."

As the kicking became wilder, the prince dropped him to the floor. Morris fell heavily, the impact hardest on his right knee. The sound of squealing aside, the first thing Thomas noticed was a definite change in the atmosphere.

Gone the resolute hatred and arrogance.

Replacing it, heavy breathing.

"Talbot?" Thomas repeated. "J-Jack Talbot?"

The question went unanswered. He considered asking again, but the prisoner was breathless.

At least he had something worth checking.

The prince straightened his jacket and headed for the door.

"You will never find them," the friar said. His voice had changed slightly; without question it was less powerful. Slowly he rose to his feet. As he approached the bars, he gestured the prince to approach.

Tentatively the prince came nearer.

"Beware the Sons of York. Beware!"

The prince eyed the prisoner for what seemed like a lifetime before turning away, heading through the door.

"They can see you."

Back at ground level, the son of the Duke of Clarence marched swiftly along the side of the River Thames, still riled by the recent episode. He got into a black Ford, parked discreetly some twenty metres from the nearest lamppost, and began heading east.

He looked to his right as he drove. Out of the window, the Tower dominated the view, its foreboding structure backlit by the night sky like a halo. Quietly, Thomas replayed in his mind the recent events in the facility below the ground.

Though it had been frustrating, he had unearthed one important lead.

Alone in his cell, the prisoner gazed up at the ceiling. The lights above were blinding, partially reflected by the white panels that surrounded them.

He lowered himself onto one knee and concentrated on the area where the walls met the ceiling.

"Forgive me, Father."

Over 250 miles north, a lone figure sat quietly, his eyes on the screen in front of him. The scene he had just witnessed had been revealing. He had already seen at least twelve different men interrogate the prisoner, but this man was by far the most high profile yet.

Part one of the plan had indeed succeeded.

The royals were taking him seriously.

12

Jen was awake by 8:30 the next morning. She heard a noise coming from the corridor, possibly another guest, possibly the maid, closing a door and walking towards the stairs.

Jen rolled over in the bed, yawning. The location was charming; in truth even better than she had remembered. The room was bathed in a bright yellow hue caused by the sunlight against the colour of the curtains. The large oak tree that had occupied the site outside her window for the last five hundred years created a shadow across the far wall, even through the curtains. Outside, she could hear the chirping of birds and the flapping of wings. It had been a long time since she had woken to such a sound.

She could tell it was shaping up to be a warm day.

She sat up slowly, placing her back against the pillow. The soft, thick duvet that had wrapped itself around her snugly, creating a nice heat against her legs, loosened slightly, allowing some of the air to escape. For the briefest of moments she considered staying there, fleeting her time away within the comfort of the soft linen.

The ringing of the telephone spoilt the quietness.

She answered.

"This is your wake-up call. Your wake-up call."

Jen smiled as she put down the receiver. The American accent of the automated voice seemed completely at odds with her present location. She wondered whether anyone had ever thought about recording a more local version: something like 'get out of bed, you big Jessie,' or 'ey up, you're gonna be late'. She laughed to herself as she considered the local candidates: Ratcliffe, Hancock . . . Harvey Mitchell.

Reluctantly she removed the duvet, at last coming to terms with her life outside the bed. She entered the ensuite and looked herself over in the mirror.

What she saw disgusted her, even though many would have said the opposite. Her shoulder-length, sandy-coloured hair was straight and surprisingly presentable, despite nine hours on the pillow. She had meant to get it cut last week; she had said the same thing the week before. Ever since moving to London, time always seemed to get away from her. Lack of vitamin D was another negative. Coming from Nottinghamshire, she was used to living without sunlight, but living in the capital was starting to play havoc with her fitness. Her skin was white, ghostly white to her, and added at least ten years to her in her mind.

She concentrated on her forehead: traces of acne were beginning to present themselves, more obviously visible as she wasn't wearing make-up. She screamed to herself in a low-pitched whine as she stared incessantly at the huge volcanoes occupying the areas between her eyebrows and hair. She rubbed against them vigorously, then decided not to proceed.

Maybe one of these days she'd finally clear adolescence, she thought to herself. Maybe then she'd find herself a real boyfriend.

Rather than the muppets she seemed to be a magnet to.

Her telephone rang for the second time in five minutes. Leaving the ensuite, she answered.

"I have that address you were asking for, Miss Farrelly," a woman began, "the one for the old school."

Jen recognised the voice of Tara Simpson, the kind barmaid/receptionist/waitress/goodness knows what else who had shown her to her room yesterday.

"Thank you, Tara, let me just write this down."

Jen left the inn at just after 9:30 and headed towards the high street. She exchanged banter with Harvey Mitchell on the way down, and told him of her wish to stay for another three nights. That was fine, the man said; it was evident from the quietness that the inn was hardly overbooked. Jen smiled at his compliment that she brightened up the place, and that the barflies will miss her when she goes. She was still to hear from her producer regarding a definite schedule for filming, but she knew from past experience it wouldn't be sooner than any time in the next two days.

On the plus side, Wootton-on-the-Moor wasn't turning out to be the worst place in the world.

Jen made her way over the bridge that led to the high street and continued left on crossing the street.

The busiest part of the village.

According to her sources, it was somewhere around here that Mrs

Susan Rankin lived – and had done for most of her life. After considering the matter carefully, she had decided to visit Rankin first. She knew from her experience at the Hog that news of her arrival in the village was becoming more widely broadcast – credit in part Martha Brown – and that was bound to escalate before the day was out. She knew it was possible Rankin was now aware of Jen's arrival, but there was nothing she could do about that. Her favourite professor at Nottingham once told her, always play the percentages: at least that way you are always guaranteed a certain amount of success. If a successful interview with Susan Rankin was possible, she figured her best chance was before the gossip column tainted her reputation.

She headed for a location called Fox Lane, a pleasant side alley off the high street flanked by red walls. Tree branches and plant life spilled over from the gardens of nearby houses, giving off a pleasant rustic vibe. The location was lonely, but not unsettling, rather like having a quiet walk in the country on a peaceful summer's day.

The end of the pathway led to a clearing, giving Jen the choice of turning either left or right. Choosing the right, she followed the pathway for another thirty metres. There were twelve houses in total, four lots of three in a row that formed a square around a cobbled courtyard. The houses were old, stone construction, black and white terraced, and dated back to the 16th or 17th centuries.

She assumed from the exteriors they were Grade II listed.

Jen double-checked the address against what she had written down and walked slowly to the middle of three houses. A small plaque on the right side of the strong wooden door confirmed the address: 8 Gallacher's Court.

She rang the doorbell, a loud high-pitched dingdong that sounded unexpectedly modern. She waited patiently for several seconds, considering trying again, before hearing the sound of metal against metal coming from inside.

A woman appeared, aged somewhere in the mid-forties. She was about five feet six – three inches smaller than Jen – and her weight insufficient for her size, perhaps partially accounting for the gaunt expression on her face. Had Jen not known the woman's back-story, she might have put her appearance down to illness.

But she knew in the case of this woman the reason was probably more straightforward.

"Mrs Rankin?" Jen asked.

"Yes."

"My name is Jennifer Farrelly; I'm a researcher for a TV productions company . . . I was wondering if you had a few minutes?"

The woman delayed her response. "I know why you're here, Miss Farrelly. Isn't a person in the whole village that doesn't."

The comment was a setback. "I'm sorry to bother you, Mrs Rankin."

"Martha told me all about you."

That was another setback. "You're good friends with Martha?"

"He was a good boy, Luke was."

"I'd love to hear more about him."

The woman folded her arms. "I've said everything I want to say."

"Mrs Rankin, please," Jen said as the woman sought to close the door. "I'm not here to take sides. I understand what you must be going through."

Jen instantly regretted saying that.

"How?" Susan Rankin replied, colour returning to her cheeks. "You know nothing of my son. Nothing!"

The woman closed the door in Jen's face and retreated hastily, her footsteps audible even outside. Jen took a step backwards and looked longingly at the exterior. She muttered the word 'great' under her breath and walked back towards the pathway.

She considered her options. There was no point going to the school: most of the teachers would be in class.

Lunch or after school was surely the best time to catch her.

She thought about visiting Ratcliffe, but she felt underdressed. Knowing him, he probably wouldn't be in anyway.

The best option was Lovell – the retired former head teacher at St Joseph's, described by the barflies as something of a character. She had learned from Hancock that the man lived on the other side of the village in a grand manor house once owned by his ancestors – all twenty-three generations of them. According to the barflies, Lovell lived in the same part of the village as Ratcliffe and Catesby.

The posh side.

Even if the man was out, it was definitely the most sensible option.

If all else failed, at least it would give her the opportunity to see where the other half lived.

Susan Rankin watched from the window as the girl from south of Yorkshire retreated in the direction of Fox Lane. She waited until the girl had disappeared completely before returning to the heart of the living room.

64

In truth, she had lied to the poor girl. She had no idea why she was there. She had not spoken to Martha Brown for over a year – she had barely spoken to anyone for that matter. The fact that the girl had bought it confirmed her suspicions.

History repeats itself.

It certainly felt like the last time. She recalled a phone call from a few weeks back: another interview request, a different company. She guessed the two were connected. Jennifer Farrelly was certainly not the first, though she was the first for a while – at least six months had passed since the last.

Susan Rankin walked across the living room, stopping on reaching the bookcase. She picked up a photograph, a nice silver frame surrounding a colour print taken about two years earlier. She looked at it for several seconds, focusing on the lad standing beside her. He was smiling in this one – he smiled in all of them. He certainly didn't look like a boy who had the weight of the world on his shoulders. Over a year had passed, but it seemed to her like an eternity.

She held the photo tightly to her chest and slowly started to cry.

13

The old man was standing by the doorway, looking outside. Catesby was in the usual place, doing the usual things. He looked completely different in his overalls. He could have been a farmer or a scientist, but not both.

That was almost unheard of.

The old man cleared his throat, but failed to attract Catesby's attention. Instead he remained preoccupied with his animals, the sound of the cough overwhelmed by the consistent clucking of chickens, not to mention other birds. The old man had never seen so many in one place, even in an aviary.

He cleared his throat again.

This time Catesby noticed. He turned away from the cages, his eyes on the door that connected the back of the house to the garden.

"Ah," he said. "I didn't see you there."

The old man did not respond. If nothing else, it was energy badly spent. And these days he needed that just to stand. Even with the stick, walking was difficult.

He hated the wheelchair, but he hated being without it even more.

There were four people with him, three dark-haired men in their late twenties, and another who was noticeably older.

"Ey up, Rowland," Catesby said to the eldest of the four. "Long time no see."

The man smiled, slightly sinisterly. As usual he wore a suit, far too well dressed for the farm. He had silvery grey hair, piercing eyes, and a face that certain members of the press had often likened to that of a gopher.

"We're not looking to disturb you long, William. We were merely wondering how's progress."

Catesby put the bucket of bird feed down on the concrete. "Follow me."

He led them through the doorway of an outbuilding. There were sacks of bird food everywhere, ranging from chicken feed to old bits of bread. He crossed the floor and continued down the stairway and through another door.

The sight was confusing, particularly for the three younger men who had never seen it before.

They had entered a laboratory, visually as good as any science institution in the world.

Catesby walked towards the other side of the lab. There were cages there as well, also housing various birds. Catesby smiled at them as he opened the fridge and removed a vacuum-sealed package not obviously identifiable to an outsider.

"This is the best so far," Catesby said. He passed two of the young men rubber gloves. "You'll need these. Keep the meat under four degrees. Otherwise the effects won't be the same."

"You've done well, my friend," the old man said.

Catesby lowered his head, almost a bow.

"How long for the rest?"

"Days," Catesby said. "A week tops."

"I want it ready in three days."

14

Clare, Suffolk

The sun was up, but it was still early. The main roads were deserted, as was the high street. Even the interiors of the ancient buildings displayed no sign of life. Drawn curtains shaded most of the windows. Should one have succeeded in peering in through a small gap in an upper-floor window, they were more likely to see a stationary bulge beneath a quilt than anything that resembled movement. It was the same story every year. Those who weren't sleeping were simply absent.

Like most areas in the height of summer, the majority had moved out, a necessary sabbatical after eleven months of hardship.

The residential areas were equally quiet. Thin mist rose from the river, crossed the banks, and coated the town in an atmospheric haze. From the castle mount, the view never changed. In the spring and summer months, the town bloomed with flowers of all sorts, its colours crossing the entire spectrum.

It was a setting that encapsulated beauty and former glory.

The town of Clare was one of the oldest in England. Situated on the banks of the Stour and fourteen miles from Bury St Edmunds, the so-called 'heart of Suffolk' was a unique amalgamation of the old, the slightly less old and the relatively modern. The community thrived on the market, particularly cloth. The Domesday Book highlighted the market, and even today it thrived on tradition. One hundred and thirty-one listed buildings, ranging from stone to timber, Norman to Victorian, stood alongside three-bed terraced houses from the 1950s and '60s, and some more modern. If the locals were to be believed, its history went back further still, even to a time before time itself.

Among its listed buildings, a large secluded Georgian estate overlooked the town from the hillside. Once upon a time, it had been far less impressive. The Norman skeletal structure that existed had long since given way to a large white Palladian design that looked like something out of ancient Greece. Large gateways surrounded it on both sides, guarded by two uniformed policemen. Locally it was known as Clarence House, but that wasn't its real name. The real Clarence House was far different. This one was not like the house of the same name that adjoined St James's Palace in either appearance or importance.

Yet nor was it unimportant. The locals knew the story and were happy to leave the family to themselves.

Just as they had done in the feudal days.

The Duchy of Clarence was one of the oldest estates in England. Originally given to the third-born son of Edward III, the title became defunct no fewer than five times before its revival by the previous monarch.

The current holder was George, son of the late James III. At fifty-two, he was the youngest of his three sons and easily the least famous. As a former soldier, he served through the Falklands, the Gulf and Kosovo before turning his priorities to domestic affairs.

The duke was up by 6 a.m. By 6:30 he had started on breakfast, the usual boiled egg with soldiers, served in the morning room rather than the dining room.

He was used to eating alone, but today he had company.

He sat at the head of the table that had been famous among his relatives for over a century. The antique wood was both hard and permanent. Large portraits surrounded the table on every side, mostly of relatives and ancestors, including his famous brother, now King of England. Like some at the palace, the walls were painted cyan, reflecting the light like a calm ocean.

Another was present, sitting adjacent rather than opposite. He was the duke's only son and child.

And the house's only other occupant.

The Duke of Clarence removed his glasses and threw them down on the book that he had just been reading.

"I think I see what you mean."

Sitting less than a metre away, Thomas looked at his father. He had scanned everything the King had given him, but most of it was still to sink in. It was not until after midnight that he had returned home, and even then sleep had not come easily.

"What does it mean to you?" Thomas asked. "The R-Ravensfield Chronicle?"

The duke returned his attention to the book. "Nothing. If it had not been for this, I doubt I should ever have heard of it."

Thomas said nothing. Twenty-eight years as his father's son had given him an advantage over most in getting to know the real him. In the family circle, the man was a scholar – not that anyone from the outside world would necessarily agree. He wasn't one to broadcast his activities, particularly in the wider circles.

It was a trait shared by his brothers.

Thoughts returned to the matter at hand. "What about the S-Sons of York?"

The duke smiled philosophically. "Your uncle first showed me these a week ago," he said, referring to the two books. "Like your uncle, I was aware of the rumours that surround our family . . . sadly after a while you begin to lose track."

He looked again at the older of the two books.

"From what I could gather from my grandfather, the story about the Glorious Rising is believed to be largely true. Apparently the Sons first came on the scene in 1684 and assisted Monmouth a year later."

"What purpose?"

"In truth I don't know; my attention span wasn't the best back then. Fortunately for us, any knowledge our relatives had probably came from these two books."

Thomas bit his lip. "So the Sons, th-they were just mercenaries?"

"I think it's fair to say that at the very least they acted the part well."

"What of now?"

"Sadly, your guess is as good as mine. To me, the damn rhyme makes no sense."

"You'd never heard of them before? Aside from . . ."

"Personally, no. Unfortunately your grandfather was not always the most forthcoming of people."

Thomas nodded. Silently he knew there were things he was still to be included on.

"You have no idea at all about Ravensfield?"

"Back in the Middle Ages, there was a small town on the coast of Yorkshire called Ravenspurn. At least two kings were known to have landed there, one being Edward IV when he reclaimed the throne from Henry VI. It was never a large place, but what had existed fell into the sea about two hundred years ago."

"What was there?"

"I have absolutely no idea. Sadly history is plagued by this sort of thing – lost villages, lost libraries et cetera. You know apparently when the Romans invaded Alexandria, Caesar ordered the fleet to set fire to the ships. This one act of stupidity not only nearly annihilated his own attack, but it eventually destroyed the library. But it wasn't the building as such that mattered, but the incalculable loss of ancient works. That is the true price of war. Back then, when a document was lost, so too was the knowledge."

"You suggest there is a connection b-between Ravenspurn and Ravensfield?"

"It's only a guess. Have you tried looking it up?"

"Yes. There was no trace."

"How about the chronicle?"

"The same."

The duke put his hand to his mouth. "In truth, the location of the priory itself is probably no longer relevant. After all, even if the priory was destroyed, that doesn't mean that a copy of the chronicle didn't survive. From what we can deduce from these," he spoke of the two books, "at least one of the authors witnessed the chronicle first hand – he even goes as far to confirm it was owned by someone in Monmouth's family. If the chronicle still exists, chances are it remains in the possession of the same family. The question is, which family?"

Thomas took a deep breath and exhaled. "There's something else that's bothering me. When I spoke to M-Morris yesterday, I eventually got out of him that he was under the orders of someone called T-Talbot."

The duke raised his eyebrows. "Jack Talbot?"

"That was my first thought, too. He didn't confirm or deny it. What do you know about him?"

"The man or the family?"

Thomas hesitated. "Both, I suppose."

The duke smiled wryly. The question was where to start. "Very well. The man was a former colonel in the British Army, served initially in the '50s and continued in service till the Falklands. Was knighted in the early '80s, and as far as I'm aware, lived a quiet, albeit not always trustworthy, life ever since.

"The family goes back further. Most of them were Catholic: one was even father-in-law to one of the gunpowder plotters. One of the Wintours, I think."

Thomas listened but said nothing.

"One of the most intriguing was in the 1400s. According to the Croyland Chronicle, it was a member of the family who was supposedly married to Edward IV. The family have a history for not loving us, that's for sure."

The prince was familiar with the story. "What of him now?"

"The man is a widower, I think. Children could be anywhere."

"How about Jack? Still the same place?"

"Of course."

"I think I best be paying Sir Jack a visit."

Thomas left the house through one of the side doors and headed straight for his car. No sooner had he reached it, his iPhone started to ring.

He looked at the caller ID and saw it was the Earl of Somerset. It was not yet 7 a.m., and the man had already called twice today.

He rejected the call and set off for the north.

15

Jen was furious – not with the woman, but with herself. She knew that convincing the mother of Luke Rankin to cooperate was always going to be a challenge, but she could've kicked herself for her handling of the situation.

She hadn't prepared, and it had shown.

She kept replaying the event in her mind. She guessed from the woman's appearance and manner that Susan Rankin was something of a reluctant recluse – almost certainly driven to solitude by the events of a year earlier. The possibility was straightforward enough. The woman was attractive.

Far too attractive for a complete recluse.

Her confidence was also far from shattered. According to the barflies, the woman was a qualified accountant and still worked from time to time. From what Jen had gathered at the Hog, Rankin was more pitied than hated. Few, if any, blamed her for Debra Harrison's disappearance – at least publicly – while others simply didn't not blame her. She had lost some of her friends – Gillian Harrison being the most prominent – but there had been no witch-hunts, no angry mobs, no poison pen letters.

Silently that had surprised her. Surely somebody would find a way of attaching blame to the mother of the prime suspect.

Whether consciously or subconsciously, the majority of the villagers either did not believe Debra Harrison to be dead or they refused to accept that she was.

Jen hated herself for blowing the opportunity.

At least she'd never make that mistake again.

She re-emerged onto the high street, heading back towards the Hog. She knew that the best way to Lovell's was to cross back over the bridge and take the footpath by the church, heading into the nearby countryside. From there on she would have to rely on guesswork. She knew from her map, and from what the locals had told her, that the houses belonging to Lovell, Ratcliffe, and Catesby were three of about fifteen in that part of the village – both the oldest and wealthiest. She assumed that most of them would be gated. That worried her.

Any slipups and she wouldn't even reach the garden.

Jen crossed the high street at a zebra crossing in front of the post office, opposite the bank, and stopped in her tracks. About a hundred metres away on the other side of the street, the hairdresser's was just opening. A young girl, probably in her late teens, was putting up the sign: a blackboard, opening up into a triangle shape, informing prospective clients that they were open for business.

Jen watched the teenager from across the street. She knew from her visit to the church that Martha Brown owned the hairdresser's, and that her daughter was on the payroll. Martha had said she was welcome to pop her head inside the door.

She checked her hair in the window of the post office.

Perhaps she could kill two birds with one stone.

Jen waited for a passing car before returning to the other side of the high street. The hairdresser's was located in between an art shop and a tearoom, and had an impressive white stone façade. The building, though old, was more recent than some – Georgian, based on the architecture.

The door opened easily, accompanied by the sound of a ringing bell, revealing a modern interior with a tiled floor, white walls, lots of mirrors, and what seemed to be hundreds if not thousands of bottles of cosmetics.

A woman in her late forties was washing her hands in one of the sinks. She turned on hearing the bell.

"Jennifer, how nice to see you again, pet."

It took Jen a couple of seconds to realise that the woman was Martha Brown. Gone the apron, the rubber gloves and the polish: instead, the woman was abundant in make-up, and her hair done up with a clipper.

Jen smiled warmly. "Wow, I love what you've done with the place."

The comment went down well. "We've only recently redecorated."

Jen held her smile while her eyes continued to take in the interior. Designer brands dominated: the posters ranging from that of cosmetics to models and celebrities. It was like looking at something from a fashionable city centre.

"Were you looking for me daughter?"

Jen was, but she decided against making it too obvious. "I was actually wondering if I could make an appointment."

Martha was practically beaming. "I can fit you in right now."

"That would be fantastic."

Jen followed Martha to a vacant seat one from the end. She hung up her jacket on the nearby peg before allowing the luxurious texture of the leather upholstery to relax her tense back.

"Is your daughter working today?"

"She's just put the kettle on. Would you like a cuppa, luvvy?"

Jen answered yes, milk, two sugars.

"Anything else?"

She declined. *Was this a hairdresser's or a café?*

"I never did thank you properly for your help yesterday," Jen said. "Had it not been for you, I'd probably still be looking around the altar."

Martha smiled as she placed a black cloak around Jen's shoulders. "It was my pleasure. We don't often get journalists or TV presenters in these parts . . . well, at least not normally."

"Just chancellors of the exchequer," Jen said, smiling.

The woman laughed. "Aye. Them and a few other politicians, but that's about it."

"I met him last night in the Hog. He was having a drink with a friend of his, someone named the Cat."

Martha giggled. "Aye, that's it, Sir William Catesby. He owns a farm down the lane. He's the chairman of the parish council."

The hairdresser ran her hands through Jen's hair, silently inspecting the damage.

"How about we start with a nice little wash," Martha said. "Would you like any highlights?"

"I really love Kate Hudson."

"Ah, butterscotch blonde – that's what she'd be," Martha said, impressing Jen with her instant knowledge.

Martha walked towards the door that connected the salon to the rear of the shop and shouted her daughter's name. "Anthea."

Almost immediately she returned to Jen with her hands full of cosmetics.

"One Kate Hudson coming up."

A young woman emerged through the doorway – evidently the same person Jen had seen from across the street. The girl was brunette, petite – no more than five feet four – and had a slender physique and pale skin. She looked seventeen, which agreed with the known facts.

If Martha was telling the truth, the girl had been in Debra Harrison's year at school.

Anthea walked shyly towards them and placed two coffee mugs down on the side.

"Anthea, pet, this is Jennifer, the lady I was telling you about."

Jen held up a hand, the outline of her fingers barely visible beneath the cloak. The girl smiled, but made practically no eye contact. Her gaze instead drifted to the walls.

"Pass me that bottle, will you, pet," Martha asked.

The girl obliged, again silently.

"Now, you hold the fort while I take care of Miss Farrelly's highlights."

"Okay, Mum."

The girl's voice was little more than a whisper. Jen smiled at her via the mirror, receiving the briefest of eye contact and another nervous smile before the girl left the room.

"She's very shy."

"She's lovely," Jen said. "Has she been with you long? As a hairdresser, I mean."

"Started the day she left school. She was never cut out for the real world."

"How do you mean?"

"Growing up in Wootton isn't the same as in the olden days. Back then, the cubs and kittens would follow the parents – most of the businesses in Wootton have remained in family hands. Nowadays, those with ambition move on: university, gap years, corporate jets . . . it's all strange to me."

The hairdresser brushed Jen's hair to make a perfect middle parting before stopping to examine the results. Satisfied, she opened the nearest bottle of hair dye and made a start on the highlights.

Jen smiled, taking the first sip of her coffee. "What do the teenagers do on leaving school?"

"Most of them go to college."

"St Joseph's?"

"That's right, pet."

Jen took a second sip of coffee before placing the mug down on the side. "I was thinking of paying a visit later – one of our researchers arranged an interview with one of the teachers. A Mrs Cartwright."

"Miss Cartwright," the hairdresser corrected.

Another admin error.

"Miss Cartwright was the English teacher there – everyone's favourite."

"I understand the former headmaster also lives in Wootton? Dr Lovell."

"Aye," Martha replied. "Another favourite in these parts."

"I've heard he's quite a character."

"That's one way of putting it, luvvy."

Jen laughed. "I couldn't help notice that many of the graves in the cemetery were of Lovells, Catesbys or Ratcliffes. I assume they all go back a long way?"

Martha nodded, concentrating on Jen's hair. "Most of us can trace our roots in Wootton. It's the same for most places on the moors, really. We never really went in for all that gentrification process up this way."

The interior of the shop suggested otherwise – less so the personality of the woman.

"You seem to be well informed of the history of the village. In London I don't even know my own neighbour."

The comment made Martha laugh. "We've never had a lot of people living here in Wootton. Most of the people have roots here."

"How well do you know Susan Rankin?" Jen asked. "If you don't mind my asking."

"All my life."

"I went to see her today. Has she always lived in the village?"

"Aye. Her mother grew up here."

"How about her husband's family?"

"No. He was an outsider – his family was originally from another village." The woman hesitated slightly. "Why do you ask, pet?"

"No reason, my producer asked me to research everything."

The answer reassured her. "He was a lovely man, at least on the surface."

"Was he a different man beneath the surface?"

The woman laughed. "No, I didn't mean it that way. I didn't know him as well as Susan, you know?"

Jen nodded. "What was she like? Before, I mean."

The hairdresser shrugged. "Wouldn't know how to describe her. Normal, really."

"Was she popular? Well liked?"

"No different to the rest of us."

Jen nodded, paying particular attention to the woman's body language. It was clear the subject wasn't her favourite.

The woman backed away, her attention on Jen's hair.

"I think this is coming along nicely. How about we leave this for now, and you can come back in a couple of hours to finish the cut."

Jen hid her disappointment. Ideally she still wanted to interview the daughter.

"That sounds super," she said, checking the time. According to the clock on the wall, it was 10:10 a.m. "You wouldn't happen to know what time they take lunch at St Joseph's?"

"It depends on the class, pet. It can be anything from 12:15 to 1:45."

That was the last thing Jen wanted to hear. "I don't suppose you know what time Miss Cartwright is likely to be free?"

"What day is today?"

"Tuesday."

"Tuesday she has a half day. She'll be finished by 12:15."

Jen smiled. "Thank you so much. I'll be back about 1:30."

16

Riverton, Lincolnshire

Riverton Court was an imposing sort of place – even in the mist, it was often visible from a distance. Located on the banks of the River Ancholme near the villages of Cadney and Hibaldstow, lying against the picturesque backdrop of the Lincolnshire countryside, it was the type of place where tourists, ramblers, or members of the National Trust might pop in for a couple of hours to admire the architecture, investigate the portraits or the bedrooms, or roam the gardens, enjoying the sparkling scenery.

Or at least they would if it was open to the public.

The word was that the owner was quite eccentric – reports varying from a bit of a crank, an egotistical bigot, or even a complete and utter wanker! Either way, not one for outsiders.

So went the local talk.

It was approaching 11:00 a.m. when Thomas arrived. He had seen the property before, at least in photographs, and immediately recognised it on leaving the main road. Like many of England's finest, the mansion was a stunning Elizabethan country estate long used by the lower gentry for fishing and game. As a minor royal, he was used to much bigger, but he wasn't as snobby as some. Since joining the army, he had got used to the barracks' life, and since taking on his new position, he had taken to living as and where. In his second year at Oxford he had shared a house with four others, two girls and two guys: none of whom were aware of his exact background. Despite the lies, that year had been his personal favourite.

Now, low-key was often his aid.

The village of Riverton was in keeping with the mansion – picturesque but slightly in decline. Its Saxon church and quaint buildings aside, it was the type of place that had prospered from tourism and fishing enthusiasts in the boom years, but fallen off the pace ever since. Most of the shops on the high street were closed, including the pub, either due to the time of year or because of the economic climate. He watched the river from the window, instantly drawn to the lack of boats despite it being July with the sun beating down and a temperature of around 23 Celsius.

It was like driving through a ghost town.

The entrance to the mansion was easy enough to find: like most properties of its type, it was situated off a quiet side road and gated from the outside. Large areas of woodland surrounded it on either side, its thick vegetation prohibiting the sun from shining through.

Thomas stopped in front of the gate, surprised to find it unlocked. He opened it and then continued driving along the driveway unhindered to the entrance of the mansion.

An elderly man, probably in his early seventies, was busy gardening. He looked up from his duties as Thomas shut the door to his car.

"We're not open to the public."

The prince continued. "Kindly inform Sir Jack that an emissary of the Duke of Clarence is here to see him."

The comment seemed to alert the man.

"Quickly now."

Though riled, the man took an age to get to his feet. He removed his gardening gloves as he walked towards the front door, throwing them down on the driveway before entering.

"Excuse me, won't you?"

The gardener walked quickly through the large entrance hall and entered the library, second on the right. An elderly disabled man was sitting in a chair, his head tilted to one side and his eyes closed.

"An emissary from the Duke of Clarence to see you, sir."

The man snorted as he came to. "What? What?"

"I said there is an emissary from the Duke of Clarence who requires an audience, sir."

The man was confused. "Does he have an appointment?"

"I believe not, sir."

The door to the library opened. "Expecting better company, Jack?"

The man laughed in disgust. "You call this an emissary? I might have known. Why pay someone to do a job when you've got a son to do it for free?"

The gardener seemed unnerved on hearing the news. After all, he didn't look like a royal.

"I suppose you'd like some tea, wouldn't you? It would be proper, after all, wouldn't it? English noble hospitality and all. Patterson, Earl Grey for His Majesty here, and see if we have any more of those lovely biscuits – you know the ones I mean."

"Immediately, sir."

The man bowed, more a half bow than anything, before both men as he retreated from the room. He caught the side of the door as he left, causing furniture to rattle.

An awkward silence followed as the two men were left alone for the first time.

"Fourteen years he's been with me; still can't do a bloody thing right."

Thomas stood with his arms folded, his focus on the man in the chair. Talbot looked older than he had – though four years had passed. The frizzy white hair, the flabby skin . . .

A large portrait in the corner of the room distracted him. Talbot was in it, standing not sitting, dressed in the uniform of the British Army – a colonel, no less.

"I was younger back then," Talbot said.

"We all were."

"You don't think about it when you're young. You never think that it might happen to you."

Thomas walked slowly around the room, his footsteps echoing off the hard floorboards. At times the wood creaked beneath his feet, affecting his balance. He watched the furniture, silently fearing one bad step would cause a breakage somewhere.

"Are we alone?"

"Of course not, you've seen the butler with your own eyes."

The prince smiled. "Beside him?"

The old man shrugged. "I don't get many visitors – I used to, back when Elsie was alive, bless her. They always came back then."

The door to the library opened. The butler returned carrying a large tray containing an antique teapot, two cups, a plate of biscuits and all the usual trimmings. The old man looked at him as he placed it down on the table, but said nothing – no sign of acknowledgement.

"Will that be all, sir?"

"Would that be all, sire?" the old man asked the prince.

Thomas bit his tongue. "Quite all, th-thank you."

The butler left the room, this time taking care not to collide with anything.

The old man looked at the young royal. "Well, don't stand on ceremony. Sit, relax, make yourself at home. That's what most of your family do."

Thomas walked towards the nearest chair, dragging it slowly as he sat down. For several seconds he waited, as if enjoying the silence.

To Talbot the pause was infuriating. "Well? State your business. Normally your family have the opposite problem."

Thomas poured tea into his cup, collecting the leaves in the silver container. He added lemon and sugar, and stirred the liquid carefully, tapping the spoon against the rim. He sipped it slowly before placing it down on the saucer. The sound of the clink was disturbingly loud, emphasising the quietness.

"Ahhh."

Talbot's face was reddening. "Well? What is it that you want?"

Thomas continued to bide his time. "Tell me everything you know about the Sons of York."

"Never heard of them."

The answer came far too quickly. "I never said they were a them."

"You said sons. That's plural, isn't it? Or perhaps they didn't teach you that at Winchester College?"

Thomas smiled. "Well, quite," he said, avoiding a stutter. "Very well, l-let's try this another way. What do you know about them?"

"I've told you before, I've never heard of them."

Thomas continued to bide his time. "Does the name Andrew Morris mean anything to you?"

"Not a thing. What's this got to do with anything?"

Again, the answer came too quickly. "Well, you tell me."

"Enough of this drivel. Get to the point."

The prince gripped both sides of the chair with his fingers. The chair was antique, wooden with a sculpted lion's head on both armrests. "Two men have recently died, Jack – I'm s-sure you know the chaps I'm t-talking about. A man has confessed – seems convinced of the crime." He paused for longer. "He claims he was working for something called th-the Sons of York."

Thomas looked at him seriously. "He also claimed that it was he who killed the King."

That seemed to affect him. "Killed the . . . you mean to say he was . . ."

"Claims to have carried out the wicked act on b-behalf of the Sons of York."

"I've told you already, I don't know any Sons of York."

Thomas rose to his feet and began to pace the room. He sipped from his tea intermittently. He could tell Talbot found the sound annoying.

"How do you know he is even telling the truth?" Talbot asked, his hands fidgeting. "For all you know, he could be just another loony."

"As a matter of fact, the man is absolutely barking – I visited him myself. Surely being mad makes one even more dangerous."

The prince walked closer to Talbot.

"He mentioned you personally, Jack," he said, speaking into Talbot's ear.

"Rubbish."

"Is it? I thought so, too. Then again, they were all friends of yours." The prince circled the man's chair. "Who was he working for? Who g-gave him the or-orders?"

Talbot's face brightened. "I see you never did get rid of that stutter, Thomas."

The prince was angry with himself.

"It only ever seems to happen to the royals. It's like a curse, a plague as Shakespeare put it: a plague on both your houses.

"I can't say I blame you. Being out in that dreadful war, it's enough to make anyone lose the power of speech. I suppose losing your grandmother made it even worse. It could've been worse still, you know. You're lucky it wasn't more; it could have been an arm or leg – no, you got off lightly.

"But they never go away – the things you see. It's enough to make one go completely mad. I've seen it happen; mad as a brush they were. Perhaps they got you, too; perhaps you're a bit mad. What's the matter, Thomas? Cat got your tongue?"

The man laughed, louder and louder. After several seconds he started banging his fist, causing the table to jump.

"Dammit, Jack!" Thomas shouted, his voice loud enough to wake the dead. "I know that you're involved; I know that you gave Morris directions."

The prince removed his Glock 17 pistol from his belt and aimed it at Talbot's head.

"Your family have a history, Jack. Talbots always have a history. Do I really need to remind you?"

He checked the gun was loaded. "Or perhaps you would rather I just shoot you here and now? At least that way we can give you an honest traitor's death."

The room fell silent. For several seconds Talbot remained rigid, visibly startled. Thomas watched him, this former soldier, now an old man. The man's lips seemed to quiver. It reminded him of a guppy.

"Well, I'll tell you one thing for nothing, waving that gun won't help you – I'm already dead anyway."

The prince brushed his finger against the trigger. "Well, let's not waste any time, then, Jack."

Talbot looked up, alarmed. "All right, all right, I'll talk. For all the good it will do."

"Let me be the j-judge of that."

This time it was Talbot's turn to struggle with words. "Very embarrassing for me, you know. There have been many proud moments in my life. Sadly this isn't one of them."

Thomas's hand remained rigid, gun at the ready.

"It was back in the late '60s I first heard of them for sure, back when all this business of Europe began – prior to that, like most people, I assumed the Sons of York to be merely a myth, a socialist's fantasy, so to speak."

"They're socialist in nature?"

"Not necessarily."

"So what are their aims and objectives?"

"No idea."

"Jack . . ."

"I'm telling you the truth; I was never involved in such things."

"Tell me about this organisation. How did you first become involved?"

Talbot's face was visibly sad. "You don't find them; they find you."

"Wh-who asked you?"

"I don't remember."

The prince aimed the Glock again at Talbot with renewed emphasis.

"It won't do you any good: he's dead anyway," Talbot said, his eyes on the ground. "And they weren't all traitors, by the way – at least not intentionally. Most were patriots."

"Who recruited you? Who's in charge?"

"I don't know who's in charge – I never did. They work through intermediaries."

"Who?"

"These are not the type of men who leave calling cards."

The prince's frustration was reaching boiling point. "What was in it for you? Money?"

"Not being killed was surely more important. Though it's the family that are most at threat – you're no use to them dead."

Thomas returned to his chair, now sitting directly opposite Talbot. "Listen to me, Jack. Right now in London we have a man who many believe to be mad, who c-claims to have murdered the King and two members of the C-Cabinet. For what purpose?"

"I've already told you, I was never involved in such things."

"Dammit, Jack!"

"All right, all right, please don't shout – my ears can't take it anymore."

Thomas looked at him seriously. "Well?"

"Apparently it all goes back to the medieval times."

"When, exactly?"

"Back to the power struggles – I don't know exactly. History was never my strong point."

Thomas took a deep breath. "Go on."

"Let's just say that some of your ancestors should have been more careful about who they offended."

"This is far too vague," Thomas replied, watching Talbot, who appeared unmoved. "You s-seem to suggest that the Sons of York hold a g-grudge against the royals?"

The old man nodded. "Yes, but that's only the beginning."

"Tell me more."

"The society has changed, even in the last twenty years."

"I thought you knew nothing."

The man exhaled furiously. "I thought you wanted my help."

"How can I find them?"

"I told you before, they find you."

Thomas held up the gun again. "I really had hoped you would cooperate, Jack."

"All right, all right, please just settle down . . . I . . ."

A loud crash, apparently coming from within the room, took them both by surprise. Unmistakably glass had broken, but the other noise was difficult to decipher. It sounded like wood, thick wood, possibly being crushed, but by what?

Acting on instinct, Thomas dived for cover, banging into the table to his right and knocking a book clean off it. Under different circumstances the prince might have regretted nearly destroying the valuable manuscript, but now he felt only panic.

For several seconds he lay still with his hands covering his head, the two noises still echoing in his ears. Looking up, he noticed that the window in front of Talbot had smashed: a hole had appeared, almost the size of a cricket ball, accompanied by a large crack. His attention moved to his left.

Talbot's head had been ripped apart.

The man had been shot.

Dumbstruck, Thomas moved towards him. The bullet had travelled through the window to the old man's head and into the wooden headboard at the back of the chair. A large hole had appeared in the wood, presumably accounting for the clunk he had heard.

Thomas moved over to the window and saw movement in the direction of the far wall – the east wing.

He left the room and ran through the large hall to the main entrance. Strangely, the front door was still open.

Outside, all was quiet except for the sound of the bullet on the wood, which still resonated in his ears. The gardener/butler was absent, which was suspicious – it seemed unlikely that he would have failed to hear the sound of the glass breaking.

Now sprinting, the prince headed for the east wing – the place where he had seen movement through the broken window. He held his gun as he ran, checking the ammo. Gun at the ready, he slowed his pace on reaching the far wall and continued round the corner, his back to the wall. The wall went on for another ten metres, turned at a right angle and on again for about thirty metres – the east wall of the property.

Whoever it was had disappeared. Heading south, in the direction of the grounds, Thomas passed several windows, each divided by mullions into panels of six, the dark, patterned glass giving little away of the interior.

It was obvious from the design that the windows could not be opened.

He found a door – evidently locked. He rattled hard against the lock and, after failing to make any progress, fired a shot at it. The wood around the lock shattered with a snapping sound, following which the door opened.

Thomas entered the kitchen: a large area with an adjacent pantry and utilities that was dirty and dated, probably dating back to the '30s.

He heard a sound close by and headed through the door, finding himself in a long corridor hung with original portraits and historical wall hangings.

He looked both ways. Again there was movement, this time at the far end, a shadowy shape moving left. As Thomas chased after it, he heard what he guessed was a door closing, followed by further movement somewhere up ahead.

Cautiously, he opened the door, gun at the ready. He had entered a small sitting room furnished with antiques. The figure was approaching the wall, moving puzzlingly slowly under the circumstances.

Less surprising was the man's identity.

The gardener/butler.

Thomas sought to speak, but his stutter let him down. Eventually he forced out the words, "Stay where you are."

The man turned, also armed. He fired without warning, missing Thomas by a matter of inches. The prince dived to his left, taking out a cabinet and smashing the crockery inside. In the melee Thomas hurt his shoulder and narrowly avoided being shot a second time, as the impact of the bullets brought debris off the wall.

He waited until the mayhem died down before rising to his feet. He saw movement from the other side of the room, but what happened next he had not expected.

The wall was moving, closing as if it was a door.

Thomas wasted no time. He sprinted to the area of the wall that had moved and pushed against it, feeling for any kind of groove – any clue. He knew that houses of that type and age often concealed priest holes from recusancy times, but he guessed that this wall contained something more elaborate:

Most likely a staircase or passageway.

Thomas retreated and examined the rest of the room. He kicked the cabinet in frustration, breaking further crockery. He considered firing at the wall, but he knew that was probably a waste of bullets.

The butler was undoubtedly long gone by now.

His mobile phone began to ring, echoing throughout the deserted room. He reached for his pocket and answered.

"Hello?"

"Where the devil have you been?"

He recognised the voice of his father. "Lincolnshire," he stuttered. "Talbot's dead – I saw it myself.

"This time the butler really did do it."

17

The drive to St Joseph's took less than fifteen minutes. Jen listened to the hairdresser's advice, and waited till ten to noon before setting off.

She parked on a quiet road outside the school, deciding against using the main car park. Her time in Wootton had already attracted unwanted interest, and the last thing she wanted was to add to it. She remembered from watching the news a year ago, how much of the footage centred on the school.

If her luck held, she would get out without causing a scene.

She waited in the car until 12:10 before making her way towards the main entrance. St Joseph's RC secondary school was an assortment of several buildings: a mixture of old and new, with blue walls and lots of windows. The entrance was obvious enough, located at the centre of the main building and guarded by automatic doors. To the right of the main building, detached from the school, was an elegant and more modern building, evidently the sixth form.

Jen guessed it was only a few years old.

She headed towards the main entrance, her presence so far unnoticed. If the woman at the hairdresser's was correct, there were still five minutes before the lunch break started, giving her an ample head start.

As Jen entered, she noticed a large reception area. A nice-looking blonde lady, probably in her early fifties, was standing, practically leaning, against the desk, a telephone receiver held to her ear. She spoke to the unseen listener for over a minute before hanging up.

She smiled at Jen. "Hi."

"Hi, I was looking for Miss Cartwright."

"She's just finishing a lesson in the sixth form."

"I know," Jen replied confidently. "Any idea what room?"

"36."

"Thank you."

Jen left the reception area through the same door and headed for the isolated building at the far end of the campus. The loud ringing of a bell, heralding the beginning of the lunch break or the end of a lesson, caught her by surprise.

Jen hurried towards the sixth form, arriving as several people exited. For the first time she felt nervous – almost as if she was trespassing. Entering through the glass door, she caught a glimpse of her reflection; Martha Brown had done a good job on her highlights, but the half-completed do was still a mess.

If the reports she had heard were correct, at least Miss Cartwright would not be overly judgemental about her appearance.

The corridor was tidy and airy – except for the students, most of whom defied generalisation. Hordes of teenagers, ranging in style from trendies to goths, made their way in and out of classrooms, many laughing and talking, some hurrying – even running – in various directions as they attempted to make it to their next destination on time. Jen ignored the come-ons of one or two, putting it down to inexperience and testosterone.

She followed the sequence of numbers on the left and right, and arrived outside number 36. The room was almost deserted, the last few remaining students just leaving. Jen caught the closing door as a young brown-haired boy left. Inside, the room was large and modern, with its desks laid out in a horseshoe, as opposed to rows, painted white and lit by natural light. At the head of the class, a large desk was situated in front of double whiteboards covered by marker pen writing. A woman was standing by the desk, preparing to leave. She was about five feet seven, with reddish/blonde hair, blue eyes and wearing rimless spectacles.

"Excuse me, Miss Cartwright?"

The woman smiled. "Hello."

"My name is Jennifer Farrelly; I'm a researcher with Raleigh Five, a TV productions company. I understand you spoke to one of my colleagues recently?"

It took a few seconds for her to catch on. "Oh, you mean about the documentary?"

"I'm sorry to bother you while you're working; I wasn't sure when was the best time to catch you."

"That's quite all right, really. I've actually just finished for the day."

The response was good news. Martha was right.

"I was hoping I might be able to ask you a few questions. Is now a good time?"

"Of course."

Jen removed a digital voice recorder from her handbag. "Would you mind if I record this? I find it so much easier than taking notes."

The request made the woman slightly nervous – nevertheless, she said that it was okay.

Jen placed her hand behind her ear, her mind briefly on her highlights. The sooner she got back to the hairdresser's, the better.

"I understand you worked with some of my colleagues a year or so ago."

The woman nodded. "Yes, that's right."

"Well, right now we're in the process of putting together a little documentary, a follow-up, so to speak, of what happened in Wootton a year or so ago."

Jen touched her hair again as she made a start scanning her notes. "I understand that you taught both Debra Harrison and Luke Rankin?"

"That's right – though Luke only briefly; he only attended St Joseph's for two years."

"Were you teaching him around the time he changed schools?"

"Yes, I taught him all throughout the time he attended the school in years seven and eight."

"How would you describe his personality and character?"

The woman shrugged. "Luke suffered with learning difficulties from an early age," she said, her expression suggesting she was slightly uncomfortable. "He was also something of a shy lad."

"I understand he was autistic."

That seemed to upset her. "No. That's a widespread misconception."

If it was a widespread misconception, it was very widespread. "Okay. So he didn't have any mental problems?"

"Not in the clinical sense."

"You mentioned he did suffer from learning difficulties."

The woman smiled ironically. "He was, as some of his classmates would have put it, slightly dumb. The fact that he was so shy probably escalated the problem."

Jen nodded. "Did he interact at all with other kids?"

"Yes, of course. He wasn't a complete loner as some of my students would say – despite what some people have made out. He had a select circle of friends – mostly people of similar identity."

"You mean learning difficulties?"

Cartwright smiled kindly at Jen. "My dear, I know exactly what you're thinking; given all the media attention, it's hardly surprising. If the rumours are to be believed, Debra Harrison was the perfect A-grade student: kind, bright, beautiful – destined for great success – only to have her time cut short by a dangerously obsessed retard."

The point was clinical, but not inaccurate.

"Come with me – there's something I'd like you to see."

Cartwright led Jen through the main corridors – now back in the main school. Most of the kids were taking lunch in the dining hall, the chaos of over a hundred people dining, chatting, taunting and screaming coming through as little more than white noise.

Jen followed the teacher along the corridor that led to the reception area, and stopped in between two classrooms – one empty, the other packed to the rafters with pupils.

"Here," Cartwright said, pointing her index finger at a boy in an old class photo. "That's him."

Jen followed Cartwright's finger. The child was small and awkward looking, standing in the third row on steps. He had dark hair, noticeably so – even compared to the Asian lad next to him.

It wasn't difficult to see where Rankin's sinister reputation came from.

"Why did he leave?" Jen asked.

If he wasn't medically challenged, the reasons made less sense than before.

"Luke was always an awkward child," Cartwright said sympathetically. She looked to her left; three students were running towards them. "No running in the corridors."

The students stopped running immediately.

The teacher gestured to the nearby empty classroom. "We can talk in here."

Jen followed her inside. The room was bigger than the last one and more in keeping with a traditional classroom. Charts of all kinds, ranging from history to maps of the world, covered the walls, accompanied by various quotes, prints of art and other learning aids.

"Luke Rankin was one of those strange boys: both bullied and a bully; fearless and always afraid; lazy but full of energy; full of hate but desperate for love. Unsurprisingly most of the teachers here didn't really know what to make of him."

Jen sat down opposite Cartwright. "You think he struggled with identity issues? Crisis of confidence? That sort of thing?"

The woman laughed. "Without question," she said, "but so do most of the pupils here. If I could use one word to describe adolescence that would be: confusion."

Jen smiled, understanding she had a point. Not for the first time she found herself playing with her hair.

"What made him leave St Joseph's?"

"The poor boy hated being here – even to the point that he would throw a tantrum just to get his mother not to bring him," she said, adjusting her glasses.

"Would you say his behaviour was far in excess of what might be considered normal? I mean, I remember faking the odd illness to get out of school myself."

Cartwright grinned. "Off the record, I do know of many people who would accept that view. However, they never taught Luke first hand. He was often frustrated – most of the time his frustration was caused by being frustrated."

"In general how were his relationships with other teachers? Did any other teachers encourage him?"

The woman hesitated. "I know that most of my colleagues found him awkward."

"How about after he left? Where did he go?"

"His mother took him to St Brendan's – about eighteen miles away. I know his mother well; it was the nearest Catholic school, and I know most of the teachers well."

Jen was interested. It sounded as if the woman was directly involved in choosing the new school.

"Was the school better positioned for dealing with children with learning disabilities?"

"No, not really."

That astonished her. "So . . . it was really just about having a fresh start?"

"The former headmistress at St Brendan's was very understanding about Luke's predicament. On Luke's arrival, she earmarked one particular pupil to be his first friend. Both had similar backgrounds – I'm sure you're aware that Luke's father passed away some two years earlier."

Jen nodded.

The teacher smiled awkwardly. "Mrs Hopegood – she was the head – thought that Luke might benefit from someone who understood his problems, someone he could open up to, rather than have to face his problems himself."

"How did he fare at the new school?"

"Better – at least according to his mother. He was certainly less troublesome. He left the school with seven GCSEs, and later three A-levels. He was all set to go to university to take a science degree."

Jen was now seriously confused. While parts of what she had learnt tallied with the early reports, the testimony of Cartwright certainly painted a more positive picture of the boy.

"How was he at primary school?"

"A bit of a maverick, but nothing dangerous."

"Miss Cartwright, in your opinion, how much of Luke Rankin's problems were down to the death of his father?"

The woman shrugged slowly. "I'm sure it was an important factor."

To Jen, her face suggested it was probably the only factor.

"How about Debra Harrison? I understand you taught her all her life."

The teacher smiled and nodded – there was clear evidence of a tear from her right eye. She wiped her eyes quickly and readjusted her glasses. It was becoming obvious to Jen why everyone loved the woman so much. She was overwhelmingly friendly, caring and sensitive. She guessed from speaking to the woman, and the miss in her name, that she was minus a man in her life.

Always a bridesmaid never the bride.

"Tell me about Debra."

"She was lovely, really: bright blue eyes, lovely dark hair – the kind like a model might have. She was always smiling, always positive," the woman said, nodding.

"Was English her favourite subject?"

"Yes – that and history. I teach A-level history here as well."

"Did you teach Debra history?"

"No. I only teach A-level."

Jen nodded. In the moment she had forgotten that Harrison was only sixteen when she disappeared.

Jen placed her hair behind her ear. "Just one last question, if you don't mind."

"Of course."

"Did Luke Rankin and Debra Harrison have any kind of relationship or friendship of which you were aware?"

The woman's expression turned colder. "No, none whatsoever."

Jen switched off her digital voice recorder and placed it in her handbag.

"Thank you so much for your time, Miss Cartwright."

*

Jen unlocked her Picanto from a distance and switched on the engine on entering. It was 1:30. The traffic was quiet, and would be for another two hours.

She had succeeded in coming and going without drawing unnecessary attention to herself.

While her eyes took in the sights of the B road, her mind was alive with activity.

Rankin had been a borderline recluse rather than anything more clinical – and apparently had no history of medical irregularities. True, Cartwright admitted he had learning difficulties, but most of them seemed attributable to his attitude – particularly since the death of his father. The fact that he had no prior record of disturbances on joining secondary school made her think that Cartwright was correct.

The boy's problems were more recent.

The move to St Brendan's had been a success – that much seemed clear. While his academic achievements were hardly spectacular, his grades were more than satisfactory. Should the media reports be believed – not to mention the barflies at the Hog – the boy had no friends and no future.

If anything, the opposite was true.

A disturbing thought entered Jen's mind. She had been asked by her producer to come to Wootton to research the facts. Yet what they were was now less clear than before.

If Luke Rankin had not killed Debra Harrison, why did he commit suicide?

In a deserted room on the third floor of Riverton Court, Thomas removed yet another document from the drawer of the antique desk and scanned the content.

Riverton Court was a curious place – that much was clear even before exploding windows and secret tunnels. He knew from hearsay that the owner was something of a maverick when it came to collecting things, and the first-hand evidence matched the rumours. Guns were a favourite: Lee-Enfields, Martini-Henrys . . . in fact, everything from revolutionary muskets to automatic weapons. That caused a raised eyebrow.

How the hell did they get through customs?

The study on the third floor was easily the most bizarre of the rooms he had seen so far. Antiques and memorabilia dominated – but not the usual kind. Most of the artwork was pornographic, and not the alluring sort. As a student of history Thomas knew that tastes change, but this was taking things to an extreme. Much of the art was of animal on animal – and not the same animal. As an outsider it was not obvious whether they were caricature or serious.

Either way, the mind boggled.

Nevertheless, among the elements of weirdness and tasteless sleaze was something more interesting. The man's diary was in the third drawer – and had a reference for an appointment later that night.

Time: 21:00.

The entry surprised him. As a former soldier, the prince knew that Talbot would not dare allow anything incriminating to fall into the wrong hands. He had heard rumours of dementia, but that was still open to debate.

Certainly nothing of their meeting had given him any indication that was definite.

The other peculiarity was the absence of any mention of the location for the meeting. Perhaps that was a secret even to Talbot; it certainly matched what Talbot had already suggested.

It was also possible the appointment would take place at Riverton. If not, a car would almost certainly be sent.

Either way, someone clearly had an appointment to keep.

18

Jen was back in Wootton just after 2 p.m. She parked her car outside the Hog, and walked back along the high street to the hairdresser's.

She entered breezily, expecting to see Martha.

"Oh," she said. The place was deserted bar her daughter, who was busy sweeping the floor. "Hi."

The girl held up a hand, a nervous wave.

"Your mum said to come back and finish the cut," Jen said, looking at the clock on the wall. "I guess I was slightly longer than I thought."

The girl answered timidly. "She just went out."

Although Jen was disappointed, she knew her visit to the school had taken longer than she had anticipated. Ideally, she wanted to see Lovell and Ratcliffe before the day was out.

After her hair was fixed.

"Okay," Jen said, slightly unsure of herself. "Do you know how long she'll be?"

The girl shrugged. "She didn't say."

"Okay . . . how about I come back in about three quarters of an hour?"

The girl moved her head, not quite a nod but close enough. Jen still wanted to interview the girl herself, but she knew that doing so without Martha being present was a risk.

Even though the girl was over sixteen, the last thing she wanted was to intimidate her.

"I'll try again in about an hour," Jen said, smiling warmly. "Thanks."

"I can cut it . . ." the girl said, just as Jen was about to leave. Judging by the girl's expression, she was equally surprised by her own outburst. "You know, like . . . or if you'd rather wait."

Jen paused for a few seconds, pretending to weigh up the situation. "Okay. Great," she said, smiling.

Secretly she was delighted.

The girl smiled widely, displaying evidence of dimples on both cheeks. "I am a real hairdresser – Mum's been training me for like a year."

"That's great. Great," Jen said – slightly dumbstruck.

"You said you like Kate Hudson, right?"

"Yes."

The girl picked up a magazine and opened it to a pre-designated page. "That would look great on you."

The magazine was *OK!*, and the photo was of Kate Hudson attending an awards ceremony.

"Oh my God. There's no way I could pull that off."

"Hell yeah. You've got great hair . . . and you're really pretty."

Jen was flattered. "Thank you."

"Can I just make one little suggestion?" The young hairdresser leaned towards the counter and picked up a designer lipstick. "Try this one."

The colour was slightly darker than Jen was used to.

"Wow," Jen said, her eyes alight. "I love it."

The girl smiled, still shyly but more relaxed than before.

"I can see the salon's definitely in good hands."

The girl washed her hands in the nearest sink and dried them before picking up the cloak.

"Okay, your highlights are set. We normally offer a wash, cut and blow dry for £35."

"Great. That's great," Jen said, now feeling incapable of saying anything else. For the first time in recent memory she felt a strange degree of freedom.

It reminded her of being back at uni.

"I'm Jen, by the way."

"Anthea."

They shook hands gently.

"Well then, Anthea, let's see what we're made of."

The butler drove slowly through the open gateway of the historic mansion and parked in a hidden area around the back.

The orders he had received were specific – not that they needed to be. Fifty years experience had taught him everything he needed to know. He doubted the precaution was necessary. In addition to the natural seclusion, the property was guarded at every corner by either concrete walls or fencing.

The master refused attracting attention.

Patterson entered the house via the back door where his opposite number, the butler of the house, awaited his arrival with folded arms.

"His Highness is most unhappy."

Patterson did not respond. The butler's expression was morbid, but that was nothing unusual. The man had been a cellmate years ago, back in the good old days: a fiery old kook named McGregor.

"I'm afraid he's about to become even more unhappy."

"Well, in that case, you can be the one to deliver the news."

"You don't even know what it is yet."

McGregor frowned. "Come on. This way."

He led the newcomer through the kitchen, into the entrance hall and up three flights of stairs.

Patterson took in the surroundings as he walked. The building was magnificent. Like most in the village it was a 14th-century manor house, though this one was clearly the largest. The stairs creaked more than most, but the rest of the interior he approved of. Valuable tapestries hung from the walls, accompanied by priceless works of art, coats of arms, weaponry and other family keepsakes. The items were old and unquestionably authentic.

Yet even to an academic in the outside world, their meaning was beyond comprehension.

McGregor knocked on the door and waited for a reply.

"Try louder."

"It's about time you learned some patience."

McGregor tried again, this time louder.

Eventually he heard a response. "Come."

McGregor opened the door, revealing a poorly lit room. Three large, typically 14th-century, elaborately decorated windows, each divided into sections by mullions, looked out onto the grounds at the front. The walls were brown, the same colour as the wood, their shade intensifying the lack of light.

By the fireplace, illuminated by the ominous red glow of a smouldering coal fire, a figure sat hunched in the chair, looking into the fire with a distant and distracted expression.

The man seemed oblivious to their arrival.

"Mr Anthony Patterson to see you, Your Grace," McGregor said. He left the room without direction and closed the door behind him.

For the first time Patterson was worried. He sensed an atmosphere, one he could cut with the proverbial knife. He looked around, his attention mainly on the walls. Like the downstairs and the staircase, the room was filled with countless historical artefacts and curiosities. A large emblem was situated above the fireplace: a yellow shrub, evidently a broom – a trademark of the man's family. Similar things adorned the windows.

Everything about the room cried out heritage.

And permanence.

The feeling of being watched had become increasingly unsettling for Patterson. He wanted to look but daren't. The man was old, but his legacy was older still. If he was the shadow, what came before was the tree.

And the roots were deeply entrenched.

The old man shuffled in his seat. He watched the newcomer, his dark eyes magnified by his large glasses.

"Why have you disobeyed my strictest rule and come in the daytime?"

Patterson hesitated for slightly too long.

"Well?"

The man's tone unsettled him. "There was no alternative. Talbot is dead."

"That is unfortunate. What happened?"

"I killed him."

"You . . ."

"I had to. He was about to confess."

"Confess what and to whom?"

Patterson hesitated for a second time. "The royals are onto us. They suspect."

"Suspect what?"

"One of them came today. He was asking questions about the Sons of York."

This time it was the old man's turn to delay. "Who came?"

"One of the king's nephews. He referred to himself as an emissary of the Duke of Clarence."

Silence followed. The atmosphere was heavy, as if a fog had descended, liable to choke the lungs. The old man breathed deeply and attempted to clear his throat, the sound developing into a cough.

"I have been expecting this."

To Patterson, the assertion was preposterous. But he knew it was not his place to argue.

"Do you know what today is?"

"Of course. 20 July. The anniversary."

Patterson looked at the old man for the first time. His white hair had almost completely thinned, leaving a bald head that was plagued by liver spots. The skin on either side of his mouth sagged, as if his face was now incapable of existing on its own.

But what struck him most were the man's eyes. It was like looking at a demon, a spectre caught somewhere between purgatory and hell.

"Where is this emissary now?" the old man asked.

"I don't know."

"You don't know."

"He came after me. He was armed."

More coughing followed, this time prolonged. Patterson detected anguish in the man's expression as he attempted to rid himself of phlegm.

He doubted that the old man had long to live.

"Send a car round to the house this evening as planned. If our friend wishes to join us, you can send him to the usual place."

Patterson bowed and immediately went for the door.

"Mr Patterson," the old man called, "do not forget the purpose of your master's appointment."

Patterson lingered for several seconds before finally leaving the room. He hurried along the corridor, down the stairs and into the kitchen.

Ten minutes later he departed down the driveway behind the wheel of a luxury limousine.

Back in the lonely room on the third floor of the ancient mansion, the butler knocked quietly against the open door. He carried a bottle of medicine and a teaspoon.

McGregor cleared his throat. "Sir, it's two o'clock."

The old man did not answer. His eyes were focused on the fire, his expression suggesting he was in the middle of a dream.

"Ahem. Sir." McGregor tapped the spoon against the bottle.

The man returned to reality. "Oh."

McGregor put his right hand to the bottle top, only to feel a hand against his left arm.

"Where is my son?"

McGregor closed his eyes and exhaled. "Sir, Richard has been dead for many years. They killed him – remember?"

The man's eyes were open, but it was evident from his gaze that his memory was all at sea.

The man nodded, but blankly. "Yes . . . I remember."

"They got Anne, too."

The man wheezed, the sound of phlegm evident in his gullet.

"Sir, your medicine."

The man turned to his right, now ready to take it. He opened his mouth widely and accepted the full spoon of black liquid. The butler didn't envy him. To him, it tasted like death.

He had only tasted it once.

He wiped the man's mouth with a handkerchief, taking away elements of spillage. No doubt about it, he was getting worse.

"Where is my grandson? Where is Edward?"

"The young man decided to go out for a while."

The old man nodded, but McGregor doubted he understood. The bouts of forgetfulness were getting worse – particularly for names and faces.

Yet other things he remembered quite clearly. Even the day before, he accurately recalled that today was the anniversary. Perhaps it was because it had been so central to his whole life that it remained with him now.

Even on the point of death.

McGregor closed the door behind him and headed for the stairs.

Midway down he stopped, his eyes alighting on a magnificent portrait. The painting was relatively new, but it could have been old. The figure's appearance was impeccable – dressed in ancient regalia, just like they all were. A fine head of fair hair was his crowning glory – at least beside the actual crown. Strange as it sounded, even to him, facially he was almost the same as the man who had lived five hundred years earlier.

At the top of the stairs he heard further coughing. Soon the young man's time would come.

A new pretender would rise from obscurity.

19

"Did you always want to be a hairdresser?" Jen asked, enjoying the warm tap water as it flowed through her hair.

The young protégé nodded. "Mum started the business before I was born. She learnt from my grandmother – she owned the shop right here."

"Wow."

"It's always been something of a family tradition," the girl said, drying some of the excess water from Jen's hair. "But even if it wasn't, I'd probably still be doing it. Never really fancied working in the city."

Jen nodded, taking the time to admire her hair in the mirror as the chair turned round. It looked pitch black as a result of the water.

"I've always wondered, what do people do around here for work?"

Anthea shrugged. "Depends, really. In the past most people owned their own shops or businesses; some have survived, some haven't. A few commute to Hull, Leeds or York. Those who commute further usually have a second home in the week."

"How about the people of your generation?"

A wry smile. "Those with ambition go to London. Most go to college or university first, though."

"Did you not fancy it yourself?"

"There was no point, really; I'd already learnt everything to know watching Mum as a teenager. I just wanted to try it first hand, you know?"

Jen nodded and smiled.

"So what about you? The big TV star, you."

"Hardly," Jen said coyly. "We'll see after the haircut."

Anthea giggled. "It must be so exciting, working in television. Have you done anything famous?"

"Depends what you mean by famous. I've worked on news programs. But mainly documentaries: history, that sort of thing. I've worked on a few for Discovery."

Anthea nodded, her eyes still focused on her scissors. Silently Jen was pleased the girl was keeping her concentration.

"Have you ever worked with anyone famous?"

Jen noticed the girl's excitement was growing. "A few – most of them have been older."

"You mean like Tony Robinson?"

"Like him, but not him."

The girl's smile widened.

"It's not like people think, though," Jen said, this time more earnestly. "Most of us work to contract – we're technically self-employed. It all goes round in cycles. One day you could find yourself working on daytime telly, six months later you could be working for Panorama."

Anthea was captivated. "Is that why you came to Wootton?"

"The company I work for now filmed here a year ago. Apparently the producer became quite attached to the story . . . do you mind if I ask you something really personal?"

Anthea stopped mid-cut.

"What was it like? A small village suddenly becoming the centre of attention?"

The girl shrugged. "In a way, it was quite exciting, really. I'd never seen a media circus before."

Jen nodded. It was the answer of a teenager.

"They asked me to be interviewed, but I said no."

"How come?"

"Don't know, really. I guess it was because she was me friend."

Jen watched her reaction in the mirror. It was obvious that the question had caused the girl to reminisce.

"Were you close?"

Back to reality. "Sorry?"

"You and Debra: were you close?"

Anthea grimaced. "We sort of was, but we wasn't. You know what I mean?"

"I think so." In truth Jen had no idea.

"I mean, we were mates; like, you know you have your best mates, then your good mates, then finally just your mates."

"Yeah."

"She was like one of the good mates. I mean, we'd talk, but we didn't always hang out. You know what I mean?"

"Absolutely." That made complete sense.

"We were distantly related through marriage. I'd been round her house. Stayed over a couple of times."

"Just the two of you?"

"No – more like six or seven of us."

Jen nodded, no surprises. "Where are they now – her other friends?"

"Most of them are at college. Others moved on."

The girl paused, this time for longer. For a moment Jen thought she was going to cry, but she didn't.

"Was it weird? Not having her about."

"Being honest, it wasn't. I think that was because we were leaving school anyway. You know what I mean?"

Until now that thought had never occurred to her. Jen knew from the reports that Debra Harrison had disappeared only three days after finishing her last GCSE exam.

"When did you last see her?"

"You mean before she disappeared?"

What else could she mean? "Yeah."

"Earlier that same evening."

"You didn't notice anything unusual?"

"Not really. We'd just finished our last exam. Or I had. My last exam was business," Anthea continued. "Debra didn't do business; she did geography and history."

The facts at least continued to agree. "What did you do on finishing your exams?"

The girl smiled uncontrollably. "Mum threw us all a party here. I've never been so wasted in all me life."

Jen laughed. "How many of you were here?"

"Just the girls, really – about twelve in all."

"How about Debra?"

Anthea paused, her mind in deep thought. "She was here – at least she came. I think she went early."

Finally a potential breakthrough. "Any idea when?"

"She was definitely here till after seven. I know that because Melanie – she's me best mate – she was really drunk, and we had to put her on the settee out back. See, I remember that because I was sober then – relatively."

Jen smiled. "What time did you start?"

"Not sure, really. Most of the girls arrived after seven. Most of the girls had been drinking all day."

Again it was what Jen had expected. She remembered doing the same thing after passing her own GCSEs.

She needed to concentrate on Debra Harrison. "Any idea why Debra left?"

"She wasn't really much of a drinker – Debra."

A new thought had occurred. Was the girl sober when she disappeared? Furthermore, was she the kind of girl where a little drink went a long way?

"Was she drunk when she left?"

Anthea shook her head. "No, definitely not. I remember she was talking to me earlier; she'd been working on a project. She said she needed to concentrate. I said, look, calm down, you need to enjoy yourself – come have some fun."

Jen was confused. "What project? I thought exams were over."

"They were. This one was different."

"You mean extracurricular?"

"Sort of. It wasn't to do with school. She was helping Lovell with something. That's Dr Lovell. He lives in the village; he used to be our headmaster . . . but not anymore."

Jen raised an eyebrow. This was the first she'd heard of any project with Lovell.

"Francis Lovell?"

Anthea nodded.

"Was she good friends with Lovell?"

"Not really friends," Anthea said. "I mean, he's well over sixty – Lovell."

"When did he retire?"

"About four year ago, I think – maybe it were five."

"So he was still the head when you all started?"

"Yeah, that's right. I think I were in year eight when he retired – just finishing year eight."

Jen nodded, digesting the information while looking at herself in the mirror. The cut was progressing nicely.

"Did you still interact with him after he retired?"

"At the end of the day, we're all local, really. We normally bump into each other after a few days."

"Where does he live?"

In truth, Jen knew the answer already.

"You know that footpath that goes off by the church – near where you've been staying?"

Jen nodded.

"Follow that and you come to a lane. Follow the lane and you come to a group of houses . . . really, really nice houses. That's where Sir William Catesby and Lord Ratcliffe live. Have you met Lord Ratcliffe?"

"They both came for a drink in the Hog last night."

The girl smiled. "I'm eighteen in October; then I'll be able to drink."

"You mean legally?"

The girl laughed. "Yeah."

Jen smiled. Anthea Brown was certainly a dark horse.

"How about Luke Rankin? Did you know him?"

The atmosphere changed, as if a switch had been flicked.

"I never liked him. He was weird."

"In what way?" Jen guessed she knew what was coming.

"He was just strange. Was a right loner. He never used to talk to people."

"Did you ever go to school with him?"

"No – he were two year older. He used to go to St Joseph's before we joined. But his mum took him to some other school."

Again, Jen was pleased that the information agreed with what she already knew.

"Do you think he really did it?"

The question came from nowhere – even to Jen. She instantly regretted asking. She feared that the girl would be overcome with emotion. And that she'd have no way of being able to console her.

"Why commit suicide a week later if you've nothing to hide?"

"Did anyone suspect anything before he died?"

Anthea thought about it. "I don't think so; I can't really remember."

"Was it definitely suicide?"

"Yeah – that's what everyone says."

The answer was less definite than Jen had expected. "Where was he found?"

"You know the lane that I was talking about?"

"You mean where Lovell lives?"

"Yeah. Well, before the lane, there's this footpath from the churchyard. If you follow the path all the way, you come to a bridge, which was part of the old railway station. They don't use that anymore."

Jen listened carefully, still watching the girl via the mirror. "Did you see it? The body?"

"No. They took it down straight away."

"What? The police?"

"No – apparently it were Lord Ratcliffe."

That seemed ridiculous. "Lord Ratcliffe took down the body?"

"I think he had help."

At least help meant eyewitnesses. "Who made the initial discovery?"

"I think that were Lord Ratcliffe as well."

"How on earth did he find him?"

"He was out for a walk."

"A walk?"

Anthea nodded. She picked up the nearest hairdryer and started drying Jen's hair. "I've often seen him walk his dogs around there. He has these great big lovely Alsatians."

Jen nodded as the force of the hairdryer blew against her scalp.

Colour and volume were returning to her hair.

As she considered the recent information, her heightening suspicion was momentarily dampened. After all, there was nothing particularly extraordinary about a man taking his dogs for a walk along a quiet footpath close to his house.

Anthea switched off the hairdryer and removed the cloak from around Jen's shoulders.

"Voilà."

Jen sensed the triumph in the girl's voice. In truth, it was not misplaced.

It was oh so different, but oh so lovely.

Jen shook her head – almost in disbelief. "I love it."

The girl was ecstatic. "You're not just saying that?"

"Seriously, it's brilliant. Thank you so much."

Just at that moment the door opened, the ringing of the bell heralding the arrival of a newcomer. Martha had returned, her hands full with carrier bags.

She was clearly unprepared for the sight before her.

"Oh my," she said, almost dropping her shopping.

"Doesn't she look gorgeous, Mum?"

Jen posed for the hairdresser. "Kate Hudson eat your heart out! I hope you don't mind us not waiting."

"Me, mind?" The woman was lost for words.

Jen smiled at the seventeen-year-old. "Thank you so much," she said, kissing her on the cheek and hugging her. She placed her bag over her shoulder. "How much did you say that was again?"

"£35."

"Twenty-five," Martha interrupted. "It's twenty-five for VIPs."

"Well, here's twenty-five," Jen said, passing over three notes. "And here is your tip," she said, giving her another ten.

The girl was even more ecstatic. "Thank you so, so much."

"No, thank you so, so much." Jen looked herself over again in the mirror. For the first time in as long as she could remember, she felt a strange sense of vanity. "I'm really glad I got to meet you."

Anthea looked at her mother. "I'll be back in a few minutes, Mum. I'm just going to show Jen where the Rankin kid was found."

20

The offer was unexpected, but not unwelcome. Anthea led the way out of the hairdresser's, across the high street and past the Hog. Jen followed a pace or two behind, still struggling to adjust to the feeling of the new hairstyle.

In truth, she was undecided what shocked her the most: how good it looked, or that the same girl who earlier that day she thought would struggle to say boo to a goose was capable of carrying out the job.

For now, she focused on the former. Every opportunity she got, she studied her reflection. Fortunately the high street was abundant in glass, so the opportunities were plentiful. The length was slightly shorter than she was used to – a fraction under shoulder length – but what struck her most was how wavy it was. That and the new colour. It was different enough for her to notice, yet also subtle enough for the average guy not to notice. As she passed the Hog, she walked alongside a row of parked cars. The tinted glass offered the best reflections so far. She grinned to herself as she looked.

Enough already with the vanity.

She followed Anthea past the Hog and then right before reaching the church. The churchyard was deserted, which was usual – particularly on a weekday. There were fresh flowers on some of the graves, a stunning bouquet on one. Flowers grew wildly throughout, the colours ranging from purple to orange, with yellow being by far the most common. The smell of freshly cut grass teased her nostrils, causing her throat to itch slightly. The one thing she hated about summer was hay fever. These days it was a minor nuisance, whereas as a kid it could ruin an entire day.

Thankfully, those days were over.

Today, she could enjoy the scenery.

It was warmer than the day before, and the village was in its prime. The afternoon sun beat down brightly on the stone church tower, casting a long shadow across the churchyard, where numerous trees moved softly in the breeze, the sunlight nestling between the foliage.

For the first time Jen became aware of the wildlife, the sound of birds whistling or squawking as they hopped from branch to branch.

It still seemed unthinkable such a tragedy could have occurred there.

They took the footpath through the nearby gateway and veered to the right. The path zigzagged, following the natural curvature of the ground as it bisected two hills. The dry mud was comfortable underfoot, while the trees that lined the path took away most of the glare. The temperature had definitely picked up – even since leaving the hairdresser's. She guessed it was about 27 perhaps even 29 Celsius.

A perfect summer's day in England.

The path curved away to the left before straightening out. The landscape was more visible now. To Jen's right, fields and farmland continued as far as the eye could see, while above the horizon the sea was clearly visible, its calm water washing gently against the rocky coast. The location was lonely, but idyllic. The odd farmhouse, occasional villages – perhaps merely hamlets – reminded her that life existed, but for now they were the only signs of civilisation.

To the adopted Londoner, it was like looking at a setting from *Wuthering Heights*.

A few metres along, the illusion became even greater. On the hill to the left were ruins: white stone, the remains of a former wall.

She had learned the day before that a castle had once existed in the village.

"Who lived there?" Jen asked.

"I think it was the Saxons first. After that I think it was the Normans."

Jen smiled to herself. Ask a silly question.

"In the Middle Ages it belonged to one of the Plantagenets. We had to do a project on it at school."

The Plantagenets, she thought to herself. Kings of England 1154–1485, ending with the defeat of Richard III at Bosworth and the beginning of the Tudors.

She knew that there was the odd illegitimate branch of the family as well.

"Anything interesting?"

"Yeah, sort of," Anthea replied, touching her hair. "Apparently it was destroyed in the Wars of the Roses."

On hearing that, Jen's mind wandered back to her experiences of the previous day: firstly in the cloisters, then hearing about Catesby, Ratcliffe and Lovell in the Hog.

She assumed the windows were relevant to the village's history.

"Who owned it? Was it one of the kings?"

"Just cousins, I think."

That made sense, despite knowing little for sure of the area's history. Nevertheless, the castle intrigued her. Though only a few minor walls survived, the outline remained visible. She approved of the setting.

Even the village's bloody history had been integrated well with the present.

The path forked, giving them the option of left or right.

"That's the lane what leads to all the posh houses," Anthea said, gesturing to the right. "It's this way to the bridge."

Staying to the left, Anthea led the way. After walking for another two hundred metres the railway bridge came into view, along with the former station in the distance.

"This is where he was found, apparently," Anthea said, pointing to the bridge. It was obvious to Jen that the place gave Anthea goose bumps.

Jen stopped to take a photo of the bridge on her iPhone before continuing towards it. It was arch shaped, redbrick and dilapidated. Her footsteps echoed as she walked beneath the arch. Although she knew they were her own, the heavy repeated thud unnerved her slightly. Worse still was the darkness. It was brilliantly light outside, the time just before 3 p.m., but the area beneath the bridge was nothing but a long void. There was a strong sense of loneliness and foreboding about the place that left her feeling uneasy.

Jen returned to the entrance and looked up at the top of the arch. She estimated there was a drop of some ten metres from the top of the bridge to the ground.

She walked to her left, following the footpath, and then left again after about ten metres, taking a scenic route through some wild flowers up the hill to where the railway line had once existed.

"Be careful."

Jen looked back. Anthea was standing near the bottom of the bridge, clearly reluctant to get any nearer.

Jen lost her footing, but managed to stay on her feet. The ground leading up to the top of the bridge was steep, the grass rugged throughout.

At least the long stems gave her something to grab onto.

She succeeded in getting to the summit, at which point the grass was far shorter. She now had two choices, left or right. She looked to her right. Some two hundred metres away, she could see a derelict building surrounded by shrubbery.

She sighed. Over fifty years after the event, the former station remained a visual reminder of the Beeching Axe.

Jen made her way left, heading towards the bridge. The imprints of the former rail tracks were evident in the mud, becoming less obvious on the bridge itself, where weeds and stinging nettles were growing profusely. Moss infiltrated the gaps between the brickwork, while the bricks themselves were decorated by random graffiti. Reference to the band Velvet Underground confirmed her suspicion that none of it was recent.

She continued all the way to the wall on the left, and leaned over the side. Anthea was standing below her, looking up nervously. She smiled and waved up to Jen, who smiled back.

Jen felt the side of the bridge with her hands before investigating the other side.

Once finished, she looked down again at Anthea. "He definitely hanged himself?"

The girl nodded.

Jen pursed her lips. Although the wall was made up of hundreds of bricks, there was not an obvious place for the rope to be tied.

Jen took some more photos on her iPhone before heading back down the slope. She made it most of the way before slipping near the end. Anthea came to meet her, struggling not to laugh.

Jen accepted the girl's outstretched hand. "Thanks."

"Can we get out of here now?"

They returned along the path in the opposite direction, and headed left on reaching the fork. The muddy pathway widened as they walked, eventually developing into a small road lined by several large houses.

"Lovell lives along here," Anthea said, gesturing somewhere to the left. "I'll show you."

The houses on both sides were secluded by a profusion of trees and thick vegetation, prohibiting observation from outsiders. Every so often the greenery would open up, revealing large metal gateways that guarded long, winding driveways.

The setting partially matched what Jen had imagined, but never before had she seen anything so private. She'd learned from her evening in the Hog that there were fifteen houses in total, but that wasn't obvious from walking in the road. For all she knew there could be hundreds, thousands or maybe just a handful. There were no addresses, no house names or numbers decorating the gateways . . .

Stranger still was the quietness – even compared to what she had just experienced.

For all she knew, she had slipped back in time.

Lovell's house was just ahead on the left. As best Jen could tell from spying through the gate, the building was a period house, perhaps Elizabethan, perhaps older, and surrounded by several acres of woodland. A large double garage was attached to the house.

From her vantage point there was no way of knowing whether anyone was at home.

Anthea approached the intercom. "You best let me do the talking. People round here are a bit suspicious of outsiders."

Jen nodded. If anything, the comment seemed an understatement.

Someone answered, a woman's voice. "Hello?"

"Hi, Mrs Lovell, it's Anthea Brown here."

"Hello, Anthea."

The voice was noticeably grand.

"Is Dr Lovell there, please?"

"He went out a few hours ago; I'm afraid he'll be quite some time yet."

Jen was disappointed.

Anthea replied, "Okay, thanks."

They started back the way they came.

"Who are these people?" Jen asked, distracted by the setting. The high level of privacy was starting to intrigue her.

"Most on this side are lawyers," Anthea said, gesturing to the left. "A couple at the top of the road are politicians."

"What party?"

"Democrat."

Jen raised an eyebrow. Originally named the Whigs and dating back to around 1678, the Democrat Party had since developed into the second strongest party in the UK. After winning one election, they were now in opposition to the Tories.

"Anyone famous?"

"Yeah, a few." Anthea pointed to another house. "That's where Rowland lives."

"Stanley?" Jen said, amazed.

Rowland Stanley was the new leader of the Democrat Party.

Hence also the leader of the opposition.

Anthea nodded. "His niece lives next door to him."

It took a few seconds for the penny to drop. "Stephanie?"

"Yeah."

"Debra Harrison's best friend?"

"Yeah."

"Debra's best friend was Rowland Stanley's niece."

"Yeah."

Jen was speechless. She hadn't picked up on that at all.

They passed another gateway on the right. "That's where Lord Ratcliffe lives. Sir William lives next door."

As she passed Catesby's house, she heard something coming from the grounds.

"Is that . . . chickens?"

"Yeah. He keeps other birds as well."

Jen loitered, distracted. The sound of clucking had got progressively louder.

"What does he do? Catesby?"

"He owns a farm. His estate is massive. I think he used to be a scientist of some sort."

Jen was interested. She tried to look through the gate, but as with the others, the shrubbery restricted her view. Next on from the Catesby estate, she briefly saw another house largely hidden by greenery. It was grand, even compared to those she had just seen. The only visible areas were the upper two storeys.

She saw a figure at one of the windows.

"What's that?"

"Wootton Court. It's really old."

Jen recognised the name; she'd seen a print of it in her room.

"Who lives there?"

Anthea glanced to her right. "That's Lord Jeffries. He's a bastard."

Jen laughed, confused by what Anthea had meant. She looked back over her shoulder and shuddered. Even though they were well past the house, the sight of the silhouette at the window had made her uneasy.

"Who is he?"

"Apparently he's a lord of some description. Being honest, I don't know much about him."

"Why's he a bastard?"

She shrugged. "I dunno, he just is."

"Has he lived around here long?"

"Yeah, years and years and years. Apparently he's another one who goes back to the Middle Ages. It's him that owns the castle."

That interested her.

"Has he always had that name? It just doesn't sound medieval."

Anthea shrugged. "As far as I know. I mean, he has a title, emblem, you know, all the works. When I was at school everyone used to call him Lord Broomshoot."

Jen was confused. "Isn't that a flower?"

"Yeah, it's his symbol."

"And they've always lived in Wootton?"

Anthea nodded and pointed up ahead. "Most of them are buried in there."

At the end of the lane, they rejoined the path. The church was now visible above the brow of the hill. Thinking about it, Jen didn't recall seeing anyone of that name in the churchyard.

"They're definitely buried there?"

"Yeah," Anthea said, emphasis on the yeah before grinning uncontrollably. "There's lots of broomshoots in the cemetery."

21

Richmond Park, London

The journalist paused on reaching the Isabella Plantation and looked to his left and right.

The scenery was picturesque, but distracting. Everywhere he looked he saw exotic flowers: purple, pink and violet lighting the way like a rainbow.

He started again and stopped, now seriously confused. Richmond Park was the largest of London's royal parks, but it was also the one he knew least well. The instructions he had received earlier that day had been unspecific, but even if he had been given precise directions, following them to the letter would have been almost impossible.

Navigating the 2,300-acre park without a map was like being lost in a maze.

He made it over one of the many footbridges that crossed one of the streams and continued through the woodland.

At that moment his mobile phone began to ring. Momentarily stunned, he looked around in every direction before accepting the call.

"Yes?"

"Keep heading to your left."

The call terminated immediately, increasing his sense of unease. The feeling of being watched was growing on him, intensified by the unfamiliar surroundings. The sounds on this side of the water were different. The voices of nature had become progressively louder, particularly the echo of hooves.

He figured he was getting close to the deer park.

Apprehensively he followed the caller's instructions, taking him off the path. Fifty metres on, he saw a bench, one of many.

But the first he'd seen occupied.

The man was old. His skin sagged slightly around his clean-shaven mouth, whereas the rest of his face was hidden behind large sunglasses.

He wore a yellow raincoat, despite the fine weather, hiding a smart suit.

The journalist sat down beside him, waiting for some form of acknowledgement. On closer inspection he saw something beneath the man's right eye.

A scar of some description.

"You understand the penalty should you have been followed?"

The journalist felt his breathing sharpen. "What the bloody hell is this all about?"

The old man folded his arms. "You've been writing about the murder of the politicians."

His articles were common knowledge. "What of it?"

Again the man didn't reply straight away. He merely looked directly forward.

"You've also been speculating about the death of His Majesty the King."

Again the man was speechless. "And?"

"What would you say if I were to tell you that your suspicions are not far wrong?"

The journalist's unease was becoming ever greater. "Look, why did you bring me here?"

The old man looked at him for the first time. "Because there are some people among the royals who fail to look beyond the end of their bloody noses."

Thomas was speechless. As expected, the house concealed its fair share of nooks and crannies, but what they hid was something else.

He removed his iPhone from his pocket and called both Bridges and his father.

22

The sun was still out at 5:30, despite the gathering dark clouds in the distance. The weather was warm, the faintest touch of wind providing relief from the humidity.

For the last two hours Jen had been alone. After passing the castle and saying goodbye to Anthea, she revisited the church and after that the churchyard.

She sat quietly on a wooden bench situated in the highest part of the graveyard. Until now she hadn't realised just how many graves there were – several hundred at least. Most dated from the 1800s, the writing on most now illegible. A large statue of the Angel Gabriel had been erected close to where she sat, dedicated to the memory of those lost in the two great wars.

Most of the graves close by belonged to war veterans.

Further to her right, the ruins of the old priory stood prevalently behind the wall that surrounded the presbytery. This was the first time she had seen the ruins properly. Strangely they were not open to the public, unlike most. A large archway, probably once a doorway, was laden in ivy and surrounded by three walls, all containing the shapes of smaller archways where windows would once have been.

She guessed she was looking at the old dormitories.

A small animal, probably a fox, was sniffing around the ruins, climbing on one of the walls and staying perfectly still for several seconds. For what seemed like an age, Jen merely sat and watched, simply taking it all in. As a young girl, her parents always took her to visit old ruins. Her grandmother, bless her, was just as passionate. For the first time in a long time, her mind recalled that ancient time: the sights, the smells, the touch, the feelings . . . life really was simpler back then.

Somehow, it seemed like a different lifetime.

Her second visit to the church had been pleasant, but so far not particularly useful. On exploring the interior, she noticed things she hadn't taken in the first time, but nothing of any connection to Debra Harrison or the families of prominence.

The biggest surprise was the lack of recognition for the Jeffries family – if that was indeed their real name. According to Anthea, the family had been a central fixture in Wootton's past, but the physical evidence so far didn't back that up. Lovells, Catesbys, and Ratcliffes were particularly prominent as she already knew – there were even more buried in the Lady chapel. On initial inspection, there wasn't a single Jeffries buried in the cemetery.

Strange, considering Anthea had said there were lots of them buried there.

A large, thick, white cloud moved in the western sky, allowing the sun to shine through more brightly. Not for the first time that day Jen regretted not having her sunglasses. Shielding her eyes, her attention turned further to the right, to a series of tombstones beneath an old oak tree. The tree was large, easily the biggest in the churchyard, and heavily branched on either side.

Jen rose to her feet and ventured closer, using her outstretched arms to move the branches. There were six tombstones in all, five looking small and bare, and one much larger and surrounded by iron fencing. Four magpies were perched at the top of it, the largest gathering she had ever seen of that type. Almost immediately two flew off, giving rise to an angry shouting match as they rose into the yellowy sky.

She circled the tomb, looking for any form of writing. She guessed from the style that it was at least three hundred years old, perhaps older.

Finally she found an inscription – the language unmistakably Latin. As she translated the words in her mind, she realised it was not a tomb but a memorial, shaped in the style of an urn. A large crest marked part of the upper portion, followed by a list of names.

According to the inscription, it had been put up to honour the Yorkists who fell fighting in the Wars of the Roses. Several names were present, many of the same family.

Suddenly she was confused. Although the wording dated the monument to the 1880s, unless her eyes were deceiving her, the leading name was *Plantagenis*.

She laughed to herself, almost in wild amazement.

"Found a long-lost relative?"

The voice came from the lichgate to her left. She heard the sound of the gate closing, followed by footsteps.

A man had appeared, his features veiled in the sunlight. As the figure approached, she could make out he was about six feet in height, with a strong build and good posture.

Jen emerged from behind the branches, trying hard not to embarrass herself escaping the foliage. Inevitably, she failed, catching about a dozen leaves in her new haircut as she caught her head against the branch.

The young man laughed at her. "Believe me, sweetheart, I've done the same thing many a time – looking for my long-lost relatives."

Jen laughed – it was either that or cry. She brushed the leaves out of her hair, worried about the state of her appearance. "I bet not within three hours of having it cut."

"You'd be surprised."

Jen looked at the man, studying his appearance. He had fair hair, not quite Swedish or German, but a light shade of blond. He was clean-shaven, including the sideburns, and had bright blue eyes.

"I hope you found him, anyway. Your relative."

Jen smirked, the sarcasm evident.

If he had been a relation, that would make me the queen.

"I'm not local," she said. "I'm from London."

"London. So that's the noise what's been coming out your mouth?"

Jen placed her hands to her hips. The man was evidently from Yorkshire, his accent slightly softer than most she had heard recently. She guessed his age was mid-to-late twenties, perhaps the same as her.

"Actually, I'm originally from Edwinstowe."

"Edwinstowe?"

"In Nottinghamshire."

"In Nottinghamshire?"

"Yes."

"Well, I guess Nottinghamshire is kind of north," the man said, grinning.

"I used to live on the boundary of Sherwood Forest."

"The boundary of Sherwood Forest?"

"Yes."

"You know Robin Hood?"

"Not personally."

"He was from up this way."

She shook her head, looking away. "I thought he was from Barnsdale."

"Nah. That was Friar Tuck."

Jen fought to avoid a smile, but failed. She flicked her hair behind her ears. "Well, you clearly know more than me."

The stranger lowered his head, his grin widening. "So, I'm guessing from your slightly northern accent and the fact that I've never seen you in these parts before, you must be this pretty new girl I've been hearing so much about."

This time she managed a stronger façade. "You've heard of me?"

"It's a small village, Wootton."

Small village or not, she doubted it. "So you think you know everyone in the village?"

The man shrugged. "Basically. I mean, I've lived here my entire life."

Jen forced a smile. "I'm Jen."

"I'm guessing that's short for Miss Farrelly."

Okay, so you have heard of me.

"And you are?"

"My name is Edward," he said, offering his hand. "Edward Jeffries."

This time she managed to avoid laughing. "You live over there, right?" She pointed in the direction of the castle.

He released his hand from hers. "I see nothing gets past you, does it, Miss Farrelly?"

"Do you live there with your family?"

"Just me granddad, really. And his carers – he's not been well recently."

She lowered her head. "Sorry."

"You're welcome to see it, if you like."

The perfect summer's day was interrupted by the rumble of distant thunder. The clouds had darkened, threatening a downpour.

"Perhaps some other time," Jen said, silently approving of the offer. She knew a trip around Wootton Court might be useful.

"How about tomorrow?"

She smiled. "Yeah, maybe."

The man smiled, not quite arrogant but not unsatisfied either. He held up his hand as he walked towards the footpath she had walked with Anthea.

"How will I know if you're in?" Jen shouted.

"It's quite easy. See we have this thing in Wootton called a doorbell."

She placed her hands on her hips and blew her hair away from her face.

"Or failing that, you could check the driveway. I'm the one with the Ferrari."

Jen smiled, walking towards the church.

And I'm the one with the Picanto.

She passed a gravestone and looked instinctively at the name.

She turned. "Hey. How come so few of you are buried here?"

The man with blond hair stopped and turned. "Most of our family live longer because of the vampire gene."

Again she fought the urge to laugh.

"You're looking in the wrong place; most families from Ravensfield have their own vault."

"Ravensfield?"

"That's technically the name for the village this side of the river."

She might have guessed.

"Just take the stairs down from the cloisters. It's through the door."

"Thanks."

She followed his advice and headed for the main entrance to the church. There was a notice on the door stating that the evening service would begin at 6:30. That gave her thirty-five minutes – perhaps less than ten before the first arrivals.

The church was deserted, as usual. She walked along the main aisle and through the door to the cloisters. For the first time she noticed a plaque on the wall, in memory of a Sir John Jefryes, apparently buried in the vaults below.

She continued along the cloisters, passing the array of stained-glass windows – the work of the priest's ancestor, no less. Ignoring the temptation to get sidetracked, she walked down the stone steps that she had seen the priest emerge from the day before, and turned the handle on the door.

It was locked. Or was it? For some reason the door opened towards her, when it looked as if the opposite would be true. Successfully inside, she entered the narrow passage lined on both sides by yellow stone, and lit only by the flickering of dim wall lights. After about ten metres, she came across the first vault, which she entered through an open doorway. The name in question was Stanley, a name she had heard on more than one occasion.

Thanks to Anthea, she knew the gist.

After a brief search, she saw that there were a few prominent graves, while most of the others had been buried behind the walls.

Leaving the Stanley vault, she continued in the same direction, passing the vaults of four other families.

The fifth name stood out a mile. Rankin.

Unlike the previous vaults, this door was locked.

She assumed from the modern spelling it was the same family.

She removed her iPhone from her handbag and navigated the options. Incredibly she had a signal, albeit a faint one. She went through her list of contacts, stopping on the newest entry.

She dialled Anthea's mobile number and immediately received an answer.

"Hey, Jen, what's up?"

"Hi, Anthea. Nothing really, just at the church. Hey, can I ask you something? Where was Luke Rankin buried?"

"I think he's buried there."

Still she struggled to process the find. "I'm just down in the vaults; there's one down here with the name Rankin."

"Oh yeah, that's right, his mum wanted him to be buried in the vault – she thought being buried outside might attract vandals."

At least that explained why it was locked. "Did he have a funeral?"

"Yeah, but there weren't that many people there."

Jen nodded to herself. "Okay, thanks."

She ended the call and for several seconds just stared at the closed door. Its very existence made no sense to her. Officially, Luke Rankin's death had been classed as suicide – she had seen the press reports and spoken to the police. He was also an alleged murderer.

Yet he had received a Catholic funeral and burial.

Next was the Catesby vault, followed by those of Ratcliffe and Lovell. All were open, elaborate and ornate, and each threw up surprises.

As expected, there were a number of elaborate graves with effigies – mostly from the 17th and 18th centuries – depicting men dressed in clothing from that time. In the Catesby vault, one name stood out from the rest.

Robert Catesby, died 8th November 1605. Famed leader of the Gunpowder Plot. Originally buried in the church at Holbeach, disinterred on the orders of the Earl of Northampton, buried in this vault 25 January 1892 by bequest of Sir William Catesby, died 1901.

She knew for a fact that the leader of the Gunpowder Plot had met his end in grisly circumstances and had been disinterred as a mark of treachery.

The reinterment amazed her. If nothing else, it seemed incredible that someone kept hold of the body.

Equally astounding, it proved that the current Catesbys were of the same lineage. She wondered how far back they went. As far as she could tell, Robert Catesby was the oldest in the vault – the majority dating back to the 18th century.

Similar dates were true of Ratcliffe and Lovell.

The Jeffries' vault was easily found – the next one on from Lovell. Most of the early tombs were more modern, 19th century the most common. Most of the graves were lengthways, with large bronze effigies above the slabs. The inscriptions indicated that the majority had been clergymen or politicians – one rising to a Cabinet minister.

The family motto was displayed prominently, accompanied by an elaborate crest. Like many from the Middle Ages, it was a flower, probably a broom based on what Anthea had told her. Thinking it over, she remembered something about the real thing being yellow. She had seen something similar scattered throughout the graveyard. An ironic thought occurred to her. Anthea wasn't kidding after all.

The graveyard was full of broomshoots.

She examined the rest of the vault. As expected, there were older tombs: at least one per generation dating back to the mid 1600s.

She read the plaques for each, finding herself fascinated by the stories. Many of them had been knights, and evidently significant landowners. One of the most prominent was a Sir John Jefryes – the same name she had seen mentioned on the plaque in the church and, judging by his effigy, an old man of substantial build. According to the plaque, the man had been notorious in the English Civil War. There were similar reports of two other members of the family: this time for the Glorious and Monmouth risings during the reign of James II. A strange pattern was emerging.

The family had a habit of opposing the monarch.

She headed left, making her way past the other graves. There was a lot of debris and floodwater in this part. The smell was off-putting, as was the appearance. She made her way through the puddles, her attention on the far wall. There was a door in it, surrounded by an exquisite archway.

She had nearly missed it, thanks to the debris.

Moving closer, she felt the door with her hand. It was sturdy – typical of an entrance to a cellar. She turned the handle, but the door didn't move. She tried again before accepting it was locked. Moving on, she felt the surrounding archway. The stone was smooth, unexpectedly so, the cold sending a chill down her spine.

She concentrated on the area above the door. It was covered in cobwebs and dust that was falling onto her pretty new hairstyle. The Jeffries' logo had been placed above the door; its appearance suggested it was perhaps 17th century. She guessed that behind the door was another section of the vault.

She looked down at the floor, the area around the rubble, and saw something sparkle, almost like a diamond.

She bent down for a closer look. It was a necklace with a cross, modern but probably inexpensive. On moving the rubble, she saw there was also a camera, a small digital 12-megapixel model, probably worth about £100.

She looked at it, lost for words.

Judging by its condition, it had been there for some time.

Nearby footsteps alarmed her. Seconds later, a figure appeared by the entrance to the vault.

"Everything all right?"

She recognised the voice before recognising the face. "Father Martin."

"What on earth are you doing down here?"

The question was accompanied by a laugh, yet his tone suggested the area was off-limits.

"I met Edward Jeffries in the graveyard," she said. "He said that his family vault wasn't one to be missed."

The priest relaxed slightly. "He certainly isn't wrong."

Jen forced another smile. She placed a hand to her hair, removing cobwebs.

"I was wondering about this door," she said, gesturing towards it. "Is there something behind it?"

"Apparently it was built for victims of the great plague," the priest replied.

That was the last thing she had expected. "Can I see it?"

"Unfortunately no. It would be against regulations. Sanitation – you understand."

She nodded, studying the priest's expression.

Something had changed.

"Sorry, Father, I hope I'm not keeping you."

The kind smile returned. "I really must prepare for Mass. It's twenty-two minutes past."

Jen looked at the clock on her phone. She had been down in the vaults for nearly thirty minutes.

"Will you be joining us this evening?"

She felt herself on the spot. "Thank you, Father."

"See you in a few minutes."

The priest left the vault and continued along the corridor. Jen, meanwhile, was deep in thought.

"Excuse me, Father," Jen said, catching him. "I noticed that Luke Rankin was buried down here."

"Yes."

"Forgive me, I didn't realise that was normal."

The priest was confused. "Normal?"

"I thought the Catholic Church refused to bury people like him in consecrated ground."

The priest's expression had become sterner. "I'm afraid I don't follow."

"Luke Rankin," Jen said. "He died by committing suicide, surely."

A pause preceded the reply. "Luke Rankin's death was a tragedy – for everyone in Wootton. Now, Miss Farrelly, I really must be getting ready."

Jen stood in silence, literally rooted to the spot. She shook her head.

Was her view of Catholics so out of date?

"Wait," she said, catching him again. "Are you saying he didn't commit suicide?"

"Miss Farrelly, please, I really must prepare for Mass."

Jen watched, almost in disbelief, as the priest made his way towards the cloisters.

Luke Rankin had committed suicide – that was the general consensus. Thanks to Anthea, she knew there were eyewitnesses – she still didn't know exactly how many – and she had also seen the area where the boy had supposedly died. She knew from talking to Martha, and indirectly from Anthea, that Rankin's position as murderer was by no means clear cut.

Evidently, the priest must have agreed with that.

Either that or she was missing something.

23

The limousine pulled up outside Riverton Court at precisely 6:45 p.m. Thomas was in the master bedroom at the time, going through Talbot's belongings. Besides the diary, he was still to find anything conclusive relating to either the Sons of York or the man's own past – aside from personal keepsakes. He was still to see everything, but he had checked all the usual places, including a badly hidden safe behind one of the portraits.

He guessed if Talbot did have anything to hide, it could well be found down one of those passages.

Thomas saw the limousine from the bedroom window. After making its way through the open gates, it proceeded along the driveway before stopping outside the door. He had taken the liberty of hiding his own car, parking it in a twenty-four-hour car park in the nearby town. He assumed from the diary entry that a car would be sent for him. It made perfect sense.

Even if Talbot knew the location, his employers would not leave anything to chance.

The driver of the limousine rang the doorbell. He was smartly dressed, all in black, with a matching cap. A thick beard, distinctly ginger in colour, covered much of his face. He also wore tinted glasses, not quite sunglasses but dark enough to cast doubt over the colour of his eyes.

Over a minute passed before the front door opened, and a man emerged. He was dressed in a large grey coat, a brown hat that covered all of his hair, and large dark sunglasses that hid much of his face. His skin was wrinkly and wet, and smelt of Old Spice. He walked with a pronounced limp and rested his weight on two walking sticks.

"May I assist you in any way, Sir Jack?" Redbeard asked in earnest.

The response was a vigorous cough, followed by "away".

Redbeard didn't ask any questions. He opened the door like a good chauffeur, and waited until the man was safely in his seat before closing it.

"Mustn't forget the cargo."

Thomas remained silent as Redbeard entered the house and returned moments later with several black holdalls. He stacked them up carefully in the boot before returning to the driver's seat.

Seconds later, the black limousine made its way back along the driveway, emerging onto the road. Conversation was non-existent, even the woman on the Satnav had been set to silent.

Sitting alone in the back, the man dressed as Sir Jack Talbot displayed an air of discontent. He crossed one leg over the other with a struggle, and sat with his coat wrapped tightly around himself. For the rest of the journey he would remain silent – his eyes focused on the passing countryside.

If luck were to have it, tonight he would meet the Sons of York first hand.

In the front seat, Redbeard concentrated on the road. Although he drove with a neutral expression, inside he was smiling.

He had to hand it to the prince. The disguise was convincing. Silently he was amazed that any twenty-something could do such a fine impersonation of a crippled seventy-something.

But seeing was definitely believing.

The prince's disguise was good, but his was even better. With the red beard and dark glasses, he certainly didn't look like the same man the prince had shot at earlier that day.

And by the time he figured it out, he'd be in no position to argue.

24

The Mass had already begun by the time Jen reached the cloisters. The soothing opening of "Immortal, Invisible, God Only Wise", accompanied by the strong base notes of the church organ, reverberated through the deserted corridors before becoming ever louder as Jen reached the door. The lock snapped upwards as she raised the bolt, allowing the door to creak open.

Unsurprisingly, the noise attracted circumspect glances from almost all of the nine people in attendance.

Among them was Martha Brown, standing three pews from the front, with a hymnal in her hand and her mouth wide open. She smiled at Jen as she sang, gesturing for her to join her.

The Mass lasted forty-five minutes. Jen's first appearance at Mass since sixth form had passed without incident, despite the continuous feeling that she was in the wrong place. She didn't recognise any others of the congregation, all of whom were women bar one. She placed most of them in their mid-sixties, if not slightly older, with the exception of one pretty woman, probably in her forties.

It took a while for her to realise it was Susan Rankin.

As the service ended, Jen spoke to Martha for the first time. Although she didn't mention her hair, Jen struggled to shake the feeling that she was looking at her – in a bad way. Ever since her visit to the vaults, she felt as though there was another cobweb there – that elusive bastard that you can never find, no matter how hard you try.

The priest was ignoring her, but he seemed to be doing the same to everyone. She guessed it was probably just his nature, rather than anything she had personally done.

Nevertheless, the episode in the vaults troubled her. Whatever the reason, Rankin's burial seemed out of place.

Even more intriguing, his mother was at Mass.

Jen left the pew with Martha, waiting until the congregation had dispersed before leaving. She watched Susan Rankin as she left the church, smiling awkwardly, but speaking to no one. She shook hands with the priest as she approached the door, the pinnacle of her communication. On this occasion, the priest appeared to be warmer – as if reserving sympathy. Despite the lack of talking, Jen didn't get the impression the woman was an outcast.

If anything, she seemed part of the furniture.

Martha Brown spoke to the priest for over a minute before finally leaving, white smiles prevailing. He held his kindness for Jen, enclosing her hand softly between his two, and whispered the words "lovely to see you" as she walked out the door. At face value, the man seemed genuine. Yet the episode in the vault still disturbed her. Either Luke Rankin committed suicide or he didn't.

There were no in betweens.

"Would you like to join us for dinner, pet?" Martha asked as they walked along the pathway.

The question caught Jen off guard. She figured it was either that or another burger at the Hog.

"Yeah, great – thanks."

Anthea was thrilled. After remedying the mishaps to Jen's new haircut, she spent the next half an hour taking her new best friend on a tour of the house – notably her bedroom. Posters of actors, models and celebs prevailed throughout – male and female. The posters were a lifestyle choice – at least that was the excuse. As a hairdresser, she needed to be reminded of style everywhere. Decent advice, Jen thought.

If it was true.

Dinner was served at just before eight, the meal traditional Yorkshire. Toad in the Hole with roast potatoes, gravy and veg came first; curd tart came next.

Fair dos, the woman could cook as well as she could sing.

"So how come Luke Rankin is buried in the vaults beneath the church even though he is generally believed to have committed suicide?" Jen asked as Martha cut the curd tart and offered her a slice.

"Suicide victims are not deprived of being buried in consecrated ground," Anthea replied. "According to the modern church, they deserve both our sympathy and understanding."

Jen was unconvinced. "Who told you that?"

"Mrs Beckworth – she was our RE teacher . . . that's right, isn't it, Mum?"

Martha retook her seat at the head of the table. "It is right, pet."

To Jen that sounded wrong. "So what about all that stuff about people being deprived of burial in consecrated ground: being born out of wedlock, killing someone, committing adultery, not being baptised?"

"You still have to be baptised," Anthea said, playing with her spoon. "You also have to be a Catholic – or at least a Christian."

Jen was still unconvinced. She took a first bite of the curd tart and swallowed it down.

Predictably it melted in the mouth.

"So where did all this stuff come from about people being buried at a crossroads in the dead of night and that sort of thing?"

"Yeah, maybe when Dick Turpin was alive," Anthea said sarcastically. "It has lightened up on some things."

"In some cases, it all comes down to the discretion of the priest," Martha said. "Any Christian is entitled to burial. That's a legal matter."

That seemed plausible. "How about murder?"

"That depends," Anthea said.

"On what?"

"On whether they repent."

"It's not as simple as that," Martha said. "Murderers are still legally entitled to burial."

"It also depends on whether they were of sound mind at the time they committed the murder," Anthea said.

Jen nodded. "That makes sense."

"So Luke Rankin would not have been deprived of a funeral and burial in consecrated ground because he was a loony."

"Anthea," Martha snapped.

Silence fell, noticeably awkward. Jen looked everywhere and nowhere, her eyes alighting on Anthea, who grimaced and returned to her tart.

Jen did the same. "So what would constitute not being of sound mind?"

Martha shrugged. It was obvious the subject was making her uncomfortable. "It can be a number of things, really. It could be someone suffering from mental illness, someone who's recently suffered something of a shock, someone who's had an adverse effect to medication . . . you know?"

Jen got the picture. "Did Luke Rankin come into that category?"

"Definitely," Anthea replied.

"Martha?" Jen asked.

Martha hesitated. "You'd have to ask Father Martin; he'd know far more than me."

"I did – he seemed reluctant to talk about it," Jen said, eating.

"When was this?" Anthea asked.

"In the vaults before Mass started."

"He was probably in a hurry," Martha replied.

"Maybe. But something doesn't add up. First, Debra Harrison goes missing; then this other lad turns up dead – and we visited the bridge; it wasn't an easy place to hang yourself from. Furthermore, I spoke to your former teacher Miss Cartwright," Jen said, looking at Anthea. "She said that Luke Rankin was not mentally retarded, he was just a little slow and nervous – particularly as his father had died."

"That might count," Anthea said. "That could count as not being of sound mind."

Possibly the girl had a point.

For now Jen decided to change the subject.

"I got your joke about the broomshoots, by the way. They're those bright yellow flowers, right?"

Anthea grinned as she placed the spoon to her mouth. "They don't often grow here in Wootton."

"Does someone plant them?"

"I think so," Anthea said, nodding.

To Jen that was strange. "I assume there is a connection? Between that and the family?"

"Probably," Anthea replied. "I think it's stupid, if you ask me. Imagine being married to a Broomshoot."

Jen laughed at her. "I met one of them today – in the churchyard."

"The person or the flower?" Anthea asked, giggling.

"The person. He said his name was Edward."

"Did he like your hair?"

"What's that got to do with anything?"

"Nothing. I just thought he might have commented, you know, whether I did a good job."

Jen grinned back at her. "He said he liked it."

"Good. Did you like him?"

"Don't know. He seemed quite arrogant, really. He kept teasing me about Robin Hood being from Yorkshire."

Anthea laughed. "He can be like that."

"What does he do?"

Anthea shrugged. "Don't know, really. His granddad is a lord of the realm, isn't he, Mum?"

Martha nodded.

"Shame about his parents."

"What happened to his parents?" Jen asked.

"Died in a car crash before I was born."

"They were only thirty-seven, the poor loves," Martha said.

"His dad was a politician. They were on holiday in Corsica," Anthea added.

Jen smiled sympathetically. "What were their names?"

"Richard and Anne," Martha replied.

"Where are they buried?"

"Under the church, I think," Anthea said.

Jen was sure she hadn't seen either of them in the vault. "Have you been down there before – either of you?"

Anthea nodded. "Yeah. Why?"

"I was down there earlier, just before Mass. I was in the Jeffries' vault and found this door – it was locked."

Anthea appeared suddenly nervous.

"What about it?" Martha asked.

Jen didn't miss a thing. "Nothing. I was wondering what was behind it?"

Martha shrugged. "I don't know."

"Father Martin said it held the remains of plague victims." Jen looked at both women in turn. "Have either of you seen it?"

Martha shook her head. "No, luvvy."

Anthea was unusually quiet, and Jen noticed.

"Have you ever been in there?"

Anthea remained taciturn. She forced an awkward smile and placed a hand to her hair.

"Have I said something?" Jen asked.

Anthea remained silent for several seconds. "This door," she began. "Was there an archway round it?"

Jen nodded.

"And had an emblem on top of it?"

Jen's excitement was growing. "Yes, that's the one."

For the second time in quick succession, Anthea became distant.

"Is everything okay?"

Anthea spoke quietly. "I got in there by accident when I was a little girl."

"What was in there?"

"I don't really remember. I just remember it was really dark – full of strange pictures and tombs and . . ."

Recalling the matter seemed to make the girl's skin itch.

"I kept screaming," Anthea resumed. "I thought I was going to be trapped down there – forever. I kept screaming and screaming and screaming . . . then after what seemed like forever, Father Martin came in . . . and he shouted at me."

The memory clearly upset Anthea – though she kept it together.

"Why did he shout at you?"

Anthea shrugged. "He just said that I wasn't supposed to be in there – and that if he found me in there again, I'd be in so much trouble."

Martha placed a hand on her daughter's shoulder. "There, there, pet." She looked at Jen. "She was only eight at the time."

Jen was horrified. Her opinion of the priest had reached rock bottom.

"I'm going to need your help getting into the vault," Jen said.

Anthea wiped away a tear. Jen was relieved that it was the only one.

"Why? What's so special? It was just a dark room with a load of old people buried in it."

Jen frowned. "I've got a nasty feeling that it might also have a much younger person buried there."

25

The limousine pulled up at the pre-designated location at just before 9 p.m. Despite the recent downpour, it was still light. A glorious sunset burned across the western sky, descending into the distant hills and painting the skyline in vivid orange and red.

The image was a photographer's dream, but not just because of the sunset. The landscape was pure green, lined with fields and dense forests that seemingly continued forever. Even the occasional villages or towns barely made a mark on the landscape – and even those that did were for the most part as old as the trees. The area had a sense of timelessness, the type of place where every house could tell a story.

But also a place where most chose not to tell.

The landscape, despite the endless beauty, was not necessarily the area's greatest feature. Merely metres from the secluded car park, magnificent walls, reminiscent of the mighty Camelot, rose impressively into the sky. The white stone structure was completely intact, though nothing more than a shell. It was a place where history merged with the present day, and where the echoes of the past continued to be heard like a song being played on a continuous loop.

And while it continued to play, peace would remain impossible.

The journey had taken a fraction under two hours – one hour fifty-seven minutes according to the clock on the dashboard. Watching through the rear left window, the son of the Duke of Clarence had been able to follow the route with relative accuracy. Motorways and A roads dominated the itinerary, making the general direction easy to follow. The M180 gave way to the M18, then to the M62 and from there the A1. As time went by, the large blue signposts, listing the distance to nearby destinations, turned into blurs. He knew the roads well – he'd been travelling them all his life.

On leaving the A6055, he paid closer attention. The destination was somewhere in Yorkshire – had it not have been, the driver would not have left the A1. As the driver negotiated a series of roundabouts, Thomas watched, concentrating hard. In hindsight, the precaution proved unnecessary. There was no doubt regarding his current location.

The poetic irony was not lost on him.

Middleham Castle.

A Yorkist stronghold.

Once home to a King of England.

Patterson parked the car south-west of the castle. It was not a visitor car park; instead, it was an area where a lorry or large van would pull up to make a delivery. In his experience, it was the only area where anonymity was guaranteed. The castle itself was integrated within the larger community: a small market town of about eight hundred people. The locals usually kept themselves to themselves, but it never did to take chances. A bad move in the wrong place – a passing car, an overeager tourist, or a local walking his dog – could put everything in jeopardy. Fate rested on such mishaps being avoided.

Just as it had five hundred years earlier.

The driver turned to face the impostor, now minus his tinted glasses. As soon as Thomas saw the man's eyes, he realised his mistake.

The man waved a black revolver in his face.

"Kindly step out of the vehicle, Your Highness."

The traditional entrance was through a tower located at the north-east point of the structure. Instead, Patterson took them in through a more discreet passage. The walls were lower there, allowing easy access to the heart of the castle.

The interior was enormous – but compact. A large curtain wall surrounded the square keep: a dense, imposing structure that still looked capable of withstanding siege. It was darker there than outside, the sunlight failing to rise above the western wall. It was approaching twilight, and a half moon was now visible.

Thomas guessed there was little more than thirty minutes left of actual daylight.

He led the way, though not by choice. The black revolver, pushed forcefully into the small of his back via Talbot's grey raincoat, limited his choices. He walked with his hands behind his head, his eyes on the walls. He knew from past visits that the main entrance was the only viable exit – aside from the way they had just entered. Even if he managed to escape, his choices were limited.

Worse still was the silence. Even on grass, noises had a nasty tendency to echo, which unnerved him further as his reality continued to dawn on him. Somewhere within these ruins, someone – or some people – was lurking: someone with the potential to do him much harm. Whoever it was, they clearly knew that Talbot was dead.

Worse still, they probably thought he did it.

They continued along the outer wall of the keep. Several birds, possibly rooks, perched on the curtain wall, the sound of their fierce squawks magnified by the acoustics of the layout. In the fading light, it was like the walls were closing in on them. The sense of timelessness seemed to escalate. For the first time that day Thomas thought back to his meeting with the King. The message: apparently a calling card of the Sons of York. In his mind he could hear a majestic voice reciting the words:

"Now is the winter of our discontent; made glorious summer by this sun of York."

Though the temperature remained warm, the prince found himself plagued by a bitter chill.

He remembered the other message.

Sing a song of sixpence, a pocket full of rye.

Four and twenty blackbirds baked in a pie.

Whoever they were, they had surely killed his grandfather.

Perhaps his aunt and grandmother, too.

The keep was similar to many from the Middle Ages: a large square structure, divided in two by an internal wall, and flanked by turrets at every corner. The original stone staircase had been destroyed long ago; in its stead, a modern wooden staircase led to the south-east corner.

His heart missed a beat. Three men, each wearing identical dark jackets, occupied different parts of the staircase, automatic weapons in their grasp. Thomas could not see their faces, but it was obvious they were highly trained – probably military.

He entered the chamber, followed closely by the butler.

"Here Clarence comes, brother, good days, what means this armed guard that waits upon Your Grace?"

The response was delayed. "We have no time for playing games," barked one of the three. "Where is Talbot?"

This was surely too good to be true. Was it possible that the butler had actually sprung this on them?

"Sir Jack is dead," the butler replied, the pause between each word lengthy. "I was the one that killed him."

Thomas was amazed by the admission. He sensed the others shared his surprise.

"You murdered your own master?" another of the three asked, his voice razor sharp.

"Forgive me, sir, I had no choice. You see, Sir Jack was being made subject of a most vicious inquisition from this minor royal," he said, the disgust evident on the words 'minor royal'.

Suddenly the man's admission made perfect sense.

"Minor royal?" the final man asked.

"May I introduce to you, Prince Thomas William Henry Winchester, heir to the Duchy of Clarence."

For several seconds there was no sign of any acknowledgement.

"Why have you brought him here?"

"Forgive me, sir, I know that you should have been informed in advance," the butler said. "But His Highness was most insistent on absolute discretion."

The words shocked the prince. "I beg your pardon."

He felt the barrel of the gun move against his back.

"Do not move," one of the voices said from above.

Thomas and Patterson both came to an immediate standstill, the prince returning his hands to behind his head. With circumspect eyes, he searched the chamber for exits. Should the tables turn, he knew he would have to move fast.

All the while the light was fading.

"Why is he here?" The question came from the man at the top of the staircase; to Thomas, the most dominant of the three.

"For the good of the society, sir," Patterson replied.

Thomas could sense the man's frustration. Whatever the reason for Talbot's appointment, he silently wondered whether it was nothing too threatening.

Despite the seclusion, it was a bad place to perform a murder.

The leader of the three moved a few steps down the staircase. "What was your business with Sir Jack?"

Thomas contemplated a response but decided against it.

"Speak."

The words stuck in his throat.

"You're wasting your time with this one," Patterson said, laughing. "We'll be here till doomsday just waiting for the first word."

"Silence!" the leader barked.

Suddenly there was movement, seemingly from everywhere. Small silhouettes moved, accompanied by the sound of flapping wings. Several rooks, perhaps half a dozen, were moving through the twilight.

A split second was enough. The prince's actions were instinctive. He moved his left foot around the other side of the butler and grabbed the man's arms, twisting to the right. The butler fired as he lost control. The bullet crashed into the upper wall, the sound echoing.

Several gunshots followed. Debris flew up from the wall behind, agonizingly near. Thomas backtracked, struggling to keep his balance. Using the butler as a shield, he placed himself directly out of the line of fire.

"Hold your fire!" the leader of the three demanded.

Thomas, meanwhile, had regained control. With his left hand secure on Patterson, he removed his Glock from the inside of his right thigh.

"Stay p-perfectly still," he said relatively loudly. He looked in every direction, taking in more of the surroundings.

The tables had turned, but the exits were still limited.

He pointed the gun, first at the staircase, then at the butler's neck. "No funny business."

The leader of the three was furious. Standing two steps from the top of the staircase, he gripped the wooden railing with both hands. For the first time the prince noticed that this man was not armed – unlike the other two.

Though the light had faded significantly, Thomas could make out facial features better than before. All three wore woolly hats, black in colour, but not balaclavas. Each man was clean-shaven, white, either late twenties or early thirties. He couldn't place the accents – they were definitely English, but the region difficult to determine.

If they were local, it wasn't obvious.

"Who are you?" Thomas asked.

"You're wasting your time," the butler said, his face turned towards the prince. For the first time, Thomas noticed the man's scent – evidently some kind of cologne, and not a nice one.

He thrashed the gun into the man's back, causing the butler's spine to arch. Several metres in front of him, the butler's revolver was lying on the ground.

There was no question of it going anywhere yet.

"Who are you working for?"

"You're wasting your time," the butler repeated sarcastically.

Thomas's patience was waning. "I shan't t-tell you again."

"Whoever you are," this time the words came from one of the others, "let the man go; we can talk about this – be civilised."

The prince didn't buy it. He started edging backwards, towards the nearest archway.

"Who are you working for?" he barked.

Who was His Highness?

The silence was disturbed by the sound of a siren, evidently close by. Up above, the three men were starting to panic. An argument had broken out between them in low voices.

Thomas was confused; he recognised the whine as belonging to a police car, but there was no logical reason for them to have been called. He was quite certain no one had seen him and the butler enter – even if they had, it could easily have been mistaken as a legitimate entry by an employee.

Had the other three been seen? No, surely that was impossible. The location had clearly been used before and probably recently. Despite the lack of communication, the three were definitely not amateurs.

Had the gunfire attracted attention?

He had to move fast – or if not fast, effectively. He considered firing a shot into the air; at least that would attract attention. Then he dismissed the idea.

The last thing he needed was for a gunfight to break out.

Unfortunately that was what happened. Shots came from everywhere. Almost immediately he lost his footing, not helped by the weight of the butler in front of him. He decided to let him go, concentrating instead on his own escape.

The bullets were now flying, the sounds echoing off the high walls. Debris moved around him, some near, some further away. The lack of light was now a significant problem.

Everything was a matter of chance.

Thomas sprinted in the opposite direction from the staircase and dived. He was now in the first chamber of the keep, separated from the other by the internal wall.

He rolled to one side and slowly regained his feet, standing with his back to the wall. Recovering his breath, he turned to his right, chancing exposure. A shot came; the bullet smashed into the nearby wall.

The shot had come from nearer than the staircase.

Thomas looked again, shielding everything but his left eye with the wall. The man firing was Patterson, standing some ten metres away, the revolver in his outstretched hand.

Another shot followed, then another – both from Patterson. Glock at the ready, Thomas fired back, the shot narrowly missing the butler. Several more came from the stairs, obviously from one of the three.

Once the mayhem died down, Thomas opened fire. Almost immediately he heard a groan from Patterson. Quiet followed, lasting several seconds. The noise of gunfire echoed again in his ear, accompanied by the familiar ringing noise. For now the siren had disappeared – strange, all things considered.

Was the whole thing a coincidence?

Was the emergency somewhere else?

Two shots in quick succession ended the silence, followed by the sound of bullets against brick. Judging by the noises, the shots were being fired from further away – almost certainly the staircase. Thomas looked out from behind the wall; a silhouette was hunched over, no more than twenty metres away.

He didn't need perfect vision to know that was Patterson.

The prince fired towards the stairway. He saw the figure drop a firearm before lunging for shelter.

The lack of light was now an advantage. He moved to the other side of the gap and was rewarded with a better view of the staircase. He saw two silhouettes on the stairs, but the third had disappeared. He fired at the nearest and immediately saw movement. The man keeled over, his momentum taking him down the steps. Amidst the sound of the man's body hitting the wooden stairs, Thomas could hear cries of anguish.

The gunfire resumed, this time from the area where the staircase met the second storey. Thomas fired another shot before ducking for cover. The gunfire was consistent and extremely powerful. The bullets came in quick succession, too quickly for a shotgun, but too slowly for a machine gun. The sound puzzled him: the weapon was certainly automatic, but unlike anything he had come across.

Whatever it was, it was in capable hands.

Far too capable.

Once the gunfire ceased, Thomas returned fire. As far as he could tell the figure had disappeared – almost certainly somewhere on the upper storey.

Chancing exposure, he sprinted to where the butler had last been seen and found the pistol on the floor, a few feet from the man himself. The butler was lying completely still, hunched up slightly, his legs at an angle.

The prince knelt down beside him, checking for signs of life. The man's eyes were open, but without movement.

No question, he was dead.

A quick rummage of his pockets proved fruitless – apart from the car keys. The old adage of name, rank and serial number was clearly at play. Should the man be discovered, there was no way of identifying him without resorting to further checks.

His other secrets, he had taken to the grave.

Leaving the butler where he was, Thomas sprinted towards the stairs. The wounded man was still on the staircase, lying on his back about a third of the way up. The man's weapon had fallen ten steps below him. It was a mid-sized object, about half the size of an AK-47, capable of firing a hundred rounds. The weapon was elegant, but baffling. He had seen it only once before, earlier that day behind a wall at Riverton.

To the prince, it was unrecognisable.

Monitoring the top of the stairway, he approached him slowly. The victim was lying practically still, wheezing, his eyes open and his expression locked in a grimace. He was holding the stomach area, possibly the gallbladder. There was a look of desperation in his eyes . . .

And perhaps of resignation.

Thomas advanced to the top of the staircase and followed the wall around to the left.

The other two men were nowhere to be seen.

From the prince's vantage point, the view, in daylight, would extend as far as the surrounding countryside, but at this time of night, it was a lot more restricted. Darkness prevailed, the outlines of the thick walls the only things he was able to distinguish clearly. The reflection of a blue light was visible from somewhere nearby.

He guessed it almost certainly belonged to the same vehicle responsible for the siren he had heard minutes earlier.

The question was why had it taken so long to get here?

Thomas retreated down the stairway. The injured man clearly needed treatment, but public exposure was a significant consideration. Should the press manage to get hold of the story, it was potentially a PR nightmare for the royals.

He had to think quickly.

He crouched down beside the injured man and tried to help him to his feet. Despite his attempt at cooperation, the man's injury was severe. Placing the firearms inside his jacket, the prince helped the man to his feet and eventually made it to the bottom of the steps. With no more railing to support him, the man fell once again to the ground.

Thomas realised there was only one option. Placing his right hand below the man's neck and his left beneath his legs, he carried him through the inner chamber.

The castle was now silent and evidently deserted. Up above, the sky was almost pitch black. It seemed like a long time had passed since his arrival, though he guessed it was actually less than twenty minutes. The stunning rays of the large moon, surrounded by a ghostly haze, were his only aid.

Thankfully the walk from the limousine had been largely straightforward.

As he neared the exit, he heard voices. Accompanying them was the sound of footsteps, multiple pairs, some running, some walking. Walkie-talkies crackled violently.

Approaching the final wall, Thomas ducked for cover, silently praying his actions wouldn't injure the man further.

In silence, they waited. Unmistakably he heard noises close by. He felt the presence of several people pass, perhaps half a dozen in total. He waited until they had gone before raising his head above the wall. As expected, he saw police uniforms accompanied by torches, batons and stun guns.

Lowering his head, he held his breath. Cradled within his arms, he could feel, but not see, the wounded man breathing against his chest. He made no attempt to attract observation, nor hinder the prince's progress.

Capture was not an option.

Thomas waited until the lights disappeared and the voices quietened. Finally he moved away, placing the wounded man on the backseat of the limousine. The engine started quietly, as they always did.

No one saw him leave, nor did anyone pay extra attention to the luxurious motor that was quietly making its way through the Wensleydale countryside.

In the London headquarters of a famous English newspaper, the *London Chronicle*, the journalist tapped lightly on the door of the editor's office and entered without breaking stride.

Had the editor not been on the phone at the time, his passing of the three-page document might have received more recognition than the cursory thumbs up.

Instead, that was his last action of the day.

Alone in his office, the head of personal relations for the Royal Family was genuinely perplexed.

That was the third call today the department had received on the subject.

Biting his lip, he picked up the receiver.

He would have to inform his employer personally.

26

No one spoke for several seconds. Across the table from Jen, Anthea sat with her hands around her face. Although she was not crying, it was obvious to Jen the suggestion about Debra Harrison had taken the wind out of her sails. The idea that her friend had been murdered and her corpse hidden away behind a locked door . . .

The reality seemed unthinkable.

At the head of the table, Martha had barely moved. Her expression suggested she was disturbed, but more by Jen's suggestion than the possible reality.

Jen had no idea what to say next. One way or another, she knew she was about to outstay her welcome.

"Who would have the key?" Jen asked after a while. "How many people have keys to the vault?"

Jen waited, but for now received no response. Realistically, she knew there were only two likely options. Firstly, the priest, who had already illustrated his lack of enthusiasm towards opening the door – even if he said yes, unexpectedly, she knew she risked exposing her true purpose. If the priest had some knowledge of the events of a year ago, she risked compromising the entire investigation.

Not to mention the documentary.

The second possibility was the Jeffries family themselves.

After all, the door was connected to their family vault.

Jen looked at both Martha and Anthea intently. "There might be another way, another door." She turned to Martha. "Please, Martha, you've been cleaning that church for years. Please tell me everything you know."

The woman's patience was thinning. "Jen, can't you see you're upsetting my daughter."

Jen looked back hopelessly. "Martha, I'm sorry, but I have a really bad feeling about this. For all we know, poor Debra Harrison has been locked in that vault for the last year and no one has even thought about it," she said, brushing her hair back over her head. On this occasion, the thought that these two women had been responsible for the cut didn't register.

"Have you ever seen it yourself?"

Martha delayed her response. "No. Not from the inside."

She looked at Anthea. "You've only seen it the once?"

Anthea nodded, incapable of saying anything. Jen was pleased to see that her eyes were still dry.

"Who would have the key?" Jen asked a second time.

This time it was Anthea who answered. "Mum has a set of keys – Father Martin gave her a set for cleaning."

Jen felt her heart momentarily stop. "Keys to what?"

Martha was angry – this time with her daughter. "I was not given those keys so that I could be party to their misuse."

"Why does it matter?" Anthea asked. "The church is usually unlocked anyway."

To Jen, getting into the church was not the problem. "Do you have a key to the vault?"

Martha's expression was stern. "I have keys to the church and to the cloisters – not for any individual vault."

"How do you know?" her daughter asked. "There's like a thousand keys on that key ring."

Anthea left her seat and entered the hallway. There was a basket near the door, full of various keys and change.

"Here," Anthea said, picking out the relevant key ring. "How will we know if we don't try?"

Martha was livid. "Give me that."

Before she could react, Anthea threw the keys to Jen. She caught them instinctively and incurred a penetrating stare from Martha.

"Martha, please, wait," Jen said, sticking out an arm. "Please, I just want to have a look. You need play no part in this."

Martha huffed. "Give me my keys."

Jen held up the keys and extended her arm. She prepared to give them back to Martha, but changed her mind.

"You needn't have any involvement in this," Jen said. "If anyone asks, you can just say I took them."

The woman placed her hands to her face and shook her head simultaneously.

For the first time Jen felt guilty. She was so wrapped up in finding a way into the vault, she failed to realise that she was pressuring the woman.

"Martha, I promise I will give you them straight back. All I want to see is what's behind the door," she said, turning her gaze to Anthea. "Is that the only way in?"

Anthea tucked her hair behind her ears. "If I come with you, I can show you."

"Anthea Brown!" Martha shouted.

"Your mother's right," Jen said. "Besides, I really have no idea what I expect to find down there."

The idea made Jen feel nervous.

Anthea was adamant. "If you do get into trouble, you're going to need the help of someone who knows the vaults.

"And I'm probably the only person who's ever seen it."

Thomas drove south on leaving Middleham. Ten minutes had passed, but his heart was still thumping. A ring of sweat had formed at the top of his brow, continuing across his forehead and dripping down the side of his face. He wiped it with his sleeve, doing his best to concentrate on the road in front of him.

For now there was no traffic in either direction.

He looked in the rear-view mirror. The injured man was still alive on the backseat; even without the mirror, he could tell by the heaviness of the man's breathing. His own clothes were stained from carrying the man, while the smell was also becoming more noticeable. He tried opening the window, allowing the blustery air to reinvigorate his stressed body.

He had to think – and quickly. Attracting attention was not an option, but the man needed a professional medic.

Navigating the options on the Satnav, he selected the wider map. About ten miles west, he had a cousin: Stephen Winchester. Like himself, the lad was of military pedigree, but, unlike himself, he'd served in the medical corps. If anyone was capable of assisting the injured man, it was him.

Better yet, Stephen had another major plus point.

He was the eldest son of the king.

Thomas removed his mobile phone from his pocket and quickly scrolled through his contacts. He found Stephen, both home and mobile, and selected the home option.

Seconds later, Stephen answered.

"I'm coming to see you in ten minutes. And I'll be needing your physician skills."

*

Inside the keep, the police officer stood hunched over the figure on the ground. The man carried no wallet, nor did he possess any keys or mobile phone. He had been shot once in the upper chest, the bullet presently unidentified, but as far as the officer could tell, the man had not carried a firearm himself. The apparent cause of death certainly seemed consistent with reports of gunfire being heard in the vicinity moments before he had received the call – he had heard several himself since his own arrival.

Whoever was responsible was long gone.

The question now was who had been found?

The other two men had escaped from a small window near the main entrance of the castle. They avoided attention from police or onlookers and twenty minutes later were driving north in a black Mercedes.

Over thirty years' experience between them, and that was the closest they had come to catastrophe. What should have been a simple, straightforward task had been compromised into a matter of lost life.

Under normal circumstances, it was the job of the last man standing to put his accomplice out of his misery: whether a sign of brotherly love, to ensure the man suffers no lasting pain, or to ensure he takes his secrets with him to the grave . . . he assumed the latter was more applicable.

Fifteen years in the business had taught him that the men at the top deemed human life expendable. He knew that was the reason he was chosen – to end the life of his best friend at a moment's notice if that was what was required. In truth, neither man was sure what had become of their accomplices. Had the light been better, perhaps he would have had to finish the job himself.

But the question remained, what caused the compromise? If the butler was correct, Talbot had died for failing to abide by the cardinal rule. That explained Talbot's absence, but it did not explain the presence of the newcomer. Bringing a royal, even a minor one, to this forbidden party was like playing with fire. Someone had dropped them in it.

His Highness would need to be informed.

27

Twenty minutes later Thomas pulled up outside an isolated farmhouse on the edge of the Yorkshire Dales. The estate was large, gated, and walled on all sides, constructed mostly of white brick dating back to the early 1800s.

The gate was open, as was the front door. A handsome man in his early thirties, with dark hair, a lean build, and smart persona was there to greet him. He helped Thomas unload the body of the mysterious stranger from the backseat before ushering them inside.

The next thirty minutes were frantic. They carried the man into an upstairs bedroom and planted him down on a double bed. The surgeon's tools were already laid out on a nearby table, accompanied by a large bottle of whiskey. Five minutes later they had succeeded in removing the bullet, but after that things became a blur. The man was gushing blood at an alarming rate.

Survival was now a matter of chance.

For the last few minutes Thomas had been sitting on his own in the lounge, a large and well-decorated room otherwise in keeping with the style of the house. The rest of the furniture pointed to the man's bachelor lifestyle: forty-eight-inch TV on the wall, Dolby Surround sound and a reclining easy chair with cup holder. Aside from their grandfather's funeral, Thomas had not seen his cousin for over two years, but he could tell from the furniture, little had changed.

Footsteps on the stairs indicated his cousin was approaching. Seconds later Stephen entered the room.

"He's sleeping."

Thomas rose to his feet. "Wh-what are his chances?"

"We'll have a much better indication by morning – assuming he's still alive, of course."

Thomas nodded, returning to his seat. He struggled to prevent his hands from shaking.

"Whiskey? Or would you prefer something stronger?"

Thomas nodded. "Whiskey."

Stephen removed a bottle of single malt from a container on top of the mantelpiece. "I was hoping to save this for a special occasion," he said, removing the lid and pouring double shots into two glasses. "But, I suppose, there's no time like the present."

He passed the second glass to Thomas and clinked it with his own. "Cheers."

Stephen downed his in one and savoured the aftertaste. Thomas began his more slowly before forcing it down. He had never been much of a drinker. The fine liquid burned his mouth and throat, the sensation penetrating all the way through his head.

"Another?" Stephen asked.

Thomas looked up at his cousin. He nodded, but said nothing.

Stephen refilled the glass to about three shots worth. After that, he did the same for his own.

"Would you now mind telling me what the bloody hell you've got yourself into?"

Thomas sipped his whiskey – this time slowly. He coughed and spluttered, forcing him to cover his mouth.

"I'm waiting, Thomas."

The prince looked up at his cousin. "It's complicated."

"Fortunately I'm exceedingly clever. Now spit it out."

Thomas continued to concentrate on his whiskey.

"I can always call Dad, if you prefer?"

"Okay, fine."

Thomas recounted the events of the past two days.

Stephen listened carefully. He had drained his glass and was halfway through the next by the time Thomas had finished.

"Who knows about this?" Stephen asked after a while.

"Hardly anyone," Thomas replied. "I'm guessing that you already know m-more than me."

Stephen nodded, for now keeping his counsel. He continued to sip his whiskey.

"Jack Talbot," he said at last, swirling the liquid around in his glass. "Why am I not surprised?"

"Whoever he was working for, I th-think he was about to come clean. At least until that b-bloody butler put his f-finger in the way."

"What was his name?"

"Patterson."

"First name?"

"Really, Stephen, how many butlers are called by their first name?"

Stephen laughed. "Could you give an accurate description?"

"Of course."

"Good. At least that way someone might be able to establish a positive identification on him."

"That shouldn't be difficult – we already know his s-second name, address, and c-car registration."

"How about the others?"

"Nothing at all."

"Not even a description?"

"It was dark; they were professionals. We really must keep this one alive – at least that way we might f-find out who we're d-dealing with."

Thomas removed the injured man's automatic weapon from his jacket. "Look at this."

Stephen was confused. "What is it?"

"No idea. Never seen one before."

Stephen was quiet for several seconds. "Tell me what he said exactly."

"Who?"

"The friar at the Tower."

Recalling words was difficult, but Thomas told Stephen what he remembered.

"Beware the Sons of York?" Stephen said.

"Among other things, yes," Thomas said, finishing his second glass. "Have you heard of them?"

"Never. Who are they?"

Thomas shook his head. "I know little more than you."

"Tell us the little – at least that'll make us even."

"Only if you do the same for me."

"Okay. Fine. You go first."

Thomas went first, then Stephen.

"Apparently they've been d-doing this s-sort of thing for years," Thomas continued.

"What sort of thing?"

"C-causing mischief. Apparently one or two were involved in the Monmouth risings and other things."

"Anything more recent?"

"Your father didn't go into d-detail. He spoke mainly about not having p-paid much attention when he was younger."

Stephen was still confused. "Who were the historians?"

"Apparently there were two of them. Wrote about the Sons of York in the early 1700 and 1900s. Your f-father seemed to believe the knowledge was r-relevant. Clearly there was s-something that the Sons of York know that others are not s-supposed to."

"How about the other thing?"

Thomas was confused. "What other thing?"

"The nursery rhyme."

He told Stephen everything, highlighting the amendments.

He didn't enjoy mentioning the King's belief that the queens in the parlour was a reference to Stephen's late mother and grandmother.

Stephen put his finger and thumb to the bridge of his nose and then to his eyes. He lowered himself onto the settee and immediately rose again to his feet. "The princess was in the . . . what princess?"

"I don't know."

"What the hell did Monmouth have to do with this?"

Thomas shook his head. "There was one other thing," he said, trying to recall the events of earlier that evening. "When the butler t-took me to the castle and introduced me as Clarence, he s-said something rather odd."

"What?"

"When they inquired of the butler as to why they had not been informed of my coming and of T-Talbot's death, he said something about His Highness insisted on absolute discretion."

The physician shrugged. "Meaning what, exactly?"

"I'm not quite sure," Thomas said, starting to get slightly worked up. "It was the way that he said it: it was almost . . ."

"What?"

The prince took a deep breath. "Reverent."

"And?"

"The two politicians were murdered – tests by MI5 on the car have all but confirmed this. But the King . . ."

"You think he was murdered by someone of status?"

Thomas failed to respond.

"You said yourself the witness was something of a madman."

"He was telling the truth about everything else. W-we must face facts, it's not out of the question."

Stephen was unconvinced. "Even if he was telling the truth, the situation hasn't really changed, has it?"

"Our grandfather's condition weakened considerably in a s-short period – we can practically catalogue the exact schedule. On the Tuesday he returned from Balmoral, the day after the family meal, still a p-picture of good health. The next ten days he b-barely left Winchester. All we know of the poison is it works slowly. If he was murdered, the day at Balmoral was almost c-certainly the day the d-damage was done.

"And I'm afraid that only leaves us with one g-group of suspects."

"The servants?"

"No. The relatives."

Still in his office at 9 p.m., the editor of the *London Chronicle* scanned the document in front of him.

The piece differed from the journalist's usual style, but the article was not uninteresting. It was just the opposite, in fact. If it was true, the revelations were startling.

Better yet, apparently he had a source.

He double-clicked on his mouse and copied and pasted the original article into the new document.

The article would be ready for tomorrow's evening edition.

28

It was dark by 9:30. Along the high street, buildings were closed for business, their interiors revealing no sign of life. The only illumination was the white glow of the streetlights, radiating a warm atmospheric haze above the pavement. Between Dovecote Ridge, where Martha and Anthea lived, and the middle of the high street, there was not a soul to be seen, apart from Jen and Anthea. And that boded well; even for such a short walk it would be unwise to be conspicuous. As they passed the estate agent's, the dim glow of what appeared to be a backlight served as a reminder that observation could come from any corner.

But as far as they could see, the building was deserted.

The light was merely a deterrent to put off potential thieves.

There was activity across the bridge. Lights were on in the Hog, as expected. Laughter and chatter resonated within its ancient walls – as it surely had done for centuries. Jen thought she heard the sound of Brian Hancock laughing boisterously, but she knew she couldn't be sure.

Among the sounds of many, those of the few were lost.

About an eighth of a mile further on, the church was dark and deserted. On warm and still nights, the sight of passing teenagers, lonely figures walking their dogs or local residents taking the night air was not uncommon, but tonight there was not a soul to be seen. Even the birds had disappeared.

Like the monks of old, a vow of silence had taken over the village.

Making her way through a cluster of gravestones, Jen headed for the main doors of the church.

A sudden glare of bright lights caught her completely off guard.

"Shit," Jen said, taking cover behind the nearest gravestone. She realised her mistake immediately. The security lights overlooking the main door were obviously movement activated.

Two minutes in and the plan had failed.

"That always comes on," Anthea said. "People'll just think it's a squirrel or a bird."

Jen was unconvinced.

"Come on, before it goes off and comes on again."

This time Jen followed Anthea, sprinting for the front door. Her gut feeling was she had made a mistake – potentially a huge one. Until this point she had not considered the possibility that CCTV cameras could be in operation. The sleepy nature of the village made her think it unlikely, but she reminded herself she was living in the 21st century. Technically, she was considering breaking and entering.

And the law was pretty clear on the matter.

Anthea inserted the main key into the lock and opened the door. She locked it immediately from the inside, and for several seconds they both held their breath. The lights outside the church went out after about fifteen seconds. Even the interior of the church seemed darker. As best they could tell, nobody had seen them enter; aside from the Hog and the presbytery, there were no nearby buildings, and Jen knew from personal experience that visibility from the Hog's windows was poor. For now she was satisfied.

At least they were in.

Jen followed Anthea towards the cloisters, concentrating on her footing. As expected, the door was locked, but that was remedied thanks to a small key on the key ring. The cloisters appeared lighter than the main church; the faint gleams of moonlight, entering through the windows, shone down on the tiled floor and reflected off the walls. The images in the glass appeared different at night, the patterns causing unique shadows. Even though she knew they were more modern than they looked, tonight they appeared somehow more sinister.

If that were possible.

"What are these?" Jen asked, now unconvinced by the priest's answer the day before.

"Heritage," Anthea replied. "People of the village were prominent supporters of the House of York."

Jen accepted the response – though still confused by the relatively modern design.

They made their way to the bottom of the steps and opened the door to the vaults.

Predictably, the tunnel was shrouded in darkness. Jen activated the flashlight facility on her iPhone, and Anthea did the same. Despite the improvement, the dense colour of the stone absorbed more light than it reflected. She remembered from earlier that the passage wound gently from left to right.

In theory, all they had to do was follow it.

They passed the vaults Jen had visited earlier and continued all the way to the one belonging to the Jeffries. Jen entered through the same open archway and into a desolate chamber that on this occasion seemed even gloomier than when she had seen it earlier. Inside, the chamber was pitch black – the dim glow of the surrounding wall lights that had lit up the vicinity a few hours earlier was no longer present. There was obviously a light switch somewhere – or switches – but even Anthea didn't know where.

Their mobiles were the only aid.

The locked door was visible in the torchlight, as was most of the debris. A large spider web had appeared in front of the door, beginning at the top corner and continuing all the way to the nearest tomb.

Jen saw movement and jumped. A small spider was floating across the torchlight. She batted it immediately, not knowing whether or not she had killed it.

She heard laughter developing into intense giggling. She pointed the light at Anthea.

"What? It was only a spider."

Jen's breathing returned to normal. She ran her fingers through her hair, assuming she had fallen victim to another cobweb. "I hate spiders."

"I'd never have guessed."

Jen attempted to regain her composure, but it was becoming difficult. Enclosed spaces were a no-no, and had been since she had become lost at Wookey Hole when she was seven. The chamber had seemed more open in the day – and certainly less dusty.

She sneezed, causing several motes to move in the torchlight. She shone the light on the door and turned her attention to Anthea.

"Try opening it."

Anthea seemed reluctant to move.

"Okay, I'll try."

She collected the keys from Anthea and slowly approached the door. There was rubble beneath her feet, making it impossible to stand without moving it first. She spent the next minute doing so before finally getting a clear view of the door.

Strangely, it looked smaller in the bad light, whereas earlier it had looked more imposing.

She concentrated on the lock. The first key was the wrong shape, the second, a perfect fit. Nevertheless, there was no sign of the door opening. There were eighteen keys in total, seven of which were the correct shape.

But none unlocked the door.

She went through them all a second time, concentrating on the seven that fitted. She tried everything she could possibly think of: turning them left, right, turning the handle, lifting it . . .

It was useless.

Jen tried the last key for longer, now rattling the handle. She pushed and pulled . . .

Useless.

"Ugh!"

She removed the key from the door and retreated several metres.

"How exactly did you get in the first time?"

The question unsettled Anthea. "Through that door, there."

Jen swept her hands through her hair. It was obvious that the keys didn't work.

"There must be another way in," Jen said, her eyes on the surrounding walls. She investigated them one by one.

Nothing but graves and debris.

Useless.

She returned to the door, trying the keys for a final time.

Nothing.

Jen rattled the lock vigorously before retreating several steps and picking up a piece of debris. She hurled it at the door, the object making no impression other than a dull thud followed by an echo.

"It's hopeless." She sighed. "Come on. Let's go."

Jen left the chamber and stopped on reaching the main passageway. She was still convinced there was another way in, probably from a different part of the vaults. Thanks to the appearance of the priest earlier, she hadn't had the chance to explore anything past the Jeffries' vault.

If there was another entrance, it was almost certainly nearby.

Movement from close by chilled her to the bone. It sounded like stone, not falling but definitely moving. She turned, the light from her phone now centred on Anthea's face.

"What was that?"

The girl shook her head. Jen could see in the torchlight that Anthea swallowed, a nervous gulp. It was evident from her expression that she had heard the noise as well.

"Can we leave now?" Anthea asked, petrified.

That wasn't going to happen.

Jen re-entered the chamber. She passed Anthea on the way back, neglecting to reply to her question. The noise had definitely come from inside the Jeffries' vault.

She scanned the room with her phone light. As best she could tell, nothing had changed. She assumed the most likely cause was falling debris.

Finding it would be like looking for a needle in a haystack.

Jen turned her thoughts to the tombs and then once again to the walls. Behind the debris was that doorway again, surrounded by the elaborate archway. The sight of it angered her – the keys that didn't fit, the peculiarities that allegedly existed on the other side. She shone the light on the debris surrounding the archway before aiming it slightly higher.

She noticed something. The symbol above the archway was different; instead of the Jeffries' flower, it was a five-pointed rose.

Was she seeing things? The darkness playing tricks?

She moved closer, hoping for a better view. She had seen the type before; it reminded her of the ones used by the houses of Lancaster and York in the Wars of the Roses.

But there was something stranger about this one. The original symbol was still there.

Only it had slid to one side.

A strange feeling had overcome her, somewhere in between excitement and sheer astonishment. Without doubt, the five-pointed rose had previously been hidden behind the Jeffries' symbol. On closer examination, there was some sort of hinge attached to it, which was why the Jeffries' symbol had been able to move. Jen attempted to rationalise how it might have happened, but for now nothing made sense. Had her throwing of the debris a few seconds earlier been the cause?

If not, she was stumped.

The excitement in her started to rise again. Unable to reach the symbol, she climbed up onto a nearby block of stone, but still came up short. Following that, she tried making a small pile out of other pieces of stone and debris that were close at hand, but it still wasn't high enough.

The extra height, however, did at least allow a better look at the crest: the five-pointed flower had a second flower at the centre and a circle within that – presumably the sun. She remembered that the white rose of York pointed downwards, whereas that of Lancaster did the opposite. While the identity of the symbol did not surprise her, of greater interest was its condition. The stone was weathered, obviously older than the Jeffries' symbol, but even more intriguingly, it contained no motto, unlike the one in front of it.

To Jen, that was itself a sign of authenticity.

She knew that mottos were not widely used until the 17th century.

Standing on the rubble, she looked up to her right at the Jeffries' emblem. The Latin motto was *dieu et mon droit*. Her Latin was rusty, but good enough to know the literal translation:

God and my right.

She heard something, somewhere in the distance. Turning to her left, she shone the light on Anthea.

The poor girl was scared out of her wits.

Jen came down from the makeshift pile and moved quickly to the entrance of the chamber. She looked both ways, not daring to expose the light. On either side she saw nothing. Whatever had made the noise had stopped. The only thing she could hear was the extended breathing of the poor girl standing behind her.

Jen pointed the light at her face.

"Okay. Now we can go."

Sitting alone before the big screen, the man with whitening hair watched as the two female intruders left the vault.

People said he had been crazy wanting to install a camera among the tombs – a lookout against would-be intruders. Even his own wife had scorned him for resorting to such drastic measures. Up to this point he had already been proven right on six occasions . . .

Tonight he could proudly make that seven.

On the top floor of the farmhouse, the door to the last bedroom on the right was slightly ajar. Thomas entered the room and sat down on the chair near the bed. The patient was still awake, but clearly exhausted. His breathing was laboured, as it had been before their arrival. Beneath the sheets, over seventeen stitches marked the area where the bullet had penetrated.

At least they had managed to remove it.

Thomas dragged his chair along the floor to the side of the bed. The patient looked up at him, his eyes displaying a mixture of fear and uncertainty. He said nothing, but the look in his eyes suggested communication.

What are you going to do with me?

For several minutes Thomas did the same. After watching him for what seemed an eternity, he asked, "Who are you?" To which he received no reply.

Just eye contact and the sound of extended breathing.

As the man tilted his head to the right, finally unable to stay awake, Thomas's attention turned to his possessions: a dark woolly hat, black combat jacket, black combat trousers, black T-shirt, black socks and black boots.

Beneath the sheets, even his underwear was the same colour.

Aside from his gun, the man carried little. There was no form of identification; the nearest was a phone.

Thomas scrolled through the contact list. The numbers were English, all mobiles, but the identity of their owners impossible to know.

The entries were written in code.

After placing the mobile phone in his pocket, Thomas got up, ready to leave, but then stopped. The man's left pectoral muscle was visible where the duvet had fallen. There was a mark on his chest, a tattoo of some kind. It was either a symbol or a coat of arms – the prince was unsure which.

Whatever it was, it matched the one he had seen on the friar at the Tower.

He walked over to the side of the bed and lifted the duvet.

After replacing it around the patient's shoulders, he walked away and left the room.

Stephen opened the boot of the limousine and unzipped the first holdall.

What he saw amazed him.

The bag was full of guns.

29

Jen was the first to make her way up the stairs, with Anthea following closely behind. After making sure the door was locked, they headed back along the cloisters, stopping on reaching the door that led back into the church.

In the distance Jen could see a light shining, quite possibly the security light outside the church, but whatever it was, it was clearly not an interior light. Less clear, the source of the sound they heard in the vaults.

If someone had entered the church, they had since disappeared.

They locked the door to the cloisters and continued towards the entrance of the church.

"Wait," Jen said, as Anthea prepared to unlock the door. There was light outside, clearly the security light.

Someone – or something – had activated it.

Jen put her eye to the keyhole, seeing if she could make it out. She could see the light, but everything else looked normal. Nevertheless, the field of vision was far too narrow to tell for certain.

She couldn't rule out the possibility that their exit could be observed.

"Tell me there's another exit."

"You've got either the sacristy or the cloisters."

"Where is the door to the sacristy?" Jen asked.

"Over there." She pointed to the left of the altar – the other side of the church.

"Perfect."

This time Jen allowed Anthea to lead. For the first time, Jen reminded herself that she was inside a church. In her mind, somehow the vaults seemed separate from the church itself. Despite the secrecy, it hadn't felt like breaking and entering until now. Behind the altar, the reredos was illuminated by light coming in through the stained-glass windows. Why had the security light come back on?

The thought disturbed her.

She genuflected quickly as she passed in front of the altar, and made a muttered sign of the cross. If anything, that had unnerved her even more. Anthea opened the door to the Lady chapel, a latch handle that fortunately didn't need locking with a key. On the other side of the chapel, a second door led to the sacristy. Anthea found the key at the seventh attempt, opened it, and locked it again from the inside. She saw the door to the outside.

In principle, it had been a good idea.

She switched the flashlight on her phone back on, and shone it on her surroundings. There were cupboards everywhere, including a large chest of drawers.

"What are they keeping here?" Jen asked.

"Stuff for the Mass, I'm guessing."

Jen continued to take in the sights. "How about Parish registers? Burial records? That sort of thing?"

Anthea shrugged.

"It would be recorded, wouldn't it? Even the old stuff."

"Wouldn't that be written in Latin?"

Jen was too busy to answer. "Check the cupboards; check the drawers."

Jen went through the cupboards while Anthea started on the large chest of drawers. Most of the content was albs and various vestments, whereas the papers were bulletins or things to do with the order of service.

Either way, no registers or anything of the sort.

She closed the door of the cabinet and looked at Anthea.

"Come on."

From the window of Wootton Court, the old man watched as the two figures emerged from the door that led to the sacristy. One, he recognised, but the other he was still to have the pleasure of meeting.

On leaving the sacristy, he saw them disappear into the graveyard.

Less than two hundred metres from the church, the long-haired brunette approached the gate that led to the footpath.

The dust of the church, accompanied by the stress of not being seen, felt extra heavy on her lungs, forcing her to stop to use her inhaler.

She could see movement near the sacristy, the door opening and closing, followed by the sight of two figures running. She watched as they disappeared towards the Hog.

*

Alone in his cousin's study, Thomas attempted in vain to control his patience as the dialling tone continued to dominate his hearing. Although it was after eleven, it was unlike his father to go to bed that early.

Finally an answer.

"I'm sending something through to you."

The prince replaced the receiver and inserted the number into the fax machine.

At the other end of the line, the Duke of Clarence collected the first three sheets. All three contained nothing but one small photograph, the contact list of someone's mobile phone.

There were eight sheets in total – each containing phone numbers.

He didn't need his son's instruction in the ninth that the clues would lie in uncovering the identities of their owners.

Moments later, in the headquarters of MI5, the DG received the same fax. Wasting no time, he picked up the telephone.

"Get me the Director of GCHQ."

Jen was back in her room by 11:30. The first thing she did was examine the photographs she had taken, the images far more visible on her laptop.

The symbol that had been hidden behind the Jeffries one definitely had the appearance of the white rose of York. According to the Internet, there was a yellow sun in the centre of a white rose with five petals that rested on a green five-pointed star, itself inside another white rose with five petals that also lay atop a five-pointed green star. The largest of the five-pointed green stars also pointed downwards, but much of the other detail on the one in the vault had been worn away. The upper part of the smaller rose, in particular, had practically disappeared, but there were enough parallels to satisfy her that the two were a match.

In theory, that much wasn't a problem. The original church – once part of the priory – dated back to the early Norman era, and she was certainly in the right county. She guessed in all likelihood, there were bound to be some graves of that era in the vaults – and just because she hadn't seen them didn't mean that they didn't exist. She exhausted Google for any hint of a secret door, local legend, old wives' tale or other, but yet again the exercise proved fruitless. If the Internet was to be believed, the church had enjoyed a relatively uneventful history . . .

Or to be more precise, a Jeffries-dominated uneventful history.

The family history seemed equally uninspiring. The family came on the scene in the mid-1550s, rising from minor to prominent noblemen in the East Riding of Yorkshire. Most were significant landowners, but nothing else to trouble the history books.

All in all, pretty forgettable.

But there were things that didn't add up. Firstly, Anthea was right. Edward Jeffries' father had been a politician, rising to leader of the Democrat Party. Several stories came up on Google, including a Wikipedia profile. The man had been a politician, only to die in a car crash prior to the 1994 election.

She tried to remember him but couldn't; she figured she was simply too young.

The second thing was even stranger. The family motto *dieu et mon droit* was not entirely original.

Nor was it even original to that graveyard.

Even to this day it belonged to an even more prominent family.

30

Oxford, England

The black Ford pulled into a parking space on the right-hand side of Museum Road, just outside Keble College. Seconds later, Thomas emerged from behind the wheel, dressed far more smartly than he had the night before. The slip-on shoes, dark trousers, and smart sports jacket did not look out of place. To a casual observer, he could have been anything from an undergrad to a research fellow – perhaps something more impressive still. There was something about the way he walked that suggested familiarity.

He turned left where Museum Road met Parks Road and left again on reaching the Porters' Lodge.

This was the main entrance to Keble College.

He flashed his old student card to the face behind the entrance window, catching a brief acknowledgement but nothing more. Instead, the woman was more preoccupied with the departing prospective students and their agitated parents as they left the college on the back of a recent guided tour.

Five years had passed since Thomas had last visited Oxford. Nothing ever changed. It was a city of elegance and beauty that continued to merge the elitist, the wannabe, the tourist, the local, and the downright drunk. In term time, he was used to every street and alleyway being packed to the rafters with students, some strutting, others ambling, making their way to the chosen port of call: the library, the lecture theatre, the dorms . . .

The bar . . .

At certain times of the year, the city had a buzz to it. The buildings of the university radiated distinction and permanence, unlike the students. The awe of the old guard lingered, whether it be in the form of a plaque, painting, or photograph of past achievements. He remembered his first week – the expectation, the stress . . . the contemplation of suicide . . .

Even for a royal it was relentless – perhaps even more so. It was difficult to shake the impression that someone was always watching you.

But fortunately today was different. The academic year was over; it was the time of transition. Today there was a different kind of environment. It was not the student, but the happy snapper, mainly from Asia or America, who frequented the famous buildings – the dinner gowns replaced by T-shirts and baseball caps, and the various wide-angle camera lenses.

In truth he knew he could not have picked a better day to return.

He continued through the main gate and stopped to take in the sights. The freshly cut lawn of Liddon Quad teased the nostrils, as did the accompanying smell of hot sun on pavement. To his right, the Gothic-revival chapel rose into the clear blue sky like a miniature cathedral, while to his left the equally Gothic library had a more foreboding feel, being drenched in shade. Like many buildings in the university, this part of the college was arranged in a quadrangle, and Gothic-revival architecture abounded. The consistent colour of the brickwork, reddish-brown or orange depending on the light, matched the consistency of the shape.

Like the joining of the past to the present, the cycle continued.

He followed the footpath that circled Liddon Quad, and reached the door to the chapel.

The interior was equally impressive. It was airy, lavish, and beautiful. Sunlight blazed through the stained-glass window behind the altar, engulfing the front of the chapel in an angelic glow. The pews on either side were empty, which was rare, even out of term time. Of all the buildings of the college, the chapel was arguably the biggest tourist attraction.

With the possible exception of one.

Thomas continued along the main aisle and turned right on reaching a door. He opened it and entered a small, airy room with light-coloured stonework and four arched windows. A handful of chairs had been placed either side of the carpet, facing the altar. An original painting hung behind the altar, depicting Christ holding a lantern, standing outside a door with no handle, surrounded by thorns.

Holman Hunt's masterpiece *The Light of the World*.

Keble's greatest treasure.

In the front row, an elderly gentleman sat with his eyes on the painting. He was balding, clean-shaven, slightly overweight and possessed striking green eyes that always seemed to be capable of looking everywhere at once. He was dressed impeccably.

As Thomas had always remembered.

"Professor Wilson, it's so g-good to s-see you."

The old man rose to his feet. "Thomas," he said, cupping the prince's right hand with both of his, "how have you been?"

"My health has been quite s-sound," he said, surveying his old mentor. "And yours?"

The old man smiled kindly. The light entering through the window seemingly caused his eyes to twinkle. "One gets old."

He lowered himself back into his seat.

"I always liked it here. In my earlier years, I would come here sometimes to look at the painting. I had a cousin who entered the priesthood, you know; he used to preach about this. He told me that the light of the world was hidden, covered by the undergrowth. But it wasn't so much what's in the painting, you know, but also what's on the other side of the door. That's why there is no handle, you see.

"It's up to us to let in the light – not the other way round."

The prince was familiar with the analogy. "I hear you retired."

"As I say, one gets old."

He knew the man's age was seventy-four. "How's Isabelle?"

"Passed away this time last year."

The news was shocking. "I n-never knew."

"Why should you? You've had far bigger things to worry about."

"I'd like to have known."

The man smiled at him. "It all came about rather suddenly. A strange bugger – cancer. You never really know how it's going to strike until it does. Fortunately for Izzy, it had already spread too far by the time it was caught. By that time there was no way to fight it. The decline was quick, but peaceful."

The prince put his hands to his eyes. "I'm so sorry."

The old man's expression was thoughtful. "So what brings you back home?"

Thoughts returned to the present. The messages to the King. Shakespeare. Nursery rhymes. Everything that had happened since.

"I was speaking with my father yesterday. There's something I would r-rather like your opinion on."

"How is the old rascal?"

"Still complains about his hip."

Wilson laughed boisterously. "I should have thought his brother might have promised him a new one."

The prince laughed.

"How is your uncle?"

The prince hesitated, preventing a stutter. "What do you know about the Sons of York?"

"HA. Do you want history or my conjecture?"

It was the answer he expected. "How about we start with history, th-then give me your b-best guess."

Professor Wilson cleared his throat. "All right. According to a source from the 1700s, they were a band of mercenaries who played a somewhat inconspicuous role in the Monmouth and Glorious risings against James II."

Nothing new. "I've seen the manuscripts myself."

"I should think so, too; they've been in your family for over a hundred years. I needed special permission myself to see them. And even then under close guard."

"I'm also familiar with the views of some more recent authors."

"So you are looking for conjecture?"

Ten years of knowing the man told him it was a statement not a question. "I'm prepared to keep an open mind."

Wilson watched him without expression. "In that case, follow me."

The library of Keble College was situated on the opposite side of the quad and was similar in style and stature to the chapel. Thomas followed Wilson through the double doors into an elegant Victorian reading room rich in hardback books, wooden panels and stained-glass windows.

"The Sons of York don't fall into the usual category of history – I know of many in the profession who would not regard them as being historical at all. To expose oneself to their follies invites criticism – particularly from other scholars."

"You mean like the s-search for the Loch Ness monster?"

"More like the man in the iron mask," Wilson replied. "Unlike the legend of Nessie, there is a general acceptance that the Sons of York were real, but the sources I mentioned never gave enough information to allow any clue as to who their members were.

"Of course, these days, since the invention of historical method, any author with a brain cell has connected them with everything from the Holy Grail to the Pied Piper to the reason that a particular tower in Pisa is slightly off balance. In many ways, the search for their true identities is a bit like a search for the Grail – in my experience, it can certainly be argued that there are as many different Sons of York as there are hunters for them."

Themselves aside, the library was deserted apart from one young blonde woman who was standing on a stepladder, stacking books.

"I say, Dr Alcock isn't about today, is he?"

The question seemed to activate the woman's hyperactive setting. "No," she replied, nearly dropping a book. "The archivist is currently away."

"Pity. Oh well, not to worry, you don't mind if I help myself, do you?"

"Access to the manuscripts is usually by prior appointment only," the woman replied.

"I am familiar with the protocol; I've only worked here for forty years. If the old boy asks, just tell him that Paddy Wilson was showing an old student around."

"Paddy Wil–?"

"That's right. Professor Emeritus of Keble College Patrick Wilson, former tutorial fellow of medieval history. He'll know the person you mean. Thanks so much for your assistance – good day."

Ten minutes later, Thomas was sitting alone at a table in the more modern reading room on the floor below. Wilson had disappeared since they had entered, and when he returned, he carried a small manuscript.

"Right," Wilson said, taking a seat. "Let's see what you make of this."

Thomas investigated the manuscript. "Richard III," he said, examining the title, "John Paston," he said of the author, "MDIX."

"That's 1509 in the modern tongue."

Thomas looked up at his former personal tutor. "I know."

"You'd be amazed how many wouldn't."

Thomas returned his attention to the manuscript. "This seems in rather good condition for 1509."

"That's because this copy was first printed in 1735. Also notice that it is written in English."

Thomas grinned as he caught the rebuke. The print was usual for 1700s – and slightly messy.

"What about it?"

"You are familiar with the Paston letters?"

"I've heard of them, but wouldn't say f-familiar."

The retired professor shook his head. "One of the best and rarest historical keepsakes to have survived the Middle Ages," he began. "The Paston letters deal with all sorts of things that happened between about 1422 and 1509. The family themselves were prominent gentry in the Norfolk area up until the mid-18th century. Upon the death of one William Paston, this large collection of letters and documents found its way into the hands of one particularly capable antiquary and over the next hundred or so years was published in six volumes – at least two of which found their way into the hands of one of your ancestors, George III."

"What sort of letters?"

"The content ranged from personal letters between members of the family, legal records, and other important observations of local life. Of particular interest was the correspondence of John Paston to various acquaintances regarding the marriage of Richard III and Anne Neville. Interestingly, the family were also the original owners of the oldest surviving portrait of Richard III."

Thomas digested the information. "And one of them wrote a biography of Richard III?"

"Unfortunately the original has never been found. The date on the cover claims 16th-century pedigree. However, the oldest surviving version is the one in front of you."

"You d-doubt its authenticity?"

"I doubt nothing – the subject has never interested me."

"So it c-could be genuine?"

"Over the years, all of the letters have been the subject of intense scrutiny. On at least one occasion, every single one of them has temporarily disappeared."

"But they were found?"

"Each edition has an original source, if that's what you mean. It's possible, of course, there were others that did not survive."

Thomas scanned the content, taking in practically nothing. "What of this?"

"This copy I came across about ten years or so ago – originally it had been in the Magdalen library along with many of the original letters, and for some reason it had never been catalogued. Most of the letters are housed in the British Library, though some are either at Magdalen or in the Bodley. I actually found this one myself; it was in the box along with several other works from the Victorian era. From what I could gather, most were bequests from friends of our great founder."

"You don't know who?"

"They were credited among the possessions of the Reverend Henry Liddon – I assume you've heard of him?"

The prince laughed. "Isn't the quad outside named after him?"

"There's no doubting the man was a genius."

"What has this to do with the Sons of York?"

"Nothing – at least in the literal sense. However, some of the content here is, shall we say, different."

"Can you elaborate?"

"According to the known sources, Richard III married once: Anne Neville on 12 July 1472. Together, they had one son, Edward of Middleham, who died in 1484. Had he survived, he would have been heir to the throne after Bosworth and a direct rival to the Tudors. Richard is also accepted as having sired at least two bastards – one John of Gloucester, and another Katherine Plantagenet."

"I'm familiar with the story."

"I've no doubt you are. However, according to Sir John Paston, Richard sired at least three more, most of who are completely unverifiable. The most famous was the story of the bricklayer from Eastwell in Kent – I suppose you've heard of that one?"

The prince nodded. He'd heard the tale of an illegitimate son of Richard III who went on to become a bricklayer.

"But even more fascinating," Wilson continued, "is the claim that Richard entered a marriage contract before Anne Neville, later annulled by the church. According to the author, while Richard and his brother were banished to the Low Countries, he married a Flemish girl in 1470 and had a son named Perkin."

Thomas looked up, his mouth now a smile. "Perkin?"

"Indeed. He also goes on to suggest that the poor woman died in childbirth – so two years before Richard married Anne Neville."

The story seemed farfetched. "What of the boy?" Thomas asked.

"Exactly what you would expect: that the boy later came on the scene in England and many other countries in Europe, pretending to be the heir to the throne of England."

"Warbeck?" Thomas asked.

"The very same."

The prince smiled. He was familiar with the historical Perkin Warbeck, an alleged imposter who began an uprising in the 1490s against Henry VII.

"Is this the only source?"

"There are possibly more copies, but certainly this is the only manuscript I've ever come across."

"No register of births? Or death?"

Wilson shook his head.

"H-how about a grave?"

Wilson laughed. "What do you think?"

Thomas thought it was a pointless question.

"No other contemporary document speaks of it."

"How about the later ones?" Thomas asked.

"Would you like history or conjecture?"

"H-how can you tell the difference?"

"You can't – that's precisely what makes the historian's job so damn difficult."

"In that case, g-give me your best guess."

The former professor looked over his shoulder, checking they were still alone. "The document you have just seen, though it cannot be dated to 1509, can at least be dated to before 1712. A local historian from the village of Shipsey in Yorkshire wrote his own account and claimed to have seen Paston's original book."

"William Stuart Lee."

"Ah, you clearly have heard of him."

"Like I said, I read the book," he stuttered.

"All of it?"

Thomas grinned awkwardly. "I also read one from the 1900s. Both made reference to something called the Ravensfield Chronicle. That was the only one that m-my uncle didn't have."

"You're not alone there. Even the British Library and the Bodleian have nothing, which is particularly strange because Bodley once had it catalogued."

The prince was astounded. "You're quite sure?"

He instantly regretted asking the question.

"You are most welcome to try."

"Have you s-seen it yourself?"

"No. But there was another author who apparently did."

"George Manning."

"I say, Tom, you have done your homework."

"Like I say, I've scanned two books; sadly they didn't tell me very much. What did he know?"

The professor shrugged. "I don't know – the poor chap died young."

"How?"

"I haven't the foggiest . . ." The professor detected urgency in the prince's voice. "Why don't you tell me what this is all about?"

"Two members of the Cabinet have recently turned up dead."

"Surely that was a car accident."

"Come on, Patrick, your intelligence is not limited to history. The men were blown up."

"Blown up?"

Thomas nodded. "Scotland Yard then apprehended a suspect – a Dominican friar, disturbing the peace, of all things. Under interrogation he c-claimed responsibility for the d-deaths of Trenton and Bates. Claimed he was acting on the orders of the Sons of York."

"Have you met him?"

"Yes."

"What was he like?"

"Mad as a hatter."

The man laughed.

"This is no joke, Patrick." The prince lowered his voice. "He also claimed involvement in the death of my grandfather. And to beware the Sons of York."

For several seconds Wilson said nothing. At the top of the stairs, the sound of the blonde woman wheeling her trolley informed them of her present location.

Thomas proceeded to tell his former personal tutor about the events at Middleham.

"What happened to him?" Wilson asked after a while.

"Who?"

"The man you shot."

"Died during the night."

The historian placed his hand to his face. "You didn't interrogate him?"

"The man was in no fit state."

"Jesus, Tom."

Silence lasted several seconds.

"And the butler was also killed?"

The prince nodded. "Our only chance is to t-trace the phone numbers."

"Where are you staying at the moment?"

"No one place."

"Come with me – I think I know someone who might be able to help you."

31

Jen had left the Hog by 10 a.m., heading in the direction of the church.

The first mission of the day was to inspect the burial registers, which she assumed were kept at the presbytery. On the way, she had intended to pay another visit to the Plantagenet monument located at the far end of the graveyard amongst the shrubbery, but she decided against it because of the weather. The downpour had started at about 5:30 a.m. – she knew that because it had awakened her. Nevertheless, the signs for the rest of the day were better. The storm had passed, the black clouds replaced by consistent sunshine.

She would look again when the ground had dried.

The presbytery was located about two hundred metres to the left of the main church, in the grounds of the former priory. The present building was about three hundred years old and built on the former lodgings of the old priors. A red brick wall circled the grounds, intercepted by a large gate.

Jen raised the handle to open the gate, and walked along the pathway to the front door. A red Vauxhall Corsa was parked on the drive, presumably belonging to Father Martin.

The priest answered almost immediately. "Ah, Miss Farrelly."

"Sorry to bother you on a Wednesday, Father. I was wondering if it would be possible for me to see the burial records for St Michael's?"

The priest barely batted an eyelid. "Okay. Please come in."

The interior was dated, particularly the walls. Despite the warmth of the otherwise pleasant day, the building had a certain coldness to it. It was the windows that did it. The single panes of glass and the dilapidated wooden surrounds were a depressing combination.

Father Martin led her up the creaky stairs and into a small room located directly in front of her. The room was cluttered, containing a photocopier, several pieces of paper, a desk with a twenty-year-old PC on it, and several filing cabinets.

The priest opened one of the cabinets and handed Jen a brown leather folder. The item was old, but she guessed not old enough.

"This is everything?"

"Everything from 1973 onwards."

"Is there any record of the earlier stuff?"

The priest returned to the drawers and removed a further three folders. "The oldest goes back to 1879."

The answer was disappointing. "Is there nothing older still?"

"1879 was the year of the church's reconsecration."

"Excuse me?"

"Between the years 1540 and 1878, St Michael's was under the authority of the Church of England."

"The Church of England?"

"Yes, of course."

"I thought St Michael's had always been Catholic."

"Well, no. It started Catholic, of course. But its ownership changed hands following the Dissolution. It was briefly Catholic again during the reign of Mary I, but Protestant again in 1559."

"But it's Catholic now?"

"Yes, the church was bought from the Church of England following the Emancipation Act."

"Why was it sold?"

"We've always had a large Catholic following in Yorkshire. Despite the Reformation, there have always been more Catholics in Wootton than Protestants."

That sounded unlikely. "What happened to them before 1879? Where did they worship?"

"Ah, that's an interesting question. You are familiar with Wootton Court?"

The large house up the road. "That's where Lord Jeffries lives, right?"

"Yes, that's right. Inside the house is a chapel – for three centuries it was the scene of Catholic worship, initially clandestine."

The priest's facial expression changed. "What's with the interest? If you don't mind my asking?"

"Nothing, really, it's just my job to research the local community – and local history has always been a passion of mine."

"Mine too," he said with a sombre smile. "Anyway, let me know if you need anything."

"Thank you, Father."

Jen took a seat at the desk. "Oh, Father."

The priest returned to the room.

"Where were the local Catholics buried before 1879?"

"Most of them are buried here," he replied. "Though the ceremony would have been Protestant."

"Would the deaths have been registered?"

"Of course. But the registers would have been moved to Bishopton."

"Where's that?"

"It's about four miles away."

"Thank you, Father."

For the next twenty minutes Jen concentrated on the folders. She found the entry for Luke Rankin in the expected place – the burial recorded as having taken place on 28 July the previous year. There were two other burials that month, but neither were Debra Harrison. In all honesty, an entry for Debra Harrison was the last thing she expected; should there be one, it would have confirmed she was dead, for a start. The only other burials for July, August, and September were for people over the age of sixty-five. At face value the details seemed to check out – she didn't know any of the names, but she had no reason to doubt the entries. She found an entry for Rankin's father, originally buried in the graveyard, but reinterred in the vault less than a fortnight after the death of his son.

Again, in theory, that checked out fine.

The older entries were interesting. She had expected a billion or more Jeffries, Catesbys, Ratcliffes et cetera, and she hadn't been disappointed. Some of the names she recognised, having seen them in the vault herself the previous day. True enough, there was no record of the older ones.

Evidently, the priest was right.

The burials before that period must have been Protestant.

The records of which were at Bishopton.

The village of Bishopton was located less than four miles away. Like Wootton, it was an idyllic symbol of Merry England that comprised a village pub, village green, cricket ground, and several thatched cottages.

The church was located on the edge of the village, overlooking the moors and the coast. The sign on the gate confirmed that the Church of Our Lady of the Rose was indeed Protestant and dated back to the mid 1200s.

The church was open. A beautiful Victorian font was the key feature at the rear of the church, accompanied by several wall plaques, their words connected with everything from passages of the gospels to the names of soldiers lost in the two great wars.

A man in his early seventies was standing at the front of the church, dressed all in black and wearing a dog collar. A list of former parish priests and vicars had been put up close to the door.

"Reverend Dennis, I presume?"

The man adjusted his bifocals. "May I be of any assistance?"

"My name is Jennifer Farrelly; I'm a researcher from London."

"Are you really? I'd have placed you more in the Midlands area."

A wry smile. "You're very perceptive – I'm originally from Nottinghamshire."

"Ah, I thought as much – I lived there myself over ten years. Are you familiar with the village of Blidworth?"

"Yes, I am."

"My first parish."

"Also the final resting place of Will Scarlock, I've been told."

The vicar smiled. "Yes, so goes the legend."

Jen brushed her hair aside. "As a matter of fact, I was hoping to talk to you about something similar."

The vicar's attitude became more sombre. "Oh dear, I'm so sorry. Did they pass away today?"

Jen laughed as a reflex. "No, no, it's nothing like that," she said, starting to feel uncomfortable. "I'm researching a documentary on the history of Wootton-on-the-Moor. I understand from the parish priest that you hold the burial records for when the church was Protestant."

The vicar nodded. "Yes, you understand correctly. I think they're in my library. It's this way."

The old rectory was a grim-looking two-storey house lying on the other side of the graveyard. Like the churchyard at Wootton, there were hundreds of dilapidated headstones, most of which were too weathered to offer any details of the deceased's past. Worse still, the area perpetually echoed with the sounds of rooks. Jen had a theory that the most broken gravestones had been put there for one purpose – just to scare her – but she knew she couldn't prove it. No matter where she went, the graveyards never really changed – at least except for the weather. The sun was still shining, which was a bonus.

If only she could shut the bloody rooks up!

The library surpassed her expectations. The room was well laid out with several large bookcases covering all four walls. The vicar's desk was located in between two of them, placed before a large window that overlooked the church. He made her a white coffee with two sugars, and sat her down with eighteen folders, all of which looked as if they were on the verge of falling apart.

She guessed they had never been researched.

"The records here go back to 1660," the vicar said. "The year of the restoration of the monarchy."

The number of books certainly looked more promising than at Wootton.

"Is this everything?" Jen asked.

"We have a few scattered fragments that go back further – I keep them under lock and key due to their historical value."

She accepted the response. "Thanks very much – and for the coffee."

"I'll be downstairs if you need anything."

The vicar departed, leaving Jen alone in the large room. She started immediately on the first folder. The handwriting was messy and difficult to read, but her time studying at Nottingham gave her an advantage for this sort of thing.

The date for the first entry was July 1871.

For the next half an hour she concentrated on what was directly in front of her. She read through the later entries quickly. The usual suspects were where she expected them to be. The Jeffries and Catesbys, in particular, more or less tallied with what she had seen in the vaults – though there were certain names she did not recognise. Her gut feeling told her it was something to do with that hidden room; unfortunately, unlike at Wootton, this register did not distinguish between the graveyard and the vaults.

Two entries caught her eye. The first was the apparent reinterment of one Sir William Catesby, died 1485. Developing what she'd learned after finding the grave of Robert Catesby, this offered further clarity that the Catesby family were indeed the same one that had once been prominent in the running of the country.

She didn't remember seeing the grave itself.

The second surprise was one Lord Jeffries, initial E, she guessed that stood for Edward, dying late 1688. There was a note in the margin, written in Latin,

Rex Angliae.

The literal translation was King of England.

She looked at the words for several seconds, confused. The idea was implausible, but thoughts of the day before continued to dominate her mind. The Jeffries' motto, she had established, was God and my right.

The same as the Plantagenets.

And the modern-day Royal Family.

The more she thought about it, the more she wondered about a connection with the Plantagenet monument. The name Plantagenet was rare – as far as she was aware it was unique only to the former kings of England and their Angevin relatives. She knew that many kings had mistresses, their illegitimate offspring later making do with substantial payoffs – and usually peerages.

Rarely did it amount to anything more.

Nevertheless, the date was intriguing.

Whoever it was had died within months of the Glorious Rising and the abdication of James II.

She also remembered from the vault that at least two of the Jeffries had fought against King James II in the same war.

She got out her iPhone and looked up both on the Internet. She started with Catesby. The original Sir William had risen from fairly mediocre beginnings to become chancellor during the reign of Richard III. He died at Bosworth, executed without trial after the battle.

If the burial record was accurate, his body was reinterred four hundred years later.

Lord Jeffries was described in little detail. Indeed, the E stood for Edward, and he, too, had been executed. According to his Wikipedia entry, the man had fought with the Duke of Monmouth in 1685, and then with Mary, later Mary II, against James II – her father.

Movement behind her roused her attention.

"Everything all right?" the vicar asked.

Jen smiled and nodded. "Fine, thank you."

The vicar smiled and sought to leave.

"How much do you know about the history of the parish?" Jen asked before he left.

"You mean Bishopton?"

"No, Wootton, sorry."

The vicar re-entered the room. "Not much, I'm sorry to say; it's never been my cure. Why do you ask?"

"It's just so many of the names seem to overlap – Catesby, Ratcliffe . . . Jeffries."

The vicar smiled. "Ah, yes, the families go back a long way . . . I know Lord Ratcliffe believes he can trace his ancestors right back to before the Norman Conquest."

That was impressive if true. "Wow."

"Lord Jeffries, too, has quite a selection of family memorabilia."

"You've seen it?"

"Personally, no. Though I have been told it's most impressive."

Jen nodded. "Who were the Jeffries?"

Who was Rex Angliae?

"Prominent landowners, minor peers . . . to be perfectly truthful, I don't really know much about them."

That makes two of us.

"You mentioned there were some other records – under lock and key."

"That's right." He gestured to a glass cabinet.

Jen left her seat and walked to where the vicar had pointed. There were ten sheets of parchment in total, all displaying contemporary Latin handwriting.

The content was illegible to her.

"What are they?"

"That document records the granting of a manor at a place called Ravensfield to a son of the king by Edward III."

"Ravensfield?"

"Yes. Not much is known of the early history. It is believed by some the village of Ravensfield was wiped out by the Black Death and modern-day Wootton built on top of it. It's dated 1352."

Suddenly the Plantagenet connection started to make sense. "Any idea who?"

"His name was Edmund of Langley, the second youngest of Edward III's five sons who lived into adulthood. When the male line died out, King Edward IV granted ownership of the manor to his brother, later Richard III. On the marriage of Henry VII to Edward IV's daughter, Elizabeth of York, the manor remained in the queen's family."

Jen listened carefully. "So the manor remained Yorkist?"

"Ah, but by then the king and queen were married. The houses of Lancaster and York were united – joined by that one ceremony." The vicar looked at her, only this time in a slightly different way. "Have you ever noticed how the Tudor rose is a mixture of red and white?"

"I thought it was mainly red."

"Contrary to popular belief, the red rose of Lancaster was not in use during the Wars of the Roses – it is possible it was designed by Henry

VII himself. Either way, Henry Tudor's claim to the throne of England was weak. He was descended of Edward III through his son, John of Gaunt, and his third wife, Katherine Swynford. Gaunt, after taking the unusual step of marrying his mistress, made his children legitimate. Henry's only claim was on his mother's side, the Beaufort line, whereas his father was merely a minor nobleman. His marriage into the House of York was necessary to augment his claim. With Richard III dead, it was Elizabeth, not Henry, whose claim to the throne was strongest."

"Wow, I never knew that."

In truth, she knew it well.

"At Wootton, I noticed there are quite a lot of burials both before and after 1879."

This time it was the vicar who was confused.

"Does this mean that some are Protestant and others Catholic?"

"Ah, I see what you mean . . . yes, anything before 1879 would have been done using the Protestant rite."

"Forgive me, I'm so confused, it seems that practically everyone in the village converted at the same time."

The vicar smiled. "More likely most of them were actually Catholic to begin with."

"Sorry, I don't follow."

"Well, it's perfectly simple, really. Prior to 1829 and the Act of Emancipation, there were many restrictions on what a Catholic could and could not do."

"You mean recusancy?"

"Up until the 17th century, yes. However, even after that time it was far easier going along with the rules."

Jen nodded, but silently she was confused. "When was the vault at St Michael's first constructed?"

"I think it goes back to about the 1600s."

Surely too late for the symbol she had seen. "I don't suppose anyone still has the original blueprints?" she asked, more in hope than expectation.

"I really wouldn't know."

Jen fought a grimace, turning it instantly into a smile. "Thank you so much for your time, Reverend. It's been really, really useful."

32

Thomas shouldn't have been surprised where Wilson took him. Rather than embarking on a one-hour drive through the Cotswolds to Wilson's three-bed Worcestershire cottage, the retired professor pulled up less than two minutes later on Broad Street and took Thomas across a courtyard to one of the most imposing buildings in the city.

The Tower of the Five Orders.

The main entrance of the Bodleian Library.

Wilson's second home.

Wilson led the way through the heavy 17th-century doors of the main entrance, their appearance more in keeping with a castle than a library. The coats of arms of several of Oxford's famous colleges marked the doors at equal intervals, intensifying the feeling that they belonged to a building of high esteem.

Wilson knew the inside like the back of his hand, whereas in three years at Keble, Thomas had only visited it once – not that he would admit it. The sheer scale of the buildings was magnificent, and practically impossible to navigate without a tour guide.

Fortunately, he had arguably the best in the business.

Five minutes later they entered a reading room somewhere in the Clarendon Building that seemed off-limits to the majority. Like the library at Keble, its appearance was predominantly Victorian with church-style windows, several bookcases, and three large desks. A brown-haired man in his fifties sat reading, the room's only occupant. He wore bifocals and a snug green jumper.

"I thought I'd find you in here, you rascal."

The man was taken momentarily off guard before realising who was talking to him.

"Well, if it isn't old Paddy Wilson," the man said, rising to his feet and extending his right hand. "I thought you'd been living it up in Spain."

"Only in the winter months," he replied with a smile.

Wilson gestured to the prince.

"Harry, may I introduce a former student of mine: Prince Thomas Winchester, heir to the Duchy of Clarence. Thomas, this is Harry Ainsworth, an old adversary from Magdalen."

Ainsworth eyed the prince cautiously, offering his hand. "An unexpected honour."

Thomas accepted it and smiled but for now remained silent.

"I was wondering if we could show Thomas the Bosworth Manuscript?" Wilson asked.

Ainsworth looked back with a neutral expression. Clearly the question was unexpected.

"Of course. Right this way."

They entered another reading room, this one more modern and located beneath the ground.

"The earl's reading room has never been open to the public," Wilson said as they entered, "nor is it ever likely to be."

Wilson sat down at a large table. Like the previous room, bookcases abounded, though these appeared older and more secluded.

"This is where we keep Bodley's more valuable treasures."

Thomas smiled. He was familiar with the Bodleian's more informal nickname.

Ainsworth removed an item from a large cupboard lining the side of the room, a thick plastic folder that clearly contained something of interest.

"Now, what you are about to see, Tom, has not been seen by your average student. Nor has it been studied in detail. In fact, it was only discovered a few years ago."

The prince watched as the professor from Magdalen removed a solitary item from inside the folder. It was parchment, unquestionably, and contained several lines of writing.

"What is it?"

"It is a rather rare legal document, and potentially one of the most important ever found. The document appears to be the last will and testament of King Richard III."

Thomas was speechless.

"We believe that the document has actually been here for centuries," Ainsworth continued, now standing beside him. "It was discovered about four years ago by accident in the Radcliffe Camera – hidden inside a medical document, of all things. How it came to be there, only God must know."

"My dear Harry, you still think it was a clerical error?"

The professor from Magdalen grinned at Wilson. "I believe it to be the most likely explanation."

"You believe it had been hidden on p-purpose?" The final word shot out of the prince's mouth.

"The Radcliffe Camera building dates back only to the 1730s," Wilson said of the brilliant Georgian structure that passers-by usually mistook for an observatory. "Since 1810 it has been devoted only to the sciences. Therefore, the document must have been moved there within the last two hundred and ten years."

"Not necessarily," Ainsworth retorted. "Prior to 1810 the Camera was used to house a much wider range of subjects. More likely, the mistake dates to that time."

"The document it was discovered within dates back to the 1650s – it must have been before that time."

"Not necessarily . . ."

Thomas was becoming slightly agitated. "Excuse me, gentlemen." He looked at both men in turn. "What does this mean exactly?"

Ainsworth took the lead. "That all depends on whether the document is genuine."

"Is it?"

Ainsworth remained on the fence. "Parchment is definitely the right age."

"How about the handwriting?" Thomas asked.

Ainsworth smiled. "Very different."

The answer irritated Wilson. "Come now, Harry." He turned his attention to Thomas. "The document itself would not have been written by the king. Furthermore, according to at least one eyewitness, the king fought at Bosworth with an injured wrist."

"What's your verdict on the signature?"

"Shaky but potentially sound," Ainsworth admitted.

"A bit like Guy Fawkes after the torture," Wilson added.

"How about the date?" Thomas asked.

"A month before Bosworth. Tell him what it says," Wilson said.

"I think it was something about the winter of discontent . . ."

"Don't be so damn childish, Harry," Wilson replied.

The prince laughed, though silently he found himself remembering events from two days ago.

The letter of the Sons of York.

The man from Magdalen translated as he read.

"I, Richard the Third, by the Grace of God King–"

"Just skip to the succession part," Wilson interrupted.

Ainsworth took a deep breath and continued.

"To decease without heirs of our body lawfully begotten, to have and inherit the said imperial crown, and other of our late brother's dominions, according and in such manner and form as in the said Act made in the said xxiii year is declared that then the said imperial crown, and all other the premises specified in the said Act, should be in the Prince Richard, until recently Duke of York, our late brother's son and brother of the late king, and to the heirs of the body of the said Richard lawfully begotten, with such . . ."

"Okay, Harry, I think we get the picture."

Thomas found himself unable to speak.

"You understand, Tom?" Wilson asked.

Though he heard correctly, he was sure that he did not.

"F-forgive me, I don't think I do."

"It's perfectly simple, my boy," Wilson began. "According to this document, Richard named as his heir to the throne one of the boys he supposedly murdered."

33

The second interview with the mother of Debra Harrison was scheduled to take place at 1:30 that afternoon. What with everything that had been happening, Jen had forgotten about it, and would probably have missed it had it not been for a well-timed phone call from her producer.

She left Bishopton immediately after leaving the rectory, and headed straight for the Harrisons' residence.

She took a seat opposite Harrison and crossed her right leg over the left. "I understand your daughter had been working on a project before she disappeared."

The woman lit a cigarette. "You clearly know more than me."

It was obvious to Jen the woman's mood had not improved during the last two days.

"Had she decided what A-levels she was going to take?"

"Yup, Latin, French, English Lit and History."

"Did she understand Latin?"

The woman exhaled smoke. "Does it matter?"

"No – it's just something I didn't know."

Did Lovell recruit her for her knowledge of Latin?

The woman's expression softened. "Debra was a natural when it came to languages – had a memory like an encyclopaedia."

"I understand her ambition was to be a journalist?"

"Yup, but she used to change her mind. When she was fourteen, she wanted to work in fashion, be a designer for one of the big firms. She loved to draw – and paint."

"I understand she also loved history?"

"Yup. That was one thing that didn't change."

"Did she have an interest in local history? History of Wootton, that sort of thing?"

The woman smoked. "Yup."

"I understand from one of her classmates that she had been working a lot with Dr Lovell. You know anything about that?"

The woman's expression changed. "Oh, that project," she said, more interested than before. "That wasn't for school."

"It wasn't?"

"Nuh uh. Debra had it in her head that she'd never get on the course she wanted or get the jobs she wanted on grades alone."

Jen was confused.

The woman sat up in her seat. "Teachers at St Joseph's are all obsessed with résumés – they don't even care if the kids don't know the subject. The current party line is extracurricular shit: climbing mountains, volunteering places, you know, the usual."

Jen smiled. "Did your daughter participate in a lot of extracurricular activities?"

"She had hobbies – lots of them."

"What were her favourite hobbies?"

"She liked to hike; that was one of her favourites. She liked art . . . oh, and photography; that was a new one."

"May I see any of it?"

She shook her head. "I could never find her camera."

"Did she upload anything onto computer?"

"We bought her a netbook for her birthday – you know, one of those little laptops. Took it everywhere with her."

"You know where it is?"

She paused before answering. "No."

"You know anything else about her project with Dr Lovell?"

"Dr Lovell is the editor of the East Riding history bulletin – it's basically a voluntary thing, kind of like one of those parish newsletters but bigger. Dr Lovell wanted to write a series of articles on the priory and the church at Wootton. He agreed to let Debra help him; in exchange he'd publish some of her articles."

Jen made a note of the fact, in addition to recording it on her digital voice recorder. "How long had this been going on?"

"Three months, maybe four. She put things on hold for her GCSEs."

"Had she had anything published?"

"No."

Jen took a deep breath as she planned her next question. She couldn't help feel Lovell was the key.

Somehow.

"I understand that Dr Lovell was her former headmaster?"

"Yup."

"How long have you known him personally?"

"All my life."

Jen was pleased to see that once again the information agreed with what she had heard earlier. "Was he close with your daughter?"

For the first time the woman's face practically lit up. "There's not a person in the village who doesn't love Dr Lovell. He's just the loveliest man you could ever meet."

Jen tucked her hair behind her right ear. "I really can't wait to meet him."

"You haven't met him yet?"

"No. Every time I call by, he seems to be out."

"Probably out walking; he often goes out walking alone on the moors. He just loves nature."

For some reason she took that with a pinch of salt. "What kind of things had they been working on?"

"Couldn't tell you. Something to do with the history of the church."

"Any idea what the research involved? Was it in libraries, archives?"

"Possibly. Though most of it was either at Dr Lovell's house or at the church."

"Any idea what part of the church?"

"Does it matter?"

Jen contemplated a response. "I'd be interested in knowing what the research involved, yeah."

This time it was Harrison's turn to be speechless. "Sorry, I really wouldn't know."

Jen forced a smile.

"You gonna start filming soon?"

"Friday, I think. Is that okay?"

She smiled faintly.

"Do you have any other photographs of your daughter that we could maybe use?"

The question was clearly expected. "Sure."

Harrison rose to her feet and made her way into the kitchen. She returned a few seconds later carrying several photographic prints.

"Thanks, Mrs Harrison."

Jen left the house and walked along the high street. She decided to take the detour to Lovell's house. She had missed him on every other occasion so far.

She grabbed a sandwich from the Co-op and ate it while on the move. She wanted an egg mayo, but decided chicken salad would be easier on the breath – even after a few Polos. The meat was moist and tender, and the tomato dressing on the salad to die for. It was her first food since breakfast, and throughout the interview her stomach had been rumbling.

Lovell was out, which she was starting to accept as par for the course. On this occasion there was no response at all, meaning his wife must be out as well, perhaps joining her husband on a long, romantic walk across the moors. As she considered her options, she felt sleepy. It was almost 2:30, and she had nothing else planned for now. She would try Lovell again after five.

That gave her over two hours to catch up on sleep.

She returned to the Hog and then went up to her room. She placed her handbag down on the chair and removed the new photographs from her pocket.

She looked at them for the first time. Without question, the girl got prettier every time. Gillian Harrison had given her seven in total, capturing her daughter from the age of four or five to a few weeks before she disappeared.

The photos were useful. Judging from them, the girl's hair had darkened as she aged, with possible evidence of jet-black dye. She was always tall, no matter what age she was, and was clearly slim, athletic, and undeniably attractive. The possibility of her being a rape victim could certainly not be ruled out. Furthermore, the photos had one very obvious thing in common.

The girl never stopped smiling.

Jen sat down on the side of the bed and scanned the next photo. As she did, something caught her eye. As she continued to look, she felt her body go cold. The photograph was more recent, no more than a year at the most before her disappearance. Debra was dressed in a black top and shorts, her hair done up in a ponytail. A small necklace with a silver cross hung around her neck.

Jen looked to her right. The camera and necklace she had found the previous day in the vaults were lying on her bedside table.

She had all but forgotten about them.

She picked up the necklace and compared it to the one in the photograph. Her breathing began to quicken as she realised they were exactly the same. She took a deep breath and tried to rationalise the situation. The necklace did not look particularly expensive and was probably store bought.

It was certainly not unique enough for her to confirm that the two were one and the same.

She looked again to her right. The camera was still there, lying on its back.

Suddenly the words of Debra Harrison's mother started to repeat themselves in her mind.

The girl had recently taken up photography – her camera had also disappeared.

A sobering thought overcame her.

If these were Debra Harrison's camera and necklace, they were potentially a vital clue in ascertaining the place where she disappeared.

Right outside the locked door in the vaults.

34

For several seconds Thomas failed to speak.

"Richard of Shrewsbury was m-murdered in 1483."

"No, Tom, the Duke of York disappeared in 1483," Wilson retorted. "Along with his brother, I might add. The debatable King Edward V."

"The Princes in the Tower," Thomas said, exasperated.

"Or as they were known to most people, Prince Edward and Prince Richard," Wilson said.

Thomas shook his head. "The Princes in the Tower were murdered."

"Says who, exactly?"

Thomas simply stared at his former personal tutor. "Croyland, Thomas More, Dominic Mancini . . ."

"Philippe de Commines," Ainsworth interjected.

"Ten out of ten on the choice of your sources, both of you, but just because someone says they were murdered does not make it so."

"Meaning what?" Thomas asked.

"Meaning exactly what I say."

"You suggest otherwise?"

"I suggest nothing, only that you must question every angle as opposed to relying on hearsay."

"Damn it, Patrick," the prince shouted, the sound of his voice echoing, "why must you always speak in riddles." He breathed deeply to control himself.

"Sorry."

For several seconds all was quiet.

"What's the significance?" Thomas asked.

"Nothing," Wilson said. "For all we know, the document is a forgery."

"You believe it to be so?"

"I do not believe either way."

A thought occurred to Thomas. "Even if the princes were not m-murdered, they had been declared illegitimate."

"By who?"

"By common council."

Wilson nodded. "Titulus Regius. The only Act of Parliament of Richard III's two-year reign."

Thomas nodded. "Exactly."

"Denounced during the reign of Henry VII, who later married the boys' sister, I might add."

Thomas was aware that was correct. Historically, Edward IV had gone against usual protocol and chosen a commoner for his wife: Elizabeth Woodville, famed for her beauty. The marriage catapulted the family into brilliant success at court. When Edward IV died, the scene was set for his son, Edward, to take the throne.

Until the revelation, later denounced, that the king had already been married, resulting in his marriage to Elizabeth Woodville being declared null and void.

"In any case, how could Richard of Shrewsbury be heir to Richard III? For that to happen, his brother must have been murdered."

"No, for that to happen, Edward must have been dead," Wilson replied, now smiling. "As for their uncle, his only legitimate son had died."

Thomas was now riled. "You said earlier he might have had another son."

"Indeed, he may. In fact, the document goes on to suggest that the son of the Flemish girl, in turn, would be next in line after Shrewsbury; the dispute over his own legitimacy on this occasion acknowledged."

Ainsworth smiled. "If the document is genuine, there is reason to believe that this was in fact an addendum to Titulus Regius. Unfortunately we don't know for sure because no copy of Titulus Regius has been found."

"They were all destroyed on the orders of Henry Tudor," Wilson added.

Thomas breathed out forcefully. "You suggest the document implies Richard III succeeded Edward f-fairly and Richard of Shrewsbury would reign as Richard IV. You think Richard III only reigned because the Duke of York was a minor?"

The thought seemed plausible to Wilson. "Perhaps, but you are forgetting, Henry Tudor won the Battle of Bosworth."

Thomas nodded. "Exactly. The document became irrelevant."

Wilson seemed to agree. "Unless . . ."

Thomas's patience was almost gone. "Unless?"

Wilson looked at Ainsworth. "Would you care to explain this one to His Highness?"

Thomas looked at the other historian.

"Unless Richard of Shrewsbury had already been crowned joint king alongside his uncle."

At around that time in the restaurant of a luxury hotel in the city of London, a dark-haired man dressed in a fine suit watched from his seat by the window as the distinguished guest sitting seven tables away displayed his discomfort. As the seconds passed, his face became evidently more flushed.

The man was clearly experiencing something of a tightening sensation in the chest region.

He departed unseen just before the sound of a crash attracted the attention of astounded onlookers.

35

For several seconds Thomas said nothing. "How exactly?"

Wilson cleared his throat. "According to the typical history book, on the death of King Edward IV, the throne of England was set to pass to his eldest son and heir, now King Edward V. However, as the new king was only a minor, he would require the assistance of a regent."

"Richard III," Thomas said.

"Brother of the late king, at that time Duke of Gloucester and commander of the king's armies in the north," Wilson agreed. "Now, as you are undoubtedly aware, Tom, following the death of King Edward IV, preparations were put in place for the coronation of his son, to be crowned King Edward V, with his uncle Richard, Duke of Gloucester, taking on the role of the king's protector.

"Within a month of his father's death, the prince had arrived in London to take up residence within the Tower of London – which at the time, of course, was normal, being a royal residence. In June, the king-in-waiting was joined by his younger brother, Richard of Shrewsbury, while the protector continued to make preparations for the young king's coronation. Yet, within a week, the young boys were declared illegitimate, later confirmed by Act of Parliament."

"Titulus Regius," Thomas repeated.

"The very same," Wilson replied. "You clearly know your family history."

"Not really. I know the facts, yes, not the reasons."

"I daresay you are not alone," Ainsworth said. "Even at the time, the reasons given were weak to say the least."

"R-remind me. Why were the princes declared illegitimate?"

The man from Magdalen smiled wryly. "Because according to the account of one eyewitness–"

"Stillington," Wilson said.

"Yes, Stillington, the king had already been married prior to his wedding to Elizabeth Woodville – thus rendering the whole thing null and void."

The prince knew the gist. "Who was she?"

"Who?"

"The first wife."

"According to the Croyland Chronicle, of which few copies survive, its author had seen Titulus Regius and made a note of its content. The woman mentioned was Lady Eleanor Talbot," Wilson said.

Thomas remembered his conversation with his father the day before. "Tell me about her. And who was Stillington?"

"Lady Eleanor Talbot, or Dame Butler, as she was following her marriage," Ainsworth began, "was a daughter of John Talbot, the 1st Earl of Shrewsbury, and later wife of Sir Thomas Butler, the son of Lord Sudeley. Eleanor was evidently something of a beauty and may have been the mistress of Edward IV."

"Stillington, on the other hand," Wilson took over, "was the Bishop of Bath and Wells – and a devout Yorkist. According to the French chronicler and diplomat Philippe de Commines in June 1483, Stillington had presided over the marriage agreement between the king and Eleanor Talbot, thus making the later marriage between Edward IV and Elizabeth Woodville null and void."

"When was the marriage?"

"History is vague on the matter," Wilson said.

"Talbot herself died in 1468," Ainsworth said, "so it couldn't have been recent."

Thomas scratched his chin. "Why did it take over fifteen years for this to come to light?"

"Because, my dear boy, the case didn't hold water."

"You think it was a lie?"

"Of course it was a lie. Henry VII himself repealed the act."

"You think that Richard III just w-wanted the throne for h-himself?"

Ainsworth leaned back slightly in his chair. "The only possible evidence before 1483 is an event that took place in 1478. Stillington himself spent several weeks in gaol during that year, apparently as a result of some association with the king's brother, the Duke of Clarence–"

"No relation to you, of course, old boy," Wilson said.

Thomas was aware that Clarence had been executed for conspiring against his brother, Edward IV.

Ainsworth grinned. "It has been suggested that Stillington passed on information about the king's first wedding to Clarence."

"If Clarence had still been alive in 1483, wouldn't that have made him heir?" Thomas asked.

"Yes, it would," Wilson agreed. "At least after the princes."

Thomas was starting to become rattled. "This makes no sense; surely there must have been eyewitnesses."

"There was – Stillington."

Thomas looked at Wilson. "Any more?"

"No."

"Hence why it was later repealed," Ainsworth added. "Stranger still, when the charlatan Lambert Simnel came on the scene in 1487 claiming to be Clarence's son, Stillington himself became involved in the plot against Henry Tudor."

Thomas breathed in deeply. He was vaguely familiar with the Simnel fiasco. A charlatan pretending to be the new Earl of Warwick, intent on reclaiming the throne from the Tudor pretender.

Thomas's attention returned to the document in front of them. "But according to this, Richard of Shrewsbury was still alive?"

"Yes," Ainsworth agreed, "according to this."

"You still don't think that it's g-genuine?"

"I told you before, it hasn't been studied in enough detail," Wilson replied.

"When could the coronation have taken place?"

"Any time," Wilson replied, "could even have been the same day as Richard III."

"According to one source, Richard had a second coronation in York."

Thomas bit his lip. "Wait a moment, the princes were found and buried in Westminster Abbey."

"No, old boy, two bodies were found and assumed to be the princes, and buried in Westminster Abbey."

"They certainly fit the profile," Ainsworth said, "and DNA testing in the 1930s confirmed that the skeletons were of the correct ages."

"It confirmed the bloodline?" Wilson asked, quite obviously rhetorically.

"You know it didn't – the technology wasn't available."

"Which just about proves my point," Wilson argued. "The skeletons could be anyone's."

Thomas decided to take a backseat as the discussion turned into an academic arm wrestle.

"The casket containing the bodies was discovered just where Thomas More said they were."

"Actually, the coffin was found where More said it had been originally," Wilson corrected. "According to More, it was moved outside."

"Perhaps there was more than one source."

"All the more reason for doubting."

"How do you explain the purple velvet that was found in the coffin?"

"There could be a number of reasons."

Ainsworth was unconvinced. "Purple at the time was the colour associated with the king – you know that."

"My dear fellow, do use your common sense. For all we know, that piece of velvet could have been put there deliberately so that people would think it was the princes."

"Then why hide the bodies so well?"

Wilson sought to reply, but the ringing of Thomas's mobile phone broke his concentration. The prince apologised to both and made his way to the corner of the room.

"Hello?

"Yes . . .

"What?

"When?"

The prince stuttered uncontrollably.

"Of course . . ."

Thomas disconnected the call.

"Forgive me, gentlemen, I'm needed back in London."

Less than five minutes later, Thomas was back in his car, heading east out of Oxford.

As soon as he was in free-flowing traffic out of the city, he selected a call on his mobile phone.

After several rings a voice answered. "Hello?"

"Stephen, we're needed back in London . . .

"The Duke of York's been taken to hospital. They think he's been poisoned."

36

To Jen, the next thirty minutes were something of a blur. Incredibly the camera still worked; if it had belonged to who she thought it had once belonged to, it had probably been lying in the vault for almost a year. The battery gauge was flashing red, signalling the charge was almost at an end.

At least this camera took AA batteries.

There were well over a thousand photographs on the memory card, the oldest dating back sixteen months. The earlier ones were of girls and boys, probably aged around fifteen or sixteen, adding weight to her theory that the camera belonged to Debra Harrison. Harrison wasn't in any of them; most likely she was the person holding the camera. Anthea was in one or two, as were some other girls she hadn't met. One appeared regularly; Jen assumed it was Stephanie Stanley, Debra's best friend who had taken the news particularly badly. Jen still hoped to interview her.

At least off the record.

Jen scanned through the majority of the images before returning to the most recent. The last forty were all of St Michael's; the last twenty inside the vaults.

The final five were all from the Jeffries' vault. Two of the photos were blurred, but the other three were all clear and sharp. Jen recognised one of the effigies in the middle of the vault, a member of the Jeffries family who had become a Member of Parliament.

After taking in the detail, Jen looked back at the previous thirty pictures, most of which were of the old priory. She was still to see the ruins herself, as technically it was situated on private property.

Evidently, Debra Harrison had been granted quite a privilege.

Five photos were of locations she didn't recognise. They had definitely been taken somewhere inside the vaults, but she was certain they included nothing she had seen before. As best she could tell, the chamber was larger than the Jeffries' vault, but also darker. There were several tombs, the designs more elaborate than the ones she had seen so far. On top of each tomb was an effigy: a figure lying on his back and carrying a sword between two closed hands.

Yet it was impossible to see much detail, so bad was the light. Whatever it was, the person who took the photos clearly thought it important enough to capture.

Now Jen had a new theory. Whoever was buried behind the locked door, it probably didn't include Debra Harrison.

But whoever they were, they certainly weren't plague victims.

37

Westminster

Thomas and Stephen were back in London by 5 p.m. On the orders of the palace, they parked Stephen's car en route before being collected and taken by another car to the King Edward VII's Hospital Sister Agnes in the city of Westminster.

The hospital was the usual port of call for members of the Royal Family. A smartly dressed nurse in her early forties met them on arrival, and led them through the hospital's immaculate hundred-year-old corridors to a clean, yet inconspicuous, room on one of the upper floors.

The Duke of York was awake when they entered. A heart monitor was connected to his chest by a series of wires, and oxygen via a tube to his nose. His daughter, seventeen-year-old Princess Caroline, was sitting on the side of the bed, stroking her father's hand. Surrounding them were several carrier bags and get-well cards.

Thomas hesitated before entering. He felt Stephen's elbow in his back, forcing him inside. The paper bag in his hand rattled as he scrunched it.

"Hello, Uncle," Thomas said, slightly nervously. "We've b-brought you some grapes, I think."

There were several others already on his bedside table.

"Yes, bloody good that driver – thinks of everything."

Thomas smiled, whereas behind him Stephen was laughing loudly. He saw Caroline smile, then the duke himself.

Slowly they approached, both shaking the duke's hand.

"Hello, Caroline," Thomas said as they kissed one another on the cheek. "So s-sorry it t-took so long."

"You missed Fred."

The Duke of York's eldest son. "I'm sorry to have m-missed him." Thomas looked at the duke, then Caroline. "How is he?"

"Not deaf for a start."

The prince smiled weakly.

"They say it was only a mild one," York said.

Thomas was concerned. "What? Heart attack?"

"No. Dosage. It was bloody poison; there's nothing wrong with my bloody heart."

The duke looked at his daughter.

"Cookie, dear, leave us for a second, will you? I'd like to have a chat alone with the boys."

The girl seemed slightly put out.

"Quickly now."

Caroline huffed as she strode indignantly out of the room. The princes watched her depart. Three years had passed since Thomas had last seen her, and clearly much had changed. Her face was prettier, but the weight greater. Her jet-black hair was now down beyond the shoulder, a spitting image of her mother.

Stephen closed the door behind her. "Why Cookie?"

Thomas bowed his head into his hands.

"Because we made her out of baking dough," the duke said, his eyes on the door. "Is it shut?"

Stephen nodded.

"Good."

He invited the princes to come closer.

"Not as close as that," he shouted, placing his hand in front of his face. "There's nothing wrong with my sense of smell either."

He turned to Thomas.

"How's progress?"

Thomas hesitated slightly. "To tell the truth, it's been quite erratic."

"What do you mean, erratic?"

"You're aware, no doubt, of his visit to me in the middle of the night?" Stephen said.

The duke looked at him, slightly disturbed. "Yes, your father did say. I assume this has something to do with the one that got away."

"Yes," Thomas said. "Stephen did his b-best with the s-surgery."

"The bullet had punctured part of the large intestine. It was only a matter of time."

The duke exhaled furiously. He tried to sit up in his bed. "Help me with this damn pillow."

Thomas moved the pillow while Stephen grabbed hold of the duke's hands.

"That's better," York said, sitting up. He removed the air supply from his nostrils.

"Is that wise?" Stephen asked.

"You're the surgeon; you tell me."

Stephen decided to remain silent.

"One of the phone numbers you faxed through to your father, Thomas, was registered. Rather unexpected, I might add."

Thomas took a deep breath. "Who?"

"The name Burghart Stanley mean anything to you?"

Thomas shook his head.

"How about Rowland Stanley?"

"Father of the British colonel who defected to the Spanish in 1586."

"Try more modern."

"What? The politician?" Stephen guessed.

"The very same. Democrat MP for the constituency of Maplewell in Yorkshire, and leader of the opposition for the past year."

"Wh-who's his son?" Thomas asked.

"Former Royal Marine: left eighteen months ago, officially of his own choice, though my sources tell me it was actually due to a breach of discipline."

"I'm sure his father approved of that," Stephen said.

York managed a smile. "Now also a politician, though not an MP – at least not yet. Stood as a MEP in the last election, but lost out to the LibDem. Apparently he's planning on standing for the real thing in Dewsbury, or somewhere of the sort."

"It's a place where the party has always been strong," Stephen said.

The duke was unimpressed. "I never knew we were a county of socialists."

"It's really not as bad as that," Stephen said.

Thomas chose not to respond.

"Even if he wins, they're still some way short of a majority," Stephen added.

"Just as they were the first time," York fired back. He felt a slight twinge as he spoke.

"I'll get the nurse," Stephen said.

"Sit down; you'll do no such thing." He looked at his nephew, this time more softly. "I'm sorry, boys. Just damn hard luck being tied up like this."

Thomas nodded. "Of course."

The duke sipped from a glass of water. "Now then, boys. The

question is, why were these phones entrusted to the people you saw? GCHQ have been informed. We're looking into past conversations."

He looked at his nephews.

"Who else was there last night?"

"Four in total," Thomas began. "The butler and the three accomplices."

The duke nodded, clearly ruing the fact they had got away.

"Any news of the butler?" Stephen asked.

The duke looked at Stephen. "Good question. According to Scotland Yard, he was named Anthony Patterson and had been butler to Sir Jack Talbot for over fourteen years. Prior to that he had served over ten in nick."

"What for?"

"Murder and arson. Brought about in the last years of the Thatcher government."

"He was a unionist?"

"No. Apparently it was something to do with the EU."

The surgeon accepted the response.

Thomas was more concerned with his uncle's wellbeing. "Who did this to you?"

The duke fought a sarcastic reply. "I don't know."

"Whoever it was, they were clearly not looking to murder. This was surely no more than a warning sign," Stephen said.

Thomas doubted that. He knew the King had not died immediately.

The duke agreed. "We've had a narrow escape, put it that way."

"Has my father been informed?" Stephen asked.

"Of course, your father's got ears coming out of every fence in the countryside." He turned to face Thomas. "I want you to check the surveillance footage. The poison was in the pie; whoever put it there must have acted fast."

"Pie?" Stephen said.

"Yes, that's what I said."

Thomas was alarmed. His first thought was the nursery rhyme.

"There were no blackbirds in it?"

"Oh, for heaven's sake, Steve."

Thomas was concerned. "Uncle said Aunty Matilda and Granny both died of f-food poisoning. The rhyme must be a clue."

The duke bit his lip. "The pie was chicken. White bird."

"You're quite s-sure there were n-no eye witnesses?" Thomas asked. "After all, it's d-different from the other s-stuff."

The duke's stare had hardened. "Perhaps you could ask your father; he was eating from the plate opposite."

Thomas closed his eyes, his jaw tightening. Almost immediately, he put the surprise behind him.

"The pie was normal?"

"Yes. And don't you worry; he's been fully checked out. Old bastard's as fit as a fiddle."

Thomas offered a faint smile, slightly reassured. "What more about the mobile phones?"

"Apart from the one registered to Stanley, all were standard pay-as-you-go."

"Network?"

"Varied. The models themselves are less than a year old. The best guess indicates they were purchased within the last six months."

"Where's Stanley now?" Stephen asked.

"Which one?" the duke asked.

"I don't know – why not both."

"Burghart, I understand, is presently in London – he has an apartment in Greenwich, though I understand it's still in the process of being built. According to my sources at GCHQ, he's been there today making phone calls. His father is alone in the family home in the village of Wootton-on-the-Moor – it's all part of his constituency."

Stephen raised an eyebrow. "That's the village where that girl disappeared a year ago."

"Blimey, Stephen, you do have a good memory."

"Did they ever find the body?" Thomas asked.

"No."

"Didn't one of the s-suspects commit suicide?"

"Yes, at least according to the press."

"Must have been around the time Stanley became leader, mustn't it?" Thomas said.

"Yes, I suppose it must," the duke began. "What are you getting at?"

The prince shook his head. "Nothing."

The duke didn't buy it. "Anyway, be sure to check it out. And be sure to find out why those mobile phones were in the same hands as those guns."

Thomas and Stephen left the room and quickly made their way along the main corridor.

"Get me the Duke of Clarence, please," Thomas said into his mobile phone. He covered the mouthpiece as he spoke to Stephen.

"I say we check out this boy's apartment tonight."

"Before he gets away, you mean?"

"Precisely."

Thomas received a response from the other end of the line.

"Text me the details, please, won't you? Thanks."

He ended the call and placed his mobile phone in his pocket.

"At least we have an address."

"The thought occurs that he might have been one of the boys firing at you. After all, Uncle said the bastard used to be a Royal Marine. Hardly incapable."

"You might have a point there. I-I wonder why he became a politician?"

Stephen laughed. "Perhaps he's one of those men of the people who wants to get the old place clean again."

Thomas grinned at him.

"Thomas."

The shout came from the other end of the corridor. Caroline was following them.

"Oh, hi, C-Caroline," Thomas stuttered. He took the time to examine her face, notably her mouth and nose. "I hear you were attacked the other week."

"I was walking through the grounds of our estate, and some fellow in a hood just came out of nowhere," she huffed. "It was nothing, just a bloody nose," she said, covering it with her hand.

Her attention turned to the present. "What's happening?" There was a look of desperation in her eyes, exaggerated by the appearance of black mascara smudged by recent tears.

"Nothing that need concern you," Stephen replied. "You can go back to your father now."

"I can help."

"Absolutely not," Stephen replied. "Go back to your father, Cookie."

"Don't call me Cookie."

Her voice was shrill and piercing, the acoustics of the corridor causing it to echo.

Stephen closed his eyes as a reflex. He turned around, coming face to face with her. "Are you out of your mind? For all we know the press could be anywhere."

The girl looked desperately at Thomas. "Thomas, please."

"Stephen's right. Your place is to be b-beside your father."

He held her gaze for an extended pause before finally walking away.

"I can't go back; the King wants to see us."

38

Finding the camera had left Jen rejuvenated. Forsaking her nap, she left the Hog and headed back across the bridge.

She wanted to know more about the history of the village. Accepting she had learned all she could from the parish registers, she entered a 14th-century building located two along from the end of the bridge. According to Mitchell, the building housed the local library and heritage centre.

Not that she would have guessed from the lack of advertisement.

She entered through an original wooden door and espied a nice open-plan room with traditional features, including high beams and stone walls. A small grey-haired woman, probably in her sixties, was sitting behind the front desk. She offered Jen a free leaflet about Wootton's history before directing her into the next room.

For the next ten minutes Jen explored everything the building had to offer. A neat display had been assembled in the next room, a visual history of the parish from the Roman era to the modern day.

Curiously it mentioned nothing of the so-called village of Ravensfield.

After learning nothing new of the castle, priory or the church, she continued upstairs to where the library was housed. She looked for anything on the church and the vaults.

Again, there was nothing new.

She had been standing in one particular row for less than a minute before noticing movement to her right. At the end of the row, she saw a face, young, brunette . . .

Almost immediately, the girl disappeared.

For several seconds, Jen stood rooted to the spot. When the surprise had worn off, she walked to where she'd seen the face and looked for her in every direction.

There was movement along the corridor, heading through one of the nearby doorways.

Jen chased after her, but the girl had disappeared. She tried the remaining rooms on the first floor, most of which were empty bar miscellaneous curiosities and writings from the village's past. Failing to find the girl on the second floor, she took the stairs back down to the main entrance. The woman on reception smiled at her as she passed, thanking her for coming.

Jen opened the door, looking in vain for any sign of the mystery girl.

Instead, she noticed something different.

Lord Ratcliffe was passing.

"Well, if it isn't the lovely Miss Farrelly."

Her dry expression warmed into a smile. "I was hoping I'd find you."

"Me?" Ratcliffe asked. "And what possible thing has an old politician done to deserve such a prestigious honour."

She walked alongside him, heading across the bridge. "I understand that it was you who discovered the body of Luke Rankin?"

The question was clearly unexpected. "Who, might I ask, told you that?"

"I have my sources."

The man's expression changed. "Aye, well, like it or not, find him I did . . . forgive me, Miss Farrelly, it wasn't exactly my most favourite of memories."

She smiled sympathetically. "I was wondering what happened?"

"What . . ."

"How did you find him?"

He took a deep breath. "Tell you the truth, it all happened so fast. There I was walking Bobby and Bernard, that's me dogs, you understand."

She smiled.

"I usually go that way, down by the old train station. Takes you down to the coast. It's a lovely walk in summer."

"I'm sure it is."

Then what happened?

"Anyway, I'd just got up as far as the bridge when Bernard started barking. I thought it strange; he never barks like that, not to me, not Bernard."

"What time of day was it?"

"Early," he said, "I always take the dogs for a walk first thing; you know what they say, old habits die hard."

A wry smile. "Any idea of the time?"

"You're not a secret copper, are you?"

She laughed. "You say it was early?"

"Aye, now that you mention it, I'd guess it were before seven."

She made a mental note. "What state was the body in when you made the discovery?"

"You mean, how did he die?"

"That as well."

"Poor lad hanged himself the night before."

Jen was confused. "How can you be sure it was the night before?"

"Autopsy confirmed it," he replied. "Said he'd been dead about five hours."

Placing the time between 1 and 2 a.m.

"Where was his body?"

"Have you seen the old railway station?"

Jen nodded.

"Well, up there, there's a bridge, you see."

She noticed the way he gestured with his hands as he spoke. "I understand it was you who took him down."

Ratcliffe hesitated before nodding. "Aye. Me and Bill, that's Sir William, you see. I called for him first. It were impossible just me."

"Where was the body found? I mean, had he fallen over the side, or was it beneath the arch?"

"Oh, I see what you mean. The rope was attached to the rocks above."

"The rocks?"

He nodded.

"Could you show me?"

He winced slightly. "I can show you the bridge. The police later destroyed the exact point."

"They destroyed it?"

The politician nodded. "It was a deterrent, you see. The last thing anyone wanted was for someone else to do the same. Very common, copycat deaths, you see."

She nodded. She walked with Ratcliffe past the churchyard, heading back to what Edward Jeffries had described as Ravensfield.

She decided to move on. "Did you know them well? Debra and Luke?"

"Not really; I've been living down in Westminster these past twenty years. I never really spent much time here before I retired."

She accepted the answer, albeit convenient. "I understand Debra Harrison was a friend of your nephew?"

That surprised him. "Gary?"

She didn't know his name. "I think that's the one."

"Must be; I've only one."

"Did he go to school with Debra?"

"Gary? No, he's thirty-two."

That amazed her. Then again, Ratcliffe himself was over sixty.

"I understand the pair had become friends."

The politician was baffled. "I'm afraid you know more than me, Miss Farrelly," he said as they reached the gate of his house. "Would you like a cuppa?"

She smiled, but decided against it.

"Thank you for your time, Lord Ratcliffe."

Ratcliffe made the short walk through the grounds of his house and crossed the threshold into the Catesby estate.

Catesby was in the lab as usual. He was dressed in grey overalls and wore goggles to shield his eyes. He held a pipette in one hand, protected by rubber gloves, while steadying a Petri dish with the other.

He looked over at Ratcliffe. "It isn't time yet, is it?"

The Rat shook his head. "No, it's nothing to do with that." He gestured with his fingers, and Catesby dropped what he was doing.

"I were just having a chat with the lovely Miss Farrelly."

39

The King was in his study at 6 p.m. Through the window behind his desk, he watched in silence as the newest batch of guards marched smartly across the forecourt. Though he had witnessed the Changing of the Guard countless times, it never failed to make the hairs on the back of his neck rise.

"Tell me, George. Is Britain at war?"

Standing behind him was his brother, the Duke of Clarence. Like most of the family of that generation, he was in his late fifties and had previously served in the armed forces before concentrating on his business ventures.

He was a dead ringer for his brother, apart from his beard.

"Aren't we always?"

The King smiled – he knew in his heart of hearts, it was the first genuine one he had managed all day.

His pondering was disturbed by a knock at the door. He answered, "Come in," and in walked the Home Secretary, followed by West.

"George, you are familiar with Mr Heston, and the new Secretary of State for Justice, Mr West?"

"How do you do?" Clarence said, shaking hands. "Congratulations on your new appointment."

"Thank you very much, sir," West replied.

"Nice to see you again, sir," the Home Secretary added.

The King checked his watch; it was now approaching a quarter past seven.

"I have spoken to Thomas," Clarence said. "He and Stephen will be arriving shortly."

The King nodded. "I had hoped Fred might have joined us as well, but understandably his place is with his father."

"Quite understandable, Majesty," West said.

The Home Secretary held his tongue.

A few minutes later the doors opened for a second time. "The Duke of Cornwall and Prince Thomas," the two men were announced.

Thomas didn't recognise the man with Heston, but the sight of his father warmed him.

"Father," he said, embracing him.

"I'm quite all right, Tom. There's no need to fuss."

"Ahem."

West was standing with his fist covering his mouth.

"I do hope it's not contagious, West," Stephen said as he entered.

Although he had never met the man, Thomas could sense a dislike between the two.

"Nothing to worry about, sir, I assure you."

Stephen removed a cigar from the box on the desk, unwrapped it, and put it to his lips. "I hear you got promoted. Medical expenses gone up, I assume?"

Awkward laughter followed.

Stephen addressed the King for the first time. "Father."

"You're not going to light that, are you?"

Stephen removed the cigar from his mouth.

The King turned his attention to the politicians. "You know my son, the Duke of Cornwall, and my nephew Thomas."

Thomas acknowledged both men in turn. "How do you do?"

"An overdue honour, sir," West said, shaking hands with Thomas.

Standing behind West, Stephen made a gesture with his mouth.

The King was unimpressed, but quickly moved on. "Well, now that we are all here, let's not waste any more time. Tim, perhaps we might start by telling me what the bloody hell happened today?"

In truth, the Home Secretary had no answers. "Sir, I have spoken personally with the owner of the Marigold, Scotland Yard, and the head of Special Branch. All have reassured me that the matter is fully in hand."

"What the bloody hell does that mean: the matter is fully in hand?" Stephen asked.

"How is he?" the King asked before Heston had a chance to respond.

"Good, already barking out orders," Thomas said, avoiding a stutter.

"Yes, good old Uncle Bill, already up to his old tricks. Giving poor Cookie one hell of a run-around," Stephen said.

The King laughed. "Well, that's certainly a relief all-round."

He returned his attention to Heston. "Do we have a suspect yet?"

Heston replied, "Special Branch has already been given footage; I understand the hotel staff are also presently examining CCTV. We should have a far better idea over the next few hours."

"During which time our man could have got halfway across Europe – if not further," Stephen said.

"Unfortunately there is still no news on the exact source of the duke's illness," West interjected. "Even with the footage, it remains unclear what we are looking for."

Stephen removed the unlit cigar from his mouth.

"My son is quite correct," the King said, his point not questioned. "We need to nail this bastard now, while the iron is still hot." He brought his fist down on the desk with a thump.

"Have you seen the footage?" the King asked Heston.

"No, sir, but thanks to the owner of the Marigold, I am now in possession of a copy on a data stick," the Home Secretary responded.

"I should very much like to see that myself, Minister," Thomas said. "After all, protection of my family is my field."

"What a wizard idea," Stephen added. "There's a good chap, Minister, hand it over."

"Your co-operation would be much appreciated, Minister," Clarence added, he had been quiet so far. "I would also like to view it myself at some stage. As I'm sure would my brother, the Duke of York."

"Your assistance will be most valued, Your Grace," West added. "With a bit of luck, you might even turn out to be an eyewitness."

"The thought had occurred to me, Minister," Clarence replied. "Now then, Home Secretary, do you have that little stick with you?"

The request made Heston uncomfortable. "Why, yes."

"Would you be so kind as to hand it over?"

The Home Secretary hesitated. "I'm still to see it myself. Perhaps West can email . . ."

"I have a better idea," Stephen interrupted. "Hand over the stick. And my uncle can email it to you."

Clarence didn't object. "Minister."

Reluctantly the Home Secretary removed the memory stick from his pocket and handed it to Clarence, who placed it in an inside pocket of his jacket.

"We should have a much better idea of what we're dealing with when we've established the exact cause of the poison," West said. "Perhaps they used a different substance this time."

"Different to what time?" Stephen asked.

"And who exactly are you referring to when you say 'they'?" Thomas added.

"Why, the people who dictated the actions of the friar," the new Secretary of State for Justice said. "I can only assume that there is a connection."

All eyes fell on West.

"Okay, West–" Heston began.

"Don't you think you're being a tad presumptuous?" Stephen asked.

"Perhaps so, sir, but surely the possibility cannot be disregarded. After all, within the last three weeks two of my colleagues have been found murdered . . . that, for all we know the King himself . . ."

"You mind your tongue," Stephen said.

Thomas placed himself in front of him. "Calm."

Stephen looked briefly at his cousin, then once again at the minister, their eyes at constant deadlock.

"Gentlemen, time is of the essence," the King said. "Home Secretary, Justice Secretary, thank you very much for coming. Do, of course, keep us informed of any developments."

"Of course, sir," Heston replied.

West nodded at the King and slowly started to leave the room.

He saved the last eye contact for Stephen.

"The insolent bastard," Stephen exclaimed once the two ministers had left the room.

"Pipe down," the King reacted. "Like it or not, the boy had a point."

"I was so busy vomiting from all the arse licking, I'm afraid I must have missed it."

"I said pipe down."

The King moved towards his son, looking him in the eye. "One day you will be king. Now grow up and start to act like one."

The King took a breath and exhaled loudly.

"What news?"

"Talbot is dead; so is the butler. So is the m-man who sh-shot at me at Middleham," Thomas said.

"Any progress with the phone numbers?" the King asked.

"Yes," Thomas replied. "Uncle Bill brought us up to speed."

"I can't deny, the topic of conversation came up earlier at luncheon," Clarence said.

"So, who is responsible?" the King asked.

"One of the numbers was registered to the account of one Burghart Stanley," Clarence confirmed. "The others were all pay-as-you-go."

The King was confused. "Why did he need an account if they were all pay-as-you-go?"

"Stanley's must have been a contract," Thomas answered.

The King accepted the answer. "Very well. Who is this Stanley?"

"Son of Rowland," Stephen replied.

"The Democrat leader?" the King asked, his eyes narrowing.

"The very same."

"You know, I actually had the pleasure of meeting him recently," Clarence said.

"Really?" the King replied. "I'm sure he took kindly to you."

"No worse than I to him."

The King laughed softly. "What of his son?"

"Ex Royal Marine, now posing as a politician," Thomas replied, "at least according to Uncle Bill."

"You think him unreliable?"

Thomas smiled. "N-not at all. In truth, I had never even h-heard of him until about an hour ago."

Clarence nodded. "Actually, that pretty much covers him. He's twenty-nine, six feet one – at least according to his former profile in the marines. Unmarried, no kids as far as we know. Praised by his former commander for his sharpshooting."

"How about now?" the King asked.

"Failed to become the 31st Democrat to enter Strasbourg last year. Rumour has it he plans to stand for parliament at the next election."

"What are his chances?"

"Too early to tell, at present – things should be a lot clearer by early next year."

The King looked at Clarence, not in the slightest reassured. "So what's his involvement in all this?"

"His recent activities have not been widely catalogued," Clarence replied. "Nevertheless, I have passed on his details to GCHQ. From what I can gather, he's been in Greenwich most of the day."

"Thomas and I thought we might pay him a visit," Stephen suggested. "Sometime in the region of now."

The King shot his son a piercing stare. "Out of the question. Cause a scene, the press will be over you in a flash."

"Father, I wasn't planning on causing a scene; I merely thought we might, you know, pay him a visit."

The King remained sceptical.

"Father, come on. After all, I'm a surgeon, not an assassin."

For now Thomas remained silent. It was obvious that the King was not buying it.

"Then I must go alone."

The King looked at his nephew. "It sounds dangerous. Very well, go with him if you must. Just be sensible."

"I'm not planning on getting killed if that's what you mean," Stephen replied.

The King turned to Clarence. "I want someone else tracking his father."

Thomas and Stephen left the palace through a back entrance to await the arrival of the car that had been assigned for them.

"That slimy weasel talks too much," Stephen said, finally lighting the cigar. "Who told him about the politicians' murders?"

"He's a member of the Cabinet – word gets around. Of course s-some things might be p-public knowledge. Freedom of information and all that."

"Hopefully not too much."

Their car appeared in the south-east part of the grounds. They got in through the rear right door, and the driver emerged on the A3214, south of the palace.

"What I can't understand is why the bastard was even there," Stephen continued.

"It's his department; technically it's his job."

Stephen wound down the window to exhale smoke and flick away ash. "I wouldn't trust him as far as I could throw him . . . what's the address?"

"742 Drake Gardens, an apartment block in Greenwich."

"Did you get that?"

The black visor came down, and the driver's face appeared.

"Caroline?"

"I told the driver he deserved a night off. I'm coming with you."

Back at the palace, the King looked over his brother's shoulder. He was looking at a fifteen-inch laptop presently showing CCTV footage from earlier that day of the main entrance and exits of the Marigold.

"Stop right there," the King said, focusing in on a man wearing a dark suit, aged somewhere between late twenties and early thirties. "Focus in on him."

Clarence paused the footage and attempted to zoom in. The man had some sort of facial hair, probably stubble.

"Ring any bells?"

Clarence looked at the image for several seconds. "I don't know."

*

Moments later, the data came through on Thomas's email. He opened it using his iPhone and seconds later was looking at the same footage.

"What's the matter?" Stephen asked.

"That's one of the men who got away."

Stephen's response was delayed. "You're quite sure?"

In truth, he wasn't.

"Positive."

40

"Ey up, it's Miss Farrelly," Brian Hancock said on entering the Hog. Jen was sitting alone at the bar, an almost finished plate of fish and chips in front of her.

"Hi ya," she said, her mouth full.

He took a seat beside her. "Haven't seen you about these last couple of days; where you been hiding?"

She pointed to her hair.

It took Hancock a second to twig. "Oh, you've had something done to your hair . . . oh, yes, it looks very nice, that does." He turned his attention to Mitchell behind the bar. "Hey, doesn't Miss Farrelly's hair look nice?"

"Very nice," he replied, pouring a pint.

"Anyway, when you have a minute, I'll have a pint of the manliest you've got on the premises and same again for Miss Farrelly."

"Two pints of lighter fluid coming up."

Jen coughed as she finished her Coke.

"Don't worry; it still tastes better than his beer."

Jen laughed.

"So what else have you been doing these last couple of days – besides growing ever more attractive?"

"Just research, really. I've been spending quite a lot of time around the church. I never knew it had a vault."

She was fishing.

"You know far more than me. Got a vault, has it? Down below, is it?"

Mitchell passed Hancock a pint of local ale and another Coke for Jen.

"Bit quiet in here tonight, isn't it, Harvey lad?" Hancock asked.

"Must be something good on the telly."

"Is that right? Not the dancing, is it?"

The statement seemed true. Themselves aside, there were only three other people in the bar area, none of whom Jen recognised. The sound of chatter was more evident from the dining area. Several people spoke in low voices, husbands talking to wives, others ordering food. One voice rose above all others, the man's tone loud and annoyingly ostentatious.

"Where's your friend?"

"You mean Gavin? I don't know . . . he must have fallen off the face of the earth." He asked the landlord, "You haven't seen him, have you?"

"What – Gavin? I haven't seen him."

"He hasn't seen him, and he would know – doesn't miss a thing, does Harvey."

Jen found herself unable to avoid giggling.

"Tell you what, I'll tell Gavin you asked about him – that'll make his day, that will, Miss Farrelly."

Jen took the first sip of her new Coke and stirred it with a straw. She placed the glass on a coaster, her mind again distracted. Laughter from the dining room had become consistently louder.

"Someone's got the giggles," Jen said, again unable to avoid smiling.

"That's just Dr Lovell," Hancock returned. "He's a bit of a minor celeb round these parts."

"Lovell?"

She didn't mishear him.

She leaned back on her barstool, her eyes on the archway that connected the bar area to the dining room. Although the view wasn't perfect, she could at least make out the man responsible for all the laughter.

She looked at him, taking note of his features. A large red shirt, unbuttoned at the collar, fit snugly around a large belly, while matching white trousers looked close to bursting point. A fine head of whitening blond hair, combed back smartly and perhaps assisted by some kind of gel or paste, was receding in some places, though she reasoned that might have been a trick of the light.

Either way, not bad for a man approaching seventy.

His face was fixed in a smile that brought joy to all around him – notably the staff. If there was a correlation between jolliness and weight, this man was Father Christmas.

"Is that him?" she asked Hancock.

"That's him."

"He's on his own."

"He often is. Knows everyone between here and the next five villages, Dr Lovell does . . . I'm guessing Alma's gone to stay with her sister again." The second half of the statement was for Mitchell.

"Got it in one."

"Happens every middle of July, that does."

"What does, sorry?" Jen asked.

"Alma, that's his wife, she always leaves Wootton this time of year to go and stay with her sister in Scarborough. They say it's the closest she ever comes to leaving Yorkshire."

Not for the first time Hancock's banter made Jen laugh. "He seems very friendly."

"Why don't you go have a chat with him?"

Jen was unsure. "Perhaps after dinner."

"Don't be shy. Hey, tell you what, if you go now, there's still time for him to buy you dessert."

The prospect appealed. "You're sure he won't mind?"

"Him? Mind? You've got more chance of being bitten by a plague rat."

The dining area was larger than the main bar area. At least twenty tables, ranging in size from two-seater to eight or more, were arranged evenly on either side of a large partition wall.

All of the walls were painted white, matching the original colour of the stone, and supported by wooden beams that dated back at least four hundred years. The room oozed periodic charm and contained two open fireplaces, neither of which were lit. Historic memorabilia lined the walls, mostly prints depicting the village from anywhere between fifty and two hundred years ago.

Lovell was sitting on his own at a four-seater table, halfway through what looked to be a homemade pie.

"Majestic, my dear, majestic," Lovell said as he delayed the passing waitress. "I daresay the cuisine of this fine establishment surpasses the cooking of any other in the county . . . but please don't tell my wife."

Jen approached the man from the left, her smile now permanent.

"Excuse me, Dr Lovell?"

Lovell turned to his left, nearly knocking over his glass of red wine.

"My name is Jennifer Farrelly . . ."

"Miss Farrelly, we meet at last," the man said, rising to his feet and cupping her hand in his. "I've heard so many very good things about you."

Jen smiled awkwardly, touching her hair with her free hand. "I was wondering if I might . . ."

The man returned to his seat, unable to hide his delight. "Of course, of course, of course, of course, of course. Please sit down. Samantha, dear . . ." He caught the attention of the thirty-something waitress as she passed by with two plates, "a second glass for my youthful companion, though please do not inconvenience yourself and carry out my request with those hot plates still in your hand."

"Be right with you, Dr Lovell."

"Lovely girl, such manners, such grace . . . now, my dear, please."

"You're most kind," Jen said, taking a seat opposite, placing her handbag down on the floor. "I've actually been trying to see you for quite some time; I've passed by your house twice, but you were out."

Lovell clapped his hands together. "How tragic I should have missed you, and to think how fate might have robbed me of this fine opportunity . . . my dear, what a pretty necklace you wear around your neck."

"Thank you," Jen replied, taken completely off guard. "It was my grandmother's."

Nobody ever complimented her like that.

"How remarkable. Such taste, such beauty."

The waitress returned with an empty glass and smiled at them both in turn. Lovell picked up the three-quarter-full bottle of red wine and poured into Jen's glass.

"That's more than enough, thank you."

The glass was well over half full.

"My dear, tell me, how are you enjoying your stay with us?"

"Oh, it's been lovely; everybody's just so friendly."

"Oh, I'm quite glad that you think so; so different from London, I'm afraid the modern world is so alien to me."

Jen smiled weakly. "I understand you're something of an authority on local history."

The man laughed as he raised his knife and fork. The aroma of steak, kidney, carrots, swedes and potatoes was simply beautiful to Jen, even on a full stomach.

"Lies, lies, all of it lies – leaving room, of course, for the occasional exaggeration. So many well-wishers, such great friends . . . please forgive me, Miss Jennifer, I do not wish for this fine cuisine to go cold."

"Not at all," Jen said, flicking her hair away from her face. "I understand you were headmaster at St Joseph's for over twenty years."

"Twenty-three years and a day – would you believe it? Oh, happy days, oh, how I miss those happy little faces."

"I understand that you're also the famed editor of the East Riding history bulletin?"

The man dropped his knife and fork on his plate. "What a most lovely thing to say," the man said, bringing his hands to his heart, "and such an impeccable piece of research on your part. However did you know?"

"I think one of your former students told me . . ."

"How incredible . . . what was their name?"

Jen decided against telling him it was Gillian Harrison. "I think it was Anthea Brown; I went to their salon yesterday to get my hair done."

"Remarkable, such talent, such grace."

"I was hoping I might be able to chat with you about the history of the village – there's still so much I don't know."

"And I, too, Miss Jennifer, it is indeed my most solemn opinion that for every nook in Wootton there are at least three crannies, all stuffed to their gussets with titbits, be it from the Romans to the Victorians."

Jen smiled, noticing his rounded pronunciation of the word Romans. "I'm actually interested more in the Plantagenets. I've been able to learn a bit about the church, but I still know little about the rest of the village. How well do you know the priory?"

"I've known it ever since I was a small boy. It used to be Dominican, you know and before that Augustinian: first built in 743 AD, one of the oldest in Yorkshire."

"Was it important?"

"I'd say not, at least compared to the great and nearby abbeys of Fountains and St Mary's. It never had more than thirty friars living there at any one time."

Jen made a mental note, but wasn't convinced it was particularly relevant.

"How about the castle?"

"Oh, goodness gracious, you have been busy. The castle was once an absolute treasure trove – and still there is much to be investigated by the archaeologist."

"Who owned it? Originally, that is?"

"Originally it was built by William II, son of the famous Conqueror. Later it was owned by the de Vaullis family, prominent Norman noblemen."

Jen was more interested in the later period. "Where were they buried? I didn't see anything in the vaults."

"Ah, you wouldn't. You see, the vaults only date from about 1540."

She bit her lip. "Who owned the castle after the . . . what were they called?"

"De Vaullis," he said. "They lost the castle and their inheritance for fighting for Simon de Montfort in the Second Barons' War. Following that, the castle spent several decades as a royal castle before it was given away by one Edmund of Langley, second youngest of the sons of Edward III, to one of his . . . one of his . . ."

"Illegitimate sons."

"Quite right."

Jen smiled; she had learned as much from the vicar at Bishopton. "I saw a Plantagenet monument in the graveyard; I assumed there was a connection."

The man was gobsmacked. "What frightening powers of observation you have. There is only one such example in the entire five-village area."

To Jen, that definitely made it more significant. "Then what happened?"

"The castle was destroyed at the culmination of the Wars of the Roses," the man replied. "It was Henry VII's intention, you know, that no physical creation would remain of connection to the House of York . . . apart from his wife, of course."

She grinned. "I understand your family traces its own history back to that time."

"You know, I do believe a link in the chain can be found going back all the way to King David of Jerusalem . . . that is a fabrication, of course . . ." the man was practically beaming, "but I am sure a more accurate representation exists of my forebears going back at least to the reign of King Henry I."

"Wow. Did you research this yourself?"

"Ah, I cannot deny I owe much to the endeavours of my forebears . . . not to mention my noble cousins Catesby and Ratcliffe."

"I understand your families once filled the entire government."

The man laughed. "Something of an exaggeration, I think, but the famous rhyme of Collingbourne was not without accuracy. It is because of my famous ancestor, I owe my own nickname, the Dog."

"How well do you know the Jeffries family?"

"I should say I've known them my entire life. Why do you ask?"

"No reason, I was just visiting the vaults beneath the church the other day. I've never seen such elaborate tombs."

"Nor, I'm sure, will you see any finer. They are the hallmarks of one of the most distinguished families ever to grace our green and pleasant land."

"When I was visiting the vault, I noticed there was a door; I assume there is a second part of the vault."

The man nodded sombrely. "That would be the one leading to the crypt of Lord Edward."

"Lord Edward?"

The waitress returned to collect Lovell's plate. "Would you like any dessert?"

"My dear, I have deliberately saved room for Mrs Mitchell's exquisite apple pie." He looked at Jen. "My dear, you must try some."

Jen accepted without argument.

"Who was Lord Edward?" Jen asked once the waitress had left. Aside from them, the dining room was now practically empty.

Though she assumed Lovell's voice travelled much further afield.

"Lord Edward was a noble companion of the Duke of Monmouth and an heir to the throne in his own right."

"How exactly?"

"Well, Monmouth himself was a bastard of Charles II, or so we believe – you must forgive me, Miss Farrelly, for my vulgarity."

A wry smile.

Lovell continued, "Lord Edward, on the other hand, we know even less of his parentage. His mother, we know, was one Mary Jeffries, eldest daughter of the previous Jeffries. Now, according to some, Lord Edward was the illegitimate son of one of our neighbours; however, there was an even stronger rumour that he was Monmouth's half brother."

Jen raised an eyebrow. "Okay."

"Following Monmouth's execution, in the eyes of their followers, Edward was now the rightful king."

The arrival of the apple pie delayed her next question.

Lovell took his first bite. "My dear, exquisite as always."

Jen tapped the pastry with her spoon. Her thoughts returned to the burial records at Bishopton. The Latin, *Rex Angliae*, was mentioned next to an E Jeffries, the dates matching what Lovell had explained.

"This is delicious," she said, tasting the apple pie. The hot sugary pastry nearly took off the inside of her cheeks before it slowly melted in the mouth.

"Speciality of the house, one of many I can assure you."

She didn't doubt it. "What happened to him? Lord Edward?"

"Executed on the orders of the usurpers, William and Mary."

She detected bitterness on the word usurpers, if that was the right word.

"And he is now buried in the vaults of St Michael's?"

Lovell nodded, his mouth full.

"Is the crypt not open to the public?"

"Alas, no, for you see, the people of Yorkshire are most superstitious."

Jen raised an eyebrow. "Sorry, I'm not following."

"I'm quite sure that you are not, as an outsider – unfamiliar with local customs – it would be impossible to understand fully. You see, Lord Edward was a particularly violent man, and due to his position of such prominence, he was sentenced to a similarly appropriate execution."

"You mean he was hung, drawn and quartered?"

"Precisely. However, Lord Edward's execution was particularly grisly. His head was placed on a pike on one of the bridges of London, while the rest of him was scattered among the four corners of the kingdom."

"Okay." She was determined not to be put off her food.

"After a period of several months, his eldest son returned to the family estate at Wootton having successfully accomplished his ambition of collecting every part of his father's body except, of course, the head. His remains were placed in the family vault, and for several weeks, so the story claims, rested peacefully. It was after that, however, a peculiar series of events occurred, which has given rise to Wootton's greatest legend."

"What is that?"

"The legend of the Barghest."

Jen's hand stopped just before the fork reached her mouth. "The what, sorry?"

"The Barghest is a legendary creature, a bit like the beast of Bodmin. According to accounts from the late 1680s, the Wootton Barghest was first seen on a wet November night by the innkeeper of this very location. Over the next few weeks, the beast was seen by no fewer than twelve independent eyewitnesses. Well, you can just imagine the commotion, can't you? Villagers were afraid to travel alone after sundown."

Jen took the last bite of apple pie. "Forgive me, I don't see how this is connected to Lord Edward. You seem to be suggesting that they believed he was a monster."

"Indeed they did, right or wrong, I cannot tell you. What you must remember is that their world was most different to ours. Folklore was still prominent, despite the advances in science. The beast captured the imagination of the public, and many believed it to be the tormented spirit of Lord Edward."

Jen accepted the reasoning. "What happened?"

"According to an account written by the parish vicar, from January 1689, the beast, after being spotted in local woodland, was set upon by the villagers. The contents of the grave were blessed and perhaps burned, accounts vary, and finally a wall was built around the late Edward's tomb."

Jen sipped slowly from her wine. It was a good yarn, no doubt, but the story made little sense. "Has anyone ever been inside to check?"

"I assure you they have not – the key has been missing since the early days."

She didn't buy it. "Why was there a door included at all if it was meant to be sealed in?"

"A most excellent point. Against the wishes of the majority, Edward's son wished to be buried in the crypt. After his death, the wall behind the door was apparently filled in."

Jen took a deep breath but for now remained silent.

The idea beggared belief.

"Wow, I've certainly learned a thing or two about the history of Wootton-on-the-Moor."

The former headmaster laughed. "I assure you, you haven't even scratched the surface. Away from the folklore, I think you'll find that history is indeed more fascinating than myth."

The waitress returned with the bill.

"I must offer to pay for that delicious dessert."

"Nonsense, my dear, nonsense, you've truly made an old man's evening."

Jen smiled. She placed her handbag over her shoulder. "Surely there is something I can do to show my appreciation."

"How are you fixed tomorrow?"

She shrugged.

"There is a fine display of medieval keepsakes at the heritage centre. What say the two of us have a morning of real history?"

She didn't know what to say. "Thanks, I really can't think of anything else I've got on."

They left the dining room and returned to the bar area. Lord Ratcliffe was standing by the counter.

"Ey up, Francis, does Alma know?"

Lovell clapped his hands together, a loud swift bang. "My dear Richard, please assure me your discretion. I fear the shock would very near kill her, and that me."

The politician laughed. "Come with us to the back room. I've just got William a brandy."

Lovell turned to face Jen. "My dear, I'm afraid I must humour the fellow. To say no to the Rat would be like saying yes to an Alsatian, with something more valuable than money, I might add."

Ratcliffe laughed loudly.

"My dear, it's been a pleasure." He kissed her on the hand.

Jen fought a blush, but failed. "Thank you, I really enjoyed it."

Jen left the Hog and walked quickly across the bridge. It was after eight, and the sun was still up, the fading light flickering behind the hill.

She called Anthea on her iPhone.

"Can you meet me on the bridge? Thanks.

"Oh, and bring your mum's keys."

Back inside the Hog, Lovell sat down in between Catesby and Ratcliffe. Three large brandies were placed on the table in front of them. With the door closed, the conversation would remain private.

"Was she the one you saw on the camera?"

Lovell exhaled lengthily. "I'm afraid so."

Catesby wrapped his large fingers around the glass. "That is a pity."

Lovell nodded. "And she was such a nice girl, too."

Anthea arrived ten minutes later, wearing trainers, jeans and her school hoody.

"What's up?"

Jen bit her lip before responding. The priest had said the vault was for plague victims; Lovell some kind of medieval monster.

At least one of them was lying.

She removed the camera from her pocket. "It belonged to Debra Harrison."

Anthea put her hands to her mouth. "You mean she's . . ."

"I don't know," Jen said. "But take a look at this."

She showed Anthea the photographs of the vault.

"I don't understand."

"Debra Harrison disappeared after finding a way into the restricted vault."

Anthea was gobsmacked. "How?"

"That's the problem:

"We have to enter it via the priory."

41

The GPS led them to a large building in Greenwich, situated south of the water and within sight of the O2, the Royal Observatory, and the National Maritime Museum.

Caroline stopped at a red light on a busy street that was rich in tower buildings and concrete, and a bitch on the parking. Scaffolding surrounded the building opposite, and traffic cones and iron railings blocked the only entrance to the multi-storey car park.

Judging by the exterior, the inside wasn't habitable.

"Tell you what," Stephen said, "why don't we get out here while you find somewhere to park?"

Stephen and Thomas departed while the light was still red, leaving Caroline without opportunity to argue. They jaywalked across the street while the traffic was at a standstill, and continued towards large double doors leading to the foyer.

It was just after 7 p.m., and they had made good time. The sun was setting to the west of the city. A blaze of red dominated the London skyline, shining in all directions and reflecting off the glass of the skyscrapers. Large shadows had formed from the Citigroup and HSBC buildings, crossing several houses and continuing all the way to the water. Despite the pleasant weather, the river was quiet, save for one lonely barge heading in the direction of where the Docklands Arena once stood.

Stephen opened the door and took his first look at the interior. The décor was half completed – unless the designers were going for the bomb-damaged look. Several hardhat symbols were placed on the walls, accompanied by other health and safety notices.

Thomas was confused. The other side of the foyer was slightly more impressive and offered the choice of either four lifts or a staircase to the floors above.

Stephen entered the lift without consultation and scanned the buttons on the display.

"What floor is it?"

"Six."

Stephen pressed the button. "Penthouse. Well, I never."

The lift began its ascent.

"At least it works," Stephen said. He removed the Glock 17 Thomas had given him from the inside of his suit and checked it was loaded.

"You best let m-me do the t-talking."

Stephen looked at his cousin. "I don't think we've got time for that."

The doors opened, revealing an unlit corridor still to be furnished. The floor was a combination of wood and plastic covering. Countless workmen's tools were scattered at random, ranging from hammers to tape measures. The upper part of the corridor had been freshly painted, the aroma evident in their nostrils. All of the doors were white and evidently double-glazed.

It was less obvious whether anyone was at home.

They tiptoed through the plastic, taking great care over their footing. Thomas removed his firearm from his jacket, holding it with the barrel facing upwards. Like the surgeon, he had gone through the same basic training that all the royals went through on reaching a certain age, but unlike Stephen, this was now his life. For some, a career in the forces began at Sandhurst and ended in a magnificent parade, the ribbons of war dangling from just above the heart – at least for the lucky ones. For Thomas, Sandhurst was barely even the apprenticeship; that stage of his life was still ongoing. Perhaps it would never end. That was both his choice and the choice that had already been made for him – perhaps even before he was born.

The curse of the Invisible Royal.

The address corresponded with the penultimate door on the left. On appearances alone, it was no different from the others. It was white, with a gold handle, and appeared to be deserted.

They stopped before the door, listening carefully. The sound of background noise was louder than it had been, most notably that of the gulls. If anything, that enhanced the feeling of loneliness.

Thomas looked to his left, then to the right.

Nothing.

They were alone.

Stephen pushed the doorbell, a high-pitched chiming sound that faded almost immediately.

Ten seconds passed, no response.

"You're sure this is the place?" Stephen asked.

Thomas didn't reply. Silently, he shared his cousin's concern.

Stephen took a step back and looked around: the floor, the walls, the ceiling . . .

"Well, if you ask me, we've been brought on a wild bloody goose chase."

Thomas took a deep breath, his eyes darting side to side.

Something was troubling him.

"Can you hear that?"

"Hear what?"

"Shhh!" He placed a finger to his lips. "Listen."

The noise was coming from nearby.

It sounded like gas escaping from a balloon.

No. It sounded like an egg frying in a pan.

No. It was acid dissolving something metallic.

Or perhaps the sound of something fizzier.

Thomas placed his ear to the door. Whatever it was, it was coming from inside the apartment.

The realisation hit Thomas immediately.

"B-b-bomb!"

Two streets away, Caroline finally found a parking space along a busy street lined with houses and shops. It said on the sign that payment must be made by phone, and required both car registration and a credit card number.

The plague of living in London.

She inserted the last three digits of the registration and huffed on realising she'd made a mistake. She listened to the options on the phone and attempted to rectify the situation.

The explosion occurred about two streets away, probably less than a quarter of a mile from where she was standing. The noise was startling, causing her to drop the phone.

A trail of dust was rising into the evening sky, the full effects partially obscured by nearby buildings. There might have been smoke as well, but she couldn't be certain.

Whatever it was, it was coming from the building she had just dropped the boys off by.

Panicked, she picked up her mobile phone and started dialling.

Thomas acted on instinct. He grabbed Stephen's left arm and dived.

The impact was horrific. Debris came from every angle, either crashing into their moving bodies or just missing.

They hit the floor and covered their heads, doing their best to keep dust out of their mouths and eyes.

Several seconds passed before visibility improved. The door had disappeared, that was obvious, as had most of the wall. A hole had appeared in the roof of the apartment, and it looked like more was about to cave in.

No doubt the debris could be seen from the outside.

Less obvious was exactly how far the damage went.

There was movement to Thomas's right. Stephen was stirring. He rose slowly from his chest to his haunches, and slower still to his feet. The sound that had dominated his ears for less than two seconds was still ringing over a minute later.

Through the wreckage, Thomas could just about see into the apartment. The interior was completely bare but, as far as he could see, largely undamaged.

He saw movement followed by gunfire.

They hit the floor immediately. The clattering of bullets from an automatic weapon, accompanied by the familiar yellow blaze, had come from the living room. The bullets missed, damaging the wall behind them, just above their heads. Stephen felt a graze to his skin, then a peculiar warm sensation.

There was blood on his arm.

Thomas kept moving to his right, practically dragging Stephen with him. The gunfire continued even after they were out of sight, confirming it was coming from the middle of the apartment.

As soon as it stopped, Thomas rose to his feet and hurried towards the wall. Stephen followed less than a metre behind, adrenalin pumping.

Hyperventilation was setting in.

"They're firing at us," Stephen stated, his back to the wall.

"No fucking shit."

Thomas felt the trigger on his Glock and edged closer to what remained of the door. Instead of a door and a wall there was now a large hole, perhaps ten metres in diameter.

"Keep quite still."

Stephen nodded, his breathing now slightly more under control.

Less than a metre away, Thomas chanced exposure, leading to further gunfire. He retreated immediately to his initial position, back to the wall.

Amidst the gunfire, Stephen's mobile phone started ringing.

He answered. "For God's sake, Caroline, not now."

"Wait," Thomas said, taking the phone. "Caroline . . ."

"Where are you?"

He could hear crying at the other end of the line. "Listen to me very carefully. I want you to get in t-touch with the p-palace. Tell them that s-someone's f-firing at us and we need b-backup."

The words stuttered out of his mouth. He hung up the phone and returned it to Stephen.

Meanwhile, the gunfire had ceased.

Thomas edged closer to the hole, allowing himself an opportunity of observation. He moved closer still, but the gunfire started again. Lunging to his right, he nearly collided with Stephen as he clattered to the floor.

He was back on his feet immediately, attempting to form a plan. The apartment was open plan; he had seen enough of it to know that. The kitchen area was to the right, the area where the gunfire was coming from. He knew he had seen a figure standing there, dressed mainly in black.

The rest was something of a blur.

He waited until the gunfire ceased before firing a couple of shots in that direction. Intuition told him at least one had been successful, perhaps fatal. He allowed what he estimated was ten seconds to go by before chancing further exposure. The figure had disappeared, which meant one of two things:

He was hit or he had moved.

Within a second Thomas had the answer. This time the gunfire came from another part of the kitchen. He took shelter immediately and waited several seconds before firing.

This time, he knew he had found his target.

He moved to the entrance, alive to the possibility that the man he had shot had a partner, and sure enough, he did.

The next round of gunfire came from the other side of the apartment. Everything about it was consistent with the last, suggesting to Thomas that the weapon was the same.

The bullets ceased after about five seconds.

Thomas reloaded. "Give it up. We have you surrounded."

"Tell him to surrender in the name of the king," Stephen said.

Thomas refused to dignify that with an answer.

"Come out on the c-count of five."

The gunfire resumed. A stray bullet ricocheted off something nearby, causing Thomas to drop his gun as he dived. He waited until the gunfire had ceased before returning to his feet and running hard towards the wall. He looked for his gun, but couldn't find it.

"Give me your gun."

Stephen didn't argue.

Thomas edged closer to the doorway. On this occasion he decided to hold back, wary that the man had changed position. He thought about firing one on spec, but decided against it.

His new tactic was patience.

Twenty seconds of silence felt more like a lifetime. His intuition told him that the man had moved. He inched closer to the hole, keeping his back to the wall. He entered the apartment for the first time, gun at the ready.

Whoever had been there was now gone.

He headed left, the lounge area. Stephen followed him, evidently now armed.

"You were just looking in the wrong place."

Thomas let the insult slide. He continued to the left, whereas Stephen went to the right. Beyond the lounge was a dining area, in the other direction the bedrooms and bathroom. Thomas concluded the gunman had entered the dining room.

There was no way in hell he could have sprinted across the lounge unseen.

The dining area was minus any furniture, confirming initial suspicions that the owner was still to move in. That begged a new question:

What was he doing there?

"He's dead."

Thomas turned, his attention on Stephen.

"Two puncture wounds: the heart and lungs."

Thomas continued to move. "Check his belongings."

There was movement outside the patio window. He fired immediately, his bullets somehow failing to penetrate the glass.

Outside, the figure had disappeared again.

Thomas continued through the dining room, looking for an exit. There was an open door to the right, heading to a balcony area.

The only option was to head right. A partition wall to the left separated the property from the next one, while directly in front of him the same wall continued along the north side of the building, preventing anyone from falling over the edge. Further afield, the property offered striking views of the north side of the water, buildings recognisable beyond the village. In the last ten minutes, the sun had completely disappeared behind dense cloud, its light replaced by the occasional glow of office lighting standing out against the background like a gigantic electronic solitaire square.

Heading to the right, Thomas followed the balcony. There was a metal fire escape descending all the way to the pavement. He opened the metallic door and began down the stairway. The structure was square, divided into quarters.

He heard footsteps, followed by a gunshot. A bright orange spark was visible about twenty metres in front of him, accompanied by the sound of metal on metal. It didn't take a genius to work out that the shot had been fired from below.

Staying as close to the wall as possible, he moved quickly down the stairs. Two gunshots followed, dangerously close.

Either he was getting nearer, or the man's aim was getting better.

Two flights further down, Thomas saw him for the first time. Without question, he was getting closer, no more than a single flight behind. The signs on the stairway told him he was now on the second floor, which tallied with his views out across the river.

A fourth gunshot followed, this one disturbingly close. Sparks appeared merely centimetres in front of him, making a mark on his wrist. The sudden occurrence caused him to fall on his back, though the fall was less painful than the burn. He returned to his feet without breaking stride, and picked up the pace as he approached level 1.

He heard something from down below. A door opened, thick and heavy judging by the sound. Seconds later he saw it himself, a typical fire escape that needed to be opened by pressing a bar.

He emerged on a side street adjoining the road where they had exited the car some twenty minutes earlier. The figure was moving along the banks of the Thames, heading roughly in the direction of the O2.

Thomas wasted no time. He followed the man at speed along the road known as Riverside, at this hour devoid of either humans or cars. Across the water, the buildings surrounding Lyle Park and the Thames Barrier Park passed by in a flash of colour.

On reaching Greenwich Peninsula Ecology Park, he headed to the left and sprinted through the greenery. Thomas emerged on West Parkside, a busy main road with cars racing by in both directions. Ahead of him, the gunman took a chance dashing across the road, barely making it unscathed.

Thomas cursed his luck. Several seconds passed before he was across himself. The shooter was now progressing rapidly along Child Lane, a smart residential area. About a hundred metres in front of him, he could see the man climb aboard a motorbike. Seconds later, he saw Caroline running towards him.

She had parked on the other side of the road.

"Follow that motorbike."

"What?"

Thomas changed direction before she was able to respond. The motorbike had roared into life, making its way south.

Caroline panicked. She attempted to follow her cousin, but that was impossible in high heels.

Across the road, the biker was revving up and preparing to make his getaway. Practically in tears, she returned to the car, throwing her heels on the front seat. The engine started immediately, and seconds later she was away.

Thomas returned to the apartment the same way he had left it. Stephen was in the kitchen, kneeling down alongside the second shooter. While the apartment itself was quiet, the high-pitched tone of the nearby sirens was becoming progressively louder. In London, it was never obvious exactly what that meant.

"Did you call 999?"

"Of course not."

Thomas knelt down alongside him. The second shooter was now topless, his upper body covered in blood.

"He needs medical attention."

"I don't need a second opinion to tell me he's dead."

Thomas remained silent. The adrenalin was pumping so hard it was affecting his thinking. Without question the man's blood flow had stopped, except for a slight oozing from the actual wound.

There were markings beneath the blood, somewhere around the collarbone.

It was the same thing he had seen on both the friar and the man he had shot at Middleham.

"Have you checked his b-belongings?" Thomas asked.

Stephen showed him a small white package contained within a plastic bag. "I found this in his pocket."

It looked like pieces of meat.

Outside, the whining of a siren had become louder.

He looked at Stephen. "Come on. The King will kill us himself if we're seen."

The first squad of policemen made their entrance on the south side. The lobby was undamaged, despite being a mess.

They had heard reports that the explosion had come from the unfinished top floor.

They proceeded up the indoor stairway, lined up two ranks at a time. The sixth floor was an even greater mess, particularly the far end. Though the dust had settled, evidence of the reported explosion was clear. Even from a distance, it looked like a bomb had done the damage. The hole in the wall was clean, far too clean for it to have been an accident. According to the manager of the building company in charge of the construction, although most of the apartments had been sold, they were still to be lived in.

Strange, then, reports of an explosion at one of them.

The squad scattered on reaching the living room, some heading left, others right.

The body was found in the kitchen. Two gun wounds to the upper chest were evident; it was estimated he had been dead for between ten and twenty minutes.

But there was one peculiarity that no one expected. Above the higher of the two wounds, below the left shoulder, the flesh was missing. It was not part of the original wound – that would have been impossible.

No question, the skin had been cut away with a knife.

The princes had escaped down the fire escape and were now heading east along the river.

Stephen carried a bag of ice in his gloved hand, taken from the freezer.

"I suppose I should congratulate you – it's not often you have an idea as good as this."

Thomas answered while sprinting. "Do I detect a hint of sarcasm?"

"Remind me, what was the point in removing the man's tattoo?"

"It was the same as on the one I shot the other night. And the friar."

Stephen was becoming breathless. "Did you keep that as a souvenir, too?"

"If the press were to see it, it would only be a matter of t-time before someone blew this wide open."

Stephen's tank was now empty. "Okay, okay . . . that's far enough."

Thomas also came to a halt. They had made it well over a mile. As best they could tell, they were alone. Traffic in the distance was the only noise.

The sirens had stopped.

Stephen was standing with his hands placed just above his knees, his breathing laboured. "Would you mind telling me what the bloody hell that was all about?"

Thomas didn't know how to explain it. "They b-both had the s-same tattoo."

"So what? For all we know, they were both in the same gang in prison."

Thomas shook his head. "I don't think so. It was the symbol of the House of York. I think it might be relevant."

Stephen remained sceptical.

"Perhaps we can get someone in the lab to have a look at it."

Stephen sought to reply, but the ringing of his mobile phone cut him off.

"Hello?

"Caroline? Where are–

"You're where?"

"Give me that." Thomas snatched the phone. "Caroline, what's happened?"

"I lost him two minutes ago. I made a note of the bike's registration and reported it to your father. It's currently being tracked as we speak."

"Good girl, Caroline."

"I might be able to catch him again when I get out of London. It looks as if he's heading north."

Thomas waited until she had finished. "Try to stay with him. F-far as you can."

"Will do. I told your father as much as I knew. They're sending a car to pick you up. Don't worry; I didn't drop you in it."

Thomas laughed. "Thanks."

"They'll pick you up at Maryon Park."

"Maryon Park is fine, th-thank you."

Thomas hung up and returned the phone to Stephen.

"Why the hell do we have to go all the way to Maryon Park?"

"Trust me, the f-farther away we are from this, the better."

42

All of the lights were off in the presbytery; at least that was how it looked from the outside. The grounds were deserted, as usual, the priory ruins barely visible beyond the far wall.

There was no danger of surveillance – of that Jen was sure. Her earlier visit, though hardly a reconnaissance mission, had been useful in that regard. The building itself was the opposite of ultramodern – the only thing that prevented it from being antique was the fact that the interior was not even interesting.

It was just plain old.

She took Anthea as far as the main gate and stopped. The air was still, the light fading, the atmosphere quiet as the grave. Speaking of which, the nearby church was forlorn and silent, even the rooks had grown tired of crowing. There was nothing to disturb the security light that had plagued them the night before. Perhaps it was too early in any case. Either way, they were alone and undisturbed.

The question was, how alone?

Jen surveyed the presbytery from the gate. The house looked dark, but she knew it was still light enough outside to prevent her from being certain.

"His car's missing," Jen said – a guess rather than a statement of fact.

"He's probably visiting the orphanage; he usually does that on a Wednesday about eight."

That was all she needed.

Jen opened the gate and walked along the pathway, heading towards the house. She rang the doorbell to ensure that there was no one in.

Anthea was nervous.

Two rings later and still no response.

That settled it.

*

The priory was located to the north of the church and east of the presbytery. A second wall separated it from the presbytery grounds, accessible via a locked gate. In its heyday, the red walls that surrounded the grounds had not been there; instead, moderately sized Romanesque buildings continued across the graveyard and were attached to the church via the cloisters.

Jen stopped by the gate. It was evident from its appearance that this one was older than the first.

"Do you have the key?"

Anthea passed her mother's keys to Jen, unsure which was the one she wanted.

Jen tried them, but clearly none worked.

She walked along the wall, looking for a way in. There was a tree near the wall, easy to climb.

Jen went first, using the branches to reach the top of the wall. The drop was about four metres.

Seconds later they were over.

Jen led the way across the grounds to the ruins. What little remained was hidden among a luxuriant growth of trees, the walls littered with occasional ivy. What remained of the chapter house – a large Gothic opening, now dilapidated and itself laden with greenery – was now the greatest evidence that the priory once had a heyday. To Jen, it was almost impossible to think that this stone skeleton, now little more than a memory of life, was once a thriving, bustling hub of activity. In her mind, she attempted to imagine it as it had been: according to Lovell, the home of over thirty Dominican friars.

The remainder of the priory's story, she did not know. As far as she was aware, no one knew – at least no one living. In the 19th century, Turner had painted it; in the early 20th century, Francis Gasquet had written about it.

But the rest belonged to time itself. Even since the era of the watercolour, much of what was once there had itself been reclaimed by the elements.

For once, Jen had a good idea where she was going. The image on the camera confirmed that the entrance to the secret vault, if that was indeed what it was, would be found in an area overgrown with greenery near the former dormitories. The building itself had practically disappeared, the outline of a large window the main exception.

As the wall ended and the next one started at a right angle to the left, she recognised the image exactly. The light was now going, whereas the photograph had been taken in broad daylight, but the similarities were evident: the height of the wall, the layout of the stone . . .

The only thing missing at present was the entrance.

"Jen, look."

Jen turned. There was a small structure located between the trees, evidently what had once been a grotto.

"Look."

The stones were grey and jagged, but on the whole well built.

"What?"

"Look."

Jen had no idea what she was looking for. She moved closer to the grotto and continued all the way around.

Finally she caught on. There was something beneath it that was not grass – it looked like an iron grille.

Jen checked the images on the camera. One clearly showed the wall of the old chapter house, the second something similar.

There was nothing of the grotto.

She could feel the frustration boiling within her. She followed the wall all the way around and then back again.

Nothing matched what she was looking for.

She returned to the grotto and then through the trees. For the first time she noticed a circular outline in the grass.

"This had once been a well."

Jen got down on her knees and felt the outline with her hands. The grass was longer in this part – at least two and a half inches in height. She could feel detail, unquestionably stone. She reasoned that it had once been part of the well, but the upper part had since been dismantled.

The centre of the well was now grass.

She rose again to her feet, heading for the wall that separated the ruins from the churchyard. The vegetation was rugged, the red brick covered with moss, ivy, and vines coming down from the other side.

"Jen."

The call was loud and excited.

Anthea was pointing at the wall that separated the ruins from the cloisters of the church.

Jen advanced slowly, the greenery so thick she could barely make out the wall.

She felt herself stumble. Though the ground was rugged, it didn't take long for her to realise what had caused her to fall.

The ground beneath her was descending.

The stairway had clearly been part of the former priory.

Jen grabbed the rugged vegetation in front of her and tried her best to move it. She made progress, not enough to see everything but enough to start her way down.

She progressed down twelve steps before coming up against something solid. She activated the flashlight facility on her iPhone and shone it all around.

There was a passageway heading to the right.

"Come on."

43

The car picked the princes up at Maryon Park as prearranged, and took them south, then west along the Old Kent Road. They dropped the driver back home on the way, telling him to take the rest of the night off.

How things had changed since the days of the royal coachmen.

Thomas took over the driving and pulled up in a large car park near a department store. There was a café nearby, quiet and secluded.

The perfect place to think.

Their identities disguised with baseball caps and padded windproof jackets, they went into the café. Thomas ordered a tea and a coffee before joining Stephen at a two-seater table near a window. About a minute later, the same person who took the order brought over the tray.

"One tea and one coffee," he said, placing the drinks in front of Thomas and Stephen.

"Thank you," Thomas said.

Stephen watched the waiter leave, thankful he didn't recognise them. He ripped open the sachet of sugar and poured it into his tea.

"Could do with this." The first sip, his face displayed his disgust. "It tastes like something out of the Thames."

"Is that really all you can think about?"

Stephen placed the cup down on the table. "What would you rather I think about? How we nearly got obliterated?" He wiped his mouth. "What the hell happened?"

Thomas shook his head. "Believe me, I've been asking myself the very s-same question."

He took the first sip of his coffee. His cousin was not wrong.

The taste was horrendous.

"The explosion was activated from the inside," Thomas affirmed, "manual detonation."

"Really, Thomas, how can you be so certain?"

"Before the explosion I heard a f-fizzing sound. Now that could only happen when one substance is added to another. The qu-question is what."

"I have an even better question: who did it and why?"

Thomas bit his lip.

Stephen took another sip of tea. "And here's another one: how did they know we were coming?"

Thomas turned to his left, looking outside the window. It was getting dark, the street illuminated in the orange glow of the streetlamps. Cars passed at regular intervals, left and right.

Turning to his right, Thomas's attention was drawn to a wall-mounted chrome rack holding a number of national and local newspapers.

The front page of the *London Chronicle* caught his eye.

He left his seat, picked it up and examined a banner headline.

"Duke of York victim of assassination attempt . . ."

Stephen was furious. "Give me that."

He scanned the early lines.

"The Duke of York, 57, was declared to be in a stable condition after falling ill while dining . . . a spokesman for the palace claimed the duke had suffered a mild heart attack . . ."

There was a second article.

"Assassination attempt linked with the murder of politicians . . ."

Stephen threw the paper down on the table. "How the hell did they know all this?"

Thomas was equally lost for words. He picked up the paper and began reading the second article. While the one on the duke was extremely short, the breaking news on the front page, the second article was far longer and continued on pages four and five.

Thomas was horrified. "According to an insider, the R-Royal Family have long been p-plagued by the threats of a m-malicious operation. They r-refused to comment on reports that the m-murders of the politicians were themselves c-connected to the death of King James III, who p-passed away less than four weeks ago."

Stephen snatched the paper for a second time, his face registering his fury.

"How dare they print this!"

Thomas took a deep breath, also struggling to control his anger. "Who was the journalist?"

Stephen checked. "Neil Atkins."

"I suggest we pay him a visit."

44

The way was shut. Judging by the condition of the bars, it had been for some time.

Jen attempted to open the gate. As far as she could tell, there was no lock on it, but the evidence of rust, particularly around the hinges, made it obvious she was in for a challenge.

She tried shaking it, pushing it and pulling it. Pulling it worked, but slowly. A couple of minutes later she had opened it about eighteen inches – not a lot, but enough to get through.

The passageway wound from left to right. The walls were made of stone on either side, as was the ceiling, cold but relatively smooth. Judging by its appearance, it had been constructed in the Middle Ages, almost certainly at the same time as the priory. The ground beneath them was solid and complete rather than made up of slabs.

Whatever it was, it had been built to last.

Jen shone the light in front of her. There were cobwebs everywhere, particularly on the ceiling. She could feel them touching the side of her face as she walked.

"I hate spiders, I hate spiders, I hate them, I hate them, I hate them . . ."

An open doorway on the left revealed a chamber. There were objects inside, possibly tombs.

She shone the light in the middle of the chamber.

"Paupers' graves," Jen guessed. Whatever it was, it was in too dilapidated a state to know for sure.

Standing by the doorway, Anthea was nervous. "Don't touch anything. You might catch something."

Jen doubted that.

Nevertheless, she decided to move on.

The passageway contained four similar burial chambers. In each case there were only a handful of tombs, all of which were ruined. As far as she could see, there were no names on the outside.

Whoever was buried there, it was unlikely they were people of prominence.

The sixth chamber was different, the archway curiously elaborate, as was the interior. The style was Romanesque, with writing above the door, illegible after centuries of wear.

There were several graves, all of which had an effigy atop the slab. Jen wandered around the left side of the room while Anthea took the right. There were puddles and debris on the floor.

It was unclear where the water had come from.

Anthea walked alongside the grave with the largest effigy. "There's writing here."

"What's it say?"

"I don't know; I can't read Latin."

Jen decided to look for herself. She shone the torch on the verge.

"There but for the grace of God . . . Edward Stanley, died 1566."

The others were also Stanleys of the same era.

Jen allowed herself a moment to gather her thoughts. "The dates are getting older; we must be getting closer."

They passed two more chambers, neither of which seemed to contain anything physical. For the first time Jen considered the possibility that there was actually something in the priest's plague victims' story, at least indirectly. The graves were old and heavily weathered. If there was any truth in it, most likely they were from the 14th century rather than the 17th.

Nevertheless, she was still to find anything that old.

The evidence came in the next chamber, the largest so far. The roof was vaulted, reminiscent of catacombs.

Whatever it was, it had clearly been built for a specific purpose.

There were tombs everywhere, arranged in some kind of order. Most of them lined the walls: they were short, flat, and contained some kind of symbol on the top. The light from their phones revealed it was a long cross, with Calvary steps at the base.

"This is where the friars are buried."

"How can you tell?" Anthea asked, joining her from across the room.

"It's obvious from the symbol," Jen said. "Only a cleric or someone of a monastic order can be buried with a long cross and botonny base. It depicts Christ's death on Calvary."

There were more graves in the centre of the chamber, these containing an effigy on top of the slab. There was also writing along the verge.

"Reginald, prior of St Michael's, died 1384."

It took several seconds for the find to sink in. The grave was nearly seven hundred years old.

"Wow."

Jen finished her inspection of the elaborate tombs. Once done, she moved on to the ones lining the walls. She finished at the far wall, opposite where they had entered the chamber. She concluded that the surrounding graves were those of the friars, while the ones in the centre, the more prominent graves, belonged to the priors.

The chamber contained a further doorway, this one even larger, leading in the same direction.

Jen sensed that this was the one she had been looking for.

At 9:45 Father Martin's Vauxhall Corsa made its way along the driveway, heading towards the presbytery. It was getting dark outside, the ruins of the priory nearly invisible.

He entered the presbytery through the front door and punched in the four-digit code to deactivate the alarm.

Something was wrong. Though he had entered the code correctly, a second red light was still flashing. He had seen it only once before – exactly a year ago.

Someone had entered the restricted vault.

45

The editor of the *London Chronicle* was still in his office after 10 p.m. Most of the journalists had gone home, and he knew that his floor was deserted.

It was something of a surprise when he heard two lots of heavy footsteps approaching his office.

The princes entered side by side, Stephen carrying a copy of the *Chronicle*. Thomas knocked, but both entered without invite.

"Care to explain this?" Stephen asked. He threw the paper down on the desk.

The editor was gobsmacked. He recognised the Duke of Cornwall, but not the person with him.

"Well?"

The editor remained seated, merely staring.

"How dare you write this sort of thing about my family!"

Thomas, meanwhile, monitored the editor from across the desk. He was bearded, brown haired, and aged probably somewhere between fifty and sixty. It looked as if the man had endured quite a long day.

"Mr Symons," Thomas said, attracting his attention, "my name is Thomas Winchester, son of the Duke of Clarence–"

"How on earth did you know that the duke had been taken unwell?" Stephen interrupted. "I demand to know your source!"

"Mr Symons–" Thomas began.

"The duke is aware of the article and has already consulted his lawyers." Stephen pointed his finger at the editor. "I swear to God–"

"Stephen, please . . . Mr Symons," Thomas spoke only to the editor, "you have an opportunity here to make the best of a bad situation. Where is Mr Atkins?"

The editor remained speechless.

"Mr Symons."

The man made eye contact with Thomas for the first time. His expression was gaunt and clearly overwhelmed.

"Mr Symons. Where is Atkins?"

"He-he's gone for the day," the editor finally muttered. "Be in tomorrow."

"We must see him tonight. What is his address?"

The man, clearly stunned by the unexpected presence of his high-profile visitors, made no reply.

"WHAT IS HIS ADDRESS?" Stephen demanded.

The editor scrambled for his mouse. "It's here, somewhere . . ." After a few seconds he started feverishly checking his desk drawers before returning his attention to the computer.

He found the address listed in a staff database.

Thomas wrote it down on a piece of paper. "Come on."

From behind his desk, the editor watched with a blank expression as the son of the Duke of Clarence left the office.

"You're, you're not going to hurt him?"

Stephen delayed his exit. "Take a good look around, editor. After all, you never know when it might be your last."

Thomas grabbed Stephen's arm. "Come on."

He looked back at the editor and could see that the man was close to tears.

"Thank you, Mr Symons."

Thomas and Stephen left the building via the staircase and through the electronic doors that led out onto the street. Like a number of other London newspapers, the *Chronicle*'s headquarters was in the London Borough of Tower Hamlets. The journey from the Old Kent Road had taken less than twenty minutes through the Rotherhithe Tunnel.

Judging from Atkins' address, the next journey would be about the same.

They had parked on the main road, about fifty metres from the entrance.

"What the bloody hell was that about?" Thomas asked as he started the car.

"What?"

"Wh-what do you mean, what? Accusations of lying, lawyers, f-for all we know, Uncle Bill hasn't even seen it!"

Stephen opened the window and began to smoke. "Never hurts to keep the bastards on their feet."

Thomas breathed out heavily. He stopped the car at a red light and entered the postcode of the address he had been given by Symons into the GPS.

The result was somewhere in between Barking and West Ham. He waited for the lights to change before flooring the accelerator. If luck was to hold, they would arrive well before eleven.

46

Jen felt her breathing become more intense. The archway was peculiarly large and seemed a suspicious and ostentatious prelude for the chamber they were about to enter.

She had never been so nervous. Or excited. The combination was alluring, but also strangely unique. It was different to a nice surprise – a birthday present, Christmas morning, the start of a holiday – but there was definitely a feeling of anticipation.

She feared the unknown more than the prospect of further graves.

The light was non-existent, even compared to a few minutes earlier. As best she could tell, the chamber was even larger than the previous one. The air had improved, despite the smells becoming more dominant. If she was where she thought she was, it was probably about the size of the Jeffries' vault. Ideally she needed to see it in the daytime.

Not that that was likely.

She heard a faint cry from several metres away.

"Anthea."

"Sorry. I just lost me footing."

Jen exhaled, relieved. The last thing they needed was an injury.

She shone the phone light in every direction. She could see objects, somehow more foreboding in appearance than the previous chamber. There were statues, possibly wall markings and other things normally found inside the church itself. There were tombs, as she had expected, but these were definitely more elaborate than the ones she had seen so far.

Without question this was what Debra Harrison had photographed.

Father Martin left the house immediately, carrying a torch and a shotgun. He decided against informing the owners of the vault. Instead, he opened the gate that led to the priory ruins and headed across the grounds of the estate.

There was a stone stairway that led into the crypt near the wall. He had never used it, but he'd been told it was there. He shone the torch on the wall and found it almost instantly. The vegetation, though thick, was not how he had expected it to be.

The vines had been moved.

Jen took a deep breath, in then out. The air was dank, perhaps less so than the other chambers, but its effects were far worse. It was the darkness that did it, her other senses accommodating for the decreased visibility.

She couldn't remember a time when she had experienced anything so pitch black.

The first tomb was located close to the entrance. It was large in height, length and depth and contained a fine effigy of an elegant-looking man lying with his hands together. There was colour on the outline, possibly maroon, the coating partially worn away. He wore some kind of headwear, though definitely not a helmet.

It looked like a crown.

Jen walked to one side and looked along the verge. There was Latin writing on it.

"*Ricardus VII, Rex Angliae.*"

She translated.

"Richard VII. King of England. 1612–1622."

She stood there, totally lost.

Richard VII?

There had never been such a monarch.

She moved on to the next, this one equally strange. Richard VI, 1566–1612.

Anthea had joined her, also holding up her phone. The extra light was useful, allowing Jen an opportunity to take in all of the inscriptions.

"I don't understand," Anthea said. "Who were these people?"

Jen shook her head, dumbstruck. She pointed the light at Anthea, causing her pupils to contract. Against the dark background, her skin looked even whiter than usual.

"Is this the room you saw when you were young?"

"I think so . . . Jen, can we leave now, please."

Secretly she wanted nothing more. The potential seriousness of the discovery, combined with the foulness of the air, was becoming increasingly difficult to stomach.

"Not yet."

Jen moved onto the next, studying the tombs one by one. She read each name as she passed, making a mental note of them. Names repeated themselves: Richards V–X, Edwards VI–VIII, Johns II–V, and Williams III–VII.

What seemed strangest was how different they were to the real kings of the same name. She had studied history; she knew who Edward VI, VII and William III and IV were.

She knew what she was looking at should not exist.

Jen continued around the far side of the chamber, taking in as much as her eyes would allow. There were things on the walls, possibly paintings or else stained-glass windows – strange considering they were so far underground. There were other decorations, swords, shields, and other things that seemed suspiciously regal.

Whoever these people were, they were clearly revered.

She followed the tombs to the far wall and found a door. She recognised the outline; it was the same one she had tried to open the day before. She tried opening it, but again found that it was locked.

She continued to explore, every tomb seemingly offering more of the same. She saw three in a row, starting with Edward IX, died 1688.

To Jen, the date stood out.

It was the man who had attracted her interest at Bishopton.

Who Lovell claimed was a Barghest.

Jen examined this one in greater detail. Based on the effigy, he was a large man, strong in stature, bearded and with large eyes. She looked for an inscription along the side of the tomb. Like the others, it was written in gold on red.

Yet again referred to as a King of England.

She took in the detail as best she could in the dim light. The effigy seemed to depict a young man of warrior-like appearance.

She now had proof the story recited by Lovell was untrue.

"Come on, let's go."

"Jen."

The cry was soft and desperate, the tone enough to make the hairs on the back of her neck stand on end. Numbed by uncertainty, she walked slowly between the tombs and stopped on reaching Anthea, who was standing by the final wall, shaking.

In front of them were four tombs, perhaps the most elaborate in the crypt. There was something on the wall behind them, though neither of them could make out what it was.

Jen approached the first tomb and read the inscription. The Latin translated:

"Edward V, King of England, March–November 1483."

She looked at the effigy in detail. It was surely the tomb of a boy.

She moved on, speechless. The next tomb was even more elaborate. The man was a fine figure, although slightly smaller than most. The first thing she noticed was that his shoulders were slightly out of line.

She translated the inscription aloud: "In memory of King Richard III of England, whose body was buried in the Franciscan church of . . ."

She froze, unable to finish the sentence. She tried to catch her breath, but doing so was becoming difficult. She moved on to the next and looked carefully for a name.

This one was a joint tomb, a man named Edward Plantagenet, 17th Earl of Warwick. Beside him was a woman. The inscription read, Lady Elizabeth, daughter of Edward IV.

Impossible! The woman had married Henry VII.

Finally she moved on to the fourth and final tomb. This was also a joint tomb, a man and his wife.

She looked at the name on the inscription.

Less than three hundred metres away, the priest navigated the tunnels with the aid of his flashlight. He was cold, despite the jacket, and completely unprepared for what might await him.

Still, he had come this far.

He remembered what the master had told him on his arrival all those years ago. Four simple words.

Dishonour leads to hell.

47

The drive was completed within fifteen minutes. The journalist's house, a typical London/Essex two-storey 1930s semi, was located on a moderately busy road and had a white garage door and a small front garden. A blue Ford was parked on the driveway.

There were lights on inside the house.

Thomas stopped briefly outside the house before continuing further along the road. He parked in the most secluded place possible, a leafy area in front of a house with a large garden.

They both got out of the car.

"You think it's safe?" Stephen asked.

Thomas grinned. "We're not in Helmand Province."

"I was talking about the car, cretin. I mean, you hear stories about these places."

"Why, they are hardly going to get away with stealing a royal B-Bentley. These things do have a t-tendency to stick out."

They headed up the road towards the driveway of the house. Aside from the lights, there were few signs of life on the street itself.

Thomas rang the doorbell and waited for a response. Alongside him, Stephen was getting impatient.

"You're quite sure this is the place?"

"It's the address we were given."

Stephen also pressed the doorbell. "I suppose he could be otherwise indisposed."

Thomas laughed under his breath. "All the more reason to be patient."

He rang the bell again.

Neil Atkins had been home for just under an hour. As a thirty-five-year-old living alone, Wednesday night entertainment consisted of only two reasonable choices: he could either stay in and watch the telly or go over the road to the White Swan. He'd spent a lot of time there recently – beer certainly took the sting out of the divorce. Tonight, however, he was in no mood to go out. His lamb rogan josh, fresh out of the microwave, was still piping hot and created a warm sensation on his lap through the tray. The TV was playing an episode of *EastEnders*, which he had Sky Plused earlier in the week.

He was halfway through his curry when the doorbell rang. He paused with his fork halfway to his mouth, undecided whether or not to answer. He waited until the second ring, followed by a third, fourth, fifth, sixth, seventh, and eighth. He placed the tray down on the coffee table and pressed pause on the TV's remote control.

Two strangers were standing outside the front door. Both were smartly dressed and over six feet in height.

"Mr Atkins?" the more athletic of the two asked.

"Yes."

"So sorry to b-bother you at home," Thomas continued, "but it is most important that we speak with you. Time is really of the essence."

The man was annoyed. "What the hell are you . . . my God . . . it's you."

Stephen took a step forward. "You don't mind if we come in, do you?"

Thomas took a deep breath and exhaled fiercely.

At least they were in.

He closed the door behind him and followed them into the lounge.

Atkins was rattled. "Look, if this is about that damn article, my information came from the best of sources."

Stephen was unimpressed. "What sources?"

"You know I can't say."

"Who told you that the duke had been taken unwell?"

"I don't know . . . I had a call from somebody who claimed to have been there."

"You mean at the restaurant?"

"Yes."

"That's funny; it happened in a hotel."

"Oh, for heaven's sake."

"Wh-what do you know about the attacks against the monarchy?" Thomas asked.

"I know nothing."

"But you mentioned them in your article," Stephen said.

"I only know what I've been told."

"What was that?"

"I-I-I can't say."

254

Stephen picked him up by the scruff of his neck and flung him against the wall.

"Stephen," Thomas shouted.

"Tell me your source."

The man was bewildered. "My God, you're both mad . . . that's criminal assault . . ."

"Tell me your source."

"I could have this all over the front page . . . West Ham knocked out by Cornwall!"

"Right, have it your way." Stephen removed the Glock from his pocket and aimed it at the man's temple.

"Stephen . . ."

"My God."

"Who told you about the politicians?"

The journalist stuttered terribly. "I-I-I-I-I only have what I was told."

"Which was?"

"What's written in the article."

"And your source?"

"I swear I don't know."

Stephen aimed the weapon and pushed powerfully against the man's head.

"All right, all right, okay, okay, okay, Jeez Laweez, my God . . ."

"Who was your source?" This time the question came from Thomas.

"He never told me his real name."

"Then how did you find him?"

"I didn't – he found me."

"Liar." Stephen spat the word out with venom.

"No."

"How?" Thomas asked.

"He knew I'd been writing about the politicians and the King . . . he told me there was foul play."

"Who was he?"

"Told you before; he never told me his real name."

"What did he tell you?" Thomas asked.

"Only what you saw in the article."

"He's lying," Stephen said again.

"How did he contact you?" Thomas asked.

"Usually by phone."

"Usually?"

"Yes."

"But not always?"

"We met once."

"Where?" Stephen asked.

"Richmond Park."

"When?" Thomas asked.

"Yesterday."

"Describe him." Again the question came from Thomas.

"He was old–"

"How old?"

"Early eighties–"

"How about appearance?" This time the question came from Stephen.

"I don't know, he was bald, some grey hair, perhaps white."

"He's lying," Stephen said.

"What else?" Thomas asked.

"He wore sunglasses. And the suit . . . old habits die hard, that sort of thing."

"What made you so c-certain he was genuine?"

"I don't know – instinct."

"Your instinct is going to find you in prison," Stephen said.

"He said he'd lived at the palace."

"Capacity?"

The man was now desperate..

"For the last time," Stephen said, "who was your fucking source?"

"He didn't tell me his name. But he said he came to me to avert a catastrophe because the royals had a tendency for not being able to look further than the end of their noses."

The words caught Thomas cold. It felt like a gun had gone off, but inside him.

"Wh-what did he look like?" Thomas stuttered. "Facially?"

"I told you before. He was going bald."

"Did he have a scar?" Thomas pointed to his right cheek.

The man did not respond immediately. "Why, yes. And not an ordinary scar."

"In what way?" Stephen asked.

"It was rather large – and cross shaped. Like a war scar."

Thomas nodded. He felt as though the air had left him.

"And he had another – on his right hand."

"You're quite sure it wasn't the left?" Thomas asked.

The journalist looked at his hands. "Yes, the left, my right looking at him. I mean, it all gets so confusing."

"Not that confusing," Stephen retorted.

The journalist looked up at him, emotionally drained.

Thomas walked closer to the journalist and offered his hand. "Thank you, Mr Atkins. My cousin and I will take it from here."

48

Jen was still shaking. The light of the phone moved like a firefly, dancing from side to side.

She grabbed her left wrist with her right hand in an attempt to control the jumpiness. With that under control, she read the name on the tomb for the second time, then the third, fourth, fifth . . .

She could not believe what she was seeing.

Anthea was now seriously worried. "What is it?"

Jen was at a loss to explain.

After failing to get a response from Jen, Anthea looked at the tomb for herself.

"Ricardus . . ." Anthea was confused. "I can't read Latin."

"In English it says Richard IV, reigned August 1485 to October 1529."

She headed to the other side of the chamber and attempted to take a photograph. Unsurprisingly, she got little more than a blur.

Failing that, she removed Debra Harrison's camera from her pocket. She changed the ISO setting and sat it down on one of the nearby tombs. She held it still and attempted to take a picture. The flash lit up the entire room, momentarily blinding.

She looked at the quality.

For the first time she saw other things hanging from the walls. It was like being in a castle, only underground.

Now she was seriously getting spooked.

"Okay. Let's go."

Anthea was visibly relieved. She followed Jen back towards the entrance, but almost immediately Jen came to a standstill.

"Jen?"

"Shhh . . . listen."

For several seconds neither of them spoke.

There was something moving in one of the nearby passageways.

Both girls were frozen with fear. There was no way out and only the darkness of the room to hide them.

"Switch off the light."

Anthea did so immediately. With the light gone, her breathing became considerably louder.

"Shhh."

Jen did the same for her phone and then the camera. As she did, she saw on the camera's LCD display something located beyond the tombs.

It looked like another passageway.

"Quick." She grabbed Anthea's hand and headed straight for the area she had seen on the screen. Despite the darkness, a vague outline was visible. Whether it was a doorway, a passageway, or something smaller, she was still unsure.

She entered it and held her breath.

The priest entered the priors' vault and paused. There was light up ahead, small but moving.

His heart was thumping. He feared the idea of intruders, but he feared the paranormal more. There was no logical explanation for the light. It was too small to be a torch – yet it moved too wildly to be anything else.

He took a deep breath.

Suddenly the light went out.

Jen edged closer to the wall. They had entered the recently discovered passageway, its appearance not unlike the previous one. The passage headed upwards and east – that was her best guess.

She prayed it was another way out.

Father Martin stopped on reaching the next archway.

The interior was impeccable. Had the circumstances been different, he might well have stayed there to admire it. He had seen them before – but never from this direction.

And never in this light.

He entered the kings' vault and shone the torch in every direction. He saw nothing unusual, aside from what he knew he was meant to see. Whatever made that strange ghostly light had now disappeared.

He walked towards the door that led back into the main vaults and affirmed it was shut.

Whatever had made the light must be hidden amongst the tombs.

*

Jen kept edging backwards. There was light coming from the vault, moving slowly. Initially it shone on the other side of the room, then nearer.

Then it came overhead.

She ducked.

The priest was stumped. There was nothing there. Nor was there evidence of anything amiss.

"Show yourself!"

Anthea felt her heart try to escape her chest. She recognised the voice of Father Martin.

Immediately she felt a hand cover her mouth.

The priest heard something.

Were his senses deceiving him?

It sounded like breathing.

Jen edged backwards, guiding Anthea with her hands. Moving without paying attention to her feet was a risk, but she couldn't take her eyes off the light.

The passageway continued upwards. Like the other corridor, it was stone, vaulted and very smooth beneath her feet.

The light from the other room was moving in a different direction.

She turned and for the first time started walking forward.

The priest called out again, his voice echoing. He considered turning off the light, but realised that would be foolish.

God knows what could happen if he exposed himself.

He shone the torch on the next wall. A large tapestry hung behind the most important of the kings, its once fine appearance ruined by centuries of decay. The sight of it made him shudder.

He breathed in deeply and then out again.

Then he heard movement from somewhere close by.

Jen's pace had picked up. She continued to hold Anthea's hand, doing her best to reassure her.

"Come on, we're nearly there."

That was a guess, but Anthea accepted it.

The tunnel passed several rooms, all of which appeared empty and contained nothing of interest. Even if they did, Jen was in no frame of mind to study them.

Suddenly the light changed. There was an outline visible in front of them, square shaped.

"Come on," Jen said. "We're nearly there."

The priest found the passageway by accident. Though aware of its existence, he had never seen it before.

He wandered about twenty metres along and stopped. He sensed there was something in front of him, but he couldn't see it, even with the torch.

After several seconds he abandoned the chase.

He knew all too well where the passageway ended.

The tunnel ended unexpectedly: no steps, no variation in the slope, no warning whatsoever. Jen knew from the incline that they had been heading upwards, probably about ten degrees.

They came, out side by side in an area of dense greenery. Though neither of them had any idea where they were, it was obvious the area had not been cared for.

There was a house to their right, large and well lit. Jen could tell from the layout that it was one of the Ravensfield mansions.

For the first time she noticed ruins around her.

"This is a castle," Jen said. She had been expecting the priory. "This is the castle."

Anthea was now seriously worried. "We're in Lord Jeffries' garden. He never lets anyone on his land."

The penny had completely dropped.

Jen looked around the grounds, studying every possible detail. Although it was dark, she was still able to make out the layout.

"Where's the best way out?"

"I don't know."

"Think, Anthea. You know the village better than me."

The poor girl racked her brain. "The church is over there." She pointed. "The path that we walked yesterday is over there."

That told Jen they needed to walk away from the house.

"Let's get out before anybody sees us."

At around the same time, the biker pulled up at the gateway of Wootton Court. Travelling all that way by bike had been difficult, but he knew he had little choice.

He waited for the gate to open before continuing along the driveway. He parked in the usual place, along the side of the house, and was escorted inside by the butler.

Jeffries was having supper at the time. He was seated in the usual place: the head of the table. The setting was ostentatious and rich in candelabra, all of which were lit. Five sets of grand silver tableware had been placed at equal intervals on a white tablecloth that covered the entire table. Numerous paintings and other works of art were hung on the walls, and a large log fire was blazing brightly in the fireplace, though, given the size of the room, clearly more for decoration than warmth.

Four other people were present.

Facing Jeffries, at the opposite end of the table, Sir William Catesby was enjoying his soup. The remaining guests were Ratcliffe, Lovell and Stanley, who was clearly surprised by the unexpected arrival of his son.

"Burghart?"

He ignored his father. "Forgive the disturbance, gentlemen; I assure you it is most necessary."

Jeffries' expression was hostile. "You think of us as dumb, or deaf, or blind? They have been talking about your incompetence on the television for hours."

"It is true that things have not gone to plan," he replied, addressing Jeffries. He then looked seriously at the man nearest to him.

"Lord Ratcliffe, I'm grieved to inform you that your nephew is dead."

Less than a mile away, Caroline pulled up on the high street and switched off the engine. She had not seen the biker for over three hours, but she was aware from her communication with the palace that the satellites had tracked it to her present location.

The village of Wootton-on-the-Moor.

She removed her mobile phone from the hands-free holder and scanned the contacts list. She had not spoken to Thomas or Stephen for well over three hours.

The Home Secretary was appalled by what he had just heard.

"Absolutely not; it's not only out of the question but illegal."

He placed his hands to his head, feeling sweat on his forehead.

West understood his concerns. "I admit it's a gamble," he returned. "But worth it."

The Home Secretary shook his head.

"If anyone asks, Minister, deny the whole thing."

49

Thomas pulled up outside a mansion in Richmond. The house was Palladian design: Georgian and grandiose with a brilliant white exterior.

Thomas monitored the entrance from the gateway. Like the previous house, the lights were on.

Stephen's expression was stern. "Shall we?"

Thomas was far more disheartened. "If it's all the same to you, I'd rather do this one alone."

The man with the scar was in the library when the doorbell rang. About three minutes later the butler entered and announced his distinguished guest.

"Prince Thomas, sir."

The man with the scar removed his monocle and turned in his seat. The prince was well dressed, but looked slightly exhausted.

He smiled at his former protégé. "Come on in, old boy, don't stand on ceremony."

"I'll bring tea immediately," the butler said, departing.

Thomas remained standing by the doorway. He forced an awkward smile, the best he could muster. His heart was suddenly feeling heavy. He had seen the library, the personal pride of James Gardiner, on many occasions. Several watercolour and oil paintings lined large cream-coloured walls that always seemed immaculate. The smell of old library-bound leather teased the nostrils. He guessed at least ten thousand books and manuscripts filled the shelves of the thirty-plus bookcases that lined every corner of the room.

The setting was the same as usual, but today it seemed slightly different somehow.

He looked at the man, a man he had known his entire life.

James Gardiner.

Earl of Somerset.

Brother of the late queen.

Uncle of his father and the current king.

His great-uncle.

The man smiled at him. "You're up late tonight, Tom. Everything all right?"

The silence was unsettling. The prince detected the man's unease.

"All these books," Thomas said, wandering one way then the other. "A life well spent?"

The old man was confused. "As you know, most of them were gifts, many from your grandfather I might add . . . forgive me, old fellow, but is everything all right?"

Thomas's grin developed into an awkward laugh. "I don't really know; it's been quite a long day." He shook his head. "And how about you, Uncle? H-how you been diddling?"

Gardiner raised an eyebrow. "Does your father know you use language like that?"

"As far as I'm aware my f-father doesn't know I'm here. In fact, there are many things my f-father doesn't know. Nor his brother, f-for that matter."

Gardiner was completely baffled. "What are you talking about?"

"You've been watching the news, I-I assume?"

"Bits of it."

"You've n-no doubt heard about the explosion in Greenwich."

"Should I?"

The prince shrugged. "I was there, you know – Stephen and I. Blown up it was, b-by the Sons of York."

The butler returned carrying a tray of cutlery and the usual tea service.

"Will that be all, sir?"

He left receiving no response.

The earl waited until the butler had left. "My dear fellow, it sounds as if you've had quite an ordeal. Sit, have some tea."

Thomas watched as the earl poured tea into two cups, followed by sugar.

"I know, Jimmy," the prince said softly.

The historian didn't catch on. "What on earth are you talking about?"

"I saw the article in the *Chronicle*. I s-spoke to the j-journalist."

He looked him in the eye.

"I know you leaked the information. I know you told him about my grandfather's murder."

Gardiner remained unmoved. His expression was stern, but his body language confirmed the bombshell.

"My dear boy, you're delirious, you–"

"Don't lie to me," Thomas shouted. He tried for several seconds to get the words out. "After all these years."

"Really, Tom, it's not as bad as all that."

He shook his head. "Why?"

The man stirred his tea, his eyes never leaving the prince. "All right, if you really want to know: because you and your silly relatives remain incapable of seeing beyond the end of your bloody noses. Ever since the death of my beloved sister I tried to warn your father, your uncle, your grandfather, about the dangers posed by the Sons of York, and all I got was to be shot down."

He pointed his finger at the prince.

"Finally I have your attention. Finally I've made you listen."

He said the final word loudly.

"What are you babbling about?"

The old man laughed. "Your speech is improving, Tom. Therapy working, is it? You should be proud of yourself. It takes great character to overcome the things you've had to."

He looked up at the prince, who was standing with his arms folded.

"Come, sit, have some tea before it goes cold."

Thomas didn't move. "You never told me about the Sons of York. I'd have listened."

"Would you? Like two days ago, when you motored past me in the grounds? The next day when you refused to answer my call?"

"I was in a hurry then."

"And now?" the old man said, concentrating on the prince. "You know, once upon a time I would have been taken seriously. You know the Sons of York were once believed by your ancestors to be the greatest threat posed to the kingdom. George III went mad with worry; Victoria nearly abdicated because of their threats."

"Don't patronise me, Jim."

"You think I'm fibbing?" He shook his head. "An historian's only aim is to find out the truth, you know that."

"There's a difference between truth and fact."

"Only in definition, come on, Tom, game playing gets us nowhere."

He agreed with that. "Go on. I'm here, listening." He checked his watch. "It's 11:45 p.m., and I have nowhere left to go. So, please, Jim, I demand an explanation."

The old man set himself up for a long story.

"I suppose in a way, like all great kings, your grandfather, too, was made to suffer the curse of the monarch. No fewer than six attempts were made on his life of which I am aware. Two, we can put down to lone wolves. Three were from abroad. The other . . . well . . ."

Thomas bit his lip. It was obvious he was talking about the event that killed him.

"Prior to the First World War, and again just after, there were a group of intelligence officers known as the OWLS. It basically meant all-seeing. There were about twelve officers in all. In the wars they moved more in military campaigns. Then your grandfather, in agreement with the Cabinet, disbanded them."

"Why?"

"Apparently they believed they served no future purpose," Gardiner said, sipping his tea. "In my opinion that was possibly the greatest mistake of the past century."

For several seconds nothing was said.

Thomas broke the silence. "Who were they? The Sons of York, wh-who are they now?"

"You know exactly who they are now; you've met them."

"I know only that they were sh-shooting at me. Who are they?"

The historian said nothing, instead concentrating intently on his tea. Thomas finally sat down. He picked up his teacup and sipped from it. "Earl Grey. You always did like tea with lemon."

"Don't patronize me, you ungrateful berk. More often than not, it's overconfidence that leads to demise."

The prince bit his tongue. "Jim, for God's sake. What happened?"

The man sat back in his chair. "I suppose in a way it all goes back to the early years."

"What? The 1950s?"

"No. The 1060s. Or perhaps of greater relevance, the 1370s.

"One might argue it all began with Edward III. Now there was a monarch. You know all about him, of course? Son of Edward II, grandson of Edward I, great-grandson of Henry III, great-great-grandson of King John–"

"Dammit, Jim." The shout caused the china to move. "Get to the damn point."

The old man saw fire in the prince's eyes.

"In many ways, Edward III was the perfect monarch. He was brave, just, kind . . .

266

"The problem was that Edward III reigned too long and had far too many children. His successor should have been called Edward IV, but unfortunately England's greatest king that never was died a year too early, in 1376. A legend in his own right, I'm sure you know of whom I speak."

"The Black Prince."

The historian nodded. "The Black Prince was famed throughout all of Europe as the next great King of England. But prior to that time, among his five adult sons, King Edward III created England's first ever dukedoms: Cornwall, Gloucester, Lancaster, York, and, alas, Clarence."

Thomas noticed the unnecessary emphasis on Clarence.

The earl resumed, "In time, on such decisions, the fate of England would rest. With the Black Prince dead, the right of succession fell to his son rather than one of his younger brothers. The problem was, the new heir was far too young, a minor by all accounts, forced to rule over an England dominated by dukes. You know, of course, of whom I speak."

"Richard II."

"Hmm. Richard II was never under any circumstances fit to rule as King of England during the 1380s. His inability to impose his authority led to revolt by peasant and nobleman alike. But even more importantly, the king failed to father an heir. Without a direct successor, the throne was set to pass to the young Edmund Mortimer. Until, however, it was usurped by another."

"Bolingbroke."

"Eldest son of John of Gaunt, and henceforth Henry IV. Indirectly, the man responsible for this whole web of intrigue and first upholder of the line of Lancaster."

The historian refilled his cup.

"You think we might sk-skip the history lesson?" Thomas asked.

"You asked me about the Sons of York."

"I did. However, I was thinking more along the l-lines of their r-relevance to the p-present."

The earl was unmoved. "To understand the activities of the present, it is vital one first understands their motives. The answers to all that has happened, recently and before, began on the battlefields of Medieval England."

Thomas remained silent.

"Rebellions by the Mortimers achieved little, and when Bolingbroke died, humbled and slightly paranoid, it was up to his son, Henry V, to pacify a still-troubled nation."

Thomas waited until he was sure that the man had stopped speaking. "Didn't he?"

"I should say that he did. But then history played its greatest trick: the perfect king died young. Thus began the reign of Henry V's infant son: henceforth Henry VI."

The earl sipped again from his tea and placed his cup down on the saucer.

"Of course, to make matters worse, the brothers of Henry V produced no legitimate offspring. When the new king's uncle, the Duke of Bedford, died in 1435, the thirteen-year-old king was left with nothing but a council of quarrelsome meddlers. In fourteen short years, the position of the House of Lancaster had slipped from secure to susceptible, while that of the House of York had strengthened considerably. The land in France was lost; the king's reputation suffered. Whereas his father had been strong, the son was seen to be weak.

"Over the next twenty years, the fate of England rested on a knife edge. During that time, more uprisings and rebellions are documented to have occurred than at any other time since the Conquest.

"Can you imagine?" he asked. "Imagine what it was like living in such uncertainty. The battles were among the bloodiest ever witnessed. Reputable men were put to death at the drop of a hat. And for what? The fortunes and grievances of unprincipled men whose own tenuous claims to the throne were tainted by the actions not only of their forebears but also their own kin."

"May I remind you that you are speaking of my ancestors."

The old man laughed. "You sound so sure."

"Am I wrong?"

Gardiner's expression was stern. "Do you have any idea what it meant to be a King of England at such a time? The Lancastrian dominance was finally cut short in 1461 when the king was usurped by Edward, Earl of March, henceforth Edward IV. This charismatic young man was on a road to prominence, until he decided his penis was more important than his realm. His marriage to the young commoner, Elizabeth Woodville, infuriated the nobles, including most importantly, the man history would remember as Warwick the Kingmaker – the most powerful and treacherous man of his day. No sooner had Warwick defected to the Lancastrians than was Henry VI back on the throne."

"But only for one year," Thomas said.

"The Battle of Tewkesbury in 1471 shall forever be remembered as one of the bloodiest to besmirch our green and pleasant land. But it is what came afterwards that would always be of greater importance.

"The Lancastrian line may have ended, but when Edward died suddenly in 1483, probably from a STD, the can of worms that had been sealed shut for so many years finally exploded. Edward V became king, then he simply disappeared . . .

"Or so the history books tend to claim."

Thomas remembered what Wilson had told him. He watched the historian rise to his feet.

"Follow me, if you feel it's worthy of your time."

Beneath the Tower of London, Edmondes heard cries of consternation coming from the main corridor. It was after midnight, and such things were unheard of.

He left his office and headed rapidly in the direction of the sound. As he did so, he heard gunfire. He went for his Glock, only to realise it was too late.

Four men dressed in black and white robes were standing in the middle of the main corridor, each armed with automatic weapons.

"Good evening, Constable," one of the four said in a voice that was both deep and hard. "Take us to the prisoner."

Choiceless, the four hooded men frogmarched Edmondes through the maximum security doors, heading towards the most exclusive area of the prison. Seconds later they were outside Morris's cell.

"Open it," the leader demanded of Edmondes.

"Are you mad?"

The leader of the four raised his gun. "You're no use to any of us dead, Constable."

Out of options, Edmondes placed his palm to the scanner, and the electronic cell opened.

"Get in."

Edmondes obeyed.

Morris bowed before his brothers.

The leader of the four threw him a weapon. "We're needed back north by sunrise."

Outside the Tower, the new Justice Secretary was sitting in the backseat of the car when the door opened. Barely able to hide his disgust, he watched as Morris quickly got in.

Seconds later, they were away.

50

They entered a room on the first floor, not quite a living room but not far off. Like most in the house, it was painted white, ornately furnished with antiques and well lit by Georgian-style chandeliers.

One feature took the breath away.

The walls were covered in masterpieces.

"Christ, Jimmy – there's more here than the Tate."

"Either a poor attempt at humour or a complete lack of scale," the man retorted. "However, they do give me great pleasure."

He walked in front of three in particular, all renaissance artworks.

"I don't expect you to comprehend their true significance. To expect that would be unfair; it takes years to grasp that kind of knowledge."

"Years well spent?"

"In my opinion, yes."

Thomas detected the comment had upset him.

"Jimmy, it's almost midnight. It's been a long day, and I'm s-starting to get somewhat sleepy. Save the p-party tricks for the anniversary."

He turned around, his eyes on the prince's. "You never did take my advice, did you, Tom?"

"Wh-what advice exactly are we talking about now?"

"The same advice I've been giving you your entire life. Never take things at face value. The legacy of the Sons of York is all around us – even in this very room."

He pointed at one of the paintings, a large original oil-based picture depicting a family scene.

"This rather nice painting is a copy of an original by the younger Hans Holbein, completed around 1527. The version here is from 1593. Notice the scene."

The prince took in the detail. "Thomas More."

"Sir Thomas More, later saint, a model of Tudor humility and excellence. Quite right," the historian continued. "Surrounding him, his lovely family."

Thomas studied the painting. The artist's name was Rowland Lockey.

"What happened to the original?"

The historian shrugged. "Lost. Though if you want my best guess, the original is probably still in the possession of the man's family."

Thomas accepted the answer, his concentration on the painting. There were twelve people in total: six men and six women. Slightly left of centre, Thomas More stood in a position of prominence, dressed in his usual attire of a black beret and an identically coloured cloak atop a red overcoat. A large gold medallion hung around his neck, denoting his position as chancellor.

Thomas looked at the historian. "What's so significant?"

"There are twelve people, Tom, in the painting: two of whom we cannot verify. See if you can guess who."

The suggestion made Thomas feel suddenly uneasy. He looked at the painting in more detail, studying individual faces. There was writing above the heads – always in Latin.

There was a young man standing towards the back, reading something. There was no writing above his head.

"Him."

Gardiner nodded. "Quite right."

Thomas tried to find the other elusive subject. The others all had writing either above or below.

"I'm afraid you're going to just have to t-tell me."

"All right. May I draw your attention to the gentleman standing to the uppermost right?"

Thomas followed his direction. There were three women sitting at the front of the painting, and three men standing behind them. The man standing furthest to the right was dressed in opulent garments, mostly dark red, and a black beret partially covered a fine head of dark hair.

He was clearly not part of the main setting.

"Notice anything strange about the man?"

The test had started; knowing Gardiner, it was possibly a trick. Thomas saw nothing unusual.

"Tell me, what is he holding?"

Thomas looked. "A scroll, s-something similar."

"Correct. What is he standing against?"

Again Thomas examined the painting in detail. "It's some kind of, I-I don't know, some kind of doorway or partition."

"A sensible answer, but quite incorrect," the historian said, walking ever closer. "Tell me what's different about the top of the structure?"

"Why, there's a small statue at every c-corner and several fleur-de-lis."

"Exactly."

Gardiner walked to the other side of the painting, his breath evident on Thomas's neck. This was the closest he had been so far.

"May I draw your attention to the second painting," Gardiner said, gesturing to the next painting on, also of the More family. "There are four key differences in this painting. Firstly, please find for me the mystery man."

Thomas looked in detail. "I can't."

"Hmm."

Thomas was now getting worked up. "Really, Jim . . ."

"Perhaps I may also divert you to this." Next on from that painting was a sketch, clearly much older and depicting the same scene.

"The original?"

"Let's call it the brainstorm. Notice anything different?"

"Well, there's no colour."

"Besides that."

Thomas had no idea.

"Give up?"

"Wait . . . he's not there."

"Nor is the lad reading in the background, often assumed to be the servant."

"Isn't he?"

"A servant reading?"

"Why not?"

"Why is surely the more important question."

"Perhaps it was a sign of M-More's personality."

"An interesting idea, but quite wrong." Gardiner took a dramatic pause. "May I ask you to return your attention to the original painting?"

"I thought you said it was lost."

"I meant this one. What is the mystery man's name?"

Thomas looked. His name was written in Latin above his head. "John."

"John what?"

He read the remainder. "It says, John the rightful heir."

"Heir of what?"

Thomas shrugged. "How should I know?"

"Notice, Tom, how the lad stands and who he is looking at."

The prince was now seriously confused. John the rightful heir was standing with his head slightly tilted and looking at a thickset man who, in turn, was looking directly at the artist.

"The man here," Gardiner pointed to the thickset man, "was one Henry Patenson, More's fool. Who does he remind you of?"

Thomas grinned. "Henry VIII."

"King of England at the time, whereas in this painting," he pointed to the second painting, "Patenson's appearance is far more low key."

"Meaning?"

The historian smiled. "Let's take another look at our friend John, shall we? The wooden structure you see behind him is not so much a doorway but a throne. The thickset fool, reminiscent in appearance of Henry VIII, is sadly covering the chair itself. Notice how Henry stands beneath the structure, but there is nothing above his head. As for John, he is standing beneath the fleur-de-lis. Meaning . . ."

"Meaning he was king?"

The earl nodded.

"That's preposterous."

Thomas looked at the painting in detail. Indeed, the mystery man and the lad reading were the only two standing in that part of the painting.

"Notice, also, how the mystery man is raised above Henry and all others."

"Really, Jim."

"It might also interest you to know that three versions of this copy survive and eight of this." He spoke of the second painting. "It cost me a pretty penny, I can assure you. This is the only one that includes the mystery man or the reader. The others appear exactly as they did on the sketch."

Thomas was confused. "Then why is this different?"

"Because in every other copy the mystery man was deleted."

"By who?"

"By Queen Elizabeth I."

Thomas laughed. "What makes you so sure?"

"They have all been tested, Thomas. X-rays, marvellous things, confirm without any shadow of doubt that the man who was once included was later marked out."

Thomas looked again, his focus on John the rightful heir.

"Who is he?"

"His name, at least to historians, was John Clement. Rose to prominence in the 1540s, becoming president of the Royal College of Physicians. I'm sure that you'll be most amused when I tell you that no paintings or documents of the man survive – the only president to suffer such misfortune."

"Means nothing."

"Perhaps. Perhaps not."

Thomas bit his lip. "Who was he?"

"Clement was the husband of this lady," he pointed to the first lady on the left of the first painting, "Margaret Clement, nee Giggs, More's foster daughter. Notice how she is also absent from the second painting."

"But present in the original sketch."

"Indeed she is. But look at how she appears in the first painting. Notice the expression on her face, and that of her husband."

The woman was clearly unimpressed. "She's looking at the fool."

The historian nodded. "Between them, husband and wife are giving Henry the evil eyes."

Thomas said nothing.

"John Clement was born in 1500 and was at the time of the painting about twenty-seven. Check the records."

Thomas didn't doubt him. "What's so important?"

"The matter of importance was John's father, the identity of whom is mentioned only in one document: the same one you have been looking for all along."

Gardiner left the room and returned with a medieval chronicle, quite obviously an original. The composition was vellum, the writing clearly Latin.

Thomas didn't need any instruction it was the Ravensfield Chronicle.

"You?"

"Try reading it."

Thomas did his best. The handwriting was old and elongated.

"Note the name of his father."

He followed the earl's finger. "Richard P-Plantagenet."

51

Jen didn't stop until reaching the far wall. The estate was large, comprising at least a hundred acres of fields and woodland, but also a number of man-made facilities and structures, including paddocks, barns and what looked to be the old village windmill beside the river. After taking a breather at the windmill, Jen and Anthea followed a line of trees and came to a pathway on the other side of a wall.

The end of the estate.

Jen used a tree stump to help herself onto the wall. She stopped halfway to help Anthea, who, not for the first time, was practically paralysed through fear. The pathway was gravel and led from the nearby woodlands back to the lane near the church.

The route came awkwardly near to the house.

They had made it back to where the path joined the lane when Anthea grabbed Jen's hand. "Jen, stop."

The girl was breathless.

Jen was also struggling. Sweat poured down the sides of her face while her T-shirt felt soaked beneath her jacket, itself now covered in dust.

"What the hell just happened?"

Jen's mind was alive with images. What had she seen? She remembered the image on the camera. She removed the camera from her pocket and turned it on.

She looked at the latest picture for several seconds before showing it to Anthea.

"I don't understand."

"Neither do I," Jen said. "Not exactly."

Jen started pacing. She ran her hand through her hair, then dusted off her clothes. She looked over her shoulder. The house remained in sight, the lights on.

It was way too close for comfort.

"Come on."

Anthea caught her up. "Jen, what's it mean?"

Still she struggled to explain it – even to herself. The image on the wall had only shown up in the photograph after using the flash. It had been far too dark to see it at the time.

"There was a tapestry hanging from the wall – three lions on a maroon background. It was the symbol of the Plantagenets," Jen said.

"I don't understand."

"The main tombs were of Edward V, Richard III, Princess Elizabeth and Richard IV. Edward V was never crowned; he disappeared in 1483 along with his brother."

Anthea was confused. "How?"

"According to most people, murdered by their uncle."

The penny dropped. "The Princes in the Tower?"

Jen passed through a kissing gate, now less than two hundred metres from the church.

"Edward V was allegedly killed, along with his brother Richard, Duke of York. Before they disappeared, Richard III declared them illegitimate and took the throne. Richard III died at Bosworth two years later and was buried in a church in Leicester. After that, Henry Tudor took the throne."

She looked at Anthea.

"There was no Richard IV."

Anthea shook her head. "Whose grave was that?"

"Richard of Shrewsbury, the Duke of York – the second prince."

"But . . ."

"Edward and Richard were never murdered. If what we saw is correct, Edward died of typhoid in November 1483. He was succeeded by Richard III, and he, in turn, was succeeded by his other nephew."

"What about all the others: Henry VII, Elizabeth I, Charles I, Victoria . . ."

"That crypt contained the bodies of an alternative dynasty." She looked at Anthea seriously. "If this is real, Richard of Shrewsbury lived on, married, had children; their children had children."

She looked back at Wootton Court, slowly disappearing into the distance as they walked.

"The original emblem of the Plantagenets is a broom. The founder of the house was named Geoffrey. There was a Plantagenet monument in the graveyard."

She looked again at Anthea.

"If this is correct, the Plantagenets didn't die out. Their offspring continued in the line of the House of York. In their twisted minds, they still think they're kings."

Jen hurried through the gate at the end of the pathway and bumped into something moving.

"Ouch."

Standing before her was Edward Jeffries. "Ey up, it's Mrs Robin Hood."

She nearly jumped out of her skin. It took her several seconds to get her bearings. She looked at him, initially nervous, then inwardly annoyed. She took a deep breath to compose herself.

She tried to remind herself, he didn't know what they had discovered.

"Don't they say hello in Nottingham?"

Jen smiled, noticeably forced. "Hey there."

He smiled. "Hello, Anthea."

Anthea grinned shyly.

He looked Jen up and down, amused by the dusty state of her clothes. "What have you two been rolling around in?"

"We have to go, sorry."

He moved to one side to let them pass. "I'm looking forward to tomorrow, Jen."

She stopped, surprised.

"I was talking with Dr Lovell. He asked if he could show you the castle and the house. You're very welcome."

She'd forgotten about Lovell.

"Actually, I'm pretty busy tomorrow; I need to finish preparations for filming."

The rebuff didn't faze him. "No worries. You can always come the day after."

She forced a smile. "Thanks."

Jen couldn't get away quickly enough. She grabbed Anthea by the wrist and accelerated through the churchyard, not daring to look back.

She headed for the nearest bench and took a seat.

And a deep breath.

"Oh my God."

"Why did you say no? He's lovely."

Jen couldn't believe what she'd just heard. "Did you not see what I saw?"

"Yeah . . ." Anthea looked over her shoulder. From there Wootton Court was no longer visible. "Yeah. It's just, he's really nice."

Jen ignored her.

"Jen?"

Jen's expression was the most serious yet. "Look! We have no idea what we're dealing with here; for all we know, he could be part of it – for all we know, he could be the next in line."

The suggestion unsettled her. "Are you being serious?"

Again Jen decided not to respond. She looked over her shoulder to see if Edward Jeffries was still there.

As far as she could tell, he wasn't.

She rubbed her temples and then smoothed her hair.

"Was it all genuine?" Anthea asked

Jen laughed out loud and replied, "I really don't know."

The answer was far less reassuring than Anthea had been looking for. "Why would they do it? I mean it was years ago."

Jen was thinking the same thing. Long gone were the days when the powers of the monarchy could shake the thrones of other princes.

Nearby, the sound of sudden laughter startled her. Along the road, two men were walking in the direction of the bridge. She recognised the voice of Hancock talking with another.

"What time is it?" Jen asked Anthea.

Anthea checked her watch. "Just after twelve."

"Oh crap, they'll be locking me out."

Jen jumped to her feet and began jogging towards the Hog.

Anthea caught up with her.

"Who around here is an expert on Wootton's history?"

Anthea shrugged. "I don't know. Dr Lovell."

Jen shook her head. "Ever since I've been here, the one thing I keep hearing is how their roots can be traced back to goodness knows when. Their family were prominent statesmen in the reign of Richard III. They've known about this for hundreds of years."

She looked closely at Anthea. "Are you sure you didn't know anything about this?"

Anthea looked back blankly. "No. Nothing."

Jen believed her. "What are you doing tomorrow?"

"Working in the afternoon."

"Meet me here at 8:30. I'll need you," she said, walking towards the entrance of the Hog. "Don't tell anyone about what we saw tonight."

Standing in the shadow of the pathway that led from Ravensfield to the church, the long-haired figure remained unnoticed. She watched as the young researcher and the even younger hairdresser went their separate ways, one heading towards the high street, the other inside the inn.

She grabbed hold of the gate to support herself. Breathing was difficult; it had been ever since that fateful day a year ago.

It felt similar – perhaps even worse than the last time.

History was repeating itself.

Jen entered the Hog through the main door. The lights were still on, but the locals had left. She heard the sound of chairs being moved, accompanied by glasses clinking together. Tara was busying herself with the usual end-of-day tasks. She smiled at Jen as she passed before heading off into the kitchen with her hands full.

Jen wandered through the deserted bar area, the dining area, and into the main hallway where Mitchell was hoovering. He nodded at her as she passed, but neither said anything.

Jen entered the bedroom and went straight to her laptop. She reasoned that if there was any truth in the things she had seen, they would have left a trail.

Even if just a vague one.

If Debra Harrison had been murdered – or at least abducted – for finding out more than she needed to know, chances were she wasn't the first to have suffered such a fate.

Anthea crossed the high street, heading back home. There was a car parked opposite the butcher's, a stunning Rolls Royce with a unique number plate.

Even on the other side of the village, she had never seen anything quite so elaborate.

She continued up the passageway, less than a hundred metres from her house. There was movement nearby. A figure emerged, walking towards her.

The wall light revealed the stranger's face.

"My God, it's you."

52

Thomas moved slowly away from the paintings and took a seat on the settee. It was old and antique, and felt more like a park bench than a couch.

"Don't feel so bad, Tom," the earl said. "Successful comprehending of the pieces of our timeline can never be achieved in one segment – no matter how talented the historian."

Gardiner sat down alongside him.

"Have you any idea how long it took me to put together the pieces of this incredible jigsaw? An entire lifetime, such was the challenge and so few the clues. And many that were clues were left by people whose connection to the Crown was so remote it barely seemed relevant."

"Yet when you found it, you said nothing."

"On the contrary. No sooner had your grandmother died than I took the search to the next level. Your father was the first person I told. Your uncle, the King, listened with a vague interest before finally concluding it was all obsolete – ancient history, he called it." He shook his head. "When I brought the subject before your grandfather," he spoke of the late King, "he, too, listened with the same polite interest before concluding that I had got too old. He told me to take a holiday – a sabbatical, he called it – a lengthy spell away to recharge the old batteries. A month later, still they refused to take my claim seriously. The reward for fifty years of dedication: a lifetime banishment from the palace, compensated by a fine pension and an extra title to shut the hell up."

Thomas was rattled. "You feel you were short-changed?"

"I never asked for any such titles, earldoms, OBEs . . . it might well interest you to know that during the Cold War, I was walking home one evening when a rather striking car crossed my path, and travelling within were two rather large Russian fellows and a long-haired brunette who would have made Clark Gable's heart beat fast. She played her role well, too, I can assure you."

Gardiner rose to his feet and began to pace.

"By the time this rather intimidating episode was over, I had been offered over £1 million to spy on my country and my king by the KGB," he said, his eyes now on the prince. "Over the next seven years the offer would be extended several times. Did I take it? I am sure that I did not . . ."

Thomas exhaled forcibly. "Well, at least no one can accuse you of being motivated by greed."

Gardiner's expression had hardened.

"You never told me."

"Two days ago I tried; yesterday I tried again – you said you were too busy."

"I was."

"Oh really, Tom. The Sons of York are among the most ghastly of people ever to have walked God's earth. I tried to tell you of the path you needed to tread; you didn't even give me a moment."

"So you leaked the story to the press."

"I did the only thing I could in order to get the attention of the people who needed to see it."

"There's a word for what you did."

"Only one?"

"In the past it was called treason."

Gardiner shook his head. "My boy, you disappoint me. All these years you have claimed to be different. How long have you claimed your wish to right the wrongs of the past, walk the path of righteousness? What was it you once said to me as a boy: he that should dare fight the king of beasts shall never fight inferior?"

Thomas bit his lip. Remembering words was difficult.

"When all is said and done, you're just like all the others. Be it too proud, too arrogant or simply too stupid, you fail to look beyond the length of your own hooter."

The prince leapt to his feet. "You forget to whom you speak."

"I'm speaking to the spoiled brat of the third child of a king who was too proud to admit his own faults. The heir to a once defunct Duchy of Middle England, the son of a minor noblewoman whose only talent in life was divorce–"

"How dare you!"

"And the ninth in line to a throne that, thanks to its inability to listen, could well be due to expire."

"My mother was a great woman," Thomas said, struggling to control his rage. He took a deep breath and raised his shoulders. "What happened to the princes?"

It was evident from the earl's expression he had been looking forward to this.

"The fate of the Princes in the Tower, as they were so dubbed many centuries later, was not recorded by the journalists of the time. Should the chroniclers be believed, it was Buckingham, or perhaps Sir James Tyrell, who performed the deadly deed, always on behalf of the tyrant immortalised by Shakespeare for being a hunchback. It has always been my belief that the majority of the chroniclers were acting with the best of intentions – doing the best they could with the information at their disposal.

"However, there was one who had no such excuse."

The realisation hit Thomas immediately. "Of course, Sir Thomas More–"

"Was the one person we know for sure who always knew the truth."

Thomas was almost speechless. "Wh-what are you suggesting? That he lied?"

"Yes, of course he did. Henry VIII was on the throne, and the Princes in the Tower were assumed to be dead. It would have been something of an inconvenience, don't you think, should the king have realised that he had a pretender to his throne."

"He didn't know?"

"Well, his father certainly did and, in the early years, went to great lengths to eradicate them. Since the reign of Edward IV, the princes were the subject of countless assassination attempts by the red rose of Lancaster. With the princes alive, Henry Tudor could never rule. There was a reason he went to such extremes to eradicate every copy of Titulus Regius. If you should read what I have read," he spoke of the Ravensfield Chronicle, "it was clear why. The princes were known to be alive."

He grinned at Thomas.

"Yet, there was another problem. With the princes dubbed illegitimate, marrying Elizabeth of York would prove no gain. Why marry a bastard? It wouldn't make any sense."

He laughed to himself.

"The relegitimization of the offspring of Edward IV and Elizabeth Woodville gave Henry Tudor a boost, but only if people believed the princes were dead. When Henry married Elizabeth, he sought only alliance with the House of York. After all, what kind of husband would seek to murder the brothers of his queen?"

"They were still alive?"

"Edward V was a sickly child, who, according to the Ravensfield Chronicle, finally succumbed to typhoid in November 1483. After falling ill while preparations were being made for his coronation, it was the best projection of the royal physicians that the king would not last the year. Fears soon began to mount that his brother had also caught the disease. With that, the entire future of the House of York depended on its ability to survive."

"Why have them declared illegitimate?" Thomas asked.

"Because only a strong figure could resist the threat posed by the House of Lancaster, and only one such man existed – Richard, Duke of Gloucester. The fledgling rule of the House of York was far too feeble to withstand the threat of insurrection, so it was decided that the Crown must pass to Richard. The Stillington conspiracy, as it was then dubbed, was the brainchild of three prominent statesmen – William Catesby, Richard Ratcliffe, and Francis Lovell. Catesby, a successful lawyer, was almost certainly the composer of Titulus Regius. But when Richard died without a surviving heir, there was only one person left to replace him. The younger brother of the former king."

"What happened to him?"

"The prince was taken from the Tower on 3 September 1483, along with his dying brother and cousin – the Earl of Warwick, son of George, Duke of Clarence. At first, we believe they sought refuge with a distant relative, one of the Woodvilles, before making their new home in North Yorkshire – in the household of one of Richard III's bastards. As the rightful king regained his strength, the family began to make moves to bring the House of York back to prominence. After the failure of the trial run by the pretenders Lambert Simnel and Perkin Warbeck – themselves both sons of Richard III – it was decided that the rightful heir would never have the military strength to retake the throne during his own lifetime. Instead, he returned to the limelight as Edward Jeffries, taking the Christian name of his deceased brother and the surname of the founder of his house, Geoffrey Plantagenet. Only this man would not be a king, but a surgeon."

"Surgeon?"

"In time the man would marry, and no fewer than six heirs were born. The eldest was John, the man in the painting. In time he would become president of the Royal College of Physicians. A subtle alternative to being king, but a fine way to infiltrate the circles of the time."

"Then More knew?"

"Of course. If you want my opinion, much of what happened next was his idea. As a Plantagenet, Jeffries had the luxury of a fine education. That in turn was passed on to More, who brought John Jeffries, known in wider circles as John Clement, into his house under the guise of a tutor. A strong marriage was needed for the prince and who better than a daughter of the Chancellor of England. And at what better time?"

Thomas was now completely lost. "What do you mean, better time?"

"In the eyes of More, the antics of Henry VIII could not continue. The feud with the papacy was large. More knew it was only a matter of time before disaster struck. This led to his own plot against the king – an action that would cost him his life."

Thomas was dumbstruck. "More was a traitor?"

"The definition of traitor is dependent on what side one happens to be on at the time. The actions of the king were about to tarnish the future of the country, and also threatened to change the landscape of Europe. More's mission was slightly different to Jeffries', but the effects of re-establishing the House of York would prove the only way forward."

"Which was?"

"To place a Catholic back on the throne of England."

The DG of MI5 had never been so confused. Despite every attempt at carrying out research, the gun just failed to come up on any of the investigations.

It had simply not been charted.

The telephone on his desk began to ring. "Bridges."

"The Home Secretary is on the line, sir."

"Put him through."

The next voice he heard was Heston's.

"Yes, Minister."

"I'm afraid we've had something of a development. The bastard from Clapham has escaped."

53

Thomas exhaled violently. He sat forward with his hands clenching his knees, his eyes fixed firmly on Gardiner.

"The Wars of the Roses were among the bloodiest times in the entire history of our beloved nation. Seldom in the centuries since, or the centuries past, has more quarter been given or asked for the cause of the 'rightful' king."

Thomas remained silent for several seconds. "Surely there have been worse wars?"

"Actually no. Over twenty thousand lost their lives that day at Towton, a number far greater than in any other battle on English soil." The earl eyed him keenly. "It is not by the death count alone that one defines a battle. Many of the Lancastrians, including the heir to the throne, lost their lives at Tewkesbury when Edward IV regained control. The Lancastrians that were captured were swiftly executed." He gestured with his hands to his throat. "In a way, you might say, it was the battle that returned stability to England."

He walked away from the prince to the other side of the room. There was a fine oil painting on the wall, portraying a battle scene.

"Magnificent, isn't it?" Gardiner said, admiring the picture. "Though right you may be when comparing the amount of bloodshed at Tewkesbury to that of Crécy or Marston Moor, there is no doubt that the effects of that day in May 1471 would go a long way towards shaping England's history for years to come. When Henry Tudor, victorious at Bosworth in 1485, claimed the throne for what remained of the Lancastrians, he did what many thought unthinkable: a man of relatively obscure beginnings became king through nothing but tenacity and self-belief. Who would've thought it then, that the most pragmatic king England had seen since the conquest would be succeeded by the oaf who married six times."

"I see your love for the Tudors has not diminished."

The man laughed. "For all the good that happened during that time, for every positive there was an aftershock that threatened to tear

Europe to the core. The Dissolution of the religious houses that followed remains to this day the most heartless and unethical event ever carried out by an English government. Today, of course, it would be illegal, right of ownership, human rights, we've heard it all before." He shook his head. "But for every corrupt abbot or prior there were thirty good men who were treated like the scum of the earth. It was in the reign of his son, most historians will tell you, that the true Reformation began, but it was during Henry VIII's time the drumbeat was set.

"If the rule of the Plantagenets taught us one thing, it was the importance of the assistance of the Pope. When Henry VIII burned that bridge, those who were once our allies became our enemies. And the ruler of England forever susceptible."

Thomas shook his head. "You have a C-Catholic sympathy now?"

Gardiner looked back coldly. "It is not I who does anything, I am only telling you what happened. When Edward VI came to the throne, it was known that the best way forward for the government of England was a monarch who could unite. The boy king, sickly though he was, would have survived a lot longer had it not been for the circumstances that put him there. The web of the papacy was far reaching; that of the House of York, cunning."

That got his attention. "He was murdered?"

"Killed by the very people he thought were his friends."

"His wife?"

"His physician."

Thomas placed his hands to his head. "Death by poison."

The historian nodded. "Perhaps manipulation would be the correct word in this instance. Baked in a pie."

Thomas shook his head, the irony painful. He looked to his left and picked up a goblet of wine from the nearby table.

Then he went off the idea.

"The young king knew that successful continuation of the Reformation in England required the right successor. Naïvely, he chose Lady Jane Grey, the poor girl who did not stand a chance. For the Sons of York, Edward's succession by a Catholic queen was at least a lesser of two evils. When Mary failed to conceive, in theory all that was needed then was a York marriage to Philip II's daughter and a York would return to the throne."

"But who? You d-don't even know if the next child would be a b-boy or girl."

"Behind the walls of the Vatican, I have no doubt that the Pope and his ally from York had that anxious wait many a time over. Fortunately for John Clement, he was blessed with both sons and daughters. The eldest was Edward, named after his great-grandfather. He's the boy in the painting."

Thomas turned to see the painting attributed to Holbein. All he could see was a person reading.

"The papacy knew?"

"Of course they knew; not only that, but they approved. Should the Tudor kings have behaved like good little boys and continued to pay homage to the Bishop of Rome, then there was no reason to believe that the eventual outcome of the Wars of the Roses would have been anything more than a footnote in the context of the Vatican's history. As soon as it became clear that Elizabeth was going to be heading the same way as her brother and father – hardly surprising given she was the daughter of Anne Boleyn – the papacy once again had a problem. The Act of Uniformity of 1559 made the position of the Roman Church untenable. In 1570 she was excommunicated."

Gardiner laughed loudly.

"Does it not strike one as strange that within a year of the queen's excommunication she was the victim of a plot, by an Italian?"

"Ridolfi."

Gardiner nodded. "During her long reign, the queen was the victim of no less than sixteen plots, perhaps more – who knows how many were swept under the carpet or failed to come to fruition. After the failure of the Somerville and Parry plots, many believed the opportunity for Yorkist revival had passed. Had the Somerville Plot been successful, carried out by the descendants of the cousins of the Princes in the Tower, the return of the Sons of York would have been set almost totally in stone. When the failure of Anthony Babington and his attempts to secure the throne for Mary Queen of Scots led to the pretender's death, there was little anyone could do but wait for a Spanish triumph or for the old girl to die."

"But Elizabeth was s-succeeded by James."

"The coming of the man from Scotland could have been exactly what all sides needed – a compromise. When that failed, it took only one hungry young wannabe tyrant to attempt to rewrite history. It signalled a dangerous new era for the Sons of York. The man's name, Robert Catesby."

"The Gunpowder Plot."

"A sixth generation descendant of the Chancellor of Richard III, known also to his contemporaries as the Cat."

The words were spoken by Gardiner in the manner of a teacher addressing a primary school student, the older man clearly amused by the prince's ignorance.

"Had it have been successful, of course, the almighty blow would have seen the end of the entire constitution. It was not only a building and a monarch that would have needed replacing, but the government."

"Swept away like the waters of the Red Sea."

"Interesting analogy – not incorrect. Even the Puritans were not averse to suggestion it was something of a judgement."

Thomas was beginning to see the big picture. "What happened next? And this time don't beat about the bush."

On this occasion Gardiner didn't dally. "Evidence suggests that the plots continued, although if they did, they met little in the way of success. During the reign of Charles I, the two actually joined forces against a much greater foe. It was Cromwell, not the Lancastrian kings of old, who oversaw the ruin of the Jeffries' estates."

"Then what?"

"The next descendant emerged, this time as part of the Monmouth Rebellion, yet he, too, met his maker following the fall of James II."

"I've heard this bit before."

"Have you indeed?" Gardiner cleared his throat. "Following that time, it is my honest opinion that the direct line came to an end. As a result, attempts against the Royal Family itself have, at least up to now, been largely non-existent. It could even be argued that in the 18th and 19th centuries the history of the Sons of York can be more easily explained by the development of the Whig movement. Even now, their influence in politics is greater than you can possibly know."

He'd heard this before as well. "You mean they're republicans?"

"Actually, no; the importance that the Sons place on their Norman ancestry is really rather admirable in many ways. They are quintessential English – that's a fact – but you are more likely to find a trade unionist in their midst than a Blackshirt. Nevertheless, word of caution."

Thomas left his seat and examined the paintings for a second time. He shook his head.

"How? How do you know this?"

"Over the years, the curiosity of the curious has led to many a fine discovery."

He showed Thomas the Ravensfield Chronicle again.

"Even to this day it is in their home county where their influence runs deepest."

Thomas breathed furiously. "How did you find this?"

"I pilfered it from the Bodleian."

He looked at it. "The Ravensfield Chronicle," he said. The handwriting was dark and murky. "Where?"

"The original Ravensfield Blackfriars Priory was located somewhere in the North York Moors. According to the end of this, something the author called the second continuation, Henry Tudor ruined the priory in 1490 due to its importance to the House of York. After that, it goes into less detail."

"Where was it?"

"In my opinion, the place referred to as Ravensfield is now a village called Wootton-on-the-Moor. According to this, the entire village was ransacked and lost."

He looked at Gardiner. Suddenly things were making sense.

"One thing still p-puzzles me. If all this is correct, why did Elizabeth of York marry Henry Tudor?"

The historian laughed. "A most excellent point."

He showed him another oil painting, this time on the far left wall.

It was a copy of a very famous painting. The subject: Elizabeth of York, artist unknown.

There was a second painting alongside it, another woman, blonde hair, elegant and beautiful, perhaps late teens.

"Notice anything strange?"

Thomas shrugged. "Who are they?"

"Elizabeth of York."

"It's the same woman?"

"Yes and no."

"Let me guess. Tudor married an imposter."

Gardiner clapped his hands together and smiled. "Another fine work credited to the great Hans Holbein."

He turned to face the prince.

"Elizabeth Woodville was cunning. And as you say, why enter an alliance with the Tudors if the princes, or at least one, were still alive?

"Thus we come to the final element of the puzzle. The deceit of the Woodvilles into making Margaret Beaufort think her son, Henry Tudor, had married a Plantagenet. In fact, he had married a lesser Woodville."

"He didn't know?"

"I believe he probably did. That is why Henry Tudor's wish to destroy every copy of Titulus Regius was so pivotal. Being barred by Attainder, his only option was to marry the princess. Thus, the Tudor's own deceit. Their claim to the throne was void."

Thomas exhaled deeply. "And Elizabeth?"

"According to the Ravensfield Chronicle, she disappeared when leaving sanctuary in 1483 on the advice of her uncle Richard. Two years later she was joined by her cousin and soon-to-be husband."

"Who?"

"The third prince in the Tower. The boy history always forgets."

Thomas bit his lip. "Clarence's son."

The earl nodded. "It is through him and Elizabeth that your noble cousins, Jeffries, claim their descent."

Thomas returned his attention to the chronicle. "Can we really v-vouch for its accuracy?"

"There is only one way."

"Go on."

"Exhume the skeletons at Westminster Abbey and carry out the tests that your grandfather was too afraid to order himself. If you're smart, you will also find a way of excavating the tomb of John Clement, who is buried in the Cathedral of St Rumbold's in Belgium. Only then will you know the truth."

For several seconds Thomas failed to reply. "And of the present?"

"By now I'd have thought that must be obvious."

"Jeffries."

"Noble cousins."

Thomas's anger was finally beginning to boil over. "You bastard. You b-bastard. All this time, you—"

The old man remained resolute. "It does not do to dwell too much on the past, Tom."

"Strange words f-for a historian."

"Who better qualified to say them?"

Thomas bit his lip and pointed. "Treason lives. As do traitors."

He left the room, heading in the direction of the hallway.

From the room he had left, he heard the sound of a lone gunshot.

He stopped in his tracks. He was suddenly numb, his body static. As he began to breathe, a cold chill ran down his spine.

Slowly he returned to the room.

The earl was standing, carrying a revolver. "Be careful what you wish for."

The prince breathed deeply.

Suddenly he started laughing.

"Enjoy your retirement, old man."

Outside the house, Thomas got into the Bentley.

"Everything all right?" Stephen asked.

Thomas turned slowly. "Peachy."

"Caroline called. She tracked the car to the village of Wootton-on-the-Moor. I was right, by the way. That is where the girl disappeared last year."

"Also the home of some distant cousins."

"What's that got to do with anything?"

Thomas bit his lip so hard it nearly started to bleed.

"Everything all right?"

"It's a long story."

Thomas dropped Stephen off at the rear of the palace.

"Remember what I said."

"Tom, I still don't understand."

"You don't need to. Jim said the tombs will prove it. The Princes in the Tower are b-buried at Westminster Abbey; Elizabeth of York is in the Lady chapel. Also, use any influence you have to s-see that a s-similar excavation is carried out on the tomb of John Clement in St Rumbold's Cathedral in Belgium."

"What are you going to do?"

"I'm going north to find Caroline."

The King was still awake at 1 a.m. He was reading in his study when he received his unexpected visitor.

Stephen entered without waiting for an invite. "Father, I need a favour."

The King didn't bat an eyelid. "Very well."

"I need your permission to exhume two royal tombs."

"Whose?"

"The urn containing the Princes in the Tower and Elizabeth of York."

"The Princes . . ."

"There's very little time to explain.

"And I need it before dawn."

54

Wootton-on-the-Moor, 5 a.m.

As always it began with the dawn. The first hint of orange had emerged in the sky behind the castle hill, its bright light distorted by distant clouds. Soon the sun would rise above the hill, illuminating firstly the ancient woodland and then the house, entering through the large Gothic windows that lined the side of the building. In the past the light had been necessary; without it, the telling of time was impossible.

These days it served only as a reminder.

The cellar was the oldest part of the estate. In its heyday it had belonged to the castle itself. Back then it was known as the court or the meeting room. It was the heart of the feudal system – the place where justice would be meted out or new laws passed. Wooden furniture was arranged along the walls, its appearance in keeping with the room's former purpose. There was a statue at the head of the room of an elegant king adorned with regal sword and crown.

Henry II. The first Plantagenet king.

The floor was also wooden, its boards prone to prolonged creaking. The main feature was an elaborate table decorated with the Plantagenet crest: three gold lions on a maroon background. The symbol represented England at a different time, back when the empire extended far beyond the channel.

How things had changed.

The table itself was worthy of mention. Instead of the usual circle or rectangle, it was designed in the shape of a shield. Thirty chairs surrounded it, all of which were taken.

Twelve sat along either side. While every man present was dressed in robes, a fitting and ancient regalia, for those on the left side the black cloaks and white habits were also their usual dress. It had been that way since the 1200s, back when the priory was in its heyday.

All sat quietly.

At the bottom of the table, three men sat spaced apart. Lovell and Ratcliffe sat either side of Sir William Catesby, who sat at the point where the tip was at its most outstretched.

Opposite him, Lord Jeffries occupied the most elaborate seat. To his left sat his namesake and grandson. On the other side, the seat was empty – a reminder of the loss of his son. To the wider world, the man was an enigma. To the people of Wootton, his reputation was less esteemed. Most of them viewed him as a crank, if not simply:

A bastard.

In this room, however, his importance rose to unrivalled heights. Within the assembled group, he was addressed only as 'Your Highness' or 'Your Grace'. It was the term used before Majesty, back in the old days. To his followers his official title was:

Edward XIII, King of England, Duke of York, Lord of Ireland, Duke of Aquitaine, Duke of Normandy, Count of Anjou, Count of Poitou.

Despite his appearance, regal but without the highly crafted trimmings of the monarchs of old, he was now little more than a figurehead. The true authority belonged to the three sitting opposite. Like their predecessors, they not only ran this show, but every show. Their ancestors had achieved immortality as the governors of England:

The Cat, the Rat, and Lovell our Dog.

Who ruled all England under a Hog.

"Martin Tolson, Democrat candidate for the constituency of Keighley, was yesterday successful in the bi-election. May we offer our congratulations to both he and his party leader."

There was no applause, but Catesby's words were taken seriously. The leader of the Democrat Party, Rowland Stanley, the gopher-faced man with smart silver hair, nodded but remained silent.

"Next week we have another bi-election, this time in East Sussex. I understand the candidate to be put forward is Mr Thompson."

"I thought he was dead," Ratcliffe said.

"This is Thompson junior," Stanley replied. "Gareth is his son."

"Is he able?" the Rat asked.

"I respect him."

"That doesn't answer the question."

The Dog sat forward. "I think what my colleague is trying to say, dear Rowland, is that the constituency in question has always been one loyal to the Tories. Is the son of a former Blackshirt really a man who will endear himself to the voters?"

Stanley took his time. "He is the best we have at the present time."

"I see."

"What are his chances?" the Cat asked.

"He is unlikely to beat the Tory candidate, but the late Mr Bates was rather popular – a former Cabinet minister, we mustn't forget," Lovell replied.

"There is no doubt that he has big shoes to fill," Stanley agreed. "But these days, who doesn't?"

The Cat stroked his beard. "Personal congratulations, I believe, are also in order for Mr Dawson. For those of you who do not know, Mr Dawson's construction company has recently won the contract for development of the South Bank. I'm sure, gentlemen, you will join me in wishing him well in his bid to add his vision to the great city."

Several people nodded, including Dawson, who sat quietly along the side. He had dark hair and wore a smart suit beneath his robes.

As did the others on that side.

"But now, gentlemen, to more pressing issues. As many of you may now be aware, a situation in London is brewing, and a minor crisis must be averted. I assume we need not waste time on the details."

Prolonged silence descended on the room. Those sitting along the sides in particular became deathly still, either unwilling to put themselves on the spot or risk appearing stupid.

"Should that be the case, gentlemen, I'm afraid you must excuse me," Edward said. "I've never been much of a fan of those twenty-four-hour news channels. There would really be little point in me staying without knowing what on earth you're talking about."

At the other end of the table, the Cat retained a neutral persona.

It would be impossible to continue the meeting without the Prince of Wales.

"Perhaps it would be wise, my friend, not to gloss over the details," the Hog said. "Historically it has been something of a curse of my family: how precision has been lost through lack of clarity."

"Very well," the Cat agreed. "Gentlemen, as many of you may by now be aware, yesterday an explosion took place in the Borough of Greenwich; most of the news channels have been reporting the issue as a gas leak. Also, thanks to a certain news article, they are presently covering the story of a possible health scare for the Duke of York. The stories are compelling, but largely inaccurate."

"Where is the duke?" the Rat asked.

"The King Edward," the Cat replied.

"Actually, the old boy has already discharged himself," the Dog said.

Catesby and Ratcliffe were stunned.

"You know this?" the Rat asked.

"How?" the Cat asked.

"I have my sources."

Neither man replied. The answer was sufficient.

"What I can't understand is how the old bastard survived," Stanley said.

"The murder of the duke was never our intention," the Cat replied sternly. "But even if it were, the substance takes time. My guess would be that he had an allergic reaction. Ironically, it might have done him good."

"The palace has already been put on red alert following the escape of Morris," the fair-haired man sitting on the right side said. "Understandably neither the palace nor the Ministry of Defence have released the news to the public. The murders of my colleagues are now common knowledge to them, as is that of the former monarch."

All present watched the politician.

"I was unaware that the palace knew," Edward said.

"Most of them accept it as likely," the new Secretary of State for Justice, Dominic West, replied. "Though the King himself is largely in denial."

"How has the Home Secretary responded?" the Dog asked.

West laughed. "Well, he's using the usual buzzwords."

Soft laughter resonated throughout the room, including from some of the friars.

"That's not an answer," the Cat said coldly.

"He knows the truth about my predecessor and his alleged involvement with terrorists." West used his fingers to quote. "For now it is known only to a select few."

Catesby looked at the friars. "What of Morris?"

"The Home Secretary had been attempting to question Brother Morris himself," West said.

Sitting among his fellow brothers, the escapee sat in silence.

"How about the royals themselves?" the Dog asked.

At the opposite end of the table, the Hog was unimpressed with Lovell's choice of words.

"The King, of course, has put his best man on the case."

"Off the record, of course?" the Cat asked.

"Of course," West replied. "They'd never let a thing like this reach the public domain."

"Who, who is this man?" the Hog asked.

"Prince Thomas, son of Clarence . . . I know very little about him," West admitted.

"Francis?"

Lovell looked at the Hog. "Prince Thomas, yes, the so-called invisible royal."

"I'm sorry, the invisible royal?" Stanley interjected.

"Yes, the so-called go-to chap: the person the King will turn to in a time of crisis. Usually a more minor royal, someone unlikely to take the throne, probably a younger son of the younger brother. Every monarch since the Tudors has had one."

"And what of this Thomas?" the Hog asked.

"Only son of the Duke of Clarence, also his sole heir. A history graduate of Keble College, Oxford; finished Sandhurst with more credibility than usual for a Winchester . . . unofficially, now a member of the Secret Service."

"A capable man?"

"Without question. I actually had the pleasure of meeting him myself once," the Dog replied. "Very nice chap, a strapping build. However, he has a tendency to suffer the same affliction as many of his ancestors."

"What?" the Cat asked. "Don't tell me he stammers?"

"More stutter than stammer; usually improves when he's relaxed or in full flow. However, unlike his ancestor, his was not from birth. From what I could gather, the poor chap was most unfortunate in witnessing some of the things he did in Afghanistan. Rumour also has it that it was he who stumbled across the corpse of his late grandmother."

No one said a word. They were familiar with the story of the queen's death.

"Nevertheless, most brutal in his own fashion. And almost certainly," Lovell turned to face Lord Ratcliffe, "the man responsible for the death of your nephew."

The Rat was clearly livid.

"What of him now?" the Hog asked.

"I saw him yesterday at the palace with the Duke of Cornwall," West replied. He hesitated before continuing. "He really is the most vulgar of fellows."

"He is a man unworthy to be referred to as Prince of England," Morris said, bowing his head towards the Hog.

Jeffries acknowledged the friar with a smile. "Why was he there?" he asked West.

"I'm afraid I was not party to their conversation."

On this occasion the Hog seemed to accept the answer.

"Has Stephen senior given any indication of a willingness to comply yet?" the younger Jeffries asked his grandfather.

The Hog changed the subject. "I understand we have a more local problem?"

The Cat turned to his left. "Francis?"

Lovell looked uncomfortable. He had seen the footage, and the footage did not make for pleasant viewing.

"She seemed like such a nice girl."

"According to you, they're always nice," the Cat said.

The Dog did not have a response.

"I saw her myself two nights ago," the Hog said. "She was making her way out of the sacristy with one of the local teenagers."

"What's wrong with that?" his grandson asked.

"It was after eleven at night."

Edward raised an eyebrow. "I saw them myself last night."

"What time was this?" Lord Ratcliffe asked.

"Not sure. About midnight."

To Lovell, the timing made sense.

"Have you spoken to the priest?" the Hog asked.

"I have spoken to Father Martin," the Dog replied.

"And?"

Sitting among the friars, the priest again allowed Lovell to respond. "It is as I suspected."

The Hog was silently seething.

"You have seen the footage?" Ratcliffe asked.

"I have," the Dog replied.

"We have no room for error here. The village is not capable of withstanding another scandal."

"That may be so," added the Cat, "but if things remain unchecked, we could be facing an even bigger one."

"How did they get in?" Stanley asked.

"The priory ruins, or at least so it would seem," the Dog replied.

"Father?" Catesby asked the priest.

"There was definitely a light within the catacombs," Father Martin replied.

"It was definitely not natural?"

"I have seen the surveillance footage myself," Lovell beat the priest to a reply. "There is no room for equivocation."

The Hog adjusted his glasses. His facial expression had strengthened, as had his resolve.

"Gentlemen, as we are all aware, the fate of our organisation, our goal, our mission, can only survive on absolute secrecy. It is for this very reason, any obstacle must be eliminated."

The men sitting on both sides of the table all looked on with discomfort. The men were professionals in their fields, but their fields rarely involved death.

"And the hairdresser's daughter?" Ratcliffe asked.

"You are familiar with our laws, Richard. Any obstacle."

Silently Lovell was suffering. He had known the girl all her life.

History was repeating itself.

"But, gentlemen, before we part this morning, I feel I must leave you with one more pressing concern," the Hog began.

"As I know some of you are by now aware, the evil that has taken my chest has spread to other areas." He cleared his throat, a lengthy cough. "I don't need any medical projections to tell me my time is nigh. I must therefore do what every one of my predecessors has done, and do what is right for the future."

He paused for breath before delivering the final command.

"It is time for the coronation of my grandson. Together we shall lead until I depart, at which point he shall rule before God without equal. This will mark the first chapter of a new and brighter future."

Silence followed. At the far end of the table, the main three were less surprised.

"My friends," the Hog said. "Bring out the crown."

Watching through a crack in the wall, the shadowy female felt a familiar sense of terror as the strange ceremony took place under the light of the candles.

The quality of the film in her camera was poor, but it was there.

She waited until the crown was placed on the grandson's head before deciding enough was enough. Departing unseen, she made her way slowly along the passageway.

Just like the last time, there was no detection of her intrusion.

55

City of Westminster, 6 a.m.

The sun was rising, but the day was still to begin. Traffic was hectic as it always was, but for now it had yet to reach gridlock. A solitary siren in the distance served as a reminder that the city surrounded them, but the chaos was far from its peak.

The city was still in slumber.

Across the bridge, the Houses of Parliament were shrouded in the usual morning haze; the broken echo of Big Ben, chiming the new hour through the mist, held its great mystique. Even when the mist was thick, their outlines were usually visible. To the artist, the picture was iconic, irrespective of the time of day, year, or decade. The quintessential British picture of fine architecture cloaked by dreariness was out in full force.

At least until the heavens opened.

Less than two hundred metres away, the royal limousine stopped briefly on the unusually deserted A3212 to allow its distinguished passenger to alight. On this occasion, four burly men in dark suits accompanied the son of the new monarch. He walked with a vague swagger. Unlike the others, he dressed in a dark jacket, jeans and shoes.

Stephen walked quickly past St Margaret's Church in the direction of Westminster Abbey. He took a shortcut across the grass and headed for the Great West Door.

He stopped to take in the sights. The famous Gothic façade towered above him, the summit covered by low mist. At this hour the tourists were absent, a rare change from what would inevitably come when the sun was fully up. He watched with little emotion as the man to his right knocked loudly on the large door, the sound echoing like a giant's footstep. Almost immediately he heard another noise from within, followed by the creaking of the opening door.

He entered and continued past the coronation chair, through the nave towards the quire.

The dean was present, walking from the altar to the quire, well dressed despite the early hour. The order had come from the highest authority.

"What is the meaning of this?"

Stephen removed a large piece of paper from his pocket. "I have a royal decree ordering the exhumation of two of your tombs."

The dean didn't flinch. "I beg your pardon."

"It's all here," Stephen said, showing him the paper. "All the usual suspects have signed it."

The dean read it quickly. At first he failed to believe his eyes.

The monuments were priceless.

"Where are they?" Stephen insisted.

The dean failed to respond.

"Very well."

Stephen continued past the quire and veered left before reaching the altar. He passed the steps that led up to the shrine of St Edward the Confessor, and the various side chapels located opposite. He allowed himself a brief glance at the tombs of Edward I and Henry III at the top of the stairs to his right. He remembered from his history lessons that those two kings had played the greatest part in the abbey's history.

Looking around, the finished article was undoubtedly impressive.

There were stairs in front of him, slightly to the right. After continuing past the tomb of Henry V, he made his way to the bottom of the stairs and stopped.

Directly in front of him was the Lady chapel, one of the newer parts of the abbey.

Constructed under the will of Henry VII in memory of his wife and queen.

The woman who united the roses.

Stephen entered the chapel, a three-aisled nave constructed in the Perpendicular Gothic style with the altar located at the apse.

The tombs of Henry Tudor and Elizabeth were located behind the altar. Their gigantic gilt bronze effigies were barely visible behind the grille that covered them on every side.

The dean had caught up with them.

"How do we get in?" Stephen asked.

The man was dumbstruck. "This tomb was designed by Pietro Torrigiano, to excavate would be sacrilege."

"Uh huh. And what of the princes?"

He was desperate not to answer.

One of the bodyguards offered the prince a leaflet.

"Thank you," he said, studying it. "Ah."

Stephen left the Lady chapel and espied an open doorway to his right. He passed the joint tomb of Elizabeth and Mary and continued to the far end.

Among the statues of what appeared to be children, he saw a plain-looking urn with a Latin inscription.

The prince looked at his four accomplices. "Let's get cracking, shall we?"

Meanwhile, in the city of Mechelen in Belgium, two well-built and suited men walked hastily through the doors of St Rumbold's Cathedral, approaching a man similar in size, appearance and stature to the Dean of Westminster.

"You have been consulted?"

This dean was far more welcoming. "Follow me."

Less than an hour later, the various men left the respective holy houses and rejoined the outside world.

In Westminster, Stephen got into the limousine and immediately dialled the phone.

"Father, we've done it."

"Already?"

"Yes, the dean was most insistent we not delay."

He smiled to himself.

"What now?" Stephen asked.

A delay preceded the answer.

"Take it to the Royal College. Telephone me when the results are in."

In Belgium a similar event was taking place. The museum usually opened at 8 a.m., though today the first arrivals were earlier.

The eminent academic had been briefed face to face and by telephone.

Now all that was needed were the results.

56

Jen didn't sleep that night. Every time she tried, it became that little bit more difficult. She tried whiskey from the mini bar; she tried listening to music on her iPhone. Everything but counting sheep.

Even when she was a kid that never worked.

Her mind was active, but not in a good way. The appearance of the bizarre tombs continued to flash in her mind like a slideshow. It was like being part of a film: the images ominously reminiscent of a police scene where the victim was still lying on the ground, surrounded by forensic experts and a dreaded white line.

It simply didn't seem real.

She turned to her right, her attention on the wall. She looked at the pictures of the priory and the castle, so quaint and charming the day she moved in. She attempted to remember things about the previous day, but the harder she tried, the more difficult it became. How many graves were there?

How many phony kings of England lay buried within that peculiar crypt?

How many phony kings of England would later be buried there?

She turned to the other side of the bed and sipped from the glass of water. The liquid was becoming stale, most noticeable on the back of her throat. Sitting up against the pillows, she switched on Debra Harrison's camera and looked at the pictures. Then she looked at her iPhone.

She knew what she saw should not exist.

The question was what to do next? The priest had followed her; she knew it was the priest. The sound of his voice, the awkwardness of his gait . . . the signs were there.

She wondered how much he knew: not just about the crypt, but about what Jen now knew herself. Chances were he guessed it was her, though she doubted he knew for sure. She thought about leaving Wootton, but that itself would surely be seen as a sign of guilt. Besides, there was also Anthea to consider. And her job.

She had almost forgotten filming was due to start on Friday.

Her eyes wandered across the room, settling on the area in front of the door. There was something white on the floor, perhaps an envelope.

How long had that been there?

She left her bed, becoming aware of a horrible feeling of cold sweatiness on her naked legs. She wiped them down with her palms and then dried her hands on her nightshirt.

She picked up the envelope and switched on the light. There was no name on the envelope, no address, no stamp, but it had been sealed. She opened it carefully, the flap coming away easily.

She guessed it had only recently been sealed.

There were three objects inside: no writing, just photographs.

She looked at them one at a time.

Five minutes later, Jen was standing at the front desk. She dressed in the first thing she could find and was still to shower or put on make-up.

There was no sign of life in the hallway. As best she could tell, the nearest noise was coming from the kitchen. She heard what sounded like water boiling, accompanied by pots and pans moving.

She rang the bell on the desk. Receiving no reply, she tried again.

Then again.

As the seconds passed, she found herself becoming increasingly nervous.

Tara appeared from the kitchen. "You all right, luvvy?"

Jen attempted to remain calm. "Hi, I'm sorry, but I need to check out."

"Everything all right?"

"Yes," she lied. "I've got to go back to London – work."

"I'll just get the gaffer."

Mitchell appeared two minutes later. By now Jen felt her pounding heart was about to explode.

"Ey up. Tara says you've got to leave."

Jen faked a smile. "Work."

He looked at her, his façade giving nothing away. "Was everything to your satisfaction?"

"It was great."

The man was taking forever.

"Sorry, but I'm really in a hurry. I've got a meeting in, like, two hours."

"You best tell whoever it is you're going to be a bit late."

She faked another smile. "Not an easy man to tell."

Mitchell offered her a form and bill. "Sign here, please."

She signed the form and put in the pin on her credit card. Suddenly she no longer cared whether her boss would reimburse her or not.

"Hope to see you again, Miss Farrelly."

Less than thirty seconds later, Jen fired up her Picanto and reversed onto the road. She continued onto the high street and turned left, the easiest thing to do.

Her eyes were blurry with tears. She tried calling Anthea, but got no response. She followed the high street, heading in the direction of the nearest hamlet.

Breathing was almost impossible. She felt she was having a panic attack, if not worse. She looked in the mirror, her gaze falling on her eyes.

She'd never seen them so red.

She drove through the next hamlet and turned down a quiet lane. The area was wooded, silent and still. She stopped in a lay-by and cried for twenty minutes.

Given the choice of staying or leaving, the choice, it seemed, had now been made for her.

The photographs were revealing. There was no date on them, but she guessed one was recent. A strange ceremony, almost reminiscent of the Masons or the KKK, but the regalia appeared somehow more ancient.

A new king had emerged, his face hauntingly familiar.

The first two photos were less obvious, and she guessed older. Four men, perhaps monks, stood around another figure with a flour bag covering her head.

Her first reaction was to dismiss it, but she recognised the clothes from the photos.

Now she knew the poor girl was dead.

57

Thomas had made it to Yorkshire by 8 a.m. Despite the chaos of the day before, he was feeling better than he had been a few hours earlier. He'd been on the road for most of the night, choosing the motorway rather than a hotel. He hadn't intended to sleep at all, but tiredness eventually caught up with him. He left the M1 at a service station north of Nottingham, and pulled up in an empty bay in the most secluded part of the car park.

He didn't emerge for over three hours.

Caroline had chosen a small hotel in a place called Titherton, less than five miles from Wootton. Like most places in that part of the world, the landscape was breathtaking and rugged, and the hamlet a hotchpotch of quiet roads, secluded woodland, farmland and quaint houses.

Chocolate boxy, as Caroline would say.

The hotel was located just off the main road, half a mile out of the hamlet itself. From the outside, it looked just like a boathouse, and sure enough, that was what it was. The river flowed quickly, surrounded by picturesque greenery, a footpath, and the hotel's beer garden. The car park was on a slope and flanked by trees. Thomas noticed the Rolls parked in a secluded spot, practically invisible from the road. Today, he drove one of his own private vehicles, a new Toyota Corolla, which was less likely to attract attention.

He entered the hotel through the main entrance and continued along the corridor to the stairs. The walls were a mixture of blue and white, and the furniture primarily nautical. He left the stairs on the second of three floors, and walked along the corridor to the far end. The final door was white, furnished with a fake round life-support cushion.

He knocked politely and almost immediately heard movement, followed by the door being unlocked.

The door opened, and he looked inside.

The sight was unexpected.

*

Over two hundred miles away, the senior physician and the leading scientist were involved in an animated discussion. The samples were still to undergo all the necessary tests, but the initial findings were revealing.

Meanwhile, in the city of Oxford, a large van turned slowly in the car park of the Ashmolean Museum. Several metres away, Professor Emeritus of Keble College Patrick Wilson and esteemed Professor of Magdalen College, Harry Ainsworth, awaited its arrival.

Both had been briefed about the possible ramifications, not that it had been necessary.

This was the second time Wilson had been asked to act as adviser to the royals.

The only time they called was in an emergency.

In Belgium, the third test was about to get underway. In a quiet laboratory, away from public eyes, the two scientists opened the box in front of them.

The results would be ready in less than an hour.

58

Jen was shell-shocked. Even though she had stopped crying, she was still shaking. The images were disturbing, but it was not that which bothered her most. Whoever had sent her the photographs had presumably witnessed the events.

Or worse yet, helped perform them.

She moved the car further along the lane, now adjacent to a footpath that led to sparse woodland overlooking the nearby valley. This was the heart of the North York Moors National Park. At the height of the season, hordes of hikers, tourists and cyclists would frequent this beautiful part of England, their accents ranging from LA to Lancashire. At this early hour, however, the land was lonely. The animals had disappeared, including the birds and the butterflies. In the quiet, even her breathing seemed loud. She sought seclusion, but part of her wanted company.

One wrong move and they could find her.

Assuming, of course, they were looking.

Composing herself, she left the car and followed the footpath for about one hundred metres before stopping on reaching a rocky outcrop that was dusty but otherwise deserted.

She felt cold, but that had nothing to do with the temperature. Normal things felt strange. She tried Anthea again, but got no response. Rationalising she was still in bed, she studied the photographs in more detail. They appeared black and white, which suggested they were intended to be atmospheric, but on closer inspection she realised that was not the case. In the background there was a light, possibly from a candle.

Whatever had gone on had done so underground and in darkness.

Jen looked closely at the first picture. The girl – she could tell it was a girl by her posture – was surrounded by four men, all of whom were dressed in some form of religious habit, though different to anything she had seen on TV or in real life.

The last photo was particularly troubling. It didn't take a genius to see the lad was being crowned. Had she not seen the vault, the ceremony would have been baffling.

The House of York had a new king.

Or at least a pretender.

She turned to the first photograph and dropped the other two. As she leaned forward to pick them up, she noticed something on the back. There was writing, numbers but no words.

Then she looked at the back of the one she hadn't dropped and saw it began with 07.

Her heart missed a beat.

Surely it was a mobile phone number.

She looked at the other two, struggling to decide on the order. She decided the coronation picture was likely to be the newest, meaning it would be the last in sequence.

She put the numbers together and entered them into her iPhone.

It rang.

Two bleeps.

Three . . .

Four . . .

"Hello?"

It was a woman's voice – perhaps a teenager.

Jen struggled to speak. "I got your note."

Silence lasted several seconds.

"You're not safe."

She knew that but felt even worse on hearing her say it.

"Where are you?"

It took Jen a while to answer. "I'm in a wood, near Titherton."

"Stay there. I'll come to you."

Back in London, the royal limousine pulled up in an empty car park. Ordinarily this part of the Royal College of Physicians was off limits to the public.

But he was hardly that.

Stephen was standing by the entrance, a large white building with automatic doors that visually resembled a giant letter T. He had arrived only moments earlier, accompanied by his guards. He watched as the driver of the limousine opened the rear door. Seconds later, the King emerged, followed by the Duke of York.

Stephen was amazed. "You should be in bed."

"Utter nonsense. All it needed was a good follow-through." He clapped his hands together.

Stephen rubbed his eyes.

The King was not amused. "Let's hope they have some good news for us."

"I'm surprised they have any news at all," the duke said.

Stephen understood the point. "I have spoken to Dr Grant personally. We should have the preliminary results within the hour."

59

Thomas followed Caroline through the bar area and into a room that was used for private functions. Although there was nobody in the bar, he was in no mood to take any chances.

Caroline took the first available seat at a large table and immediately started running her hands through her hair. Thomas sat down opposite, his posture altogether more rigid.

"Do you mind telling me what the hell has been going on?"

Caroline stared at him for several seconds. "We could hardly talk with her there, could we?"

His patience was wearing thin. "Who is she?" he asked of the teenage brunette he had seen lying asleep in one of the beds.

"I don't know. I only met her last night."

Thomas was unimpressed.

"Whoever she is, she could be the key to blowing this whole thing wide open," she said, pausing. The atmosphere was so heavy it seemed to be affecting her breathing. "How's my dad?"

"W-well, I hear. He's already left hospital."

She smiled, touching her nose. "Sounds like him."

Thomas took a deep breath. He rubbed his eyes, but tiredness was no longer a problem.

"I'll get us a coffee."

"Later," he replied, louder and more aggressively than he had intended. "Tell me what happened."

"The bike continued to Wootton," she said, repeating what he already knew. "I followed it as best I could, but it was difficult to stay with it the whole time. Did you know they sometimes skip red lights?"

"I assure you they're not supposed to. I assume he was tracked."

"Yes, that's what led me here. Our intelligence informs me his destination was a large house in Wootton-on-the-Moor. It belongs to a relative of ours."

"Jeffries."

"What's he got to do with all this?"

The question was where to start. "Believe me, I've been asking myself that s-same question." He shook his head. "What of the girl?"

"I stopped on the high street after following the directions from the palace. The house itself was quite secluded – I thought it best not to park too close."

Fair enough. "Then what?"

"After stopping on the high street, I spoke to your father and some other fellow, I forget his name, and he told me to stay where I was . . . I only went out to get a bite to eat. And I really needed the loo. I found myself in a quiet little alleyway. Thinking I wasn't attracting attention, I . . ."

"I get the picture."

"Then I was walking back, and she recognised me."

Suddenly he was alarmed. "She's a J-Jeffries?"

"No," she said, disgusted. "She recognised me from a magazine."

The prince exhaled furiously. "Why on earth did you drag her in on this?"

"I assure you I had no intention of doing anything of the kind. Turns out she had a rather strange experience the night before."

"Go on."

"Yes, seems she's become friends with a journalist of some kind. Jen, I think her name was."

"Get to the point."

She smiled. "I will. And you are going to love this."

60

The girl arrived twenty minutes later. Jen had been sitting in the same place, her attention on the moors. She hoped that the heavy dark cloud, moving progressively nearer, was in no hurry to unleash its fury. The wind had also picked up slightly, and she knew from past experience that the weather in these parts was often hard.

A deluge was the last thing she needed.

The girl was about five feet eight, slender build, and had dark brown hair. From a distance, she could have been any woman in the UK: a student, a doctor, a housewife, a celeb . . .

Even one of her friends.

It wasn't until she saw the girl up close that Jen was confident enough to know for sure.

In truth, she had expected it.

She had seen the girl before: first on the camera, and then in the heritage centre.

And now here.

The girl stopped several metres away. Jen was still to move; she merely watched, taking in her features. An awkward silence overcame them, not just them but the entire valley. The girl was nervous, just as Jen had expected. It was obvious from the photographs that she knew something important, but the girl's agitation seemed somehow more permanent. It was the eyes that did it: a striking shade of hazel that seemed excessively wide and paranoid. Against the backdrop of her pale skin and dark hair, the effect seemed greater still. Her hair was long, but lacking in volume. Either the girl had the flu or she neglected herself.

Jen sensed it was the latter.

"You're Stephanie, aren't you?"

The girl hesitated.

Jen decided not to push her. Remaining on the rock, she adjusted her position, making her body language more open.

"I wanted to see you," Jen said, testing the water. "Anthea told me about you."

Again the girl did not respond.

"She said you were Debra's best friend."

The girl she thought was Stephanie was becoming increasingly drained. "This was a bad idea."

Jen leapt to her feet as the girl began to depart. "Wait, please . . ." Jen grabbed her arm. The girl stopped, but Jen immediately released her.

For several seconds she had no idea what to expect. The girl was rattled, but Jen could see as she looked more closely that there was no malice in her eyes. Just like the Rankin kid, reports of mental instability appeared premature. The girl was not crazy.

Just afraid.

"Why did you send me the photographs?" Jen asked, waiting for a response that never came. "You know what happened, don't you?"

Again the girl remained quiet. The longer this went on, the faster Jen's heart was beating.

"Did you take the photos?"

The girl's breathing had become noticeably louder, almost to the point of hyperventilation.

"Come here." Jen guided her to the rock where she had been sitting.

Stephanie removed her inhaler from her pocket and inhaled urgently for several seconds.

Jen's heart filled with pity. She used to suffer hay fever in the pollen season.

But the girl was struggling on another level.

Two minutes passed before her breathing settled down.

"Thank you."

Jen moved closer, trying not to invade her space. "I saw you in the heritage centre. Why were you following me?"

This time the pause was brief. "It's not safe for you in Wootton."

That was surely an understatement. "What's this all about?"

"The Sons of York have never been one to tolerate outsiders."

Jen was confused. "Who are the Sons of York?"

Stephanie lowered her head. "Debra was my best friend," she said, this time with strength in her voice. "Most people in Wootton are unaware of the true history of the village. For many years, it's been restricted only to the same families."

Jen was interested. "What was happening in the photographs?"

"Debra was abducted because she stumbled on the Sons of York's greatest secret."

"The tombs in the vault?"

She looked at Jen, but said nothing.

"What did they do to her?"

The question went unanswered. Jen knew from the first photograph that whatever it was, it was far from good.

"What were they doing to Edward Jeffries?"

"The Jeffries family hold much prestige in this part of the world. They are distantly related to the Royal Family."

"You're kidding?"

Stephanie shook her head. "In the past, their influence was greater still."

"I found a monument with Plantagenet names on it."

"The village began when the manor was given by Edward III to his son, Edmund of Langley."

"Is that from where the family originated?"

The girl brushed her hair back behind her ear. "Some of the distant family claim ancestry from him, but other branches have a stronger claim. If you've seen the vault of kings, as they call it, then you must already know what it means."

Jen didn't linger on the point. "How do you know all this?"

"My uncle."

"Stanley? He's a Jeffries?"

"No. But my family have always been members."

"What is it they want?"

Again the girl hesitated.

"Stephanie, please, I need to know."

"The Sons of York were founded when the House of York was defeated in the Wars of the Roses. In the early years, the aim was to retake the throne."

"They still covet the throne of England?"

"Maybe. But not since the 1600s has an actual attempt been made to usurp the throne. But despite their fall, the influence of the families has been great. Many of its members are prominent people: politicians, businessmen, lawyers . . ."

"You mean like Lord Ratcliffe?"

She nodded.

"What's so special? What's so important?"

The girl took a deep breath and composed herself. "It all goes back to the Second World War, and even more directly to the formation of the European Union."

*

Thirty minutes later Jen was back in Wootton. She parked in a lay-by in a quiet lane just outside the village and continued on foot along the high street.

She followed the same alleyway she had walked a few days earlier and stopped before a quiet cottage.

She rang the bell, and a woman answered.

"I know what happened to your son," Jen said. "Stephanie told me everything."

Standing by the doorway, Susan Rankin seemed initially unmoved.

"Come in."

61

Thomas thought he was hearing things. "You can't possibly be serious."

Caroline thought it was funny.

"What?"

She tucked her hair behind her ear. "Nothing."

Thomas watched his cousin for several seconds, trying to digest what she had just told him.

What he had just heard beggared belief.

"She told you all this?"

"Yes."

He failed to accept the answer.

"What?"

"She saw a vault?"

"Saw it and described it in detail."

Thomas left his seat and wandered towards the window. He looked at the landscape, his mind in a daze.

It didn't seem real.

"You knew. Didn't you?" said Caroline.

Thomas turned around. Caroline was sitting with her arms folded, her expression suddenly cold.

"Why didn't you tell me? You could have trusted me."

He exhaled deeply. "I didn't know myself until last night. I assume you saw the article in the *Chronicle*."

She nodded and touched her nose. Thomas had noticed that she often touched the area where the surgery had been even though evidence of where the stitches had been was now practically nonexistent.

"It was our great-uncle, the Earl of Somerset."

"The historian?"

"Yes."

She was gobsmacked. "He wrote the article?"

"No – he was the source."

That made more sense, at least. "Why? Why would he do that?"

"He said it was to get our attention," Thomas replied, laughing to himself. "Apparently s-some of the older members of our f-family have not been particularly willing to listen to his advice."

"He always was a bit of a coot. What did he say?"

Thomas filled her in, but she didn't fully understand.

"But why?"

"I don't have all the answers. Clearly it stems back centuries."

"You think they killed Granddad?" Caroline's eyes watered.

He placed his hand on top of hers and rubbed them. "Stephen is carrying out tests on the tombs. Apparently they can test for DNA."

"What if they come back positive?"

He delayed his response. "Let's hope they don't."

For several seconds neither of them spoke. Thomas focused on his cousin, then the situation.

"You said there was another? With the girl."

"There was. A researcher or something, researching a documentary on the girl who disappeared."

"Name?"

"Jennifer Farrelly."

"Where is she now?"

"In Wootton. She's staying at an inn called the White Boar."

"I think I best be paying Miss Farrelly a little visit."

Standing alone in his office, Dr Maurice Grant was practically speechless. The results were now in, and right there before him.

He looked at his watch, then the clock on the wall to confirm.

The King would have been waiting for over twenty minutes.

62

Jen simply stared at the woman sitting opposite, stunned by what she was hearing.

"Why didn't you say anything?"

The woman laughed, but without humour. "You think I didn't want to?" she asked, her tone becoming ever louder. "You think I didn't want to expose the evil that has plagued this village for over five hundred years. You think . . ."

Her voice trailed off as she failed to prevent herself from crying.

From across the living room, Jen watched awkwardly. There was a sudden distance to the woman, even though, so far, she had been warm.

At least warmer than a few days ago.

Rankin wiped her eyes. "Perhaps it's unfair of me to expect you to understand. You're from London; you didn't grow up in a small close-knit community."

Jen was sick of people saying that. "I grew up in Nottinghamshire. It was a village, but larger than here."

The woman didn't respond. She sipped her tea and replaced the cup on a saucer.

"What happened to my son was unfair and unnecessary. Even for the Sons of York, it was an act of unique violence. Historically they have been at war with the royals throughout the ages. I had never come across anything so bad in my lifetime."

"What happened?"

"I guess Luke was in the wrong place at the wrong time. It was known that he had taken something of a shine to Debra."

Jen decided not to push the issue. "How was he doing at school?"

"Good. He was going to university in the autumn."

"Had he decided where?"

"Keele."

Jen nodded, impressed.

"He was bright enough for Oxford – at least that's what the

predicted grades were. But he decided he liked the area. He wasn't cut out for the stress of the top two."

Jen took that with a liberal pinch of salt. It certainly didn't tie in with the earlier reports she had been given about Luke's academic abilities.

She also decided to avoid questions of his mental state.

"I spoke to Miss Cartwright."

Rankin's eyes lit up. "The one person at that awful school who saw Luke for what he really was: a victim."

"She suggested he would go far. Particularly science."

The woman smiled faintly.

"Mrs Rankin, please forgive me for asking, but why would the Sons of York do what they did? If it was simply to frame him, why wasn't Debra Harrison also found?"

The woman paused for several seconds. "I guess you'll have to wait until the body is found."

The answer was clinical.

Even without seeing the photograph, it was clear that the woman assumed Debra Harrison was dead.

Jen got to her feet. "Thank you for your time, Mrs Rankin."

"Be careful."

63

Thomas drove slowly along the high street of Wootton-on-the-Moor, following the directions of the Satnav.

The setting was enough to make his skin itch. Visually the village was a fine example of Middle England: grade II listed houses, rolling hills in the distance, and practically no cars on the road. It was the kind of place where his relatives were found – particularly on their holidays.

Or even when not on holiday.

He left the high street about midway down and continued over the bridge. There was a church directly in front of him and a few other buildings, one of which was an inn. According to the GPS, he had reached his destination.

The first thing he noticed was the sign.

The White Boar. Accompanied by the character of a white pig.

He couldn't believe what he was seeing. He knew for a fact most inns named the White Boar had changed to the Blue Boar since Bosworth.

The symbol of the House of York was running strong.

He pulled up in the car park and entered the inn through the main door. Fearing being recognised, he wore a black baseball cap, dark jacket, and decided to leave the shave till later. The bar area was surprisingly deserted – it was Thursday and surely the height of the tourist season.

There was a man behind the bar, thickset and evidently a northerner.

Mitchell looked at the prince and smiled. "How do?"

Thomas smiled back. "Morning. I'm looking for one of your guests. Miss Farrelly."

Mitchell didn't bat an eyelid. Yet another of Jen's admirers.

"Who's asking?"

"I'm a f-friend." He cursed the stutter.

Harvey looked at the young man, for now deciding against replying. "Well, friend, I'm afraid you're a little late. She checked out this morning."

Now he was cursing his luck. "Did she say where she was going?"

"I thought you were her friend."

He bit his lip. "Thank you for your time."

Thomas left the Hog, and not a moment too soon. Just being there made him nervous.

He returned to the car and reversed out onto the road. He started back towards the high street, but something was on his mind.

He didn't have a clue where he was going.

In a small laboratory in Belgium, the two prominent scientists studied the results in front of them.

The results were startling, but not for the reasons they had expected.

The King would want to know about this.

64

Jen left the house and walked quickly down the hill towards the high street.

To say she was unnerved was an understatement. The words 'be careful', completely harmless, perhaps even warm and caring depending on the person who said it or the circumstances, seemed distinctly cold and serious.

The reason needed no clarification.

It was approaching 11 a.m. The high street was deserted, but today she noticed a far more sombre presence in the air. There was a noticeable silence about the place, not only that but an unnatural stillness. There were clouds in the sky, perhaps a precursor to rain, and a steady breeze that caused a rustling noise through the trees. Jen could hear every individual sound, be it leaves caught in an updraft, a window rattling or the echo of distant machinery. Even the wildlife was silent.

She shook her head, doing her best to dismiss the feeling.

She rationalised the situation was getting to her.

For the first time that day her stomach was acting normally. The sickly feeling that had engulfed her from the larynx down had faded in recent hours.

Now she was ravenous.

She bought a ham and cheese baguette from the Co-op and ate it as she walked. She saw no one in the shop bar the shop assistant, and more importantly detected nothing amiss. She tried phoning Anthea again as she walked and once more got no response.

She figured she was probably working.

She passed the road to the Hog, doing her best to ignore the buildings on the other side of the bridge. Keeping her head down, she walked on, continuing to the hairdresser's.

The door opened, accompanied by the usual ringing of the bell. Martha was inside, clearly beside herself.

She looked at Jen. "Where is she?"

"Excuse me?"

"Where is she?"

"Where's who?"

The woman was livid. "What do you mean, 'where's who?' Where's my daughter?"

Although she retained a calm exterior, silently Jen was feeling panicked. "I . . . I was just about to ask you. I was going to meet her."

The woman was practically in tears.

"Martha . . ."

"What happened last night?"

Jen decided not to be truthful. "Nothing . . . we just went for a walk . . . Martha, what is it?"

"Anthea didn't come home last night." She was struggling to control herself.

Inside Jen felt cold. Though the tiled walls gave off a cool feeling, she knew they were not the cause of the goose bumps that she could now feel across her arms, back and neck.

She tried desperately to remain calm. "Martha, I don't understand."

The woman's eyes had turned violent. "She never stays out without calling . . . if anything has happened to her."

Jen was dumbstruck. Had she not seen it herself, she'd never have believed the woman was capable of such hostility.

Suddenly she remembered the light in the vault, the one she assumed belonged to a torch carried by the priest.

Had someone discovered it was her?

"Where did you go last night?"

This time Jen didn't answer. Afraid of saying anything, she left the shop and headed back up the high street.

"Jen!"

Jen quickened her pace. Seconds later Martha called again, this time more desperately, surely loud enough for others to hear. Jen looked at her iPhone, hoping, praying, that Anthea had got back to her.

Nothing.

Martha had left the shop and was following her, her cries now even louder. Among the cries were tears.

Jen did her best to ignore her. Increasing her pace further still, she thought about what Susan Rankin had said.

How many people knew the real truth about the village?

Did Martha know what she now knew?

"Jen!"

Jen burst into a jog. She passed the road that led to the church, now two-thirds of the way along the high street. The shouts of the woman had aroused no attention whatsoever.

Was everyone deaf, or did they choose to ignore her?

There was movement up ahead. A man had appeared, seemingly from nowhere. He was about six feet tall, if not a few inches more, and had a visibly strong physique.

She stopped, rooted to the spot.

The man was dressed in the robes of a monk or friar, black and white, clearly a Dominican.

Seconds later the man removed a firearm from inside his habit.

Thomas followed the road away from the church, heading back to the high street. As he drove, he looked into the rear-view mirror. Ignoring the unshaven shabby appearance that he barely recognised, he focused on the road behind him.

There was a building beside the church, perhaps several, though most were further away. The buildings were grand: like manor houses or something of equal prestige.

He guessed Jeffries lived in one of them.

He continued to the T-junction, his mind still on the area behind him.

Then something startled him.

Out of the silence, he heard a gunshot.

Jen screamed, a high-pitched whine. Two shots had been fired, the bullets missing her by a matter of inches.

She ducked to one side and stumbled, barely making it to the pavement. She felt the impact on her knees, but also her left shoulder.

She rolled, trying to get to her feet. As she did, she felt the asphalt graze her cheek. She feared to look, or even open her eyes. She could hear the man's footsteps accompanied by the sound of the weapon being reloaded.

She scampered to her feet and screamed as loudly as her lungs would allow. She moved towards the T-junction, looking for any sign of life. Incredibly she was still alone, the hooded gunman the only person close to her. Even the recently furious Martha Brown had disappeared from sight.

Please God to call the police.

She continued forward, but her progress was interrupted by another fall. She rolled instinctively, her nerves going into overdrive as she heard the sound of the gun going off. As before, she heard two shots in close succession, the latest uncomfortably close. Her left ear felt hot, particularly at the top.

She knew the bullet had grazed her.

Sure enough, it had drawn blood.

Thomas eased forward, unsure what had happened. He heard another shot, perhaps two. Instinct told him it had come from somewhere in front of him, but buildings on the left and right blocked the view to the high street.

He drove forward, stopping on reaching the junction. To his left, a man dressed in the habit and cloak of a Dominican friar was reloading what looked like a double-barrelled shotgun, his target a blonde woman aged somewhere in the mid-twenties. He saw him fire twice in quick succession.

The woman was on the ground, evidently still alive.

Thomas reacted instantly, ramming through the gears and flooring the accelerator. He braked as late as possible, the screeching tyres smoking as he took the corner and emerged onto the high street.

The girl was on the road, trying to get to her feet. She saw the car as Thomas took the turn, her expression one of bewilderment.

He slammed on the brakes and leaned across to open the door.

"Get in."

65

For what seemed like a lifetime, the blonde girl did nothing.

All the while, the friar was reloading.

Thomas shouted, "Come on."

This time Jen obeyed. Keeping her head low, she sprinted towards the door and dived across the front passenger seat.

Thomas wasted no time. He floored the accelerator, and the tyres spun furiously, causing smoke to rise from the front two. The smell of burning rubber momentarily overwhelmed that of disused shotgun cartridges as the smoke permeated through the open window.

The gunman had reloaded and was aiming directly at the car. He unleashed one at the windscreen, causing the glass to break.

Jen screamed loudly.

"Stay down," Thomas shouted.

A second round came, also a direct hit. Glass entered the car, but the windscreen itself remained intact.

Just.

The gunman was forced to reload.

Thomas put his foot down, now on collision course with the shooter. He was less than twenty metres away, fifteen, ten, five . . .

The friar dived, far too late. The impact occurred on the left side, more a passing blow than a head-on collision. Thomas could see from the rear-view mirror that the man was flat out on the road, motionless but probably not dead.

Thomas guessed the injury was to the upper body rather than the head.

He continued through the village, his eyes alternating between the road and the rear-view mirror. Seconds later the high street was no longer in view.

He turned his attention to Jen, surveying her appearance for the first time. She was crying, the tears ruining her black eyeliner. She was more attractive than he had expected, but in a state.

He guessed from her lack of make-up she'd had a bad day.

At least the hairdresser's story checked out.

"It's okay; you're safe."

Jen didn't respond. She tried to control herself, but doing so was becoming more and more difficult. She wiped her eyes, doing everything she could to keep the floodgates shut.

The last thing she needed was to lose control of her emotions.

Thomas, meanwhile, watched with pity. His natural instinct was to pull over and comfort her, but he forced himself to be disciplined.

He knew further danger was probably still close at hand.

Jen looked as though she was going to vomit.

"Here, drink this." He passed her a half-full bottle of mineral water from the cup holder.

Jen opened the bottle and coughed immediately. The liquid simply refused to go down.

"Slowly."

She tried again, this time with more success. She spilt some on her jeans, but most of it went down, calming her nerves slightly.

She closed the bottle and placed it on the floor, concentrating now on her breathing. She wiped her eyes, composing herself.

Thomas watched her, convinced she was in a fit state to be questioned.

"What happened?"

She looked to her right at the stranger. She tried to speak but failed.

"Wh-who was that man?"

She still had no idea.

"What happened?" he asked, slightly louder.

She sought to reply, but the words just refused to come.

What on earth had just happened?

"Who are you?" This time the question came from Jen.

Thomas was determined not to stutter. "I'm the son of the Duke of Clarence – nephew of the king."

You're kidding.

No, he isn't kidding.

"Okay." For several seconds she merely sat and watched as he drove her through the isolated roads. Although the route was familiar from her earlier journey, she had no idea where he was taking her.

"I take it you're Jennifer Farrelly?"

She nodded, incapable of anything else. "And you? Do you have a name?"

He hesitated. "T-Thomas."

She studied him for the first time. He was handsome, as expected – what royal isn't? Or at least that was the fantasy.

He was well built, his figure befitting an army pedigree – or at least something from the forces. He was handsome – wait, she'd established that – though slightly ragged. She guessed he hadn't slept much recently.

Thomas looked to his left. "What?"

"What are you doing here?"

He didn't reply. Silently he guessed she already knew, assuming the hairdresser wasn't lying.

"How did you know my name?"

"I m-met your friend."

"Friend?" Suddenly it dawned on her. "Anthea?"

"You needn't worry. She's safe."

If anything, that made her even more insecure. "You abducted her?"

"Of course not, it's a l-long story."

"I'm in no hurry."

"I'm afraid that's where you're wrong," the prince said, his tone firmer than before. "Time is the one thing that we don't have. Wh-what are you doing here, anyway?"

"I was being shot at – remember?"

He let the comment go. "Your friend said you were researching a documentary on the g-girl who went m-missing."

"That's right." She looked at him. "What?"

"You seem to have outstayed your welcome."

He turned down a quiet lane, heading towards the boathouse.

"There was a man dressed in the habit of a Dominican friar firing at you."

"Yeah. I noticed."

"Had you seen him before?"

"What?"

"The friar – had you seen him?"

Jen was appalled. "Of course not."

"So you didn't recognise him?"

"No," she said, apparently baffled by the question. "Had you?"

The prince was not amused. "You're quite certain you had never seen him before?"

"Yes, I've only been here a few days."

"That's often quite long enough. What happened? Just now, wh-what happened?"

Jen took a deep breath. She told him everything that had happened after leaving the hairdresser's.

"There was no warning?"

"None."

"And you're certain you didn't recognise him?"

She looked as if to hit him. "No."

This time he believed her. "Okay. But why was he shooting at you? Come on, you must have some idea? Things like this don't j-just happen without good reason."

This time it was Jen's turn to be coy. She guessed the prince, if indeed he was a prince, probably knew more than she did.

"I've never seen him before."

"You've established that," he said. "Tell me about the vault?"

"The what?"

"Your friend told us there was a vault – she also t-told us about the churchyard."

The surprise was etched all over her face. At least she knew that Anthea was safe.

She told him everything – finishing with Stephanie Stanley and the likely murder of Luke Rankin. She could tell by the prince's reaction that he was taking it seriously.

Perhaps extra seriously.

He pulled up in the car park of the boathouse and removed his seatbelt.

He looked at her sternly, remaining seated. "Tell me everything you know about the Sons of York."

"I only heard of them for the first time earlier today."

That makes two of us. "What do you know?"

"Probably less than you."

"Actually, I know very little."

She didn't buy it. "We got into the vault via a secret passage – it started in the priory, and another ended up at the castle."

"Go on."

"There's a door in the church vaults, but it's locked. When I asked the priest for the key, he gave me some cock-and-bull story about it being unsafe."

"In what way?"

"He said it was used to house the remains of plague victims."

"You mean he lied?"

"Obviously."

"What sparked your interest in the vault?"

"I thought Debra Harrison might be buried there."

"Is she?"

"No . . . well . . . I don't know."

In truth she had never considered that since yesterday.

Thomas was equally uncomfortable. "Wh-what was there?"

"You're a member of the Royal Family; how can you not know?"

"Just because I'm royal . . ." His voice trailed off. "Just answer the question."

"Why?"

Did she really just demand that?

"I spoke to her best friend today – her name's Stephanie; her uncle is a member."

His interest heightened. "What's his name?"

"Rowland Stanley, the politician. All of them live in houses east of the church. Ravensfield, it's called."

The prince couldn't believe what he was hearing.

Verification of the location of the mysterious Ravensfield.

To him it was also confirmation that the society was close knit.

"Go on."

"Their most prominent members are Lord Ratcliffe, Sir William Catesby and Francis Lovell. Lovell is a former headmaster of the school, Catesby is a scientist or something, Ratcliffe . . . well, I guess you know."

Thomas bit his lip, this time harder than before.

The Cat, the Rat and the Dog.

It was all too incredible.

"But why? To what purpose?"

"According to Stephanie, among their ranks are many politicians, particularly from the Democrats."

Everything he heard agreed with what he had learned the day before. "To what end?"

She sighed. "According to Stephanie, their long-term agenda is to re-establish the Angevin Empire by taking power in the governments of Britain and Europe – including ridding England of the Royal Family. It wishes to gain control of both the UK and the EU through the establishment of a Democrat government."

"That's preposterous. There have already been Democrat governments."

She nodded. "Apparently this all goes back centuries; back to the

Whigs. Besides, I think the Democrat movement is just the flagship. According to Stephanie, their influence spans all parties. They have support from many in the Tories."

"Impossible. We'd know."

She raised her eyebrows but said nothing. Silently Thomas was worried.

He still had no idea why the politicians Trenton and Bates were murdered.

"How does she know?"

Jen delved into her handbag and removed the photographs Stephanie had given her.

She offered them to the prince.

His attention centred on the coronation photo. "Edward."

She nodded.

He looked at Jen, then to his right. Caroline was running towards them.

"Stephen called. The results of the DNA test have come through."

66

The Duke of York was pacing up and down the room and had been since their arrival. By now it was starting to rile the King.

"Sit down, for goodness' sake; you're making me nervous."

The duke refused to comply. "It's all that lying in a hospital bed. The linen's too tight, I tell you."

Stephen smiled. "I'll be sure to mention that to Aunt Victoria next time I see her."

The King looked at his son, but on this occasion did not smile. He checked his watch, then the clock on the wall.

"Where is Grant?"

York checked the time himself. "Reminds me of the last time we were here."

"Shut up, William."

Moments later the door opened, and Grant entered. As before, he carried several papers in his hands.

"Sorry to have kept you waiting," the physician said.

At least this time there was no Home Secretary there to snigger.

"I have the results."

The King leaned forward, his eyes firmly on the physician. "Well?"

The physician removed his glasses from his pocket and began reading the top sheet. "As per Your Majesty's instructions, the urn containing the bodies of the two children was removed from the tomb, along with that of the former queen. After having proceeded to remove the bones deemed not of human origin–"

"Human origin?" York interrupted.

Stephen nodded. "Yes. According to the original accounts from 1674, on finding the bodies under the tower stair, there was evidence of animal bones, probably an ape from the Tower menagerie, along with that of the boys. Not to mention rubble from the excavation."

He looked at the King. "Thomas told me that."

The King was in no mood to smile.

"Wasn't there also a purple rag?" asked Stephen.

"I believe so," said Grant.

The King leaned forward. "Go on, Maurice."

The physician returned to the results. "After identifying which bones were human and which were not, bones of both human skeletons were separated into two batches. One was sent to my colleague here, the other to the Ashmolean. Both tests have been completed, and both, I might add, have so far come to a similar conclusion."

York looked up at the man. "Well, friend, what's the verdict?"

The physician hesitated. "The results confirm beyond doubt that skeletons of both boys possess a minor biological link to what is commonly dubbed the 'Plantagenet line' used, of course, to distinguish descendants of Henry II. They also confirmed that the skeletons were of two boys, definitely brothers," the physician added, attempting to keep his composure. "It is the considered view, however, of all who have studied the results that the link is insufficient for what we had expected."

The King's eyes narrowed. "In English?"

"The boys, sire, were definitely not of direct relation to Edward IV. Furthermore, the subjects in question both died of natural causes."

All present looked at the physician.

"How about the time period?" Stephen asked.

"Again, Your Grace, we can only speculate . . ."

"Then give us your speculation."

"The likeliest age range, based on the probability of a high-protein diet as would be usual for a noble, we could be looking at any time between 1515 and 1600."

York was the first to speak. "You are quite sure?"

"We can never be one hundred per cent sure, Your Grace, particularly after only a few hours of testing. However, it is the esteemed opinion of my colleagues–"

"And what do you think?" asked the King.

The physician paused before answering. "I think that their conclusions are almost certainly correct."

The King nodded. He controlled his disappointment well.

"And Elizabeth?"

"It would seem the body of the woman did indeed have a biological similarity with what is known of the Woodvilles, but we could find no trace of a family connection to what we know of the Plantagenets."

The King nodded, remaining calm. "How about Clement?"

"I have spoken to the scientists who managed the proceedings at St

Rumbold's. I have only the preliminary results, but it appears that what they tested were the remains of another man."

Stephen rose to his feet, a reflex. "What?"

"Sit down," the King said.

"You're quite sure?" Stephen asked.

"Again, at this stage, it is difficult to say with any degree of certainty," the physician replied. "Nevertheless, the results were most surprising. The age of the subject was noticeably different."

"How different?"

"Perhaps even forty years."

The result was conclusive.

The King rose to his feet. "Thank you, Maurice."

The black limousine left the car park, heading back towards Westminster.

Stephen shuffled in his seat, his eyes on his father and uncle. "In truth, this confirms nothing."

"It confirms one thing," the King said, clearly distracted. "It confirms we are all in severe danger."

York was unconvinced. "If the skeletons were not of the princes, then who?"

"Montagu," the King said. "Disappeared at the Tower during the reign of Henry VIII."

No one argued.

The hypothesis seemed plausible.

Back in the city, the Home Secretary took the call immediately.

The events of earlier that morning had already left him somewhat bewildered.

Now things had just got worse.

67

Thomas flopped down on the bed, dumbstruck. Despite being aware of the hypothesis, the result of the DNA test was still difficult to digest.

Jen moved slowly to the corner of the room. It seemed unthinkable that she had stumbled on a matter of great importance to the Royal Family.

It was obvious she was not supposed to be there.

Caroline took a seat on the other bed, alongside Anthea. The hairdresser was wide-awake but clearly dazed.

She still couldn't believe that was the real Caroline.

Thomas sat with his head in his hands, his fingers massaging his temples. Almost immediately he rose to his feet.

"I need to make a phone call."

He left the room, heading somewhere along the corridor. With Thomas gone, Caroline asked, "What happened?"

The question was for Jen. She let out a deep sigh before speaking for several minutes, leaving Caroline shocked and Anthea mortified.

Particularly the part about Anthea's mum.

"I need to give her a call—"

"No, no, absolutely not," Caroline interrupted. "Nobody can know we're here."

"But she's me mum . . ."

"I know it's difficult, but trust me." She put on the most reassuring smile she could manage.

Jen didn't approve, but she didn't have a better idea. She wanted to suggest something, but what? The atmosphere was extremely tense, the silence worse than conversation. As soon as she stopped talking, images flashed in her head.

She'd danced with death and survived.

Just.

Had it not been for the man who had recently left the room, she knew she wouldn't have.

She felt her fingers beginning to shake.

There was a knock at the door, followed by the sound of a voice, obviously Thomas. Caroline answered, and the prince re-entered the room. He took a seat on the bed, his attention on Jen and Anthea.

"You have to show me the vault."

He wasn't joking.

"Are you mad?" Jen fired back. "Did you not see what happened?"

"It's because of that we must go back," he said, his expression stern. "Where is it?"

"Beneath the church."

"Can you show me on a map?"

"Do you have one?"

"Here." Caroline picked up something from the desk and offered it to Thomas. It was a tourist information leaflet she had picked up from the hotel lobby. There was a map of the local area in the middle.

Simple, but good enough.

Jen looked at the pamphlet and tried to get her bearings. She fingered her hair nervously, conscious that everyone was looking at her.

"Here." She pointed at the area marked priory ruins.

"You're quite sure?"

"That's where we got in."

"How did you manage it?"

"We did it at night. The priest had been out."

Thomas nodded. "Could you do it again?"

Jen doubted it. "For all we know, they've put a massive rock in front of it."

That seemed unlikely, but surveillance was now surely inevitable.

"I can show you the photos."

She removed her iPhone and showed him all she had. Following that, she showed him Debra Harrison's camera.

Thomas scrolled through the photographs on the screen. "It's very dark."

"It was a vault."

He looked at her, not taken by her flippancy. He held her gaze, this time for longer.

Her appearance had improved since her visit to the bathroom.

"What good is the vault?" Caroline asked after blowing her nose. "After all, we already know it's there. And we have photos to prove it."

"What is your objective?" Jen asked. "Assuming you have one."

Thomas bit his lip. Now she was annoying him again. Nevertheless, he kept his patience. "We have reason to believe that the Sons of York were responsible for the murders of two p-prominent politicians."

It took a few seconds for that to sink in. "You mean Bates—"

"Exactly," he cut her off.

Jen watched him as he began to pace. The man had a restless streak, a strange determination: almost as if he was allowing the burden of the world to be placed on his shoulders.

"What's that got to do with you? Surely that's a police matter?"

"It's complicated."

"I'm not getting involved in this unless you're straight with me."

He took a breath. "We also have reason to believe that they were responsible for the murder of my grandfather."

Jen was speechless. She attempted to breathe, but inside she felt numb, almost as if an icy storm was blowing through her chest. Whatever the reasons for the abduction of Debra Harrison, this was the last thing she had expected. Whoever they were, this cabal of men whose roots dated back centuries, their potential impact was clearly mind-blowing.

And had been for centuries.

Her phone began to vibrate, followed by the ringtone. Feeling like a fool, she rummaged through her handbag and looked at the phone's display.

It was the number Lovell had given her.

She smiled ironically. No doubt hoping to reschedule his neglected appointment.

"Who is it?" Thomas asked.

She looked at him as if he was prying. "Dr Lovell."

"Answer it," Caroline said.

"What?"

"Answer it," Thomas agreed. "Let's see what the bastard wants."

Jen was unsure.

"Go on."

She answered. "Hello?"

"Ah, do I have the pleasure of addressing the lovely Miss Farrelly?"

You know you bloody do.

"Speaking?"

"It's Francis Lovell here – you might remember we dined together yesterday evening. I must say it was a most memorable occasion."

I remember.

"Put it on speaker," Thomas said.

Jen covered the mouthpiece.

"I want to hear what he's saying."

She agreed.

"Hi, can you hear me, Dr Lovell?"

"Quite clearly, my dear, and quite heavenly. You do have the most angelic voice."

Thomas looked at Caroline, guppy mouthed.

"My dear, I hope I haven't inconvenienced you in any way."

"Not at all." She grimaced. "Just been caught up doing a little research."

"I'm so pleased; I do hope I have not found you unwell."

"Not at all. Sorry, I've just been . . . sidetracked."

"You really are the most charming of creatures. Now, Miss Farrelly, or may I be so bold to address you as Jennifer, I was wondering if you were free for a little get-together in about an hour at the home of my good friend, Lord Jeffries. His is one of the most delightful homes in all of England, and Lord Edward was only too pleased to grant my request to show you his splendid house and chapel."

Jen was horrified.

The man was trying to kill her.

"Ummm . . ."

"Say yes," Thomas whispered.

"Are you crazy?"

The words were louder than she had intended.

"I beg your pardon?" Lovell asked.

"Ummm, sorry, just a sec . . ." She was furious with the prince.

"Tell him you'd be delighted," Thomas said.

"You tell him."

"Go, he's offering you a way in."

"He's trying to kill me."

"He won't; I'll be there with you."

"Hello, I say, is everything okay?" Lovell asked.

Jen took her palm away from the mouthpiece. "Hi, can I call you back in a couple of minutes . . . thank you."

She disconnected the call and looked at Thomas. "Are you kidding me?"

"The home of Edward Jeffries is one of the m-most d-difficult to enter in the entire Commonwealth. You've been offered easy access. This could be the b-break we n-need."

Jen was still horrified. "He wants me dead."

Caroline was equally nervous. "Thomas, this is madness."

"Madness would be not taking it. While you enter the house, that l-leaves me easy access. You can be my diversion."

Suddenly Caroline liked what she was hearing.

Jen was not. "I'll be killed."

"No, you won't because you'll be wearing one of these." He showed her an object from his pocket. "Not to mention one of these."

"Is that a wire?"

"Similar. And this," he showed her a small red microchip, "is what's commonly called a tracker. MI5 uses it to keep an eye on things."

"Oh my God."

"Use this, and the palace, MI5, Special Branch, not to mention several others, can keep a track on you. Meanwhile C-Caroline can listen in."

Jen looked at him, appalled. "And what about you?"

"Like I say, I'll be in there with you. While you keep them distracted, I'll be able to s-search for evidence."

"What kind?"

"That's hardly your concern."

"I'm actually very concerned."

They eyed each other.

Deadlock.

Jen sighed forcefully, the air moving her hair. She looked at Caroline, then Anthea.

One mistake and she would surely not make it out alive.

She looked at Thomas and fought the urge of a rebuke, instead focusing on his eyes. Not for the first time he displayed the persona of a man who carried the weight of the world on his shoulders.

She took a deep breath.

"What's the plan?"

At around that time, the small helicopter came down in the grounds of the large Scottish castle. Stephen left the cockpit immediately and jogged across the immaculate grounds towards the main building.

The sight was familiar. Green lawns were surrounded by ancient woodland, basking in the glow of the sun above the mountains. He had stayed there every year of his life. It was the Scottish home of the Royal Family.

The castle of Balmoral.

A large bald-headed man walked out to greet him. "Master Stephen."

"Hello, Douglas, I have a favour to ask."

The man listened attentively.

"I need to see the surveillance footage of the dinner on the 17th June."

"The 17th?"

"Yes."

He decided not to question it.

"You best be heading this way, sir."

68

Jen rang back several minutes later to accept the invitation. Despite her concerns, the decision had been made. Had it been up to her alone, she would probably have declined.

But it was not up to her.

At least that was how it felt.

The car pulled up outside the gate. Jen checked her appearance in the mirror on the sun visor and began to fiddle with her hair. Showering had made a difference – that and make-up. Gone the ravages and dirt; even the cuts from the concrete were now completely invisible. Instead, the reflection was more what she recognised. The new do had actually lasted well in the circumstances. It certainly brought out the strengths in her appearance.

She looked to her right.

Not that anyone else had noticed.

Thomas checked his watch. It was approaching 3:30 p.m., and all was quiet. He had never seen the road before, but he felt as though he had – many times. Visually it was fantastic. Secluded but opulent.

Pretty – most would say.

He knew that the buildings represented much of what was to be loved of British history, but equally important was the knowledge that in such seclusion, evil and malcontent can spread. The houses were old; the trees older still. Despite the calm surroundings, he felt a sense of apprehension: not nerves, but something more permanent. It was instilled deep within the landscape, perhaps in time itself. He remembered Wilson had once told him, or perhaps it was Gardiner, his mind was confused, that the true lesson of history was not so much what happened, but why and, in certain cases, what happens next time. If one thing is to be learned from history, more often than not it is the following sobering truth:

Nothing is ever learned from history.

He looked at her. "Have you ever done anything like this before?"

She guessed he meant aside from breaking into vaults. "No. You?"

He grinned.

"My parents didn't bring me up to break and enter."

His grin became even wider. "Neither did mine. I went to school at Winchester College."

"Well, la di da."

He laughed, which made Jen feel better. He looked her in the eye, and a strange feeling of calm came over her.

"It'll be okay, you know."

The statement came from the mouth of a stranger, but with the concern of a friend. She looked at him and found the strength to smile.

"Let's get this over with."

Jen got out of the car and walked slowly towards the main driveway. The property was gated in two places, located approximately fifty metres apart. The one on the right was smaller, and perhaps older, whereas the one in front of her was modern, electric and seemingly impenetrable. Though it was modern, the design was classical and, to her eyes, vulgar. There were cherubim at either side, while the gate itself was symmetrical. Each side rose equally in height before reaching a pinnacle at the centre.

There she found the greatest peculiarity. A large animal, not quite a bulldog but not dissimilar. Had the last few days been different, the design might have left her confused. Today, however, the dawn of realisation was upon her.

It was not a dog, but a pig.

She was entering the home of the Hog.

The latest of a long line.

She walked towards the right side of the gate, her eyes on the intercom. There was a red sign with black writing saying 'Strictly no trespassing'.

Perhaps this was a bad idea.

A voice called from nearby. "Why, Miss Farrelly, what excellent timing."

She couldn't decide if she was scared or relieved. Lovell had appeared from along the road, dressed in white trousers and a smart yellow jacket.

At least he was alone.

She mustered the best smile she could. "Hi."

"My dear, you look a trillion pounds."

Though she held her smile, inside she was angry.

How could a man so charming be part of something so evil?

Were you one of those who stood around Debra Harrison that night?

"Are you sure this is okay? I really wouldn't want to intrude."

"Nonsense." He gestured with his hand. "As luck would have it, my dear friend Lord Jeffries is away for the day, along with his fine grandson. It seems we shall have the place to ourselves."

She didn't buy it.

"Shall we go in?"

Several hundred metres away, Thomas listened to every word.

Proof, at least, the wire was doing its job.

If his luck was in, the family was away, and all he would have to contend with would be the CCTV cameras.

Silently, he wasn't convinced Lovell was being truthful.

Back in the boathouse, Caroline sat in the bedroom with Anthea, their eyes focused on the laptop.

The tracker was doing its job.

Jen had entered the house.

69

"What does it mean?" Jen asked of the hog symbol, on seeing it for a second time.

They were now standing outside the entrance, a fine wooden door flanked by two statues, both identical to the one on the gate.

"In celebration of the family motto," Lovell replied. "By now I'm sure you are aware that every family in the village seems to have one."

Jen smiled and nodded. The symbol was subtle, irrelevant to the average passer-by.

But its significance was clear.

The walk along the driveway had taken longer than she had expected. Though she was aware that the estate was by far the largest in the village, the walk itself was well over half a mile. Unlike most, the driveway zigzagged. The land to the front of the house was abundant in greenery, once part of an ancient forest, its trees reaching heights of well over fifty metres.

It was warmer than it had been; the sun was beating down through the densely covered branches, causing long shadows across the muddy ground. The forest was alive with nature, the sound of birds a permanent feature. Rabbits, squirrels, and perhaps other things scampered through the undergrowth. Most of what she could hear, she couldn't see. She guessed there were at least ten different types of bird, chirping, singing, and wailing to one another. The forest was timeless.

Just like the situation.

Close up, the house surpassed her expectations. Unlike most in that part of the village, it was a hotchpotch of various eras. The exterior was mainly a yellowy sawdust hue, but mixed with several other colours and a variety of features. The property was described as a manor house, yet if it was, it had certainly developed. The oldest part was the centre section: not quite Tudor, but not far off. According to Lovell, every part was constructed of Yorkstone, four types in total, and with its countless turrets, the elaborate roof was highly picturesque. The exterior had something of a Gothic feel. To Jen's surprise, the east wing had one even greater peculiarity.

"Is that a church?"

"It is the chapel of Lady Jeffries. Commissioned in 1872."

"What was it built for?"

"It is used as a private place of worship; even today the family are staunchly Catholic. In years gone by, another, less elaborate chapel existed. In its day, it was the heart of recusancy for this part of the Riding. It might also interest you to know that since the early 1900s, a small brotherhood of Dominican friars has lived in the adjoining building." He pointed to the second smaller building that joined onto the chapel. "In their day, the Dominican order was staunchly loyal to our families."

She nodded, not knowing what else to do.

The explanation made sense. From her studies, she knew that every Plantagenet up to Richard II had a Dominican for a confessor.

Lovell unlocked the door and allowed Jen to take the first step. She followed the hallway past a sitting room and into a large foyer, comprising a large staircase, bright blue walls, countless antique pieces of furniture and more paintings than one would normally find in a gallery.

"Wow," she said, gaping at the vast interior. For a moment she almost forgot the implications of her visit.

"Are you musical, Miss Jennifer?"

She nodded. "Yes. I love music."

"Then perhaps you would care to try Lord Jeffries' piano." He gestured to the corner of the room. Sure enough, a fine Steinway was located in an alcove beneath the main stairway.

She walked towards it, slightly nervously. It was clearly 19th century.

Probably priceless.

"It's amazing."

"Restored it myself not two years ago."

Jen forced a smile. "You're clearly a man of many talents."

"A most pleasant way to begin one's retirement . . . perhaps you would care to give it a try."

She dismissed the idea, but felt conflicted. She walked towards it and pressed middle C. The ping resonated for several seconds, making the hairs on the back of her neck stand on end. In her mind the sound made the entrance hall feel even larger, as if the nearby staircase would never end. She composed herself and tried a D, then an E.

Then she played the beginning of Beethoven's Piano Sonata 14 in C sharp.

She looked at Lovell and laughed.

He applauded, five short claps. "Bravo."

She tucked her hair behind her ear, her focus returning to the task at hand.

She wondered how Thomas was getting on.

Thomas had entered the grounds via the Catesby estate and was making his way north. He had parked in a secluded area and continued on foot towards the grounds.

Both estates were outstanding. The grounds comprised more outbuildings than a hamlet, ranging from an aviary and dovecote to a small mill.

He spoke to Caroline using the hands-free facility of his mobile phone. "How's she doing?"

"They're just exploring the ground floor."

"Good. Keep this line open. Tell me when they get up the stairs."

He continued on foot across the Catesby estate, suddenly confused. He could hear something nearby.

It sounded like birds.

He changed direction, heading for a red farmhouse building surrounded by woodland. For the first time he realised there was no partition between the Jeffries and Catesby estates except for a small fence among the trees.

He approached the building and stopped. A well-built man was dressed in large overalls, his face disguised by an all-in-one protective suit. The man walked up and down the concrete several times, his trips to replenish whatever was in the bucket he carried.

He guessed some form of bird food.

The prince stopped by the next wall. He could smell something, strong but not obviously recognisable. He looked at the birds. The nursery rhyme he had heard the other day began playing in his head.

He didn't need clarification he'd found the source of the poison.

70

Jen walked to the other side of the kitchen and stopped in front of the largest window. In the distance, she could see the remains of the castle, the site of her recent late-night escape. She muttered to herself as she moved; to Lovell the sound was little more than mumbling. Every now and then she spoke to him as well. While many would forgive the former headmaster for assuming this was just part of her charm, to Jen it served a purpose.

If all was going well, Thomas was hearing every word.

Thomas's progress through the grounds had been without obstacle. The land in between the mansion and the wider greenery that adjoined the Catesby estate was mainly a series of lawns, the latest of which was a bowling green. There were hedges on either side, most featuring topiary of different styles and designs, depicting anything from ornamental archways to figures from mythology. There were pathways in between, leading to a swimming pool, two large tennis courts and other immaculately cut lawns. The sports facilities had surprised him.

He couldn't believe anyone in the family would use them.

The final lawn was the most open, and the most exposed. He crouched behind a hedge and considered his options. The grass area offered no cover apart, possibly, from a medium-size stone birdbath located at the centre. He considered moving towards it, but decided against it.

Knowing Jeffries, there was probably a camera there.

He moved to his right, circling the lawn instead of crossing it, and approached the patio. The windows were small and Gothic, clearly not meant to be opened. From what he had learned from Bridges and MI5, his best options were either the kitchen or the garage.

As he waited by the hedge, he saw movement. A man had left the house, white hair, bearded, clearly the butler.

He saw him walk in the direction of the lawn.

*

Sitting alone in his favourite part of the house, Edward Jeffries was a wretched figure. He hated intrusion of any kind, but particularly when he had personally agreed to the invitation.

He looked at his watch, attempting to make sense of the little hand and the big hand as they passed the Roman numerals. In the past, telling the time had seemed such a simple thing.

These days it caused endless confusion.

As best he could tell, it was approaching 3 p.m.

And the plan would be fully into operation.

In the surveillance room at Balmoral, Stephen watched as the scene before him continued to unfold.

The footage had been recorded over a month earlier, using at least twelve different cameras, all concentrating on different parts of the castle. Most of the surveillance had been on the dining room, the place where the main event had taken place. The table was large, even compared to what he was used to. There were at least thirty people in attendance, all of whom were in some way related – at least through marriage.

He focused on the man at the head of the table. His grandfather was impeccably dressed, on this night wearing his ceremonial naval uniform, including his many medals. Whether standing or sitting, the man's presence was immense. His expression was nearly always thoughtful, and his lips permanently displayed a smile. The sight caused Stephen to choke slightly with emotion.

He knew it was only a matter of time before something was about to change.

He was watching a replay of the night of his grandfather's assassination.

He was there, sitting not five seats away.

And he knew he could do nothing to prevent it.

71

Lovell showed Jen another room.

"Wow," Jen said, faking interest for the umpteenth time. She had lost count of how many times she had used the word.

They were now on the fourth floor, the highest except for the attic. Unlike the earlier rooms, the third and fourth floors were clearly unused and possessed something of a museum quality. The rooms were darker than the others. Most of the curtains were closed; swarms of dust motes danced in the faint sunlight as it pierced the gaps in the shades.

Judging from their appearance, little or nothing had changed in a hundred years.

Jen checked her watch, again thinking about Thomas. Surely he would have made it inside by now.

She walked to the centre of the room, concentrating on nothing in particular. She muttered beneath her breath, hoping Thomas was listening.

As far as she could tell, Lovell was still buying it.

"So what exactly is a drawing room?" she asked Lovell.

In truth, she knew and had no interest in the answer.

"As the name suggests, it was a room often used for withdrawing, usually after a meal."

No surprises.

Just as she had done in every room, she moved towards the window. While most of the shades were shut, one was open. She looked across the grounds. On every occasion so far, she had seen no signs of life outside – not even wildlife.

She hoped that was a good sign.

Thomas sprinted in the direction of the nearest hedge and held his breath for several seconds. He watched as the bearded butler entered the topiary-style maze and began to water the plants with a hose.

Thomas's actions were immediate. He sprung from the traps before the butler had even turned.

Seconds later the man was unconscious.

Thomas hid the body in an area of dense shrubbery and sprinted across the patio towards the partially open door. He entered the house via the kitchen. The room was older than he had expected, he guessed unchanged since the 1920s.

There were cobwebs everywhere, including the pantry area.

A large utility room was located just off the kitchen, while on the other side of the hallway were several sitting rooms, including what appeared to be a study.

He completed a reconnaissance of the downstairs in less than two minutes, and headed for the stairs. He was aware from listening to Jen that Lovell had taken her to the top floor, a fact also validated by Caroline, who was still monitoring the tracker. He kept the earpiece firmly in his right ear. Lovell had taken her to one of the old servants' rooms; Jen was asking questions about the paintings. The subject matter was dreadful, but he admired her tenacity.

The girl had a talent for faking passion in the boring.

He completed the first and second floors in less than three minutes. Most of the heavy oak doors led to bedrooms or bathrooms, the majority of which were unused. He opened the drawers and doors of the wardrobes just in case they contained something of interest, but so far everything appeared normal.

He took the staircase to the third floor, paying extra attention to his earpiece. If Caroline was correct, Jen and Lovell were only one floor above.

He climbed the staircase slowly, taking as wide a berth as possible. Visually the interior was magnificent. Priceless works of art hung from the walls, the subject matter ranging from equestrian, history, landscapes far and wide to members of the family dating back through the centuries. Impressive antiques, particularly coats of arms, were also prevalent, in keeping with the houses of his own family.

Suddenly he stopped. Level with the third floor he saw a painting of his cousin Edward, adorned with glittering regalia and a crown.

He bit his lip, anger swelling.

The last ounce of doubt had left him.

From there, he had a decent view of the landing of the fourth floor: like the others, it was about five metres in width and was protected by a wooden banister. Thomas listened carefully but heard nothing through either his earpiece or his other ear.

Which probably meant Jen and Lovell were checking out one of the rooms.

He entered the first room on the left of the third floor, another bedroom. He checked it quickly, and moved on to the next. He did the same for the next seven: all bedrooms, all ensuite, all unused.

It was like walking through a bad hotel.

The next room was a study, classy and ornate, but also seemingly abandoned. Dust and cobwebs covered every corner, mostly floating from the gaps between the walls and ceiling. The room had no obvious use, but Thomas knew that appearances could be deceptive.

He started his search with the desk. The drawers were empty, as was the nearby cabinet. He moved on to the brown-coloured bookcases, all of which were Victorian, caged, and locked. The books were library bounds, and included everything from Darwin to the original Jane Austen novels.

Thomas guessed they had never been opened.

He left the room to try the others on the third floor, all of which were bedrooms or simply empty.

Convinced there was nothing in the bedrooms, he returned to the study and started checking things a second time. Despite its bare appearance, instinct told him the trail was getting warm. To all outward appearances, the entire house harboured nothing of interest – but that was impossible. Even if recent rumours were untrue, the family was old. As a relative, he was aware that many of the family had been famed hoarders.

Surely anything incriminating would be well hidden.

He examined the room fully, carrying out a final check of the bookcases, which revealed that they were firmly shut.

On the other side of the room was a fireplace. It was made of marble, which was strange . . .

Even for the family it seemed elaborate.

It was large, at least three metres in width, with markings of knights, archers, foot soldiers, squires, and other figures of military pedigree that Thomas couldn't quite place.

The prince was now seriously confused. He moved along by the fireplace in both directions, feeling the figures with his palms. The substance was smooth and precise, slightly cold.

To him, the structure seemed misplaced.

He moved to the left, feeling the ornamentation with his right palm. The wall to the left of the fireplace was made of wood: beige-coloured panelling that continued all the way to the next wall. He placed his hands against the wood and pushed, gently at first and then more firmly. Several thoughts were building.

The episode at Riverton had opened his mind to moving walls.

He bit his lip. Something wasn't right, and the fireplace was the key. He looked at it again, then the wood.

He tried moving it left and right, then up and down before giving up.

He studied the room again, his eyes wandering from the bookcases to the right wall. He pressed things, now more furiously. Again he found himself in front of the fireplace, the lack of ornamentation on the mantelpiece now his key focus. He moved the items from the fireplace and knelt down to touch the coal.

Or at least what he thought was coal.

The presence of fake things confirmed his suspicion that the fireplace was only for show.

He pressed the artificial pieces of coal. Failing that, he tried to move the accessories.

Then he found a second poker attached to the fireplace itself. He moved it and heard what sounded like a key turning in a lock.

He smiled to himself.

The left wall had opened.

Alone in the surveillance room, Stephen hit the pause button. He rewound the footage ten seconds and pressed play again.

He repeated the process four times.

The action had taken place in the dining room. The King had made a toast, following which all present had stood. Others followed, making toasts about something or other. Though he couldn't hear what was going on, he remembered the subject matter from personal experience.

The usual drivel, he had joked afterwards to his father.

The key event had taken place nearly three minutes later. Dessert was about to be served, and the dessert wine was just being poured. Now it was another proposing a toast, the man once referred to by the late king as his favourite nephew three times removed.

Or some number of the kind.

Stephen bit his lip, angry with himself for not seeing it at the time.

He remembered the message from the Sons of York.

Wasn't that a dangerous dish to set before a king?

72

What Thomas had assumed to be a small priest hole was, in fact, something far greater. The passageway was short, leading to a large chamber that was clearly an extension of the study.

The room was dark but not pitch black. His first impression was that a curtain or blind was pulled shut, but there was no such thing in the room. There were no windows at all.

Whoever used it clearly had no issues with claustrophobia.

He worked his way along the wall to his left, searching for a light switch. He found one and pressed it. Something flickered above him, and seconds later light engulfed the room.

At first he questioned what he was seeing. Unlike the study, this room was far busier. A large desk, the central feature, was cluttered with countless papers and pads and other items of stationery. A large Apple Mac computer was located on the right side: the model noticeably old, he guessed mid-90s. Alongside it was a projector, its lens focused on a rolled-down white background. Surrounding it were hundreds, if not thousands, of photographs. Each one was different, but the theme consistent.

Richard Jeffries. Son of Lord Edward, father of Edward.

1957–1994.

Former leader of the Democrat Party.

Died in a car crash in Corsica, apparently.

Thomas studied the photographs one by one. Accompanying them were countless newspaper clippings, ranging in subject from the man's life as a newspaper magnate, minor royal and later MP to his untimely death and the conspiracy theories that surrounded it.

One of which caught his eye, a tabloid piece from 1995.

It told of how the Prime Minister in the making and third cousin of the late king was murdered for his possession of hidden knowledge regarding the King and future plans for the eradication of the Royal Family.

Thomas read the articles carefully. Though he remained sceptical, the content was disturbing. Strangely, he hadn't heard the accusations before.

Nevertheless, the events it described had happened largely before his time.

The next item of interest was the projector. He pressed play, and the film started immediately. The scene was a boardroom, the setting sometime in the early evening.

He recognised the room, and also two of the people present. Someone was in conversation with the late king, and whoever it was had decided to film the meeting. Also present was Gardiner, the Earl of Somerset.

The last person of note was a woman: brunette, late forties, dressed smartly.

He didn't recognise her.

The sound quality was slightly muffled, but it improved within seconds. From then on the conversation was cold and extremely businesslike. He didn't recognise the final voice, but it was evident from the accent that the man was English. By now viewing was physically uncomfortable.

He looked at the date at the bottom of the transmission.

8 October 1991.

Alone in his favourite part of the house, Lord Jeffries checked his watch.

If the time was what he thought it was, his grandson should be arriving home any time.

Stephen left Balmoral through the rear entrance and headed straight for the grounds. The helicopter was in the same place, the pre-flight checks already made.

He tied up the loose ends of his conversation with the King, and turned off his mobile phone. He had tried Thomas on his mobile, which went straight through to voicemail.

Either he had no reception, or more likely, his phone was turned off.

He entered the helicopter and took a seat beside the pilot. He could see from the clock that it was well after 4 p.m.

If all went to plan, he would be back in London before six.

On the first floor of the boathouse, Caroline and Anthea continued to focus on the laptop.

Assuming the information they were getting was correct, Jen was on the fourth floor, still complimenting Lovell on the tapestries.

The data for Thomas was stranger. The red dot confirmed he was somewhere on the third floor, but where exactly was another matter. The blueprints the palace had on file suggested he was near a study.

They also suggested the area where he was standing was nothing but wall.

Jen was moving on the fourth, possibly towards the stairs. She changed direction halfway along the corridor, entering what was apparently a toilet.

It was impossible to know for certain that she had gone alone, but it seemed most likely.

It was also not possible for them to see that someone had entered the house.

73

Jen left the bathroom on the fourth floor and nearly collided with something.

"All right, Jen?"

She froze, shocked.

Edward had appeared from nowhere.

She looked at him, her skin crawling. "Hi."

What the hell was he doing there?

More importantly, *where was Lovell?*

He grinned at her, his expression typically adoring. Even though she'd only met him twice, she already viewed it as his usual expression. Other things didn't change either. His hair was nicely gelled and clean cut, while a tight T-shirt and jeans flattered his firm physique.

A bit different from the photo taken earlier that day.

"I hope you've not been making a mess in there."

Charming. "It's quite some place you have here."

"I'm really glad you like it. I hope Dr Lovell has been true to his word."

The smile was now permanent. It was no different to usual, cocky but harmless.

Or so she thought.

One floor below, Thomas listened to Jen's side of the conversation.

She had been silent for some time. The resumption of speaking had almost escaped his notice, how taken he was with the footage.

He heard a second voice. Although the sound was weak, he recognised it immediately.

He feared things had taken a nasty twist.

Jen smiled awkwardly as Edward began leaning against the door, partially blocking her path.

"I'd better find Dr Lovell; he's probably wondering where I am."

"Let him wonder," Edward said, moving closer. He placed his finger and thumb to her chin. Even though he did it gently, the sensation was repulsive.

"You've got gorgeous eyes."

She looked at him, not quite terrified but close enough. Was this planned? Had Lovell left her deliberately?

"I really must be finding Dr Lovell."

"What's your hurry? If I didn't know better, I'd say you were trying to avoid me."

She was doing the best she could. She moved to one side, heading for the nearest door. Lovell had left the last room. There was no sign of him in the next either. Nor the next.

Silently she was starting to panic.

Thomas was alarmed.

"Caroline," he whispered, his hand covering his face. "Where is she?"

"Fourth-floor corridor."

"Thanks."

"Wait."

He stopped before leaving the room.

"She's moving towards the stairs."

"Would you like me to give you a tour of my room, Jen? It's where I keep all my guitars. It's kind of my hobby. I always wanted to be a rock star."

She sought to reply, but the words refused to come. She remained on the other side of the corridor, trying to avoid him.

Suddenly he blocked her off, again keeping his distance.

"I hear you nearly paid us a visit last night," he said. "You should've asked me when we crossed paths; I'd have given you the whole tour."

"Let me go."

She spoke with emphasis that Edward found amusing. He looked her in the eye, his grin ever wider. In all honesty she didn't think he was going to hurt her.

The question was, who was?

"I thought you were only here to film a documentary?"

She looked at him but said nothing.

"Do all your documentaries involve running around in dirty great vaults?"

Again no response.

"Did you like what you saw? Were you impressed?"

Nauseated more like. She tried to speak but couldn't.

"I've never really been down there myself. But I've heard it's worth a visit."

Again she refrained from speaking. In her mind she continued to see the photograph Stephanie had shown her.

It still refused to sink in.

"You have to be careful down there, though. According to some, there's a monster living there."

"That and plague rats," she retorted.

He smiled. "I have also heard that there's a few other things buried down there as well."

The words shocked her to the core. Taking the words literally, she elbowed him in the stomach and sprinted for the stairs.

In a large office in Westminster, the Home Secretary was hard at work when the visitor entered.

"Are you busy, Minister?"

It was West.

Heston threw his pen down on the desk. "I might have known . . . do you have any idea how angry the PM is?"

"I'm afraid we've had rather a startling development. I'm glad you're sitting down. You might want to brace yourself."

Ten thousand feet above the ground, Stephen watched the scenery from the window. The mountains and lakes beneath were instantly recognisable.

Picturesque Cumbria, spoilt only by the rain.

"How much longer?"

The pilot considered the question. "Probably fifty minutes."

Stephen nodded, satisfied but concerned. The development was so big, every second counted. He tried Thomas again, but once more got only voicemail.

Failing that, he tried Caroline.

Caroline was speechless.

Her body shaking, she passed on the information to Thomas.

At the other end of the line, Thomas was confused. If his cousin was correct, someone who lived in the house he was currently intruding had been directly responsible for the King's death.

He asked again, convinced he had misheard.

"Stephen saw the footage. The whole thing was caught on film."

Thomas refused to accept it. "H-how," he stuttered. "Edward Jeffries can hardly walk."

Over four miles away, Caroline shook her head.

"Granddad wasn't killed by Edward Jeffries Senior.

"It was Edward Junior."

74

Instinct told Jen to go for the stairs. She changed direction on reaching the third floor, and immediately started checking rooms.

Still no sign of Lovell.

Edward had appeared, though clearly not running.

"Why are you running, Jen?"

She ignored him.

"Whatever it is, we can talk about it."

She entered the next room, then the next.

It was useless.

Lovell was gone.

She returned to the corridor and stopped. The lad with blond hair was now standing there.

She took a deep breath and ran past him.

Thomas listened intently to the sound in his earpiece. Without doubt Jen was near, possibly on the same floor.

He sought to leave the hidden study when something made him stop. In between the wealth of photographs and newspaper clippings, the wall concealed something else.

Something older.

In the corner of the room was a small staircase leading to the floor below. He descended quickly, giving little concern for the dilapidated state of the metallic stairwell. Seconds later he entered an even darker room, packed to the rafters with manuscripts.

Without question he had found the family archives.

He moved towards the nearest selection and began sorting through them. There were countless manuscripts and records, mostly paper but also parchment. He looked at the content: most of it was handwritten. The nature of the material, the brownish colour, the rough texture, the smell . . .

It all cried out authenticity.

He turned to the other side of the room, his attention on the most dominant item. Incredibly, he had seen an identical copy before.

It was the same thing Wilson had shown him at the Bodleian.

Jen reached the second floor. As far as she could tell, she was alone, but she couldn't be certain. Urgency had given way to panic, made worse by her lack of knowledge of the house.

Despite Lovell's tour, she was still unfamiliar with the layout.

She searched every room, all of which were empty. Though she remained alone, the sound of footfalls on the stairs confirmed company was imminent.

Then she heard a gunshot.

She turned, terrified.

The same hooded figure who had attempted to kill her earlier that day was standing at the end of the corridor.

Thomas was startled. Even through the earpiece he could hear the gunfire.

Instinct guided his actions. He dropped the manuscripts and sprinted back up the stairs, through the study and down the main stairwell. Care had given way to haste.

He no longer cared if he was being observed.

The second bullet missed by inches. She dived with her arms at length, cushioning the impact and preventing herself from going over completely. Logically she had only one destination.

The end of the corridor.

There was a door at the far left; the only one Lovell had not shown her. The door led to a corridor, this one more ecclesiastical in nature. There were windows on the left side, stained glass, ornately decorated and placed in between arches that looked like they belonged in a monastery.

If she didn't know any better, she would have guessed that they were cloisters.

She upped her pace, her feet pounding against the wooden floorboards. She found a door on the right, locked, and another just ahead.

Also locked.

She heard the door behind her open, but on this occasion there was no gunfire.

Clearly the man had orders not to shoot in that part of the building.

She turned to her right where the corridor ended and followed it, her only option. Ten metres on she came to double doors on the right: brown, antique and also religious in nature.

She opened the right door using the large handle and slammed it shut. For the first time she took in her surroundings.

She had entered the family chapel.

Thomas stopped on reaching the end of the corridor before retracing his steps. He could hear breathing in his earpiece, but visually there was no sign of Jen. The info from Caroline was ambiguous, and clearly Jen was in no state to say where she was.

At least he knew from the breathing in his earpiece she was alive.

The rooms were empty. The corridor was equally deserted, strange considering what Caroline had just told him.

Clearly Jen had moved on.

He heard sound coming from the far end, a man singing. Though he was still to see who was responsible, he recognised the song immediately. It was his old school song, Winchester College's famous *Dulce Domum*, being sung in Latin.

"Who's there?"

A figure emerged close to the far window. Though Thomas could tell the figure was moving towards him, his features remained veiled by the bright sunlight in that part of the corridor.

Thomas removed his Glock from his belt and pointed it. "Show yourself."

The figure emerged, blond and smiling.

Finally he recognised him.

"How do, cuz?"

75

Jen felt as if she had no control of her movements. Her eyes were fixed on her surroundings, guiding her as if locked in a trance.

Even compared to the vaults, she had never seen anything so bizarre.

A large stained-glass window was located behind the altar, accompanied by at least twelve others on either side of the main aisle. Off the altar was a large choir area containing several wooden pews, portraits from the Middle Ages and a large Victorian baptismal font. There were eighteen pews on either side of the main aisle, allowing a capacity of she guessed five hundred people.

A chapel, Lovell had said of it.

She walked towards the altar, taking in as much as her vision would allow. The iconography was immense – ranging from paintings of the Apostles or the saints to scenes from the Old Testament.

Whoever created it clearly knew the subject well.

She passed the altar and stopped. There were stone slabs beneath her feet, all of which included names, each ending in Jeffries.

All were women, the dates anywhere between the 1700s and twenty years ago.

Lining the walls were several effigies, clearly more modern than those in the vaults. Most of the men had a knighthood or a peerage before their names, which made sense considering what she knew of the family history.

She had a feeling it also answered her question about why the hidden vault only went up to 1688.

Behind the altar was another door, wooden and slightly ajar. She walked towards it, nudging it open all the way.

From the doorway, she saw several other tombs, male and female, many of which included effigies on top of their slabs, the figures either clutching a sword or lying with their hands joined.

She investigated the nearest one, instantly recognising the names. Richard and Anne. Rather than seeing the name of a pretender king or queen, she saw only name and title. Each man was a lord, but nothing more.

Nor was there any hint of a crown covering their heads.

She took a deep breath and looked all around. The colours were bright: red, green, white, gold and perhaps several others. Priceless artwork hung from the walls, mostly oil based. She recognised one immediately, a family painting of the More family, signature Hans Holbein. There were others from the Middle Ages, including various representations of the Plantagenet kings from Henry II onwards.

The last was Richard III, looking far less sinister than normally depicted in portraits.

Without question the room had a feel to it. The light was transfixing, caused by a unique yellow glow as sunlight entered through glass panels in the ceiling. It was like being in the centre of a temple, a place where she could feel the presence of God. For the first time she noticed that the room was circular, a bit like an ambulatory – enclosed on every side. The ceiling was vaulted and extended upwards like a dome.

To Jen, it was like a miniature version of St Peter's Basilica.

While the architecture might have explained the room's bizarre acoustics, she sensed there was another presence.

Something was in there.

With her.

Then she heard a voice coming from her right.

"Good afternoon."

76

The King returned to the palace. He ignored a request from his personal secretary and headed straight for his office.

Clarence and York were already there when he arrived, both standing.

The King closed the door behind him. "I swear I will never know why my father ever hired that berk."

Clarence and York exchanged glances. Neither of them knew who he was referring to or what they had done to arouse his displeasure.

It was probably nothing, they mused.

The King turned to face his brothers. "Well now, chaps," he said, his tone much calmer, "what now?"

York was the first to speak. "The question is, do we really need to do anything at all? As far as I can see, the situation hasn't really changed."

The King walked over to his desk and placed his finger against the intercom. "Get me the Earl of Somerset, will you? Tell him to arrive here within the hour."

The person at the other end acknowledged his request.

"Perhaps this time he can finally do something right," the King said before returning his attention to his brothers, emphasis on York.

"William, you were with me this afternoon?"

"The Princes in the Tower, if indeed that is what we are dealing with, died over four hundred years ago whether at the hands of their uncle or otherwise. Their remains lie somewhere, be it Westminster Abbey or not."

"But their descendants still wander."

"Whose don't?"

The King was starting to get angry.

York continued. "If the Sons of York really exist and have carried out what they claim to have done, then our knowledge of the truth will for now make no difference."

"Except to ourselves," Clarence agreed.

The King looked at him but said nothing. He returned to his desk and opened a small cigar box, antique with the royal crest marked across the lid. He removed one of the cigars, placed it to his lips, and lit it.

"I find it absolutely extraordinary," he began, as he removed the cigar from his mouth and exhaled, "that something so big can remain hidden for so long."

"I've often found the dead to be particularly skilled at keeping secrets."

"I assume that's an attempt at humour?" he asked York. "If you don't have anything useful to say, I suggest you say nothing at all. If we don't move now, God knows what might happen."

"If we do move now, we risk exposing what we already know."

The King looked at Clarence. "Well now, George, what would you have me do?"

Clarence took his time. "The identity of their descendants is known – according to Thomas, Gardiner has known for some time. We know of their past and also their present. What we don't know is exactly what present ambitions they harbour."

"I notice neither of you came to visit me yesterday," York replied brusquely. "Maybe had you done so, you might have known whether we were dealing with fact or rumour."

Clarence beat the King to a response. "Your own experience proves only that you were targeted – not that it was the responsibility of Jeffries. The only words we have to go by are those of the friar."

"And if they are not responsible, then who is?"

The King's interest had heightened. "Come on then, George, let's hear it?"

Clarence sought to respond but failed.

"Just as I thought." The King laughed as he inhaled the smoke from his cigar. To him, the aroma had always been comforting.

"What word of Jeffries?"

"I have spoken to Thomas," Clarence said of his son. "I understand that both grandfather and grandson still reside at the same place. Caroline was with him as well."

This was news to York. "My God, he hasn't dragged her in on this, has he?"

"I'm afraid I don't have all of the details; it all seemed rather hurried."

"Where is Thomas now?" asked the King.

"Paying them a visit," Clarence answered.

"Let's hope they don't cause a scene. What of the man at the apartment, by the way?"

"Nothing since his arrival at Wootton-on-the-Moor," Clarence replied.

"And the other man?" York asked.

"Other man?"

"The man from Greenwich?"

"Well, he was dead to begin with."

The King remembered. "What of that gruesome scar?"

"Yes, I've asked Dr Grant to take a look at it," Clarence said. "This might take a bit longer."

The King accepted the answer. "What of the man who Stephen treated the day before?"

"Also dead."

"Any identity?"

"As a matter of fact, yes, Corporal Mark Percy: twenty-eight, white Caucasian, blond hair, single . . . his father owns a house on the same street as Jeffries."

The King gave him a piercing look. "Another boy of recorded ancestry."

"I know what you're thinking, Stephen . . ."

"What of the firearms?"

"According to Bridges, the model was not on record. Inquiries remain ongoing. However, most interestingly, a search has already taken place at the home of Jack Talbot. They found over a hundred more concealed behind a wall."

"What of the meat found in the man's pocket?"

"Also new," Clarence admitted. "And almost certainly the source of the poison. Tests are being carried out."

"What do they know?"

"Nothing – at least nothing definitive. Though MI5 have speculated the bird might have been genetically modified."

"Genetic . . . meaning what exactly?"

Clarence's response was interrupted by a buzzing sound on the intercom.

The King answered. "Yes?"

"The Duke of Cornwall is about to land, Majesty."

The helicopter came down in the grounds of Buckingham Palace.

Stephen left his seat immediately and sprinted towards the nearest entrance. He carried a small box, worthless in monetary value.

Priceless in everything else.

77

This time Jen really couldn't move. So many sensations had hit her at once . . .

It was like being choked all over.

Her pulse was beating so fast she thought it was going to explode. She felt it in her ears, her wrists . . . even her temples. Worse still was her breathing. Her chest felt so tight it seemed to physically close her throat.

The old man was sitting in an armchair by one of eight circular columns, each a support to the vaulted ceiling. Jen had already formed a perception of him from seeing him that day in the upstairs window, but she was actually quite surprised how small he was. His frame was hunched, and his hands prone to bouts of shaking. He obviously suffered from Parkinson's, but she assumed there was some arthritis thrown in there as well.

But what struck her most was his breathing. Inhaling was particularly lengthy and plagued, even compared to the sound as he breathed out that reminded her of a passing train. Signs of illness were unmistakable, be it cancer, bronchitis, an underperforming alveolus . . .

For all she knew, it was all three if not more.

Nevertheless, his eyes were alert, suggesting his mind was active.

"You were admiring the architecture of the late Reverend Malcolm Pritchard. He was a local man, a good friend of my grandfather. He was responsible for many similar buildings in the Riding but never really received the acclaim he deserved. I don't expect you to be familiar with the name."

Jen looked back, mesmerised.

"Do you like my little chapel?"

Jen attempted to respond. "Yes," she managed timidly. "It's magnificent."

The man showed no emotion. "I'm most sorry I have been unable to meet you until now; in my condition it's rather difficult. Fortunately these days I'm not completely isolated. There are other ways to receive news."

She swallowed, saliva nearly going down the wrong way. She cleared her throat but avoided a complete cough.

"I understand you're a TV producer?"

She wasn't, but she decided it was close enough. "Yes."

"Here to film a documentary on a missing teenager."

The way he said the words 'missing teenager' troubled her. They were slow and cold, a little too precise for her liking.

"Yes."

"The family have a long history in these parts – particularly on the mother's side. The girl's great-grandfather went on to be rather a skilled tactician in the British Army – rising to colonel, or thereabouts. You know I went to school with him."

She couldn't tell whether that was a question or a statement of fact.

"Really?" She felt incapable of saying anything more.

"They were a much different family back then."

Jen had no idea what he meant by that remark. She had no intention of pursuing the matter.

An awkward silence descended on the room, if anything even worse than talking to him. The hairs on the back of her neck were standing on end, as were the ones on her legs and arms. It was cold, despite the warmth of the day. She desperately wanted to leave, but she realised that was impossible.

She sought to speak, but had nothing to say.

All she managed was an awkward clearing of the throat.

"I hope that Dr Lovell has not been neglecting you as a guide," he asked, another rhetorical question.

In a way, Jen was relieved. Even if she was being lured into a trap, at least the old man knew why she was there.

"No . . . actually he's just gone to the loo," she lied. "He left me to visit the chapel."

She watched for a response, again not forthcoming. The man had a tendency to tilt his head forward, his eyes looking permanently upwards through his bifocals. She sensed great melancholy about his character. There was sorrow in his eyes, the feeling emphasised by the sagging of the skin around his lips. To Jen, it appeared like a permanent frown that she silently believed to be genuine.

Was his physical condition to blame? No.

She sensed it was something more personal.

She moved her legs, firstly in no one direction before finding herself examining the tombs.

"Are these your ancestors?" she asked, already knowing the answer. There were twelve tombs in total: nine joint graves containing married couples, three with just a single name. Again she felt herself drawn to the one of his son.

The oldest dated back to the 1700s.

"I never realised chapels like this were legal in the 1700s."

His answer seemed to take an age. "That's quite correct. The chapel to your left was only commissioned in 1872. It was completed in 1877, and the room where we are now added later."

The answer seemed plausible. "What about these?" she asked about the graves.

"Everything dated before 1895 was reinterred at the turn of the last century."

"Why wasn't it used right away?"

"At the time, my ancestors preferred the thought of being buried in consecrated ground."

"Is this not consecrated?"

"Only since 1895."

"Is that usual?"

"Is it usual to have a monastery or a chapel within one's own house?"

She let the subject pass and continued to inspect the writing on the tombs, her focus on the names. As before, most of the men were named Edward or Richard, and many of the women Elizabeth.

She avoided the temptation to ask why.

Suddenly she remembered she was wearing a wire.

"So how come these are not buried in the hidden vault?" she asked, making firm eye contact for the first time. "And how come they don't have king before their name?"

The man remained speechless, but on this occasion Jen detected venom in his eyes. She knew the question was unexpected, but more importantly she knew the old man must have known about her intrusion into the vaults.

Why else lure her there?

Why else try to kill her in broad daylight?

She asked the same question again, doing her best to make sure her speech was perfect.

She prayed Thomas was listening.

78

Thomas didn't feel how he expected to feel. Yet how, exactly, he expected to feel, he was still unsure. The information he had received from Caroline, though he was sure he heard correctly, was difficult to digest.

He looked intently at the face in front of him.

The face of a murderer.

Edward was standing about ten metres away, his frame leaning against one of the walls. He stood with his arms folded, as he always seemed to do. To Thomas, he was like the stereotypical student.

It was like looking at a man who had just got out of bed.

Thomas walked slowly towards him, doing his best to listen to what was around him while still trying to concentrate on his earpiece. Jen was no longer talking, but her breathing was loud.

His primary concern was locating the missing gunman.

He turned in the opposite direction.

"Aren't you even going to say hello?" Edward asked in his soft Yorkshire tone.

Thomas stopped, returning his attention to Edward. Again he looked, but said nothing.

"Didn't your father ever tell you that it's rude not to show honour to your host? Dear me, our standards must be slipping. Must be all that common blood you've let into your family."

Thomas heard him speak without really listening, choosing to concentrate instead on his earpiece. Nevertheless, the feeling was strange. Technically, the man was his flesh and blood: third cousin once removed, or something of the sort. In truth, he was unaware of even half of the branches that made up his unique family tree.

Edward moved closer, his gait not quite a swagger, but not far from it. It was like the walk of a teenager who had just punched far above his weight.

"Can I offer you a drink? Something to eat? Smoke?"

Again the prince said nothing.

"Don't you remember our old school motto, Tom? Manners makyth man?" Edward smiled. "Cat got your tongue?"

Thomas wetted his lips. "Where is she?" He managed to avoid a stutter.

"Who?"

"Who do you think?"

Edward pretended to ponder the question. "What? Jen?" He laughed aloud. "Blimey, I knew some of you royals liked it rough, but I never realised she were your type. How long have you even known her?"

"Where is she?" he asked again. The lack of talking in his earpiece was causing him concern.

Edward shrugged. "I couldn't tell you – she keeps running away from me."

The smile had returned, only this time Thomas found it even worse to deal with. His recent conversation with Caroline still dominated his thoughts.

The idea seemed impossible.

"What brings you here, anyway? I never realised you were capable of making it this far north," Edward said, laughing at his own joke. "I hear you had rather a narrow escape yesterday? Down in Greenwich – I'm guessing that was you?"

Thomas was surprised by the accuracy.

"Any idea who they were?"

"Cut the crap!" His voice echoed.

Edward looked at the prince, dumbstruck. "Wow. Okay. Did you say you would like a drink, by the way?"

"Just stop," Thomas shouted. "Just s-stop."

Thomas took a deep breath, in and then out. He knew he needed to calm himself, but doing so wasn't easy.

Thomas looked him in the eye. "Which one of you is responsible?" he asked, this time more quietly. "You or your g-grandfather?"

"I'm quite sure I don't know what you mean."

"Don't lie to me," Thomas shouted, with intense anger in his eyes. "I've seen the photos, Edward. I-I've seen them."

Edward shrugged. "I have seriously no idea what you're talking about."

"She showed me everything. I know about the girl that disappeared. I know about the Sons of York. I know about your c-coronation."

Thomas looked at him with a resigned expression.

"And I know that it was you who murdered my grandfather."

For what seemed like several seconds, Edward didn't flinch.

"Are you feeling all right? Did that explosion give you brain damage or something?"

"Stephen told me everything," Thomas replied, a partial truth. "He's s-seen the footage from Balmoral. The King knows."

"Stephen's s-s-s-s-seen the f-f-f-f-footage?" Edward mimicked. "Are you out of your mind? Can you even hear yourself? What footage, Tom? What footage?"

Thomas squared up to him, their faces almost touching. "How dare you," he said, a look of staunch determination present in his eyes. "Do you have any idea what you've done?"

Though Thomas centred his attention on Edward, he heard something in his earpiece. Jen was speaking to someone, he didn't know who.

Nor could he hear the other person.

At least the gunshots had ceased.

"Now wh-where is she?"

Edward's expression had hardened slightly, as if he was finally taking things seriously.

"I know what you're thinking, Tom. Honest to God, I do. But you still don't understand, not really. You might say you do, but you really, really don't," he said, moving away. "It's not your fault, Tom, you can't possibly understand – no one can."

Thomas watched him as he began to pace from side to side. He knew it was impossible to predict his next move.

"What are you talking about?"

Edward laughed. "Oh, Tom, I only wish I could explain – I know what you must think of me, but even I wasn't brought up with this.

"You remember when we were at school and our history tutor would tell us things: when was the Battle of Hastings, when was the Great Fire of London, when was the Battle of Trafalgar, you know, all that kind of stuff . . . imagine learning all that, only to find that there's this other side, a side practically no one knows existed. And then, imagine finding out not only that it exists, but that you're part of it."

Thomas stood with his arms folded. Unbeknown to Edward, he was also listening to Jen's voice.

"It was never my intention to hurt anyone, believe me. I'm not like that; you know that," Edward said, making passing eye contact. "If I wanted you dead, I could have shot you just now in the corridor – you would never even have known it was me. For all I knew, you were never to be involved."

"What in God's name are you talking about?"

"I know what you must think about the Sons of York; I expect you heard it all from that silly historian years ago. I saw the article in the *Chronicle* – I expect it was actually him. I'm right, aren't I?"

The prince said nothing.

"In all fairness, Tom, it's true: in the past, members of my family did try to usurp the throne – the same throne, had it not been for some guy named Tudor, would quite possibly be mine right now."

Though he heard correctly, what was said beggared belief.

Edward Jeffries, King of England.

Or Edward XIV, as he was known locally.

At least according to Jen.

"The original Sons of York actually expired in about 1688 – just after the Glorious Revolution. In a sense, that really was the end of the Plantagenets and the Woodvilles. The direct male line had died out. Ironic, as your blood now is mostly German."

Thomas bit his lip but again said nothing.

"I was eighteen when I learned the terrible truth about the rift that has plagued our separate families. All through school I didn't have the slightest inkling. My initial thought was to dismiss it. I mean it sounds ludicrous, doesn't it? The offspring of the Princes in the Tower, or the offspring of the son of Clarence and Elizabeth of York, still walking the earth, looking to wreak their vengeance on the ones who betrayed them . . . it's oh so perfect . . .

"But there's something else, Tom; something that, in all fairness, you probably don't even know."

He guessed Edward was talking about the projector in the hidden room. Based on the footage, it didn't make for pleasant viewing.

"So in return, you commit regicide?"

"Call it by whatever name you wish, it's all the same. A man's life is a man's life – king, lawyer, a worker in McDonald's . . . the feudal system ended centuries ago, but in some ways not much has changed. The same things happen, things that could be avoided. Why should there be one rule for one and another for others."

"When you p-poison the K-King of England, the penalty is no different to any other: one or the other it's life in prison, prince or p-peasant."

"Is that right? One or the other, the penalty is no different. No exception."

The pretender came slightly closer.

"Then tell me why the former King of England never did gaol time for the murder of my mother and father?"

Three guards stood outside the office, their eyes focused on the corridor in front of them. The orders were specific, as always.

No one would be allowed to enter under any circumstances.

Inside the room, York, Clarence and Stephen all stood hunched around the desk, their eyes on the TV screen. The King was sitting. Despite the gravity of what he was seeing, his façade was calm, his hands clasped loosely together as though in deep contemplation.

"Switch it off."

Stephen did so, and the screen went blank. He had seen it many times already, but it still made for unpleasant viewing.

"Who knows about this?" York asked.

"Possibly only us – and Caroline," Stephen replied. "I assume the guards at Balmoral may have seen it without understanding its importance."

Clarence agreed. "How often the subject of enquiry appears much clearer to the person who knows what it is they are looking for."

The King looked at Clarence, then at his son. "Get me the DG of MI5. Then, if you can manage it, the son of my third cousin."

79

"Have I the honour of addressing the real King of England? Or is that office now the sole preserve of your grandson?" Jen asked.

The question was far too condescending. Jen immediately sensed the old man's anger. His jaw had tightened; the sagging skin that flanked it on either side was now somehow smoother than it had been. If the malevolent expression was not enough, the extension of the man's breathing made it all the more obvious. The combination was enough to make her feel threatened.

She reminded herself she was wearing a wire. If she played her part well, Thomas would hear everything.

"Well?" She pushed him.

Across the room, the sound of laboured breathing had become steadily greater.

"How dare you!" he said at last. Although the words came out as little more than a mutter, his tone pierced with aggression. "You enter into my house, into my family chapel, and pay insult to the memory of the greatest family in the history of England!" The volume of his voice picked up, which unsettled her further. "Do you not realise, had a certain battle been won by the opposing side, I, and not my snivelling distant relation, would currently be king."

The response left Jen momentarily speechless. Till now she was still to consider the possibility that theoretically at least he could be right.

Her thoughts turned again to finding a way out.

She still had no idea what had happened to the gunman.

Or Lovell.

For now, at least, she and the old man were alone.

"Is that what this is all about? All these deaths? Just to satisfy your lust for what might have been?"

"I don't expect many people to be capable of understanding even the most elementary of truths. People come and people go, but for every man who lives well, a mark is left that betters the fabric of mankind. And when a man lives badly, there are repercussions."

He spoke strongly, but she was still to grasp the relevance to the modern day.

"You're angry at Henry Tudor?"

"My dear, having broken into my family vault, I shall spare you the insult of preserving the importance of my lineage. It is unfortunate, shall we say, that fate was at its most stupid in depriving my family of their royal birthright. But please spare me the ignominy of addressing me like a common cook."

Secretly, she was still undecided. "But that would depend. I mean, it's either that or you have a pretty extreme case of narcissistic personality disorder . . . after all, you are the people responsible for Debra Harrison's murder."

The man took a deep breath but remained silent.

"What happened to her?" she asked. "Her parents have a right to know."

"Ah, yes, to be a parent." He cleared his throat, a lengthy and chesty cough that she feared might be contagious. "Only when a loving parent has had their son or daughter taken away from them can they possibly understand the unique hurt and longing for the loss of the irreplaceable."

Jen was confused.

The man continued. "In the past, as a member of the Wootton community, any person would have been able to count on the protection of my friends and family. For centuries, we have overseen the safety of our neighbours. However, there have been times when even our own citizens have chosen to betray their roots."

Jen crossed her arms. "Are murderers not deserving of contempt?"

"Precisely," he said coldly.

The comment threw her slightly. "But you are the people responsible for Debra Harrison's murder, for her mother's unbearable pain."

"It may surprise you to learn that many years ago, I, too, found out firsthand what it is like to suffer the unbearable pain of losing a beloved child.

"My story began on a cold day in November 1991, and in many ways the story is still to end.

"Listen if you will. For what good it will do you."

Back at the boathouse, Caroline stared at the motionless screen. The two red dots continued to flash consistently, only now they barely moved.

Whatever Thomas and Jen were doing, it didn't appear urgent.

She could hear Thomas's voice in the earpiece. He was clearly speaking to someone, but the conversation had no flow. She asked him a question but got no answer.

Her mobile phone began ringing on the desk, the caller Stephen.

"Stephen," she answered, "what's happening?"

"Stay where you are. We'll be with you in an hour."

80

Thomas heard every word.

Surely he hadn't heard correctly.

The accusation was preposterous.

"What?" Thomas asked.

Edward laughed, this time without humour. "He never told you, did he? Not that I expected him to. Why would he? I mean, it would be the end of him, wouldn't it?"

Thomas controlled himself well. "Whatever game you are playing, believe me, it will not work."

"You think I'm playing? Let me ask you something, Tom; imagine the following hypothetical scenario:

"Suppose, just for a second, there's this newspaper person, let's say a journalist. Eventually, this journalist goes into politics. One day, he finds out something so incredible, the whole world would shake if they knew the truth. This person, let's call him, I don't know, Richard."

His father's name.

"Richard tries to reason with the person responsible. Listen to his side of the story. After all, even if he's guilty, it doesn't necessarily make him a bad person."

"What in God's name are you babbling about?"

"In the eyes of the public, King James III will go down in history as one of the most beloved English monarchs – even though he was half-Scottish." Edward grinned. "Everywhere you go, the eyes of the adoring faces would watch. The man who could do no wrong." His expression turned more sinister. "Only he wasn't, was he?"

Edward walked slightly closer.

"I assume you were aware of Joanna?"

"Joanna?"

"Joanna Fletcher."

Thomas had no idea.

"The King's mistress."

Thomas laughed, a reflex. "Don't be absurd."

"You think I'm lying?"

Thomas avoided a stutter. "Even if you're not, he'd hardly be the first."

"First or not, what happened is hardly right . . .

"You see, the Queen was getting suspicious back in about 1989 – at least that's what Granddad tells me."

"You're basing your story on a story?"

Edward laughed. "Alliteration, Tom, I like it, I like it." The smirk died into a frown. "The marriage was never loveless, no one could say that, but it had got somewhat complicated. In the late 1980s Joanna was an MP for the Tories, but years earlier she'd actually worked for the King on one of his estates; I forget which one."

"Get to the point."

Another laugh. "All in all, the affair lasted about four years, though I must admit, in my opinion it was probably a lot shorter – four years does seem quite a long time to get away with it, particularly when you're the king. According to some, there was even a child involved, but if there was, it was almost certainly miscarried . . .

"Anyway, after it was over, Joanna moved job, eventually ended up out in the cold. Then one day–"

"She revealed everything?"

Edward placed his hands out with his palms up. "But the affair was only part of the story. You see, there was actually another even more serious event that you, yourself, are not even aware of.

"Answer me this, Thomas: where does the king get all his money from?"

"Where . . ."

"You heard me. Where does he get all his money from?"

"Why the Privy Purse . . . obviously."

"Correct answer, well done, Tom. But what makes up the Privy Purse?"

Thomas had no idea where this was going. "The Crown Estate. The Duchy of Lancaster–"

"Exactly." Edward snapped his fingers together. "You know all about the Duchy of Lancaster, of course."

Thomas guessed there was a War of the Roses jibe coming.

"See, initially the Duchy of Lancaster dates back to the disinheritance of Simon de Montfort in 1265, but after that it became more significant. Henry IV, and later Edward IV, when he was king, made it separate from the Crown, but ever since it's been passed down pretty much to the next descendant, i.e., the king . . . what's it worth today, Tom? £350 million?"

It sounded reasonable. "Okay."

"But, and correct me if I'm wrong, Tom, but the Duchy of Lancaster, though technically it belongs to the king, can't be given away."

That confused him. "Can't . . ."

"Okay, let me rephrase. The king can profit from the income, yes. But he can't sell the capital and keep it."

Thomas bit his lip, slightly disturbed.

"We can always check . . ."

"Yes, that's right."

Edward grinned. "He liked helping people, your grandfather, didn't he?"

"He was a n-nice man."

"He certainly got on well with you. Is it true that you used to call him Popup when you were a kid?"

"Get to the point."

"Oh, believe me, Tom, I will. See, the Duchy of Lancaster must be one of the largest trusts in the world. Investments, land, buildings . . . but, like I say, he's only entitled to the profits. Technically, any money profited from a sale wouldn't legally be his.

"And there was one little deal back in the early '90s that was just a little over the edge. See, Joanna had actually been made Chancellor of the Duchy of Lancaster, which technically made her a member of the Cabinet, albeit a minor one. And there was this rumour–"

"Do you base all your suggestion on rumour?"

"Not at all, as a matter of fact, I've seen the footage myself."

Thomas assumed he was speaking of the projector in the hidden study.

"See, it was around 1992, the time when all the Common Agricultural crap came into play. See, that benefited the King no end. See, much of the Duchy's land was farmland, so when this came in, his income exploded.

"But around the same time the King was offered a deal for some of the farmland the Duchy owned: build a shopping centre, flats, that kind of thing. Only problem was the land wasn't his to sell. So what he and Joanna did . . ."

It was obvious to Thomas what was being suggested. "What you say is slander."

"Is that what you think? Would you like to see the footage? The land was silently transferred, documents were forged, people tricked into thinking the King had actually bought the land with his own money years earlier. We're talking five thousand acres, by the way."

Thomas huffed. "That's rather a lot of land to lose."

"What do you mean, lose? Tom, have you seriously learned nothing about being a royal? You people never lose. Unfortunately for the King, or perhaps fortunately, depends what side you want the coin to land, the builders went bankrupt and the site didn't go ahead. Only now he had a different problem."

Edward moved closer.

"Joanna decided to tell everything," Edward said, his sunny side returned. "It's not good, is it? I mean, the King of England up to no good with government property."

Thomas took a deep breath. "What has any of this got to do with your parents?"

Edward's expression turned more serious. "After the company was liquidated, my father got wind from an acquaintance of some of the things that had been happening. Later that year he asked the King about it directly: literally, just like that, came out and asked him. Of course your granddad denied it."

"Perhaps he was innocent."

"You would say that, wouldn't you – I don't blame you; after all, you're his grandson," Edward said, pausing. "Only now, it was no longer that simple. You see, the King and my father had something of a falling out – as a result my father threatened to expose them. Only then something strange happened.

"A few months before the general election, my father and mother were on their way back from a night out in Corsica. They were driving along this coastal road; you'd recognise it if you saw it – they always use it on the Tour de France . . .

"Anyway, they were driving back, and well, something happened, and the car went over the edge. Apparently Dad died immediately."

Thomas noticed sadness in his voice.

"Never forget the day – not ever. I wasn't with them in Corsica – I was here, being looked after by my granddad. He always looked after me, did Granddad. He's dying himself, you know," he said, making eye contact for the first time in a while. "The cancer started with the lungs, but then it spread. They caught it too late, you see. I've never had to be without him before. I don't know what I'll do without him.

"They called in the middle of the night: about three. He didn't answer straight away; it just kept ringing and ringing. I knew something was wrong. It's never good when someone calls you in the middle of the night, is it?"

Thomas remained unmoved. He could see there was sadness in Edward's eyes. Strangely it reminded him of their time at school.

"Never forget the funeral. He was there, His Majesty, and the Queen, she was there. Your dad, he was there . . . you, you were there."

"I'm sorry."

Edward laughed. "What are you apologising for? You were only eight, same age as me." He shook his head. "Never forget when the King got up to the lectern and made a speech. I loved him then: I was so proud that the King was there at my parents' funeral – making a speech about how great they were. I thought it was brilliant."

His expression hardened.

"It wasn't till after we'd left school I finally found out – not for sure. Granddad, he'd always known, at least had his suspicions. They found the car in the sea; it had gone off the road. Initially the police thought they'd been involved in a car crash."

"What makes you so s-sure they weren't?"

Another ironic laugh. "You're always the same, you are, aren't you – Mr Cynical. I seriously don't blame you, Tom; I'd probably say the same thing if I were you.

"It took years to find out what happened. Their deaths had actually been caused by sniper fire. The evidence was found on the right side of the car. Incredible, isn't it that so many people can miss something so obvious? They found him three years later – the sniper. He was dead – his corpse found in the front seat of a car. Apparently he'd died of fumes."

The story seemed familiar.

"They found me mum. She didn't die in the crash. She had a bullet lodged right there." He pointed to the right side of his head.

Thomas took a deep breath. "What happened?"

"No one knows, not for sure." He shrugged. "But the Sons of York were determined to find out. They'd only restarted again in the late '40s. The original Sons of York had an incredible network; apparently in the Middle Ages it was the best the world had ever seen. Apparently it extended all the way to the Vatican. Wherever you went in Europe, there was a Yorkist hiding somewhere.

"About two years later a cousin of one of our neighbours heard a rumour that the sniper had turned up. Rumour also had it that he had once been an employee of the Duke of York. Ryan Tomkins, his name was; there's no record of him."

"If there's no record, he didn't work for us."

"Ah, I knew you'd say that; I swear, Tom, you're easier to read than a bloody Kindle.

"A few years later, someone got to view his tax record at the HMRC. And guess what?"

No response.

"Yep, that's right; he worked as a chauffeur to the Duke of York 1989 to 1993."

Thomas exhaled deeply. "You think he shot at your parents' car? Do you have any idea how absurd that sounds?"

"Absurd or not, that's how it happened. It took me years to get the proof – even now I still don't know everything."

Edward removed a piece of paper from his pocket.

"Dad wrote this letter to Granddad less than a week before he died. You can read it if you like."

Thomas snatched it and read it quickly, all the while continuing to listen to the earpiece. Jen had been quiet for some time, but he could still hear breathing.

He looked at Edward after finishing.

"Interesting reading, isn't it?"

"You conceited baboon," Thomas spat. "You expect me to s-stand here and swallow this crap. You manipulative little–"

"Steady on, Tom, steady. You have to consider yourself lucky. After all, your father is the only one not mentioned."

Thomas tapped the paper. "Show me the original."

"Why? So you can destroy it?"

Thomas grabbed hold of Edward's shirt and pinned him against the wall. "I am not interested in the paranoid ravings of a pitiful insecure sneak. What happened to your parents was a tragedy, but it has nothing to do with the King."

"You found the projector, didn't you? I know you did; we've got cameras everywhere. And the library, did you find it interesting?"

Edward pushed him back.

"Great thing, history. Archives – brilliant. It makes things so much easier to follow when you have a trail that goes back centuries. Everything is there, going back to before Bosworth. Maybe next time you should wait around and see the whole thing."

Thomas was livid. He raised his head as far as his neck would allow. He sought to speak, but was distracted by something in his ear.

Jen was screaming.

81

"Wait, hold on a second," Jen interrupted. "The King ordered the murder of your son and daughter-in-law?"

Lord Jeffries remained composed in his chair. "Being but a junior member of the media, I suspect it highly unlikely you can ever understand my distant relation's true motive. We are the descendants of a once great dynasty – the once and future rulers of a kingdom that once spanned beyond the sea.

"It is in some ways both a blessing and a curse to be a Plantagenet. Just as it is to be a Winchester."

Jen failed to get her head round the idea. "Maybe it hasn't dawned on you yet, but accusing someone of something so great – it's a pretty big deal. After all, you're talking about the King of England."

Still the idea refused to crystallise. She reasoned that sitting in that chair for so long had driven the old man potty.

"I assume you have proof?"

"The man who shot at my son and forced his car from the road was once well known to everyone in my family. He had previously served as chauffeur to one of the earls of Northumberland – it was only in later years that he went on to work for the Duke of York.

"However, the man's true talent in life had been to serve in the Royal Marines. The man was not only fighting fit, but he was also highly intelligent for his station. His skill was in reconnaissance, showing particular talent for photography. It was that what caught the eyes of the Duke of York, and later those of the King."

Jen lowered her eyebrows. "Sorry, you've lost me."

"As soon as word began to spread that the King had been unfaithful to the Queen, things started to become quite uncomfortable for him. When rumours of a miscarried or aborted child, too, began to circulate, what began as a rumour threatened to escalate into a PR disaster for the family.

"But of all the people who knew the truth, one stood out both in calibre and in annoyance."

"Your son?"

"Had the articles my son threatened to publish indeed been published, any thread of credibility that failing house still held would have been practically wiped out in a single day. By the summer of 1994 my son had been leader of the opposition for less than a year, but his rating in the polls was staggeringly high. It was, therefore, vital not only to the King but for every member of his family that the rumours be quashed."

"So he paid the chauffeur to shoot your son?" Her tone bordered on sarcasm. "There was no guarantee he would even succeed."

"The original plan, I'm sure, was by no means quite so drastic. As I have already pointed out, Mr Tomkins, if indeed that was his true name, was something of a dab hand when it came to photography. His time in the marines had been cut short due to a landmine incident leading to his requiring a prosthetic limb. Nevertheless, it did not prevent him from carrying out surveillance of my son and daughter-in-law."

"You're saying he was sent to spy on them?"

"Many of the photographs that he took were taken prior to their visit to Corsica; some were even mailed directly to my son's address in a bid to threaten them. Fortunately, as an experienced journalist and politician, he knew better than to waver at such idle threats."

She begged to differ. "But the threat was genuine?"

"My son and daughter-in-law died on the ninth day of their fourteen-day holiday. My son wrote to me at the end of the fifth day, declaring his love for the scenery, but his contempt for the petty little man who would not leave them alone. He also spared a note for the man he knew had sent him. In a separate letter, he speculated that the man had been with them on every occasion . . . my son even photographed him once."

Jen folded her arms and blew her hair away from her face. "If he felt threatened, why didn't he tell the police? After all, Corsica is out of the king's jurisdiction."

If jurisdiction was the right word.

Jeffries looked back coldly. "Let me tell you a little story; not that I expect you to believe it. Many years ago, I had an ancestor . . ."

She guessed his name was Edward. Either that or Richard.

"He had married a French aristocrat in the late 1780s, and brought her back to England along with certain members of the family.

"As the Reign of Terror reached new heights, the brave young man returned to Paris in a bid to save one of his wife's relatives – otherwise certain to be guillotined. No sooner had he made it to Calais than the man was arrested and taken to Paris. Despite his obvious Englishness, he was charged with being an aristocrat and guillotined. His father pleaded with the King of England to aid his safe return, but unbeknown to my ancestor he had taken his pleas before the very person who had ordered the execution."

Jen took a deep breath. "Again, how do you know all this?"

"I have in my possession the letter written in the king's own hand to the Constable of Dover Castle. Prior to that time, relations between the two families had been slightly better. Never again has a Jeffries been so unwise as to trust the descendants of the red rose."

Jen listened carefully, knowing that was the best thing she could do. She assumed Jeffries probably had proof somewhere.

"What happened to the sniper?"

"When the bodies of my son and daughter-in-law were discovered, it was established that they had both been dead for at least seven hours; however, the discovery was made by chance by a passing motorist; no previous call to the emergency services had been made. The car had overturned and fallen into the sea; there was evidence of a blowout from at least two tyres, one of which was caused by gunfire.

"For over ten years I did all that I could to trace the man. When I finally succeeded, his medical records confirmed a past history of alcoholism ever since his dismissal from the forces."

"So he might not have been under orders?"

The man clearly felt nothing but contempt for the suggestion. "My daughter-in-law had been shot in the head."

Jen moved on quickly. "But he could have acted the way he did because he was inebriated rather than under order?"

"The exact methods that led to the death of my son and daughter-in-law are known only to the man responsible. Sadly, he is in no position to be questioned on the matter."

Admittedly his death seemed suspicious. "How can you be sure he didn't just commit suicide?"

Suddenly Lord Jeffries no longer felt like talking. He pressed a button on the side of his chair. It made a high-pitch shriek, not dissimilar to the setting of a burglar alarm.

She heard someone's voice, though clearly not in the room.

"Brother Morris. Perhaps Brother Daniel and yourself would be so kind as to join me in the chapel. I think that it's time our guest was leaving."

The words alarmed her. She left the room hastily and ran frantically down the main aisle of the chapel, desperately looking for exits. There was a door on the left, smaller than the main exit.

Jen tried to open it, but it was locked. She rattled the handle, but to no avail.

She looked around, her mind racing. There was another door on the opposite side.

That, too, was locked.

The main doors opened.

Seconds later, she heard gunfire.

82

Jen's only reaction was to dive. The floor in this part was tiled, rather than carpet, and well over a hundred years old.

She crashed down on her right side, her elbow taking most of the impact. It jarred, but suddenly pain was no longer her biggest concern.

Sparks were flying everywhere. Debris was falling, both near and on top of her. She tried to scream, but air refused to enter her lungs. Instead, she lay on the floor with her hands over her head, trying as best she could to keep still. The sound of gunfire was deafening, its impact sending vibrations along the walls and floor. She was desperate to leave: run, or at least crawl.

She moved to her right, the area that offered the most cover.

As the gunfire ceased, she heard voices.

Thomas moved in the opposite direction. He had nothing to guide him, other than instinct.

Edward was speaking, but Thomas ignored him. Instead, he dashed along the corridor and through the first door in front of him.

The room was a bedroom, clearly unused.

His fingers on the hands-free, he spoke to Caroline.

Caroline was still looking at the screen, struggling to make sense of the house's layout.

"Come on," Thomas shouted in her ear.

Caroline was struggling to keep calm. "Don't rush me."

"Left or right, it's not difficult."

It was to her. As best she could tell there was no easy way to get to where Jen was.

"Go back to the corridor and through the last door on the left."

Thomas followed her instructions. Edward was still standing close by, shouting at him.

The second corridor was different, more like a medieval cloister.

There were stained-glass windows on the left side, depicting everything from Moses and the Ten Commandments to the Dominicans and the Inquisition, whereas the right was nothing but wall, painted brown and largely unfurnished. The acoustics were impressive: the sound of his footsteps travelled, but so did something else.

Gunfire.

He came to another wall. His only options were to turn right or go back the same way. The gunfire continued, obviously close.

Within a second, it had stopped.

Although the gunfire had stopped, the ringing sensation that replaced it was equally insufferable to Jen. She heard various noises, though without any sense of where they were coming from. It took several seconds to figure out what was making the noise.

Sure enough, someone was shouting.

And not at her.

Two men had entered the chapel, both armed and dressed in white habits and black cloaks.

She crawled along the side aisle, using her hands to support herself. She stopped on reaching the tenth pew and elevated herself, the first opportunity to view the altar.

Lord Jeffries had appeared, standing just inside the doorway.

The old man was furious. He was barking out instructions at the two hooded friars, both of whom were standing before the altar, weapons at the ready. Despite being less than twenty metres away, Jen struggled to hear anything, so bad was the ringing in her ears.

It was like being under water, only without the floating sensation.

She scampered further along the aisle, reaching the fifteenth pew. She ducked down instinctively as she saw Morris turn, and failed to avoid sliding on the smooth floor.

She didn't need a second look to know they had spotted her.

Jeffries was livid. The debris had created a minor dust storm rising from the floor. It looked like a bomb had gone off. A large crack had appeared along one of the walls, liable to split wide open at any moment. But it wasn't the safety of others that concerned him.

The damage was sacrilege.

He saw movement to his right, somewhere in the corner of the chapel. He saw blonde hair slowly disappear behind one of the pews.

He looked at the two idiots who had nearly destroyed his chapel.

"Just kill her."

Jen heard those words clearly. Her heart pounding, she frantically slid her way to the back of the chapel, less than ten metres from the doors. Still, she had a problem.

Leave cover and she was a sitting duck.

The gunfire resumed, this time unsettlingly close to her head. Fragments of plaster fell from above, the debris covering her clothes and hair. There was another noise coming from behind her, this time far more substantial. One of the pews had literally blown apart. There were splinters everywhere, accompanied by the smell of burnt wood.

It hurt to breathe, but this time for a different reason. She tried to move, but her limbs refused to comply. As the gunfire faded, she heard someone shouting, the words on this occasion aimed at her.

She couldn't make out what he was saying.

Another round of gunshots followed, this time from her left and right. None were close, but the sound was unbearable.

Her instinct guided her behind the final pew. Her biggest fear now was allowing herself to be closed in.

She placed her hands over her head, trying to stay as small as possible. If there was a time and a place for prayer, this was surely both.

In her terrified state, she didn't notice the main doors opening.

The scene that greeted Thomas as he looked into the chapel was like a bomb site. The lectern to the side of the altar had been totally demolished, as had much of the wall. There was still dust in the air, but it appeared to be settling.

The question was where were the gunmen? And more importantly, where was Jen?

He nudged the right door open slightly, and immediately spun behind the left. Would the gunman attempt to kill him immediately, or would he wait?

If it were up to Jeffries, he knew it would be the latter.

But where is the bastard?

Eyeing the chapel from behind the door, he saw movement to his left, behind the nearest pew. There was blonde hair sticking out from behind one of the kneelers, dirtied by recent debris.

At least Jen was still alive.

He opened the door all the way, allowing himself a view of the entire chapel. In terms of visual splendour, it was magnificent, but he knew that images can be deceiving. Countless rich families from the Georgian and Victorian eras upgraded their otherwise unremarkable mansions with romanticised follies or unfinished walls, but he had never seen anything so elaborate.

Silently, he wondered whether it was genuine.

There was movement around the altar by two hooded figures.

One of them Thomas recognised.

He couldn't believe the man's identity.

"Good afternoon, sire," Morris said coldly. Then without warning he fired.

Thomas dived to his left, the bullets just missing him. On this occasion the damage occurred outside the chapel, destroying a priceless work of art and at least one stained-glass window.

Back in the chapel, he could hear shouting.

Thomas got up slowly, first to his knees, then all the way. He stopped on reaching the door, peering in tentatively.

Immediately he heard a voice.

"Thomas, my lad, come in."

The invitation came from Jeffries. Incredibly the man was standing, the altar supporting his weight.

"Come in, come, come."

Thomas edged forward, gun at the ready. He kept an eye on Jen, but also the two armed men.

How the hell had Morris escaped?

He saw movement from the other friar and fired. Immediately the second friar keeled over, his gun sliding beneath the pews.

He aimed at Morris.

"Don't move," Thomas shouted. He inched forward and stopped, allowing his eyes to take in the interior, worried there might be another gunman or surveillance equipment watching him.

He heard shuffling behind him.

83

Edward had entered, carrying a semi-automatic pistol pointed at Thomas's head.

"All right, Tom? You find the place all right?"

Thomas couldn't believe his stupidity.

"No sudden movements, mate."

Thomas dropped his Glock and watched it bounce away, still less than a metre from his foot.

"Kick it away."

Reluctantly Thomas did as instructed. His eyes on the altar, he felt himself being frisked, far harder than necessary.

Edward turned his attention to Morris.

"Hey," he said, gesturing to a sign on the far wall that said 'Peace, perfect peace, is the gift of Christ our Lord.' "Can you not read? This is a house of prayer."

"Edward." The old man was still standing against the altar.

Edward looked at his grandfather, concerned. "You need to take it easy."

Edward turned towards Thomas and laughed nervously. "Got me through a lot of tough times this chapel. And my family. Did you know that this was the first new Catholic Church since emancipation in the Riding?"

Thomas really didn't care. "It's magnificent."

"I'm glad you think so, Tom. It was also the site of the first new Dominican convent, three hundred years after the last. Just think, my ancestors were building this when good Queen Vicky was telling our troops to charge the Light Brigade."

Thomas found the inaccuracy irritating.

"And do you know what else—"

"Edward," the old man interrupted, shaking his head, "perhaps it would be wise to leave this in the hands of the authorities."

Edward eyed his grandfather, then Thomas. He laughed again.

"You know, my mum used to work for the authorities. She was eight years working in the magistrates before she met my dad. She was brilliant, Mum was. She could have been anything she wanted to be."

Thomas glanced at his gun, trying to remain circumspect. Unfortunately Edward noticed.

Jen had made it to the middle of the pews, so far unnoticed. Progress was only possible beneath the pews, and that required moving the kneelers. She moved the next one gently, trying her best to keep quiet.

Her nerves were starting to get the better of her.

One wrong move and it could all be over.

"Oi, oi, oi," Edward said, picking up the gun and pressing his own weapon firmly into Thomas's neck. "I'll frogmarch you in front of a beak myself if I have to. Better yet, how about the vaults beneath the church?"

"You wouldn't dare," Thomas said after a while. "The secret's already blown. One wrong step, your entire family will be serving time."

"You royals with your stupid threats. You're not even real military. You're chocolate soldiers in every sense of the word."

Edward licked him on the side of the face.

"Um. I was wrong. Butterscotch."

Thomas flinched. Edward responded immediately, again pressing the gun into his skin.

"Careful, Tom, careful. Enough playing games."

"You're the one p-playing."

"Uh, uh, oh," he tutted. "Let's not forget where we are."

Thomas could feel Edward moving around him, circling him like a shark. What fazed him most was the slowness of his footsteps. They echoed softly, as if trapped in the atmosphere. It even sounded like a church. To the prince, it felt as if time was slowing down, if not stopping altogether.

He needed a contingency plan.

Jen couldn't believe it. The object was there, less than five metres in front of her.

If she could make it under the next pew, she would have it.

Edward looked around the chapel, horrified by the debris. "Mum and Dad used to love this spot. Sometimes Mum used to paint, particularly the windows. She'd set up her easel over there." He pointed to the back of the church. "Would you like to see some of the pictures, Tom?"

A loud noise from one of the middle pews caught their attention.

"Jen," Edward said, elated. "I forgot all about you. Come join us."

Jen rose slowly from her knees to her feet, knowing she was helpless to argue. The waving of his gun was particularly persuasive. She walked down the aisle, grimacing awkwardly as she approached Thomas.

Edward watched her as she made her way alongside the prince. Another quick smile had withered into a frown.

There was new movement behind them, this time much quicker. A large bird had entered through the broken window in the corridor and perched itself on one of the pews.

All eyes looked towards the bird.

"Oi, oi, how did you escape?" Edward asked.

Thomas was confused. He remembered seeing various birdlife in the grounds of the Catesby estate, but he didn't associate them with the bird in front of him.

"That's a razorbill," Edward said, clearly paying it the most interest. "Sir William, that's Catesby, he breeds them. You often find them in Yorkshire. It's because we're only four miles from the sea – you only ever find them near the sea. Mum used to love painting them, too, but she could never quite get the colours right. They have this thin white line, there," he said, pointing to the area between the eyes and the bill. "Sometimes it's whiter than that; I think it has something to do with the mating season."

Thomas's patience was almost exhausted. If there was such a thing as a fate worse than death, this was surely it.

"Mum used to paint it whiter than that," Edward said, looking again at Jen. "Would you like to see some of my mum's paintings, Jen?"

She had no idea what to say. "Yeah, okay."

The smile returned. "They're in the other room."

"Wh-what do you mean b-breeds them?" Thomas interrupted.

"That's right. Breeds them; he lives over there." Edward pointed.

Thomas was confused. "You mean they're not wild?"

"Nah, not these birds. Sir William breeds them specially. They're really tasty, razorbills. I think he's got some prepared if you'd like a taste."

The sickly grin of the blond man confirmed Thomas's suspicions.

He had identified the source of the meat found on the man at Greenwich.

"It's particularly good with chips. As long as you're not allergic to poultry."

"Speaking of which. How's the medication going, Edward?"

Jen looked to her right, even more alarmed.

What medication?

"I'm sure he's already told you," he said to Jen. "When we were at school, Edward used to suffer from homesickness. Took him two full terms to settle in at Winchester."

The hurt was visible across Edward's face.

He laughed, his usual laugh. "You are so predictable," he said, quietly but with venom. "You think you're not? You think you'd be any different if the same happened to you? Do you?"

The volume of Edward's voice had risen considerably, sending an unpleasant shiver down Thomas's spine. Twenty-eight years as his cousin had taught him Edward Jeffries was unpredictable at the best of times.

"For the record, Jen, it wasn't just me that suffered. You know I had heard, Tom, members of your own family didn't care too much, for starters. Of course, back then fagging was still legal.

"I've always wondered what it was like, having to undergo such terrible cruelty," he said, waving the gun. "Care to try it out, Tom?"

"Why don't you p-put the gun d-down? Then we can t-talk p-properly."

Edward's smile returned. "You want to t-talk p-p-properly, do you? Well, let me t-tell you, T-Tom. I can t-talk p-p-properly with or without a gun."

Thomas attempted to remain calm. "Put it down, Ed."

"Don't tell me what to do; honestly, anyone would think you're the king."

The choice of words caused Jen new anguish. How much had changed in less than a day.

"It's you that's under orders, Tom, and you know what happens if you don't obey."

Edward marched in front of them, this time displaying complete concentration.

"I think the time for games is over. Backs against the wall. Move."

He shouted the last word, which made Jen jump. They followed the gesture of the waving gun to the left of the open double doors and stopped behind the final pew, in between two bookcases that were filled with hymnals.

Jen moved in alongside Thomas, her breathing quick. The large puffin-shaped bird was still in the chapel, its large feet padding up and down the penultimate pew. Every so often it would flap its wings, but not take off.

A gunshot filled the chapel, followed by frantic flapping.

"Missed," Edward said.

Jen was livid, while Thomas looked on in terror. The bird took off and escaped into the corridor, either making its way through the broken window or somewhere back along the cloisters.

"Honestly never knew what Mum saw in them." He turned his attention back to his prisoners. "You all right there, Jen? You seem nervous."

"Don't answer," Thomas said.

He fired again, this time into the air. "What did I say about giving orders?"

Thomas took a deep breath. He heard Caroline speaking in his ear. She wanted a response, but that was impossible.

Edward turned to Morris. "Come here."

The friar jumped to it.

"Frisk him. You never know, I might have missed something."

"Yes, Your Highness."

Morris carried out his objective in rapid time: under the arms, waist, and legs . . .

"He's clean, sir." He looked at Jen. "How about her?"

Edward laughed. "Where would she be hiding anything? There's nothing there." He gestured to her breasts. "Have you ever fired a gun before, Jen?"

No answer.

"Would you like to try?"

She took a deep breath, her expression turning malevolent. "Only if you promise not to move."

Edward seemed hurt by the comment. He looked her in the eyes for several seconds before ending the sequence with a trademark laugh.

Thomas was quiet; instead, his mind considered the present reality. Edward was hardly a field agent; his family had no experience in the military whatsoever since the war. Nevertheless, the more time passed, the more he was becoming concerned by the threat. The stories Caroline told him earlier that day continued to replay over and over in his mind. The possibility seemed unbelievable.

Edward Jeffries, killer of a king.

"Where did you g-get the g-gun from?"

Edward avoided the temptation to sneer. "Does it matter?"

"Only to Scotland Yard."

Edward laughed. "It's always seemed to me, Tom, that the more thinking you royals do, the more trouble you make for yourselves. I mean, take a look at the situation regarding Edward IV. All he ever really wanted was to marry for love."

He laughed.

"In the late 1700s, I had an ancestor called Martin Jeffries."

"I thought you guys were only called Edward."

The comment seemed to rile him. "Cheap blow, Tom, cheap blow. He wasn't the eldest son, if you were wondering . . .

"Anyway, he had been arranged in marriage to a fine lady from Lincolnshire – at least I think it was Lincolnshire. That Martin was something of a traveller, not that type of traveller."

"I know what you mean."

Edward grinned. "While he was abroad, he fell in love – as you do. The woman was French, but without title. And when he returned, he said to his father, his name was Edward, that he was going to marry her anyway. And you know what he said?"

Thomas had no idea.

"He sat him down, and he said to Martin that he should never underestimate the importance of choosing the wrong woman. And do you know what he meant by that?"

"He c-couldn't m-marry her?"

"No, you're wrong, Tom. He said the opposite. He said that it was his opinion that the biggest mistake of the royals was that none of them married for love. It was that which made them cheat; it was that which made them unpredictable and violent. He said that there was never a man in history who reached the top without the support of a loving woman.

"See, my ancestor, Edward IV, married Elizabeth Woodville. Now she was a commoner. Drove the nobles mad, that did, the king marrying for love. Only what they failed to realise was that Elizabeth brought out the best in him."

Again Thomas was confused. Edward seemed to have gone off at a tangent.

"Sounds reasonable."

"Ever since I was fourteen, I've spent hours and hours reading the biographies of great men. You should try it yourself, Tom. You never know, something might rub off on you."

"Well, you always did want to be the brightest student in class, didn't you?"

"Don't patronise me, Tom. And tell me honestly, what's the need for it? Does it really make you feel superior?"

"Does pointing a gun at an innocent woman make you?"

Edward bit his lip. "Not really. Sadly some things are necessary, even if we don't like it."

The sound of flapping wings from the corridor returned, though without any sign of the bird.

"Do you like riddles, Tom? Here's one for you:

"It lives without a body; hears without ears; speaks without a mouth, to which the air alone gives birth.

"What am I?"

Remembering words was difficult.

"Speaks without . . ." Thomas had already forgotten.

"Give up: An echo."

Both Thomas and Jen looked at him, not knowing how to respond.

"Here's a better one," Edward began. "When a bird flies over water, a part of it touches the water but doesn't get wet. Which part?"

Thomas heard this one more clearly, but still he had no idea.

"Give up?"

The prince shook his head. "I don't know. The bones? The organs?"

"Wrong. The shadow."

Thomas breathed out, almost in disbelief.

"Here's another one, Tom.

"Sing a song of sixpence, a pocket full of rye,

"Four and twenty blackbirds, baked in a pie,

"When the pie was opened, the birds began to sing,

"Wasn't that a dainty dish to set before a king?"

Thomas's fury escalated. "That's not a riddle. It's a confession."

Edward smiled, but said nothing.

"Death by pie," Thomas said. "It's unique, I'll give you that much."

"You haven't heard the best part.

"The King was in his counting house, counting all his money,

"The queens were in the parlour, eating bread and honey."

He said the last part slowly, forcing the painful truth to return to Thomas.

"I hear it was you that found your grandmother?"

"You bastard."

"Oi, oi, oi." Edward waved the gun. "Now, now."

Thomas took a deep breath, struggling to remain calm. The horror of three years earlier, he realised for the first time, had still to sink in fully.

"You?"

Edward shook his head. "No." He looked over his shoulder. "Him."

Beneath his hood, Morris smiled like a maniac, the lines on his face appearing extra malevolent in the shadow of his vestment.

"Care for some more, Tom?

"The princess was in the garden, nattering on her phone . . ."

"No. It's the servant," Jen interrupted, confused. "Hanging out the clothes."

Edward shook his head. "You're wrong, Jen. It's definitely the princess."

"Blackbird," Thomas said, looking at the razorbill.

"They're Dominicans," Jen said. "Dominicans were nicknamed blackbirds."

Edward smiled. "Well done, Jen."

Suddenly it dawned on Thomas. "Caroline."

"What?" the voice asked in his earpiece.

As much as Thomas wanted to respond, he forced himself to keep his attention on Edward. "Caroline was attacked in the duke's garden."

"Was she really?"

"You know bloody well she was; wh-what of it?"

"Listen to the rhyme."

Thomas muttered the rest of the rhyme under his breath.

The princess was in the garden, nattering on her phone,
When down came a blackbird and pecked off her nose.

They sent for the duke's doctor,
Who sewed it on again;
He sewed it on so neatly,
The seam was never seen.

"That's the clue," Edward said. "He sewed it on so neatly, the seam was never seen."

At the other end of the line, Caroline felt her heart palpitating wildly. She touched her nose, feeling the area where the surgery had been carried out.

"I can't breathe."

*

Thomas heard her. "Caroline?"

Edward was confused.

"Caroline?"

Anthea was beside herself. "Calm down; it's okay."

"Oh my God, oh my God, oh my God." The girl was in a fit of panic.

"Relax, breathe."

"Caroline?"

Edward moved forward and ripped away the earpiece before doing the same to Thomas's shirt.

"A wire, oh, that's cheap."

He did the same to Jen, revealing a blue bra but also Sellotape above her cleavage.

Edward yanked it and ordered them back towards the wall, his anger rising.

He looked at Jen's breasts, then Thomas. "Good guess, mind: what you said about the bones. I guess you're right, in a way. But then again, technically, do they actually touch the water? Really, they sort of don't.

"But see, it's the shadow you've got to watch for, Tom. There's nothing more dangerous in life than the shadow. It's everywhere, stalking your every move. But it's at its most dangerous the one time you can't see it – at night. Nothing hides a shadow like darkness, Tom.

"Everything in life casts a shadow. For over five hundred years the Royal Family has cast a shadow. We, Tom, are that shadow. You can't always see us, but we're always there – right alongside you."

"And if you're our shadow, then where, might I ask, is your shadow? Huh. You are, after all, living things?"

"I've got a riddle for you," Jen said to Edward. "Why did the bubblegum cross the road?"

Thomas looked at her, bewildered. Edward, on the other hand, was far more taken.

"I have absolutely no idea. Go on, Jen, why did the bubblegum cross the road?"

She hesitated, distracted by Morris standing with his gun at the ready. The other friar was lying on the floor, no longer moving. Close by, the old man was walking slowly towards them; he had made it as far as the fourth pew.

"Because it was stuck to the chicken's leg."

Edward looked at her. Though he remained silent, his expression slowly began to change. He started laughing, softly then uncontrollably.

"It was stuck . . ."

Laughter got the better of him.

Across the chapel, Morris started laughing, at first softly, then more farfetched.

Jen grinned, albeit nervously. Edward had taken the joke far better than she had expected.

Edward was laughing hysterically. He wiped his eyes; tears either real or fake, she was unable to tell.

"That's brilliant. Jen, you should be on *Mock the Week.*"

She grinned, whereas Thomas was far more concerned. He edged closer to Jen, then closer still. He saw movement from Edward, followed by the noise of a gun going off.

Standing by the altar, Morris fell to the floor, blood immediately appearing around his upper thigh.

The man had been shot.

By Jen.

84

It was impossible to know who was the most surprised.

Standing near the fifth pew, the bang had caused Lord Jeffries to lose his balance.

Morris had been floored, losing his firearm in the process. He cried out in pain while clenching his wounded thigh.

Edward's eyes were solely on Jen. Jen, meanwhile, looked to her right at Thomas. His expression was strangely normal, yet his eyes were inquisitive. She could tell what he wanted to ask her.

Where did you get the gun?

Jen blew her hair away from her forehead, finishing the job with her left hand. Her blood was pumping fast, intensifying her breathing. She felt alive. She was thinking straight, perhaps for the first time in her life.

She had made up her mind.

She would be leaving here alive.

"Why did you kill Debra Harrison?" she shouted. "Do you always prey on teenagers?"

Edward looked suspiciously at Jen, finally realising she must have taken the friar's gun when it slid beneath the pews. Though momentarily stunned, he was still armed and in control.

"Is that what you think this is about? Sex?" He looked at Thomas. "Jen, his grandfather murdered my parents. I don't expect you to understand."

"That man murdered your king. My grandfather. You're nothing but a common thug."

Edward aimed the gun at Thomas. "And how about him? Huh. How many more innocent lives would've had to be lost before you finally understood? How many more mistakes need be made? It wasn't just them, Tom; my father had intelligence on hundreds, perhaps thousands, ranging from pig farmers to nuclear scientists. The monarchy is a leach on this country."

"They're your relatives, too."

"Aye, you're right; they are – and that's what makes it so tough," he turned and looked at his grandfather. "That's the rightful king, right there. But no, fate changed because loyalty had forsaken us. That's the real history of this country.

"Do you know what they used to call the Wars of the Roses, Jen? They called it the Cousins' War – see that's effectively what it was. Did you ever hear what happened at Bosworth? The reason my ancestor lost? Because five of the families who said they would fight for him betrayed him. Worse, they watched on the sidelines until the battle was nearly over. Then they took the side of that Welsh prick Henry Tudor. It's their descendants that govern this land. Their descendants who've ruined it.

"History is full of people like them: liars, traitors." He looked at Thomas. "Kings who command other people to do their dirty work."

He looked again at Jen.

"It's not too late, though. The future is still unwritten; it can be anything we make of it."

The photograph she had seen earlier that day continued to flash in her mind.

Edward Jeffries,

Edward XIV of England.

"The choice should be with the people."

"You murdered the King of England," Thomas repeated.

"He killed far more than me." He laughed again, always the same laugh. "Would you do the same?" he asked of Thomas. "The same as your grandfather?"

Thomas bit his lip, trying his best to delay giving an answer. "You think it's easy being king?"

"Sitting on the fence."

"I am sorry about your parents. Whatever the circumstances."

There was sincerity in his voice, which Edward found distracting.

"Why do you think you're in the position you're in: the invisible royal, the king's loyal aid. In the past you'd have had another name: Henchman."

Thomas straightened his shoulders.

"How many have you killed?" He looked at Jen. "Did he tell you what he did? On behalf of King and Country."

She stood quietly, still with the gun held out.

"Your hand getting tired, Jen?"

She rose her arm, the gun aimed at Edward's eye line. She loosened her shoulder, trying as best she could to remain vigilant.

Edward laughed, his eyes again on Thomas. His question of "how many have you killed?" remained unanswered.

"Not got an answer, Tom?"

"Being king is about priority. There are some th-things that can never be c-compromised." He looked up at the reredos behind the altar. "Everyone makes sacrifices. Even he had his cross to bear."

The parallel went down badly. "I was that pissing sacrifice. He robbed me of everything. My mother . . . father . . . I could have had a brother or sister; there was still time, they were only thirty-seven."

Jen watched uncomfortably as tears began to fall from his eyes. She tightened her grip on the weapon.

"I heard a rumour once, Tom, that MI5 has a process for people like you: kind of like the royals' own version of training. Basically, once you're through Sandhurst, they take you to this place in Scotland, one of the castles or palaces, and simulate that your entire family is being held hostage. You have to choose the best way forward. Did you ever take that test?"

"It wouldn't even be necessary. And besides, telling you would be a b-breach of official s-secrets."

"Official secrets." He laughed. "Okay, you're right; that was naughty of me. The funny thing is, either way you're guaranteed an admiral's uniform and a brass chest; me: even if I were a war hero, I'd be guaranteed nothing but a shit pension and shrapnel in the arse."

"Maybe you should try it first hand before making stupid insinuations."

Edward grinned. "Have you ever seen the film *Bambi*, Tom? My least favourite bit is the part where his mum died. Even though that one event began his development as a man, he was robbed of his security. Just like I was."

Thomas exhaled deeply. "I've never seen it."

Edward laughed again. "Why do people do it? Why all the hurt?"

"A strange comment from a man who is aiming a gun at an unarmed man."

He pointed it at Jen. "Better?"

"At least she's armed."

Jen shot him a look of disbelief.

"Can I offer you a seat, Jen?" Edward asked softly.

Jen blew out forcibly. Nerves had now completely left her, but the uncertainty was greater than ever.

"Who was responsible for killing the politicians?" Thomas asked. "You?"

Edward shook his head. "Not me, Tom. I understand you've met Morris."

Thomas looked at the recently escaped prisoner still nursing a bullet to the thigh.

"Why do it? I still don't understand. I mean, it's not as though you have any chance of actually claiming the throne."

"Well, you know what they say, Tom. If I tell you, I'll have to . . ." He tapped twice against the side of the gun.

"Are you sure? Okay. Well, you see, the thing is, Tom, it's like you say, really. I have practically zero chance of becoming King of England. It's not going to happen, even if I am the rightful heir. I'm what, eighteenth in line? Perhaps seventeenth."

"You're twenty-second," Thomas replied.

Edward nodded. "Okay, so twenty-one graves stand in my way. Including yours . . .

"But there is one thing the Sons of York can do. Stand for parliament."

Thomas laughed. "So that's what this is all about. Your father, S-Stanley, Lord Ratcliffe–"

"Historically, Tom, their families have always been involved. It goes back six centuries. But it's not just about the Whigs, Democrats, or any other party. The goal is England."

Thomas lowered his eyebrows. "You want to conquer England?"

"Not conquer, Tom. Reclaim. Ever since the Tudors, England has become contaminated. The Tudor rose was supposed to be a symbol of purity, but it was contaminated. The true heir still lived, and the marriage between Tudor and Elizabeth was a sham. But, worse still, less than fifty years later things were damaged beyond repair when one fat arrogant pig couldn't have a son. Throughout Plantagenet England, we saw nothing but evolution. When Edward IV came to the throne, it developed even further. Had Richard and the princes ruled, the progress could've been out of this world. England could've had its own Renaissance: great commerce, a thriving art scene, geniuses like da Vinci and Michelangelo. The Tudors didn't create; they destroyed. Then if that wasn't enough, it was taken over by Scots. When Cromwell failed to take on the job, it was taken over by Germans."

He laughed.

"The situation may change, but the scenario is always the same.

406

Contamination. England was once the greatest country in the world. Look at what's happened. Great Britain, I'll give you that, but the EU, human rights, gay marriage, mass immigration . . . that isn't the country my ancestors fought and died for. In the last twenty-five years, the EU has torn this country apart."

"What do you want? A referendum?"

Another laugh. "When my ancestor Henry II sat on that throne, he ruled an empire that stretched from here to the Pyrenees. But do you know what the best part was? Come a century later, people finally knew what it meant to be English. That still exists; every time I go to Wembley, I feel nothing but pride. Then it goes, all gone in the drop of a hat.

"The new world we were promised is disintegrating before our very eyes; to deny that is to look upon the truth and lie," he said, conviction in the statement. "To be fair, fifteen years ago I even bought into it: a united Europe, single currency, the end of boom and bust . . . I mean, it's brilliant, isn't it when you hear it like that . . . but it's not real, is it, Tom?"

"And just what exactly do you propose to put in its place? A Fourth Reich? A police state? Fascist England? Surely you're not planning ships to invade Normandy?"

"Europe has the potential to be anything we want it to be. I bet you didn't know that once upon a time even Tories like Bates and Trenton agreed with us. Hundreds do in the Commons. Only sadly those two decided they were unhappy with our plans; both knew far too much of our existence. But, since their deaths, the bi-elections have already gone to plan."

Thomas couldn't believe what he was hearing. "Who do you even support? The Democrats or the Tories?"

Edward's smile widened. "Perhaps I'm not the right person to answer that question."

Thomas turned to his left. Two newcomers had entered the chapel.

West was waiting outside his new office in Westminster when the car arrived. It was a long, black limousine that he recognised immediately.

He opened the door. "You?"

"Get in," Stephen replied from the back seat. "I hear you've done some sterling work."

The new Secretary of State for Justice got inside.

"Tell me everything that's happened since yesterday."

85

Jen and Thomas looked to their left. Two men had entered the chapel. Jen had seen them both recently, whereas for Thomas several years had passed.

"I'm sure you're familiar, Tom, with Sir William Catesby and Lord Ratcliffe, former Chancellor of the Exchequer. Jen, may I present to you, the Privy Council."

She looked at them in disbelief.

He wasn't joking.

Catesby entered first, his demeanour characteristically cold. He wore a large protective white jacket, the sort of thing she associated with a lab. Ratcliffe wore his usual suit and appeared the more annoyed of the two. He carried nothing, while Catesby held a brand-new, slick-looking revolver.

Thomas examined both men top to bottom, strangely amused by what he saw.

"The Cat and the Rat," Thomas said. "Where's the Dog?"

Catesby's expression hardened. "A most unreliable man; probably skulking away somewhere."

"Not exactly."

The voice came from somewhere nearby. One of the side doors opened, one Jen had tried to open earlier that day.

"You've been there the whole time?" Edward asked.

"Yes, sir, I have, and listening to every word, I might add. Might I please suggest we get some medical attention for Brother Morris and Brother Daniel."

Catesby removed a bandage from his jacket and approached the injured men. While Jen was baffled, it seemed obvious to Thomas that Lovell had already informed them of what had been going on.

Catesby bandaged Morris, a makeshift job at best, before walking to the other hooded gunman.

"He's dead," Catesby affirmed, checking his vitals. He moved away from the dead friar, heading towards Lovell. The former headmaster had made it to the centre aisle.

"You chose not to participate?"

"I thought it wise, William, to observe and take in the proceedings from a distance. I see you both got my message."

Ratcliffe was confused. "What message?"

"I sent you a text message, as well, Richard; you really must learn to use your phone."

Catesby's hard façade faded. Unlike the Rat, he was a man of science.

The grin had returned to Edward's face. "That's the full set. The Cat, the Rat and the Dog, Tom."

"What would that make you? The Hog?"

"Not yet." He gestured over his shoulder. Lord Jeffries had finally resorted to sitting down. Even over ten metres away the heaviness of his breathing was evident.

"So if he's the Hog, then what does that make you? The little piggy that went wee, wee, wee–"

Edward thrust the gun into Thomas's neck. "Just watch yourself. Didn't Popup ever warn you not to antagonize someone holding a gun?"

Thomas arched his neck, the force of the gun pressing uncomfortably against his skin. Since the arrival of Catesby, there were now two guns aimed at him.

And only one at them.

"Give me the gun, Jen," Edward said.

She refused, silently concerned she had little choice.

"I won't wait this time, Jen."

"Do as he says," Thomas said.

Jen looked at him, reluctant. She tried to speak, but the words were trapped in her gullet.

"You can't win; just d-drop it," Thomas said.

She took a deep breath and finally obeyed, throwing the gun on the floor. It bounced past Edward, stopping inches from Lord Ratcliffe's feet.

Ratcliffe picked it up. "You're a woman of many talents, Miss Farrelly. It's really quite a shame things had to turn out this way."

"It's a shame the same can't be said about you," Thomas said, taking extra care to compose each word without a stutter. "I always knew you'd sell your own mother, Richard. But your country?"

"Actually, sir, it is because of my love for this country that I agree with what you have just heard. And because of my love for my family I must seek revenge on the man who killed my own flesh and blood."

Thomas was confused. "You think I killed someone from your family?"

"Yesterday at around 7 p.m. there was an incident in Greenwich involving a small group of men and a large building; I understand you were the one with the gun."

"They were relatives of yours?"

"The lad that died was me nephew."

Thomas strengthened his resolve.

"Don't get me wrong, Tom; I can call you Tom, can't I?" he said, receiving no answer. "I know that you had no idea who it was you were shooting, and I know that you were under orders. If you want the truth, I didn't initiate the commands yesterday; I just didn't disagree with them."

"So you agree th-that you also have b-blood on your hands?"

The comments seemed to sadden Ratcliffe. "Should I have my time over again, I daresay there are many things that I might do differently. But despite what some people may say, I've always stuck by my cause. Never been one to take a bribe, nor profit from another's misfortune – at least not intentionally. If the press says otherwise, that's up to them."

"The man I killed was himself a k-killer. Had he not been f-firing at me I'd have left him alone," Thomas said with fixed determination, accompanied by a cold expression that brought fear to the heart of Lord Ratcliffe. "Who gave the order?"

"That would have been me."

The voice came from the fourth pew.

Thomas looked at Jeffries elder. "There's bitterness in your voice, old man . . . in all of you."

"How dare you address the King," Edward said, his fury building. "You're not in the palace now, Tom. This is white rose country."

Thomas ignored him. "Why did you want to kill me?"

Lord Jeffries laughed. "You think I would waste my time on such a minor relation?" the old man asked, coughing. "Heavens no. My greater interest was, and still remains, the men responsible for the death of my son."

But the King is dead.

Thomas shrugged. "Why go to the bother? Your grandson said it himself: you have no chance of claiming the throne."

"You really think this is merely about reclaiming the monarchy? Sitting on an old throne, accompanied by dust and memory." He shook his head. "I lost my son, and one of the men responsible has paid."

Again, he was confused. "You really think my grandfather was responsible?"

"My dear sir, your words betray you. I know you have seen the footage of many years ago with your own eyes. Had I simply wanted your grandfather dead, then, believe me, I would have completed the task long ago: be it in a cloud of smoke, a long and hardened anguish, or at the hands of an unfortunate motorist . . . the choices seem unlimited. Throughout my life I have been forced to endure hardships, as most men would put it, and I have at times been forced to come to terms with personal loss. But only a man who has spent the latter years of his life mourning the passing of his son can really understand the torment that I have been through these past years. The man himself may no longer be with us, but for every son, there is an heir. And until the chain is broken, the past repeats itself."

Thomas was now becoming alarmed. Clearly he meant the rest of his family.

Suddenly it dawned on him. "Was that why you tried to kill us at Greenwich?" Thomas bit his lip. "Stephen?"

Though Thomas laughed without humour, the idea brought new hatred. "I can honestly say I thought better of you. But when all is said and done, you're nothing but a sad old man."

He looked to his left at Jen.

"I tell you what, what say a trade? The great-nephew for the grandson. Only, let her go."

Jen felt goose bumps all the way from her neck to the bottom of her feet. She could see from the prince's expression that there was certainty in his eyes, as if he was prepared to carry out a great duty, perhaps even destiny.

The old man laughed, coughing again. "You are not in a situation capable of negotiation."

He looked at Ratcliffe, then Catesby. "Come on, chaps. No more playing games. Let her go."

Jen was still standing rigidly, her eyes locked on the two newcomers. "I assume you were two of the participants in Debra Harrison's death ceremony?"

She looked at Lovell. "And you?"

The former headmaster was looking particularly uncomfortable.

"Who was the fourth?"

"I'm afraid that was me," Edward confessed, remorse absent from his eyes. "There will always be sacrifices, Jen. Nobody likes them."

"You don't give off the impression you dislike them."

"On the contrary, hopefully one day they will no longer be necessary. What's the saying: if you want peace, war is inevitable."

"An old saying," Jen said.

"Still as true today as it was then."

A strange silence had overcome the chapel, almost religious in nature. The sound of shuffling was the only disturbance, again coming from Morris. Nearby, Lovell was kneeling by his side, tending to his wound.

"So what's your involvement in all this?" Jen asked.

The question was for Catesby. "It was my noble ancestor's grand ambition to oversee a great transition from the turbulence that plagued England following the schism of the House of Plantagenet. Like his noble cousins, he understood that things like pestilence and bad harvest that contributed so greatly to the turmoil would be only temporary measures, leaving the developments of the realm safe among the prudent. I don't, of course, expect you to be familiar with the work of my great namesake; his private writings have rarely made it out of the family."

It saved her a question.

"But I daresay, not everybody lost in the result of the great schism. Our families perhaps had the most to profit. When the feeble Henry VI lost power to the great Edward IV, England briefly became a country of great enterprise: the flair of the merchant was rewarded as much as the toil of the industrialist, including that of the common man. In the past, the greatest mistake a man could make was to try to profit by someone else's work. It was that which failed the feudal system.

"When Edward IV died, his son had the potential to be one of the greatest kings who ever lived, but even God could not prevent his slide into darkness. When the mantle fell upon the greatest general of Medieval Europe, England could have been secure for another twenty or thirty years. It's been estimated that the Wars of the Roses saw the end of the great noble families. Less predictable, alas, the end of a great nation."

Jen couldn't believe her ears. "Most people would call it the shaping of a great nation. Let me guess. You're going to deliver another diatribe about religion. Save your breath, I've heard them all before."

Catesby's indignation was apparent. "An understandable misapprehension, but a misapprehension nonetheless. In truth, the religious fires that came after were merely a by-product. By the time the bastard of Henry VIII took the throne, the Reformation had already gone too far to be countered altogether. It was never my ancestors' intention to destroy the new. Only to make room for the old."

He took a step forward.

"It is never possible to live peacefully through conquest. Only compromise."

The sound of a helicopter interrupted Jen's intended response. The atmosphere changed in a heartbeat. Glass shattered from the broken window, accompanied by a sudden gust of wind as the force of the blades passed by.

Edward was horrified. "You called MI5," he said, unclear whether he was speaking to Jen or Thomas.

Standing alongside them, Ratcliffe and Catesby were both alarmed.

"You must've done." Panic was written all over his face.

Thomas, meanwhile, was edging to his left, now touching Jen.

His next move was instinctive. Taking advantage of Edward's brief look over his shoulder, Thomas pounced, taking Edward with him to the floor.

They landed heavily, Edward taking most of the damage on his back.

He lost his gun on impact.

Catesby was still armed. He aimed at Thomas, cocked and poised to shoot. He felt a thud on the back of his leg and fell over instantly, losing his gun. It skidded along the aisle, landing at Jen's feet.

"Stay where you are," she said, picking it up. "You too."

Ratcliffe obeyed without hesitation. He lowered himself to the ground extra slowly and placed his hands over his head.

Jen looked to the side of the chapel. Lovell had disappeared, as had Morris. She heard the sound of a door closing, then locking.

She cursed her luck.

Now they could be anywhere.

She returned her focus to her new prisoners. "I told you to keep still."

The gun went off, the sound echoing. Catesby flinched as a bullet ricocheted off the floor, barely a metre away.

Jen was so surprised she nearly dropped the gun.

She had no idea it was even cocked.

She turned and aimed at Jeffries, then Edward, but refrained from firing. The two cousins were still at deadlock, their hands gripping each other around the shoulders. Edward's face had turned bright red, whereas Thomas was in better control.

It was obvious who the fitter of the two was.

Fitness was proving the key. Thomas flipped Edward over and pinned him to the floor. He punched him twice in the face, drawing blood. Edward kicked back hard, making contact with the ribs. Thomas felt the force. He fell backwards, sliding about a metre before regaining himself. He jumped to his feet immediately and charged at Edward.

Edward was riled. He attempted to run in the other direction, but struggled to keep his feet on the tiled surface. He leaned forward for the gun, stretching himself to the utmost.

Grabbing it, he rolled onto his back, pointing the gun upwards.

Thomas stopped. He thought he was about to be shot, but Edward delayed. To Thomas's left, Jen was alongside him, still in possession of Catesby's revolver. He looked again at Edward, now a melting pot of rage.

"You stupid son of a bitch," Edward said. He rose slowly to his feet, his eyes locked on the prince. He cocked the trigger and aimed at Thomas's head.

He heard movement from behind, causing him to panic. He turned and fired instinctively.

Only then did he realise his mistake.

Less than half a mile away, the helicopter landed outside one of the mansions. Stephen was the first to exit, followed by West.

"Where is it?"

The MP knew the way well. "Follow me."

86

Edward was horrified on seeing what he had done. His grandfather was lying on the floor, oozing blood.

Edward collapsed to his knees, his vision clouded by tears. The bullet had entered the skin around the right shoulder area, close to the collarbone. The wound gushed quickly, clearly visible despite the man's thick suit jacket.

Edward placed his hands to the wound and pushed hard. Blood escaped through his fingers, covering his hands.

"Granddad." His voice was barely audible. His hands shook violently, as did the rest of him.

The old man coughed, a chesty cough, though much weaker than before. The reflex was different, noticeably without conviction.

"Quick," Edward shouted to no one in particular, "call an ambulance."

He returned his attention to the floor. He sought to speak, but the old man silenced him. He grabbed his grandson's outstretched hand and held it with both of his.

"Edward," he said, the words audible only to them, "we are undone."

His lip quivered, as did the young man's. Edward watched as the man who raised him took a deep breath and lowered his head to one side.

Either dead or just unconscious, it was impossible to know.

Thomas and Jen watched, mesmerised. Jen struggled to breathe. She tried to move, but her legs had gone to jelly.

Thomas's first concern was for Jen. He grabbed her hand and backed away towards the doors. Ratcliffe and Catesby were still on the floor, neither daring to move.

Thomas led the way through the open doors, turned right immediately and sprinted along the corridor.

He stopped on reaching a dead end. He was on virgin ground, the only part of the house neither of them had explored.

He instantly regretted his choice.

He replaced the earpiece and tried to contact Caroline.

"Caroline, I need guidance."

No response.

"Caroline?"

Anthea heard the voice. She put the headset on and replied.

"Caroline?"

"Try the third door on the right."

"Where's Caroline?"

"She's fine."

That wasn't the question. Nevertheless he took the instruction.

"It's just an empty room."

Anthea cursed her mistake. "Try the next one."

"Wh-where's–"

"She fainted."

"What?"

"She's okay, I'll explain. Try the next door."

Thomas tried it and saw a large cluttered room with bay windows and a mini balcony that overlooked the grounds and a winding stairway by the far wall. Once upon a time it would have been part of the old servants' quarters.

He descended the stairs and came to another corridor.

"Where now?"

She wasn't sure.

"Anthea?"

"Stop yelling," she yelled herself. "Go left. There's a doorway at the end."

He opened it and found a third corridor. Unlike most in the house, the wall was a dirty shade of white and the carpet older and messier. Numerous religious artefacts decorated the walls, ranging from watercolour paintings to crosses.

Immediately there was gunfire.

Thomas dived behind the door, taking Jen with him.

"Give me the gun."

She obeyed.

He waited for the gunfire to stop, using the door as a makeshift shield. The bullets penetrated the wood, destroying the upper half.

When the sound died, he inched it open, then fully.

Immediately the gunfire resumed, coming from the end of the corridor. Whoever it was had clearly been waiting for them.

Thomas fired twice, more in hope than expectation. He could tell from the cries the second shot had been successful. The man fell, slumped against the wall.

"Stay here."

Thomas ran towards him, the revolver trained on the gunman. The man was hooded, clearly a friar, and evidently still alive. Cautiously he approached. Satisfied the man was unconscious, he stole the firearm. It was automatic, modern and, most importantly, had three magazines of ammo left.

He looked at Jen, who was still crouching by the door.

"Come on."

Kneeling by his grandfather's side, Edward felt a light hand on his shoulder. As he looked up to his left, he saw the cold eyes of William Catesby staring down at him.

"They must not escape."

Edward looked back at him for what seemed in the circumstances a lengthy pause before placing his hands to his eyes. He dried the tears, but failed to mask the stains.

He rose to his feet and loaded his gun.

Thomas and Jen were about halfway down the main stairs when the gunfire resumed. A swarm of bullets battered the wall behind them, ruining three pieces of art.

Debris fell like snow.

Edward was screaming at the top of the stairway. "Don't run from me, you bastard."

Edward fired again, the closest yet. Thomas dived instinctively, forcing Jen off balance. They rolled for several steps, the jagged edges of the wooden stairway hard on their sides and back despite the carpet.

Jen was the first to her feet. She grabbed Thomas with her left hand, doing her best to sprint and keep low. As the gunfire ceased, she heard running at the top of the stairway.

Then more gunfire.

Thomas picked up the pace, concentrating on the floor above. He could hear but not see Edward Jeffries descending at a fast pace, the bullets from his gun destroying the nearby decorations.

Thomas let go of Jen's hand, allowing her to get ahead of him. They both ducked as a new barrage of gunshots caused debris to fall from above, landing on the stairs and ruining the carpet.

No question, the bullets were getting nearer.

They made it to the first floor. Thomas considered making a run for the corridor, though Jen had already continued for the stairs. As the gunfire ceased again, they heard running from above, the sound confirming Edward's location.

The gunfire started again.

Thomas turned as he ran, and fired upwards. Sparks flew off the railing, whereas others hit the wall. He looked briefly to his left as one bullet made contact with the large painting of Edward hanging on the next wall, the bullet entering the forehead.

He took aim once more as the angle opened up, but dismissed firing again.

A clear shot was impossible.

Jen reached the bottom of the stairs. The large hallway was the only thing that separated her from the front door. She pulled on the handle, but it was locked.

She had no idea how to open it from the inside.

Gunfire resumed on the stairs. She had two choices, the lounge or the kitchen.

She chose the kitchen.

Thomas had the same idea. He jumped the last four steps, narrowly avoiding a volley of bullets.

Sensing Edward was getting closer, he sprinted for the kitchen, aware that Jen was already outside. He found her again less than twenty metres from the door, visibly relieved he'd made it.

They had made it into the grounds.

Outside the main gate, Stephen stopped. He looked at West alongside him.

"Where to now?"

"There's an entrance around the side."

87

Where to next? Thomas knew his life depended on the decision, and he had zero time to decide.

And that had almost elapsed.

Instinct had guided them close to where Thomas had earlier made his entrance. Drawing on experience, he headed for the mazelike hedges.

"Head west; there's more shelter." The instructions came in his ear.

"Which way is west?" Thomas asked.

"Hundred degrees left, you should be aiming for a tennis court," Anthea said.

"I see it."

They went for it, taking a pathway to the right before changing direction across one of the lawns.

"If you follow your current path, you might be exposed," Anthea continued. "Stick to the left."

It sounded like decent advice.

"Thanks."

Edward had finally made it outside. He eyed the grounds from the patio, looking for any sign of movement.

The grounds were deserted, the vague sounds of animal life the only exception.

He crossed the first lawn and continued towards the tennis court. He reloaded as he ran, giving him forty bullets in one magazine.

Surely more than he needed.

Anthea's advice had taken them into woodland, a good choice, all things considered. The grounds continued for two miles in certain directions, whereas, according to Anthea, the nearest border was less than half a mile away.

"We can get out there," Jen said, pointing. "It's where I got out the other night."

Thomas took her word for it. They passed what remained of the castle, neither of them showing any interest in the former ruins. Thomas had never seen it, but he was familiar with the rumours.

He guessed they were probably true after all.

The woodlands were a thick assembly of briars and thickets, encompassing over a mile in area. The evening sun was slowly setting over the distant fields to the west, shrouding the woodland in partial gloom.

With the light going, the woodland offered ample hiding places.

They heard gunfire, loud but not particularly near. Instinct told Thomas it was a shot in anger, almost certainly from Edward. Nevertheless, the sound was still unnerving.

Thomas veered left among the trees and over a small brook, followed closely by Jen. The pathway wound from left to right, and then over open ground. There were several outbuildings at this point, most of which Jen had seen before.

"Here," she said. "It's this way."

She grabbed Thomas's hand, and this time didn't let go. They passed the mill and then the barn.

Gunfire.

This time much closer.

Bullets marked the walls of the barn, a permanent scar, causing splinters to fall. Thomas stopped by the wall and cautiously looked to his right.

Edward had emerged from the trees, now less than a hundred metres away.

Thomas wasted no time. He led the way to the other side of the barn. His heart sank on seeing what awaited.

At least three hundred metres of open ground separated the barn and the edge of the estate.

They stopped on the other side of the barn, allowing one final deep breath.

"You ready?"

Jen looked him in the eye and nodded.

He grabbed her hand and then went for it, keeping as low as possible. They heard gunfire behind them, but it wasn't close. Edward was tiring, and it showed. They both heard shouting, something out of anger.

The exact words were lost on the wind.

They reached the wall that circled the west side of the property. Jen looked for the area she'd used the night before but found nothing but bricks and stone.

"Here, I'll push you over," Thomas said.

"What?"

"There's no time."

Edward had reappeared close to the barn. He saw them and fired while on the run.

"Now," Thomas shouted.

Jen jumped immediately and came down with a crash. She hit her head as she came down on the path.

Fortunately nothing more than a scratch.

Seconds later Thomas was also over. He caught his right leg as he came down, nearly losing a trainer.

"Come on."

Edward cursed aloud. Catching them in his condition was now impossible.

He came to a standstill on reaching the wall and took several deep breaths.

As he composed himself, he heard something. Was his hearing deceiving him? In the distance, he heard consternation.

He jogged in that direction. Access to the pathway was still restricted by the wall and various hedges, but a view across the churchyard presented itself.

In the distance, he saw it; it was happening around the church. The sun was setting orange and red, just as it said in prophecy.

He turned away, heading for the castle.

88

They followed the same pathway Jen had taken with Anthea the night before. The rusty gate creaked as she opened it before doing the same as it closed.

They now had a straight choice, left towards the Ravensfield houses, or right to the churchyard.

The answer seemed obvious.

Jen led the way into the churchyard and came to a sudden halt. The atmosphere was electric, shouts of terrified voices, anger and uncertainty.

It wasn't until they reached the front doors of the church that they saw what was happening.

A large gathering had assembled, perhaps as many as thirty people.

"There she is."

Jen felt her heart literally try to jump out of her mouth. She grabbed Thomas's arm instinctively, her eyes cemented on the gathering. Although she was unsure who had spoken, the body language of the crowd was clearly hostile.

Martha Brown was standing amongst them, her expression like thunder.

"Where is she?"

Jen was absolutely wrathful. *You left me to die and did nothing.*

She tried to compose herself. "Anthea? She's fine. Look . . . just relax, I can explain."

Martha moved closer, her expression even angrier than before. "Where is my daughter?"

Jen did not respond. Instead, her attention was taken by the large gathering. She recognised some but not others. Harvey Mitchell from the Hog was there, his arms folded and his expression stern, but none of the regular barflies were with him. There were several men she didn't recognise, mostly dressed in black and white robes.

Another man stepped to the front. He was about five feet eleven in height and wearing a smart suit, despite the warmth of the summer's evening. He had a fine head of distinguished grey hair, but his face looked like that of a gopher. Jen recognised him immediately.

Rowland Stanley.

Leader of the Democrat Party.

"Why don't you let me handle this one, Martha," he said, placing his hands on her shoulders. He smiled at her reassuringly.

Evidently convincing her.

He walked forward a few paces. "You needn't worry, Miss Farrelly, nor you, Your Royal Highness. The phone call came through not fifteen minutes ago. Everything has been explained to us."

His words made Jen even more nervous. As she listened to the man, she also found herself listening to the sounds of nature.

For the first time it dawned on her.

The helicopter had mysteriously disappeared.

"Someone needs to call an ambulance," Jen said. "At least two people are injured – badly."

"All taken care of," Stanley replied calmly. "The police arrived several minutes ago; they have a few questions."

Jen shrugged. "I'd be happy to. Where are they?"

"Inside the inn." The politician gestured to the Hog. "If you would be so kind."

Jen didn't buy it. Worse still, Thomas was whispering something in her ear. She looked over her shoulder, her eyes on the pathway.

Three more men dressed in black and white robes had appeared by the gate.

Back in front of her, the gathering was encroaching. She heard a clicking sound, then several more.

Had the last hour been different, she might not have realised it was the sound of a gun being cocked.

She looked nervously at Thomas, then again over her shoulder. The friars by the gate were also moving towards them.

She moved a few steps to her right, the only option. The way ahead to the high street was blocked, as was the pathway behind.

She whispered nervously, "Thomas."

The prince, meanwhile, was yet to move. Instead he remained focused on the gathering in front of him. He didn't need any introductions, it was all too apparent.

This was the heart of the Sons of York: a secret brotherhood of friars and men, fifteen families whose allegiance had been tailored by history, money or geographical proximity.

Even to them, he knew such things were both a blessing and a curse.

Thomas saw several hands move at once, followed by the sound of another gun cocking. The gathering aside, what hit him most was how few other people were around, as if the rest of the village was turning a blind eye to what was happening. How on earth did the friar get away with shooting at Jen in the middle of the high street?

It didn't seem possible.

Looking over his shoulder, the three friars were also armed.

He realised now he had only one option.

He removed his gun from his pocket and fired.

Stephen came to a sudden halt. Something had caused the birds to fly away. Whatever it was, it had left an echo.

He hadn't heard the original sound.

West stopped alongside him, listening to the silence. They had been walking along the pathway close to the Jeffries' estate.

"Did you hear that?"

West nodded. "These moors are like a plague. It could've been from anywhere."

Stephen spoke into his mouthpiece. "Hello, can you hear me, Caroline . . ."

"We're just getting out of the car now."

He had no idea who was talking to him. "Where are they?"

"They're in the churchyard. They seem to be heading towards the presbytery."

He disconnected without saying goodbye and sprinted after West, stopping on reaching a gap in the hedge. He entered first before helping West through the brambles.

They were now in the grounds of the Jeffries' estate, less than half a mile from the house.

"Stop."

West did so. "What is it?"

Stephen strained to hear any sign of life.

"I thought I just heard gunfire."

89

Jen sprinted across the field and dived into a depression close to the wall.

Her breathing was almost out of control. In the fading light she could sense but barely see Thomas coming in next to her.

Unmistakably the crowd was getting nearer. She could hear voices, several people speaking at once. For the first time she could hear individuals distinctly, Martha Brown, Rowland Stanley . . .

She saw movement near the entrance to the presbytery, just to her left. Lights glowed like a series of small halos, spookily reminiscent of a 15th-century mob carrying torches.

She cursed herself for getting into this mess.

Thomas was ready to move. "Come on."

Jen felt herself being dragged to her feet. Thomas was keeping close to the wall, heading for the priory ruins.

They stopped on reaching the next wall, crouching down as low as possible.

"Which way?" Thomas asked.

Jen focused on the presbytery. The masses had scattered and were starting to cover the grounds. She guessed they had less than ten seconds.

"The vaults – it's our only chance."

This time Jen led the way. She moved through the trees, trying to remember the entrance from the day before. Guessing the gate was still locked, she climbed the tree and helped Thomas to the top of the wall.

"There they are."

The voice was that of a woman, not Martha Brown. In the distance, Jen could see a blonde lady leading the rest. There was energy in her charge.

Jen had no idea what she'd done to upset the woman.

They made it over the wall and headed straight for the ruins. Jen remembered from the night before that the opening had been covered by thick vegetation, and located close to both the south wall of the former dormitories and a small cluster of trees.

She found it almost immediately, exactly the same as the night before.

Thomas was alongside her. "Is this it?"

"Come on."

West led Stephen to the castle ruins. Although the light was fading, he was convinced by the outline that he was looking at what the mystery girl had described.

"Have you seen this before?"

West shook his head. "No. The meeting place was beneath one of the houses."

Stephen accepted the answer. Through his mouthpiece, he spoke to Anthea.

"I've found the entrance."

"We'll be with you in two minutes."

"Are the squaddies with you?"

"Yes."

"Good. I think we might need them."

At least this time Jen knew the way. Despite the darkness, the tunnels were definitely lighter than they had been the day before, the outline of the walls visible thanks to the lights on their phones and the last rays of daylight that crept in through the partially hidden doorway.

On reaching the bottom of the stairway, she followed the tunnel, ignoring the side chambers.

"Where are we heading?" Thomas asked.

"The main vault. It comes out in the castle."

They could hear noise coming from the grounds nearby.

Someone clearly had access to the locked gate.

"It's this way," Jen said.

They increased their pace. The further they continued, the darker it became, the light coming from the flashlight facility on their two iPhones now the only aid. It was hardly as good as a regular torch, but, for Jen, enough at least to jog her memory.

Thomas kept his distance, watching the rear. He could hear, but for now he was still to see, the large gathering that was pursuing them.

Judging by the sound, they were still some way behind.

A steady jog had taken them to the priors' vault. On any other day, the plethora of stone tombs, wall patterns, and ornate architecture would have attracted the prince's interest, but today they just kept running.

On the other side of the chamber he saw an elaborate doorway, vaguely reminiscent of the sort that usually leads into a medieval great hall. The chamber was dark, but he was able to see outlines, mostly of tombs and wall decorations.

He didn't need clarification that this was the place in question.

"Look here," Jen said, pointing to the four tombs at the head of the room. She shone the light on the one at the far left.

"Edward V," Thomas read what was in front of him.

"This was Richard III." She pointed to the next one.

"But his body was found r-recently in Leicester."

"That's right. I think this is just a memorial."

Thomas read the inscription. It agreed with what she said.

"This one made less sense to me," Jen said.

"Elizabeth."

"I thought she was married to Henry VII."

He looked at her philosophically, deciding against an explanation.

She led him to the final tomb. "This was the killer."

Thomas read the words under the torchlight. "Richard IV."

"The other Prince in the Tower."

The dates made sense.

Now he knew that Gardiner was right.

The King was alone when he heard a knock at the door. He answered come in, and waited for the person to enter.

Gardiner entered gingerly, aided by a walking stick. He nodded at the King as he closed the door, and continued towards the desk.

The King waited patiently, gripping the desk with both hands.

"Now then, Jim. You'd better have some bloody good explanations."

90

They could tell from the sounds that their pursuers had almost caught up with them.

"Come on," Jen said, grabbing Thomas by the hand. She led him to the next passageway, the same one she had taken with Anthea the night before.

They started up the slope, expecting to see light at the end of the tunnel.

Something was different.

On the other side of the same tunnel, Stephen started the descent. Two soldiers guarded him on either side, while six more followed, all of them armed.

Anthea led the way, the only person who had seen it.

Or so she had thought.

She stopped almost immediately.

"What's the matter?" Stephen asked.

Anthea was confused. "It's different."

"What's different?"

"This. Someone's closed it up."

Jen could feel panic escalating inside her. If the way was shut, there was no way out.

She looked at Thomas, her face appearing increasingly nervous in the torchlight.

"Oh my God."

Thomas hugged her, preventing her from shaking if nothing else. The muffled sounds on his chest, a mixture of sighing and weeping, he prayed wouldn't be heard beyond the corridor.

He grasped her cheeks, and looked into her eyes. "You're sure this is the only way out?"

Thinking was now impossible. She wiped her eyes and shook her head.

"I don't know."

Double-checking the exit, Thomas realised they had only one option. He returned to the chamber, this time without the torchlight. He knew they had seconds at best before the gathering would be on them.

The only option was to hide.

He moved around the tombs, aided only by his sense of touch.

He heard something nearby, a shuffling noise, followed by a blaze of light.

It came from the centre of the chamber.

"Not lost, are you, Tom?"

The light became brighter, revealing the man's face. Thomas tried to speak but managed only a prolonged stutter.

Edward laughed. "I have one advantage over you, Tom. Local knowledge."

Thomas looked around, searching in vain for another exit. Even if there was one, finding it was almost impossible.

"Would you like to see it, Tom? In all its glory, so to speak."

Without waiting for an answer, Edward Jeffries increased the light. For the first time Thomas saw what was making it all possible. He carried what looked like a lantern: either a portable lamp or a halogen lamp. The effect was grand, as if an angelic halo was illuminating the room.

For the first time Jen could see everything. The vault was elaborate, including wall carvings of scenes from the Middle Ages. The stone tombs were also easier to make out.

In truth there were even more than she had expected.

She counted over fifty in total.

And not just kings.

Thomas took in the sight, awestruck. He focused on the far wall, where a large tapestry had been hanging for centuries. In his dazed state, he was almost oblivious to the pitter-patter of feet from nearby.

"Richard the th-third?" Thomas looked at Edward. "Side by side with the Princes in the Tower."

"A brilliant man and a brilliant leader – but ultimately a man who had limited choices. In many ways the same might be said for many of my ancestors. Their unequivocal loyalty to their country and cause was something that England needed during the darkest hours, even if ultimately it came to nothing."

He rubbed his brow with the back of his hand.

"For what it's worth, Tom, I am sorry that your family thought it best to lie to you all these years. I'm sure there could have been a better way . . . I mean it's not like there could have been a worse way, right?"

Any second now the gathering would enter the chamber. For those who hadn't seen it before, the arrangement had the potential to blow their mind.

If they had seen it before, chances were they were already dead.

91

Thomas had a fifty-fifty chance of getting it right, but the last thing he expected was the answer to be both. On entering the chamber, the friars and suits of the Sons of York showed nothing but indifference to the site they had seen surely hundreds of times before.

There were others, however, on virgin territory.

The question was why were they allowed in?

Martha Brown looked as surprised as any. Her eyes immediately wandered to her left, the four main tombs.

The second in particular caught her eye.

Edward was noticeably unimpressed at the number of new arrivals. Nevertheless, he said nothing as the Sons of York assembled in an arc shape around him, like the Yeomanry of old gathering around their leader. At least four of the friars were armed, though Thomas knew it could be more. Despite their hard expressions, none seemed willing to take the lead. He guessed that accounted for the intrusions.

All were afraid to take the lead.

Martha Brown was clearly speechless. After struggling to adapt to the new surroundings, she centred her attention on Jen. "Where is she?"

"Dead," Edward answered. "Saw it with my own eyes."

The woman's expression turned to one of anguish.

Jen was livid. "No, wait, she's okay; she was with me earlier."

The poor woman didn't know what to think. She looked desperately at Jen, then Edward, overcome by the coldness of his outburst.

"She speaks the t-truth," Thomas added. "She's with my cousin. You can see her soon."

Martha focused on Jen. "Where is she?"

"Martha, trust me, she's okay."

Edward's anger was visibly building, the sight of which made Thomas increasingly nervous. Then, in the corner of the chamber, they saw movement.

A girl with dark hair had just entered.

"Stephanie," Jen said.

Rowland Stanley was clearly shocked by the arrival of his niece. "Go home, Stephanie."

"Why don't you tell her?" Jen said furiously. "Why don't you tell her what you did to her best friend? That four of you dressed up in God-knows-what and murdered her, simply for discovering this very vault. That you hid her body, invented the story she went missing. Then murdered poor Luke Rankin and pretended it was suicide."

A shocked silence overcame the dark catacombs. Thomas felt his insides both boiling and freezing at the same time, as if an inescapable storm was about to be unleashed.

He took a deep breath. "It's over, Edward. Even if you kill me, you can't win. The palace knows, Scotland Yard knows. MI5 will be on you in a flash, not to mention the regular beat. This has to end."

Edward cricked his neck to one side, then the other. He cocked his gun and fired twice, the bullets missing Thomas by inches. He continued to fire, but got only blanks.

He was out of ammo.

Jen looked at Thomas, his face barely visible in the darkness. She moved towards him. As she did, she noticed that he moved in front of her.

Shielding her.

"Kill them," Edward said.

His order went unanswered.

"Did you not hear what I said? Kill them."

All who surrounded Jeffries looked on uncertainly.

"Dawson, Percy, Stanley, what are you waiting for?"

Again they refused to comply, infuriating Edward. He snatched a gun from one of the friars and immediately began firing.

Jen and Thomas both hit the floor, taking shelter behind one of the tombs. Sparks flew throughout the chamber, ricocheting off the stone and creating holes in the walls. Several people screamed, some scattered, heading back down the corridors.

Again he was out of ammo.

He looked at another of the hooded gunmen. "Give me your fucking gun."

As the gunfire ceased, Jen noticed movement from the blocked passageway.

"Mum."

Martha looked around, recognising the voice. "Anthea."

Several silhouettes had appeared in the doorway, the sound of shoes on stone accompanied by that of guns locking.

The next person to appear was Stephen, surrounded by his guards, two of whom approached Edward.

"Edward Jeffries, I'm arresting you on suspicion of murder, attempted murder and treason. You don't have to say anything–"

"Get him out of here," Stephen shouted. He looked at his distant cousin as he was cuffed, wrestled and pressed up against one of the tombs.

"Wait." Stephen moved closer. He punched him in the face.

"Now you can take him."

The guards took Edward out through the previously blocked corridor, now well lit thanks to the evening sun that was still visible beyond the distant hills. Thomas looked Edward in the eye as he passed. His nose was disjointed; blood streamed down his face, congregating around his mouth.

Still he smiled, only different than before.

The man was broken.

Anthea entered timidly. She saw Martha immediately and ran to her open arms.

Stephen, meanwhile, continued to Thomas. "You okay?"

Thomas nodded. "Fine. Thanks."

Stephen looked at Jen for the first time.

"You must be Miss Farrelly?"

92

Buckingham Palace, two days later

The King was in his office at 10:45. He had barely slept for forty-eight hours, and exhaustion was taking its toll.

In recent days he had got used to the view through the window of his new study. The forecourt was deserted, but it wouldn't stay that way. Any minute now the bands would arrive, as would the new dispatch of guards. Today it was the Coldstream Guards, or at least that was what he thought. Then the crowds would arrive, usually around 11:30. It was funny. People flocked from all around the world to witness the Changing of the Guard. It had been described as one of the most iconic British moments.

A moment when the past meets the present.

He remembered the first time he saw it. He had been a child then, and a prince. Images came to him, still frames, like photographs in the mind. Whether ghosts of the past or of his own imagination, he was in truth unsure.

The two seemed to merge into one.

He turned away from the window and moved towards his desk. He had a visitor, as usual. In the past, a visit from his nephew would have been a joyful occasion.

Today, it was merely enlightening.

The King placed the iPad down on the desk and raised his hand to his eyes. This was the first time he had seen the images. To him, it was like looking through a telescope at a distant planet, but not knowing which one. The crypt could have been anywhere in the world, from any time.

And of anyone.

"You're quite certain there is no alternative explanation?"

The visitor was in no doubt. "No," Thomas replied.

Sitting on the other side of the desk, Thomas watched the King pace across the room. He had been doing that a lot of late.

"Did you speak to Jim?"

"Oh yes," the King replied, still pacing.

"Did you find his words enlightening?"

The King took an extended pause. "Well, I suppose I no longer doubt them if that's what you mean."

In truth Thomas didn't know what he meant. Like the King, images kept flashing through his mind, though his were different. He thought about Edward Jeffries, the grandfather and grandson. According to official reports, the old man was still alive, albeit in a bad way. If the medical reports were accurate, he didn't have more than six months anyway.

But that was now down to weeks.

"What happened?" Thomas asked.

"Actually, I was hoping you could tell me. After all, you seem to have been in the thick of it."

Thomas bit his lip, his mind still on Edward. "I meant with his mother and father."

The King stopped, now standing in the middle of the room. He looked at his nephew, and then walked on, passing a grandfather clock from the Georgian era. It chimed eleven o'clock, accompanied by a bell sound.

"I never realised their deaths were caused by anything other than what is common knowledge."

"Were they murdered?"

The King lowered his head slightly, his attention once again on the window.

"Father was a difficult man in many ways. At least that's what my mother always said." He laughed. "Obstinate, I think was the word she used to use."

"Did you know?"

"What? About the affair?"

The prince bit his lip. "Well, that as well, I suppose."

"There are certain things that one shouldn't ask."

"There are other things that one surely can't ignore, or at least shouldn't."

The King turned away from the window, lowering the curtain. The ceremony would be starting soon.

He sat down, leaning forward on his desk. "What difference would it make? Huh. You're a student of history; you tell me what usually happens? Better yet, what happens when the vultures begin to circle?"

He breathed out deeply, somewhere between a cough and a sigh. Sitting opposite, Thomas sensed the King's tiredness.

Just as he felt his own.

"I had my suspicions," the King said after a while. "In truth, I wasn't around much at the time."

Thomas decided not to push the issue. "How about the other thing?"

The King looked up, his eyes wide open. He had seen the video footage only the day before.

"No."

Thomas watched the King's facial expression. There was withering around his cheeks and eyes. Without question it was an expression of a man who was exhausted. But also one who had been betrayed.

An honest answer.

"So Tomkins was sent there?"

Again the King took his time. "When I was seventeen, I met an old Gurkha. He had been living here for about twenty years, after which time he won a medal, bravery or something of the kind. On his day of presentation, your grandfather took something of a shine to him. Later awarded him the King's Medal, you know, gallantry, acts of bravery, whatnot . . ."

Thomas nodded, but remained silent.

"As time passed, the man got old. And when he approached retirement, my father offered him a job – nothing official, just a job."

Thomas smiled. "Eyes and ears."

"Something of the type. It just so happened, one night in the early 1990s, he should be in the same room as the president of a certain African nation – I'll leave it to your imagination which one. He had the opportunity, so to speak, to take him out."

"Did he?"

"He put a call through to the palace. Father was dining at the time and had given orders not to be disturbed. But the man must have been most persuasive on the telephone, because within ten minutes Father spoke to him in person. The man told him about the predicament and asked what he wanted done."

"How could he be s-sure that the line was safe?"

The King smiled thoughtfully. "Perhaps that thought influenced Father's decision. But one way or another, the chance was declined."

He leaned back in his chair and then forward again.

"It's been something of a recurring theme over the years, you know," he resumed. "Stories often sound a lot better in the press. I daresay in some parts of the world this sort of thing happens almost on a daily basis.

"In the early 1990s, Father was under a lot of . . . stress. It was a difficult time for the country: the recession, the start of Europe, Thatcher . . . a number of celebrities had fallen foul of PR stings. Mother and Father were fighting more, I suppose."

Thomas nodded. He tried to picture the other woman, his mind on the film he had seen in the hidden study.

"What was she like?"

"Joanna? Don't know how to describe her, really. She was a Tory, of course."

Thomas laughed. "How about Richard Jeffries?"

"Different to his father: more outgoing, for a start. He enjoyed the social set, partying with the stars and whatnot. As a magnate, he was powerful . . . of course, sport was his passion," he said, laughing softly. "I went to an Arsenal game with him once in the late '80s, you know. Oh yes. He wrote an article later that evening, which appeared in one of the nationals the following day. Didn't go down well with Graham, I assure you."

Thomas laughed, as did the King. As the laughter faded, an awkward silence overcame them. There was something different about him now.

It was as if he was talking about a friend.

"Then he went all high profile – went into politics. He bought the *London Issue* in '87 and ran the place like a bull in a china shop. I fell out with him myself in '92 when he accused your uncle Bill of having a gambling problem." He shook his head.

"Was he a problem?"

"Richard Jeffries was a problem for everyone who Richard Jeffries didn't like. Other journalists hated him, politicians either hated him or idolised him. He did a sting on two Tory ministers in early '89. Now that was particularly nasty. Apparently the poor idiots got mixed up in some rather bad business in Soho that the PM didn't approve of – nor did their wives, of course. As far as I'm aware, it was something of a one-off, though once Jeffries had his way they were both made out to be the devil incarnate."

Thomas grimaced. "Was Granddad ever, you know, threatened?"

The King considered the question. "I don't think Father would ever let on even if he was."

"But Jeffries was a problem?"

"Well, he clearly found out about the affair, and obviously he knew about this other business as well. Which is more than me, so I suppose I have to hand it to him."

Thomas searched his memory, but again he failed to picture the man. He'd seen photographs on the Internet, but as far as he could tell, they had never met.

"Perhaps I'm being a tad presumptuous, but it sounds to me as if our cousin had our family in a position where he could, you know, blackmail."

The King took a deep breath. "Exactly what he wanted to think. He only had one problem, at least so it would seem."

"Proof?"

The King rose to his feet and made his way across the room, stopping at the ornate fireplace. He poured whiskey into two glasses and added ice.

"So Granddad decided to fight fire with fire, so to speak?"

The King offered him a drink. "I suspect it rather the case that Daddy got some rather poor advice. And that Mr Tomkins, instead of keeping our friend under surveillance, forgot himself."

Thomas wrapped his fingers around the glass, but for now refrained from drinking. "Do you think it's possible that Jeffries became aware of his presence, and perhaps, you know, threatened him?"

The King took a deep breath before drinking. "That would seem plausible."

Thomas raised the glass to his mouth. "And what of our friend Mr Tomkins? I'm pretty sure he didn't, y-you know, d-die of natural causes."

Thomas eyed him, lengthily.

"Well, clearly," the King replied. "But even in those days he was an alcoholic."

"You knew him?"

"Oh yes, he would often drive me whenever I was in a car with your uncle."

"Was he a g-good man?"

"In the early days, yes; his military record speaks volumes. I think that was his problem, you know, he was never really cut out for the civilian life."

"So it was accidental?"

The King seemed to hesitate.

"If Tomkins had gone rogue, there would have been a motive," Thomas said.

"If that were so, surely the same motive would exist for all of our enemies. And we can't exactly see off all of them, can we?"

Thomas pondered the statement before finally sipping his whiskey. It was far too early for that sort of thing.

"Still one thing puzzles me. The Sons of York. You really had no idea they existed?"

The King put his glass down on the desk and returned to his seat. "Gardiner warned me about them once, about ten years ago. Did again when Mother died."

"You didn't take it s-seriously?"

For several seconds the King's expression was soured. Then from nowhere, he laughed. "Even in those days he was a boring old bastard."

The prince laughed, perhaps more so knowing the situation was at an end.

"Looking back, did they ever have a claim?"

"The past is the past. And his was another country. Perhaps it's just something one can never get out of one's head."

Thomas massaged the fine glass with his fingers, watching from across the desk as the King drained his glass. The trials and tribulations of recent days had left their mark, and not just around the eyes.

"Does it make a difference?"

The King didn't understand.

"That the princes survived. That Tudor was a usurper."

The King looked at him for several seconds and smiled. "According to Gardiner, the prince's line died out in 1688. What remains are of the weaker line, as he put it. The son of Clarence himself was barred by Act of Attainder. When Elizabeth I died without an heir and the Crown fell to the Stuarts, the Crown also fell to the next surviving descendant of the alleged Elizabeth of York, but also now the best surviving line of Edward III. Should the Tudors have been above themselves, as soon as the male Jeffries line died out, so too did the Plantagenets."

He took a deep breath, his attention on a painting behind him. It so happened to be of Elizabeth I.

"But between you and me, I think she happened to be a damn good queen."

Thomas took a second to take it in, carefully weighing up each point. He guessed some would put forward an alternative argument, whereas others might agree.

"It doesn't make any difference, you know. Granddad."

The King smiled weakly. "I know. I just . . ."

"You think if people knew, they'd think less of him?"

He looked up and nodded.

Thomas smiled sympathetically. "Granddad was a good king," he said, rising to his feet.

"But I daresay England might now have a better one."

Thomas left the study and descended the stairs to the second-floor corridor. Gardiner was sitting in a chair, studying one of the paintings.

"I've always admired this painting," he began. "Without question Anthony van Dyck will always remain one of the geniuses of European art."

Thomas didn't break stride.

"Shut up, Jim."

93

Wootton-on-the-Moor

It was cold, despite the warm temperature. It was cloudy, despite the clear skies. A shadow had engulfed the village, at its most prevalent between the churchyard and the castle. Everyone was aware of it.

That was why they avoided it.

The village was literally a ghost town. The high street was largely deserted, including the shops. The few who did walk it did so slowly, and with their heads down. There was no hint of communication. If a passer-by should come across someone they knew, a friend or neighbour, the interaction would be limited to a nod of the head or a forced smile. Should a newcomer so happen to chance by on this of all days, an intended visit or as a journey break on their way elsewhere, they would find no source for their confusion. No evidence of two days earlier remained. The crime scene had been patched up, and the entrance to the vault shut – at least from the outside. The press had been warned about asking questions, and on this occasion none dared to dispute the matter. It was the way the words were spoken. It was more serious than usual. A footballer caught cheating on his wife or girlfriend might set about to prohibit print by dangling a piece of paper in a journalist's face, but such things rarely worked long term. And in such cases, the matter was usually over before it was begun.

There was once a saying in these parts:

Today's news is tomorrow's chip paper.

But where there is silence, there is often inquisition. And the role of the inquisitor is often taken by the curious mind. It was a practice that spanned centuries, if not millennia; countries, if not continents. The search for truth is human nature, just as the tendency to lie. And when history fails to exclude the liars, the truth becomes contaminated.

For those who lived in the village, there would be no public inquisition. Should a young man, the latest descendant of a family of high esteem, go on trial for murder, attempted murder, aggravated assault, or something along those lines, then so be it. Should a prominent politician and scientist be taken into custody as accomplices, then the same applied. Should a further twenty men be taken in for questioning regarding their affiliations with the men in question, it made no difference. It was a tradition that had lasted five centuries. And if a king should become famed for walking with a hunchback, born with hair already down to the shoulders, a full set of teeth, and a withered arm in order to hide the truth, the same rule applied. In England, history has a knack for somehow concealing its most dubious events, even if it calls for framing its participants. Even if such mishaps were to leave a stain on the families, it was a small price to pay. Life in the village would return to normal – at least in time. That was another pattern that had spanned five centuries. Should a curious individual from outside suspect contamination, then their research will itself be subject to the same thing. For the contamination began even before the village was born. It had grown up with it.

Even thrived on it.

Jen removed her iPhone from her ear and disconnected the call.

"Everything all right?" Anthea asked.

"Yeah, fine," Jen replied, "it looks as if I'm going to be leaving sooner than expected. Filming's been delayed."

"Why?"

Jen looked at her with a unique expression, not quite annoyed but not quite humour.

"Oh, right, yeah."

Jen laughed and shook her head simultaneously. As she did, she allowed herself to enjoy the scenery.

They were sitting in the churchyard, on the bench below the largest tree. Since her arrival, it had become her favourite spot in the village. The view was different than it had been, not visually but the way it felt.

Memories of recent days continued to plague her mind.

"Do you think you'll ever be back?"

Jen nodded. "Yeah. My producer still wants to do a follow-up. He just wants to see how things develop first."

Anthea nodded and smiled. "You didn't really need your hair doing after all."

Jen laughed. "Absolutely necessary. Thanks for doing it again, by the way. I still can't believe how much damage I did to it."

"You're welcome."

Silence overcame them, not awkward but pleasant. Though she had known the girl less than a week, strangely it felt like a lot longer.

"Any idea what happened to . . . you know?"

Jen shrugged. "Nothing, other than he'd been arrested. Along with the others."

Anthea smiled coyly. "Not them."

Jen was confused. Then it hit her. "Oh. Nah. I'd forgotten all about him."

"Who was he?"

"Don't know, really. One of the royals."

Anthea's smile widened. "You do know, really."

Jen looked at her and laughed.

There was movement on the bridge. A figure emerged through the sunlight, heading towards them. As the person approached, they both saw it was Martha.

"That's my cue to get back to work," Anthea said, laughing. She hesitated before leaving. "Will I see you before you go?"

"Sure."

The teenager smiled and waved before making her way in the direction of her mother. Jen saw them talk briefly before Martha continued in her direction.

The hairdresser stopped on reaching the bench. "I never really said sorry . . . you know . . ."

Jen smiled philosophically. "You were right. Looking back, I don't know what came over me. Anything could have happened."

Martha smiled weakly. It was obvious to Jen that she had said the right thing.

"Look after yourself."

"You too."

Jen held up a hand, a parting wave as Martha retreated in the direction of the bridge. Anthea had waited for her, leaning against the wall. Jen saw her wave, and she waved back. She watched as the girl waited for her mum before disappearing over the bridge.

Jen took a deep breath and sighed. Once again she was alone, and that made her nervous. Three days earlier, she would never have even thought about it. She was used to being alone; most of the time she enjoyed it. Despite what had happened, the village was visually still the same. As her ears adjusted to the quiet, she found herself listening to the sounds of nature. The river was running quickly, the birds were chirping to each other in the trees, bees were pollinating the flowers. A long shadow crossed a field in the distance. There was a heavy presence of white throughout the greenery. She had seen it often since she'd been there. Often throughout the county.

It was a perfect Yorkshire rose.

"Ahem."

Jen spun around, wondering what made the noise. "Oh . . . hello."

Thomas was standing a few metres away, smiling. He was dressed casually: blue jeans, trainers, and polo shirt.

"I wanted to give you this," he said, taking a seat beside her.

"A red rose," she said, accepting it. "You are aware that we're in Yorkshire?"

He laughed. "Actually, this is what historians call a Tudor rose. Apparently it signifies the merger of the two houses."

She smiled. "I believe that is correct. Thank you."

"I'm sorry I had to leave so quickly the other day." He held his palms up. "The life I chose."

That made her giggle. "You mean you have a say in the matter?"

"Well, so my uncle keeps telling me."

She laughed softly, flicking her hair with her hand.

Now she was extra glad Anthea had seen to it again.

"I wanted to thank you, for everything. My uncle asked me to pass on his appreciation as well."

She frowned, taken aback. "Your uncle. Wow."

He smiled at her, convinced she didn't believe him. "So wh-what happens to you now?"

"How do you mean?"

"Do they still plan to film the documentary?"

"Oh. No, that's been postponed."

"So you're heading home?"

"Yes."

"And whereabouts is home?"

"You mean you don't have my details on the database?"

He grinned at her. "Sadly I've always been useless with computers."

She laughed again, almost a snort. She placed her hand to her face as a reflex, and turned away.

She couldn't believe she'd just done that.

That was it.

Conversation over.

She placed her shoulder bag over her arm and got up from the bench.

"Well, thank you so much for coming back," she said, offering the prince her hand. "Tell your uncle it was a pleasure."

She couldn't believe she said that.

He laughed. "Well, I'm very much looking forward to your documentary. If there's anything I can do . . ."

"Actually, yes," she said, rummaging through her handbag. She removed a business card. "You never know when it might come in handy."

He accepted it. "Thank you."

She looked him in the eye and slowly walked away. She had nearly made it as far as the pathway when . . .

"Hey, I was just wondering . . ."

"My number's on the card."

Jen had spent the last two nights back at the Hog, despite some initial apprehension. She checked out at just after 2 p.m., easily the latest she had ever done so. It was the least he could do, said Harvey Mitchell, perhaps feeling some degree of guilt for a couple of days earlier. That said, the place was hardly heaving.

Ironically it could do with some publicity.

She left the Hog through the main entrance and headed straight for her Picanto. As she put her case in the boot, she noticed someone had entered the car park.

"You're leaving?"

It was Stephanie. "Hi," Jen said tentatively. "I was thinking of coming to see you."

A half smile. "I needed to get out of the house. My cousin got bail this morning."

"How is he?"

"Better than he deserves."

"Has he been charged with anything?"

"Accessory to murder," she replied coldly. "I'm sure they'll find something else before too long. My uncle is still being questioned."

"Sorry."

"Don't be. They're not nice people."

Wow, Jen thought. She could never imagine saying something like that about her own uncle and cousins.

Then again, they were nice people.

Jen looked at her, her attention on her face. There was slightly more colour in her cheeks than there had been. A hint of a smile touched her lips, which she hadn't seen before. Her hair had more volume, the curls more deliberate.

"You look better."

Her smile widened. "Thanks. Anthea did my hair."

Jen laughed. "That explains it . . . I should be back in a few weeks. Maybe we could meet up."

"I'd like that."

"Take care."

Stephanie smiled and began to walk away. Jen, meanwhile, waited by the car.

"Hey, can I ask you something?"

The girl stopped.

"Did you ever find out what happened . . . to Debra?"

"Not after the photo . . ." She shrugged.

Jen bit her lip.

"You didn't find anything?"

Jen looked at her. "I have a theory."

They entered the church through the main entrance and headed straight for the cloisters. Jen led the way down the stairs into the vaults, stopping on entering the Jeffries' vault. The door to the mystery vault was closed.

But no longer locked.

"You found the key?" Stephanie asked.

"No. I think one of the coppers picked it. They couldn't find the key."

"Father Martin didn't have one?"

"I don't know."

Strangely the priest had disappeared.

Jen walked slowly through what remained of the rubble, careful to avoid losing her footing. The kings' vault was far brighter in the daylight, particularly with the door open. She was able to see the large tapestry draped across the far wall. For the first time she could see colours, maroon with three gold lions at the centre.

The flag of Plantagenet. Soured by centuries of decay.

She walked towards the four main tombs, stopping at the middle left. Ever since she had first seen it, it had bothered her.

Richard III.

Discovered under a car park in Leicester.

Jen stopped alongside it and took a deep breath. She placed her hand upon the lid beneath the effigy. It was cold and rough, typical stone. It looked heavy.

"Try to help me lift it."

Stephanie stood on one side, placing her hands beneath the lid. They tried to lift it but failed.

"Try the other end."

Stephanie moved to the end, directly opposite Jen. They both placed their hands to the corners, and tried to lift it as best they could. For several seconds it looked as if nothing would happen, but slowly it came free.

They placed the lid down as gently as they could, careful to avoid doing any damage. Jen looked inside the tomb for the first time, not sure what to expect.

There were bones inside, collarbones, ribcages and several skulls.

Even on initial inspection it was clear there was more than just one body.

She switched on the flashlight on her phone. There was a large bag lying across the bottom: the kind she associated with gangster movies where the victim was placed in one before being moved to the boot of the car.

The stench was awful. Holding her nose, Jen placed a hand inside and attempted to move it. The bag had split, and not recently. There was something black inside, some form of material.

It looked like a dress.

She had seen it before. In a photograph.

She retreated a few steps and looked at Stephanie.

"I think we best be leaving this one for the experts."

Epilogue

One month later

"She's dead; I know that she's dead."

They were the first words she had ever said on camera. They were the words that made her famous.

She hadn't had time to consider the implications. Nor had she experience of the press.

The following week, she said the opposite. By then she'd had the time, and the experience. 50, 60, perhaps even 100 million people watched. They heard her say it.

But nobody remembered.

They remembered only what she had said the first time.

"She's dead; I know that she's dead."

They were the words that she'd be remembered for.

Whether she meant them or not.

Gillian Harrison had been standing alone in the churchyard for over an hour, considering the implications. Over the last thirteen months, she'd had plenty of time to consider them. The cameras had gone, as had the press . . . as had all the other intrusions. The only thing that hadn't gone was the implications. Not for the wider world, but for her.

During the last year, the churchyard hadn't changed very much. A new cross had been erected in the far corner, a memorial to a war hero. Just like any other village in England, such things were prevalent. There was a new hole in the ground close to the wall as well, this time for someone's ashes. She didn't know who it was for, or who the relatives were.

Though she guessed that she probably knew them.

The monument in front of her was the only other new addition. It was angelic in every sense of the word. It was large, at least three metres in height, making it one of the largest in the cemetery. The only thing greater was the cost, but that had been taken care of by others. It was a tradition in these parts. Some called it generosity. Some, community spirit. Others used a far simpler word.

Love.

It wasn't just the locals who contributed. Money came from America, Canada, Australia . . . all around Europe. And not just adults, either. Some had even been in coins, sometimes pennies.

But it was the cards that touched her the most. That and the messages.

Messages of love.

She had incorporated some of them into the body. The face of the angel was also familiar. It was her face, appearing as though it was a genuine statue. That, too, had been a gift from outsiders. No way could she have afforded it on her own. That was another implication of the words she'd said.

This time a positive one.

But among the positives remained the overwhelming negative.

She had been right the first time.

She really was dead.

Gillian Harrison put her hand to her face and felt tears. Once they started, they wouldn't stop, at least for a while. She felt her eyes close, incapable of reopening. Her cheeks were wet on both sides, and would only get wetter.

When the worst of it was over, she turned to her right, feeling a presence nearby. She wiped her eyes. Despite clearing her vision, she was still to see anything other than a vague outline. The woman had blonde hair, just like her own.

Wiping her eyes again, she walked towards her, not stopping until reaching her. Though the woman said nothing, it wasn't the silence that was awkward.

It was the implications that were awkward.

Despite not being her fault.

"I'm so sorry, Gillian," Susan Rankin said, placing her hands on her shoulders.

Gillian Harrison said nothing.

Despite the hardship, she somehow managed a smile.

The Mall was packed, as were the other streets that marked the route between Buckingham Palace and Westminster Abbey. Estimates for the number of bystanders ranged from one hundred thousand to a couple of million, depending on the network that covered the event, or the location they were actually looking at.

In reality, it was impossible to count.

In every direction, the view was glorious. It was a ritual unlike any in the world. Nothing brought out the crowds like a coronation. None carried out the job quite like the British. Even the foreign media agreed.

The fact was indisputable.

At just after 2:30 p.m. they finally saw him. The royal carriage emerged from the gates to make its journey along the Mall to the abbey. A large armed guard moved on horseback, dressed as redcoats like their predecessors. Cameras flashed, the crowds waved, people cheered as they got their fleeting glimpse of the new king and his son.

It was a picture. Dressed in a crimson surcoat like that of his forebears, he appeared just like his father, oozing charisma.

Today, nothing could hide the smiles on their faces.

Inside the abbey, the crowds had gathered. The soft sound of the organ dominated as the organist continued to prepare for the service.

The most important guests sat at the front. Most had arrived recently, while others were still to make their way inside.

Those at the front received the attention. Sitting alongside the Duke of York, his daughter, Princess Caroline, had rarely been out of the spotlight. The gossip columns continued to speculate about her appearance; rumours of plastic surgery the most prominent.

Even if it were true, the work had been carried out so neatly the seam was barely seen.

Even a row back, anonymity was almost guaranteed. Behind the Duke of Clarence in the front row, the brown-haired man in his late twenties remained silent. The crowd would be forgiven for not recognising this minor royal.

Even less, the blonde sitting beside him.

In another part of the city, four men were being marched along a well-lit corridor. The lieutenant waited for the high-security door to open before allowing the armed guard to lead them to their cells.

The blond man in his late twenties led the way; following him, the three were much older. They were still to receive an official sentence, but they didn't need a judge to tell them release was out of the question. While those deemed accomplices had escaped with comparatively light sentences, ninety days for being an accessory to five years in Wandsworth for conspiracy to regicide, these four had no such luck.

To the wider world, their fate would remain a mystery. For them, incarceration would be different.

While clarification of their location would never be made known, even to them the choice was painfully ironic.

It was the same place traitors to the Crown had always been kept.

Over two hundred miles north, two large cars moved up the driveway of the ancient mansion. Under the seclusion of the trees, their arrivals did not arouse suspicion. Even if they had been seen, it was nothing out of the ordinary. The villagers had grown up on such sights. In centuries past, stories were told of large carriages coming and going in the middle of the night, leaving like ghosts, never to return.

In front of the house, the former headmaster of the local school was standing perfectly still, anticipating their arrival. He had not been seen recently in the village, nor did he wish to change that.

The questions, he knew, would have been numerous.

He waited for the drivers to park before showing the new arrivals inside. Unlike most visits, the location of choice was below. After descending a winding staircase, the witness would be greeted by the sight of something from Medieval England. It was not quite a courthouse, but not dissimilar. Several chairs surrounded the strange table, all at present unoccupied. At the head of the room was the most important chair, its decoration in the manner of a throne.

Today that would remain empty.

Directly opposite were three vacant seats. As the newcomers entered, Father Martin nodded his head and gestured in the direction of the seats. Though he had never met two of the three, he recognised them immediately. Their faces were just like those of their fathers, perhaps even their fathers' fathers. Lovell sat on the left, the two younger men in the middle and right.

The seats of Catesby and Ratcliffe.

They were the trinity. In the past songs were sung about them. The great significance of the Cat, the Rat and Lovell the Dog. Who ruled all England under a Hog.

And so it remained . . .

John Paul Davis

The Facts Behind My Fiction

As with my previous thrillers, the story is a work of fiction. Much of what you have just read was entirely made up; however, there were times when the story was inspired by fact and history.

For those of you who are interested, what follows is an insight into my research into *The Plantagenet Vendetta*. Thanks for reading.

See you next year!

Wootton-on-the-Moor/Ravensfield

The main location in the novel was a village called Wootton, based in the rugged North York Moors. The village itself is made up and bears no major similarity to any real location, apart from the obvious general similarities of any English village. In the past, there was a real town named Ravenspurn located on the Yorkshire coast, but that disappeared into the sea due to coastal erosion in the 1800s. The town was relevant as at least two medieval kings of England landed there, but it had no connection to my made-up Ravensfield. Ravensfield Castle and Priory are therefore also fictitious. Nearby Titherton, Shipsey, Maplewell and Bishopton are also made up.

The House of Winchester

Obviously fictitious. Unlike the present House of Windsor, the Winchesters were a fictitious continuation of the House of Saxe-Coburg since around the reign of Victoria. In keeping with their names, every generation attended school at Winchester College. This is a real establishment and is one of the four top public schools in the country, dating back to the reign of Richard II. In real life, the royals have had a tendency to go to Gordonstoun, whereas the sons of the Prince of Wales went to Eton. References to Buckingham Palace's interior are mainly fictitious, whereas the general observations are researched.

Royal Titles

In truth, something of a mixture. As the new monarch Stephen II has only recently come to the throne and is still to be crowned, various investitures are still to occur. The son of the king, Stephen, Duke of Cornwall, would have inherited that title, including the Duchy of Cornwall, as right of blood succession. The more famous title, Prince of Wales, is a title that requires royal investiture; therefore he is unlikely to gain the title immediately. The Duke of York is usual for the second son of the king, and usually falls upon that person instantly.

The Duchy of Clarence

A famous title in English history, though now more or less defunct. It is generally a junior title: the most famous example was George, third son of Richard, 3rd Duke of York, middle brother of Edward, 7th Earl of March, later Edward IV and Richard, Duke of Gloucester, later Richard III. The most recent title was given to Prince Albert Victor, son of Edward VII, henceforth Duke of Clarence and Avondale, who died without issue.

George Winchester, Duke of Clarence, in this novel is, of course, fictitious, as is his son, Thomas. As son of the Duke of Clarence, Thomas would probably be heir to his father's estates and titles. Reference to Clarence being located at Clare, Suffolk, is historically correct.

The house, however, does not exist.

Real-life buildings

Many places mentioned in the book are real. Middleham Castle still exists and was once the home of Richard III and Anne Neville. Westminster Abbey is accurately described; the urn containing the bodies of two children commonly assumed to be Edward V and Richard, 1st Duke of York, is located just off the Lady chapel, close to the joint tomb of Mary I and Elizabeth I. The tombs of Henry VII and Elizabeth of York are the main feature of the magnificent Lady chapel.

Riverton is made up, while the nearby villages are real. References to Keble, Magdalen and the Bodleian are all based on fact, though I have, of course, used them fictitiously. The earl's reading room in the Bodley is made up, but the other references, such as the Radcliffe Camera, are fact.

The King Edward hospital exists and is a usual port of call for the royals. The interior is largely made up. The same is true of the Royal College of Physicians, whose accurately portrayed exterior and history is merged with a fictitious interior based on my personal research.

References to the Tower of London are largely accurate, except for the Cromwell Tower beneath the surface. As far as I'm aware, this is fictitious. Also made up is my suggestion that the Chief Yeoman Warder and the Constable of the Tower of London are the same role. They are separate.

The Dominicans

Used fictitiously, though the real order still exists and has done so since it was established in the early 1200s by the Spanish monk, St Dominic, on the back of his undertaking of a mission in the Languedoc, preaching against heresy. Pope Honorius III approved the order in 1217 and the first base in England was set up in 1221. Dubbed the Watchdogs of God, the blackfriars – so named due to the colour of their dress – were successful in their attempts to rid the Languedoc of the Cathars thanks largely to their hard approach. They were the official interrogators in the Inquisition, during which torture was promulgated. In England, every king from Henry III to Richard II had a Dominican as his confessor.

Politics

The political parties in this book are fictitious. The Democrats were loosely inspired by two of the main political parties in the UK, while the Tories are a fictitious use of the Conservative Party. The Whig Party indeed existed and was once the main opposition to the Tory Party. The Whigs ceased to exist in 1868 when they became the Liberal Party.

Edward III and the Wars of the Roses (1377–1461)

Describing this period of English history in detail would require a book of its own. For those of you who are satisfied with a short overview, here goes:

Edward III, who inherited the throne from his father, Edward II, in 1327, reigned till 1377 and had fourteen children with his queen, Philippa of Hainault, including five boys who lived into adulthood. They were, Edward (The Black Prince), Lionel of Antwerp, John of Gaunt, Edmund of Langley, and Thomas of Woodstock. To placate his sons, Edward created England's first ever dukedoms, respectively Cornwall, Clarence, Lancaster, York and Gloucester.

With the Black Prince dead, the Crown eventually fell to his young son, henceforth Richard II. With Lionel of Antwerp also dead, Richard's main adviser was John of Gaunt, Duke of Lancaster.

The unpopular government of Richard II, notably Gaunt, coupled with England's loss of what remained of the Angevin Empire, eventually led to the Peasants' Revolt. Richard exiled Gaunt's eldest son, Henry Bolingbroke, in 1398 and, following Gaunt's death in 1399, denied him his birthright. His return and rebellion won him the throne, and Richard died, probably starved to death, in Pontefract Castle.

Following Henry IV's death in 1413, Henry V ruled for nine years. Following him was his infant son, Henry VI. Despite Henry V's general popularity, he did have to contend with one plot shortly before Agincourt, by one Richard of Conisburgh, son of Edmund of Langley, Duke of York. Conisburgh's execution left his four-year-old son,

Richard, later 3rd Duke of York, fatherless.

Henry V's younger brothers themselves produced no heirs, apart from Humphrey, Duke of Gloucester, leaving the distantly related Beauforts as the next upholders of the House of Lancaster. With this, ineffective meddlers surrounded the young king. When his uncle the Duke of Bedford died in 1435, Henry's one remaining uncle Humphrey, Duke of Gloucester, sought to become protector. Gloucester encountered opposition from the Duke of Suffolk, who had Gloucester arrested for treason. Gloucester died awaiting trial in 1447, while Suffolk was murdered soon after being stripped of office and was replaced by the Lancastrian Edmund Beaufort, 2nd Duke of Somerset.

At the time, Henry VI's lieutenant in France was Richard, 3rd Duke of York. With the war in France going badly, York sought a change in policy. In 1452 York returned to England and marched on London, demanding Somerset's removal. Despite being gaoled, York was released in 1453, and as Henry VI's mental health deteriorated, York became Lord Protector and one of a new council of Regents. Two years later, Henry's queen, Margaret of Anjou, forced York from court. Soon after, York resorted to hostilities. The Battle of St Albans saw the beginning of the war, and the end of Somerset. York's victory saw him reinstated. In 1456 Henry then ousted him and, after a brief reconciliation between Yorkists and Lancastrians in 1458, plotting resumed. In 1459 battle occurred at Blore Heath in Staffordshire, and again at Ludford Bridge, forcing York to flee to Ireland. Plotting between York and the powerful Earl of Warwick (later dubbed the Kingmaker) allowed York to return in September 1460, after the Lancastrians were defeated in July at Northampton. While York's desire to claim the throne was met with mixed response, he was installed by parliament as Henry VI's successor.

York and his forces left London later in 1460 to counter Margaret of Anjou having sought assistance from the Scots. Richard of York did indeed give battle in vain, and was slain at Wakefield at the end of December. As York's eldest son was subsequently executed, Richard was succeeded by his next son, Edward, henceforth also heir to the throne. Edward was victorious over Jasper Tudor's army (Henry Tudor's uncle) in the Battle of Mortimer's Cross. While the Yorkists lost the second battle of St Albans in 1461, better luck was to follow when a panic-stricken London closed its gates on the Lancastrians, fearing plunder, and later that year Edward was welcomed and unofficially crowned Edward IV. Edward and Warwick marched north with a large army and met the Lancastrians at Towton. The battle was the bloodiest ever recorded, at least 20,000 dying on a single day. Edward's victory was consolidated by his march to York and later coronation in London.

Wars of the Roses 1461–83

Various attempts to regain the throne for Henry VI took place 1461–64. The government of England turned on its head, however, when Edward IV went against Warwick's attempts to secure a French bride, and married the commoner, Elizabeth Woodville. As the Woodvilles gained favour at court, Warwick's allegiance came into question. After entering an alliance with Edward's brother, George, Duke of Clarence, Clarence married Warwick's daughter, Isabel, and defeated Edward at Edgecote Moor. After a brief imprisonment at Warwick's hands, Edward returned to London. Rebellions in Lincolnshire were quashed, and Warwick and Clarence banished, leading to an alliance between Warwick and Margaret of Anjou. Warwick invaded England in 1470 and restored Henry VI to the throne, forcing Edward and his brother, Richard, Duke of Gloucester, to flee to the Low Countries. Edward returned at Ravenspurn in 1471 and reconciled with Clarence. The forces of Edward and Warwick met at Barnet in thick fog, at which point Edward defeated the Kingmaker. The forces led by Margaret of Anjou were then defeated at Tewkesbury, thus leading to twelve years of peace under Edward IV.

The Cat, The Rat, and Lovell Our Dog

Three of the key characters in this book. While the modern-day antagonists are fictitious, their famous namesakes were anything but.

William Catesby (the Cat), 1450?–85, was both Chancellor and Speaker of the House of Commons during the reign of Richard III. Historically, the family seat was Ashby St Ledgers in Northamptonshire, not Wootton. Like many in his family, Catesby was a talented lawyer and quite possibly the person responsible for the Titulus Regius document. He fought alongside Richard at Bosworth and was executed. Among his descendants was Robert Catesby.

Richard Ratcliffe (the Rat) was originally from the Lake District and became a key confidant of Richard III while still Duke of Gloucester. Like Catesby, Ratcliffe benefited from the bounty of many forfeited estates when Richard took power, and also served as Sheriff of Westmorland. According to some sources, Ratcliffe was responsible for Richard's execution of Earl Rivers, brother of Elizabeth Woodville.

Francis 1st Viscount Lovell (the Dog), 1454–88?, was another close friend of Richard III prior to Richard's enthronement; he was also related through marriage as his wife was Anne Neville's cousin. On Richard's ascension, Lovell became Lord Chamberlain and also inherited large swathes of land. Unlike the Cat and the Rat, Lovell survived Bosworth. He played a dominant role in the Lambert Simnel rebellion and was also present at the Battle of Stoke Field in 1487. He fled to Scotland and was granted safe passage. At that point he disappeared from history.

The three were among the most important of Richard's councillors. Around 18 July 1484, a rhyme, purportedly the work of one William Collingbourne, was nailed to the doors of St Paul's,

The Cat, The Rat, and Lovell our Dog

Ruleth England under a Hog.

It is possible that the trio still have family/descendants alive today. Their descendants in this novel are, of course, products of my own imagination.

The Paston Letters

Mostly true. The exception to this is the biography of Richard III mentioned by Wilson, which is made up. The Paston Letters are without question among the most important historical documents to have survived the Middle Ages. The majority are held in the British Library, with some in the Bodleian, Magdalen College, Oxford, and Pembroke College, Cambridge. The suggestion in the novel that Lambert Simnel and Perkin Warbeck were sons of Richard III is pure speculation.

The Sons of York

The order is fictitious, along with their political wing. It is inspired by the legacy of the House of York and my own premise that Richard, 1st Duke of York, along with the young Earl of Warwick and the real Elizabeth of York continued to live, and later sired offspring.

Edmund of Langley did indeed exist, and references to him in the novel are accurate apart from any illegitimate family who lived in Wootton. The Duke of Monmouth was a real man and his rebellion against James II in 1685 did happen, as did the Glorious Rising in 1688 which toppled the king. Monmouth's connection with a Yorkist revival is fictitious. Incidentally, a Barghest is a genuine part of Yorkshire folklore, its appearance usually that of a hound or large dog.

The Princes in the Tower

Perhaps the greatest mystery in English history. Prince Edward, later Edward V, and Richard of Shrewsbury, 1st Duke of York, were the only biological sons of Edward IV and his queen, Elizabeth Woodville.

Following Edward IV's death on 9 April 1483, the ascension of Edward V should have been a formality. The prince was proclaimed King of England in London two days later, and Richard, Duke of Gloucester, the only surviving brother of the late king, was, according to most sources, named in Edward's last will as Protector of the Realm, much to the dismay of the Woodville faction. The will of 1483 does not survive, but the content is attested by many contemporary sources.

Richard and Edward were set to meet for the first time since Edward IV's death at Northampton on 29 April. However, during the course of the day, the new king moved on to Stony Stratford, located fourteen miles south in Buckinghamshire. Richard, accompanied by his loyal supporter the Duke of Buckingham, learned of the change of plan from the new king's uncle, Earl Rivers, and subsequently dined with him in Northampton. The following day, Richard arrested Edward V's Woodville-dominant retinue at Stony Stratford. The arrest and later execution of Earl Rivers, brother of Elizabeth Woodville, and Sir

Richard Grey, Edward V's half-brother from Elizabeth Woodville's first marriage, saw Elizabeth take her children into sanctuary. Richard and Edward entered London on 4 May and announced plans for the coronation for 24 June.

It is here things become misty. Edward's incarceration since 19 May might seem strange to many, but the act was nothing out of the ordinary. Stranger still were Richard's actions around 8 June, when plans for the coronation changed. It has been suggested that it was on this day that Richard learned for the first time, through Stillington, Bishop of Bath and Wells, of the precontract agreement between Edward IV and one Dame Eleanor Butler, nee Talbot, prior to Edward's marriage to Elizabeth Woodville. Most of the information here comes from the French chronicler Philippe de Commines, and is absent from all other chroniclers. On 9 June, a letter written by Simon Stallworth, servant of the Bishop of Lincoln, suggested business was taking place 'against the coronation'. There is evidence at that time that dialogue between the council and Elizabeth Woodville, in sanctuary at Westminster Abbey, had broken down, while the coronation was brought forward to 22 June. Further letters over the next two days confirmed Richard's problems with the Woodville faction, while a council was called for 13 June at the Tower. The council convened at 9 a.m., lasting some thirty minutes. When it reconvened at about 10:30, Richard's mood had apparently changed somewhat, and he seemed convinced of a plot against him. Lord Hastings was probably executed that day, allegedly for his involvement in a plot against Richard. Sometime between 16 and 21 June, Edward's coronation was postponed, allegedly to November, almost certainly due to the events of three days earlier. By 21 June, Richard, 1st Duke of York, is recorded as having come out of sanctuary and joined his brother at the Tower.

Exactly what happened next remains a mystery. The chronicler, Mancini, while still in England refers to how the two brothers were seen, shooting and playing, in the Tower garden (the Bloody Tower was named the Garden Tower at the time), yet they were apparently never seen again after mid July. After the executions of Earl Rivers and Sir Richard Grey on 25 June – the day of the aborted parliament – a meeting at Westminster occurred, led by the Duke of Buckingham, at which accusations against Edward IV's first marriage came to light. The following day the lords met at Baynard's Castle and petitioned Richard to take the throne. Eventually he accepted, and on 6 July he was crowned at Westminster.

While providing a detailed insight into the events at the time would be largely impossible without a second book, doing the same thing for what happened to the princes would be doubly difficult. At least one attempt at rescuing the princes occurred, the Sanctuary Plot in July, which may or may not have contributed to the princes' deaths. The Italian chronicler Dominic Mancini had left England before the end of July, and was already writing about the disappearance of the princes. While it can be confirmed the princes were still alive at that time, according to Thomas More, they were both shut up and isolated except for one person who served them, named William Slaughter or 'Black Will'. More suggests there may later have been three others, including one Miles Forrest – possibly the same man who was recorded as Keeper of the Wardrobe at Richard III's Barnard Castle in Yorkshire.

What fate awaited the princes comes down to the period of late August, early September. According to the chronicler Commines, the princes were murdered. How exactly, depends on the version. Commines refers to the Duke of Buckingham acting under orders from Richard. According to another source found in the College of Arms, they were murdered on the *vise* (advice/direction/undertaking) of the Duke of Buckingham, one of Richard's closest allies. Another manuscript, Ashmole ms 1448.60, refers to the prompting of Buckingham, while Jean Molinet suggests it was actually Buckingham.

Sadly, the opinions are far from consistent. The author of the second Croyland continuation is irritatingly silent on the matter, while More goes into far more detail. More's unfinished chronicle specifically states the murder to have occurred on 15 August, while Alison Weir suggests More was correct in everything bar the date, 3 September being the key event. More's detailed description includes a letter being given to Richard III's faithful servant Sir James Tyrell, ordering that the keys to the Tower be given to Tyrell for that night only. After this, More states it was one John Dighton and Miles Forrest who smothered the children in their beds. The chronicler Polydore Vergil also accuses Tyrell of the murder, though he mentions nothing of More's detail. Other versions tell of the murder being by the sword or else drowned in wine – Clarence was executed that way. On his return to England in 1502 and subsequent incarceration, Tyrell is alleged to have confessed involvement, later included in More's chronicle.

More is the only author who details what became of the bodies. He wrote that they were buried at the foot of the Tower stair and moved into the garden. In 1674 when work was being carried out at the Tower, the bodies of two small boys were found at the location where More claimed the princes had originally been buried. Also present was purple velvet rag, the colour of the monarch. Charles II was convinced the bodies were those of the princes, and they were henceforth interred in Westminster Abbey, in the urn the work of the great Sir Christopher Wren. DNA testing on the bodies in the 1930s confirmed the ages to be in the region of twelve and nine respectively.

In all likelihood the boys were indeed the sons of Edward IV. Yet until DNA testing takes place, the matter can never be put to rest. The recent discovery of Richard III's body under a car park in Leicester has generated new interest. Of Richard's appearance, the gaps have finally been filled in and legend and history can at last agree.

In all likelihood, the princes were murdered. In all likelihood, Richard was the man who was ultimately responsible. But he is not the only candidate.

Between Richard and Buckingham, and perhaps Tyrell, if indeed he was the man in question, there remains one even more compelling candidate whose need for the princes to be dead was even greater than Richard's. For Richard had the throne regardless. Though rebellion may one day have awaited him, for Henry Tudor the demise of the princes was pivotal. Thus leading to the even greater candidate.

Margaret Beaufort.

Titulus Regius

Titulus Regius was the only Act of Parliament of Richard's reign, dated 1484. In short, it allegedly confirms a marriage contract between Edward IV and Eleanor Butler, nee Talbot, prior to Edward's marriage to Elizabeth Woodville, thus making the marriage invalid. It also speculates of Woodville's use of witchcraft in luring Edward into marriage and also suggests Edward and George, Duke of Clarence, were themselves illegitimate and only Richard, Duke of Gloucester, was the true heir of Richard, 3rd Duke of York. The Act was repealed on the ascension of Henry VII and every copy ordered to be destroyed. Only one copy survived, transcribed into the Croyland Chronicle.

Its authenticity is purely dependent on the validity of the chronicle and the chronicler.

The Holbein Theory

The Hans Holbein connection was actually pointed out to me by a family friend, who once visited one of the nunneries in Belgium. From what I can gather from my research, researcher Jack Leslau first conceived the idea in the 1970s. Among other things, Leslau claimed that both Edward V and Richard, 1st Duke of York, survived and continued to live under the guises of one Sir Edward Guildford and one Dr John Clement.

Historically, there are far too many holes in this intriguing theory for it to hold water, but it is unquestionably a fascinating one. According to Leslau, Clement survived and entered the household of Thomas More and later married his foster daughter, Margaret Giggs.

The main problem here is age. Richard, 1st Duke of York, was about nine when he disappeared and would have been well into his fifties at the time the Holbein painting was done. The man in the painting, also mentioned in the novel, is far too young to be York. According to most biographies, albeit vague ones, Clement was born in 1500, and parts of his early years are documented, including his education at St Paul's. Richard of Shrewsbury was himself born in August 1473, making him twenty-seven at the time of Clement's alleged birth. While that alone should draw things to a conclusion, Clement's death in 1572 equally stretches a point. Though technically he could have lived to ninety-nine, it seems doubtful for a man living at a time when life expectancy was around forty.

That said, there are interesting observations, the best of which I have picked up on in my novel. John the rightful heir is mentioned in the main painting, standing beneath a fleur-de-lis. He is also standing at the highest point. Intriguingly, his identity has never been satisfactorily explained. While I congratulate Mr Leslau on some interesting points, Clement is too young to be Richard, 1st Duke of York. If there is any truth in the theory, surely Clement was his son.

On a sounder historical note, the painting in question by the famous Hans Holbein the Younger was lost in a fire in the 1700s; the copies by Rowland Lockey that survive are therefore all the more important. They were completed around 1593 and now hang at both Nostell Priory in Yorkshire and the National Portrait Gallery. Suggestion in the novel that there are multiple copies in existence is false. The suggestion that Elizabeth I in some way tampered with the paintings is also made up.

The other Prince in the Tower

Edward Plantagenet, 17th Earl of Warwick was the son of George Plantagenet, Duke of Clarence, and hence grandson of Richard, 3rd Duke of York. As Richard's grandson and a nephew of Edward IV, Edward himself had a claim to the throne and would have been next in line after Edward V and Richard of Shrewsbury. Edward was made Earl of Warwick shortly after his father's death in 1478 and was made a ward of Edward IV's stepson, Thomas Grey, 1st Marquess of Dorset. When Richard III died, the ten-year-old Warwick was taken to the Tower of London on Henry Tudor's orders. Though he had no role in the Lambert Simnel rebellion – Simnel himself had claimed to be the real Warwick – he was alleged to have been involved in a plot with Perkin Warbeck, which led to him being sentenced to death.

When Edward was executed, the House of Plantagenet came to an end in the male line!

The Duchy of Lancaster

I'm guessing this will be new to a lot of people, yet its importance cannot be overstated. To this day, the Duchy of Lancaster remains, along with the Crown Estate, the main form of income for the monarch. Held in a trust, it comprises some 46,000 acres of land including everything from farmland to historic buildings. While the history of the duchy can technically be traced back to Henry III and his granting of the Earldom of Lancaster to his son Edmund, including the forfeited Leicester estates previously owned by Simon de Montfort, the creation occurred when the new Lancastrian king Henry IV declared land of the Duchy of Lancaster, of which his father John of Gaunt was the first inheritor, should remain separate from the Crown and be automatically passed down to his male heirs. Edward IV confirmed this on taking the throne in 1461. Due to this distinction, it remained the personal inherited property of the monarch rather than the Crown.

The duchy is controlled by the Chancellor of the Duchy of Lancaster, a minister without portfolio, and remains to this day in the same hands. The monarch is entitled to the revenues of the estate, but not the capital.

The Duchy of Lancaster remains the main source of income for the monarch. The House of Lancaster continues to reside on the throne of England.

In 2010 the Duchy was estimated to be worth approximately £348 million. In 2013 that figure had risen to £429 million.

Acknowledgements

Researching this book has been an enormous pleasure, and I am grateful for the kindness and assistance of many people who I have met along the way. In particular, thanks go to all who offered their expertise and advice on my visits to the various places mentioned throughout the UK. A special thank you must also go to Pauline Nolet for her work as copy-editor.

Thank you for reading. As for every author, readers are the lifeblood of our existence. I hope you enjoyed the book. If so, please look out for my other titles:

Fiction

The Templar Agenda, 2011
The Larmenius Inheritance, 2013
The Plantagenet Vendetta, 2014
The Cromwell Deception, 2014
The Bordeaux Connection 2015
The Cortés Trilogy 2016

Non-fiction

Robin Hood: The Unknown Templar, Peter Owen 2009
Pity for the Guy – a biography of Guy Fawkes, Peter Owen 2010
The Gothic King – a biography of Henry III, Peter Owen 2013

For more on me, please check out my websites,
www.johnpauldavisauthor.com and www.theunknowntemplar.com.
There, you can also find a link to my blog.
All my books above are available on Amazon.

If you have any questions or you would like to get in touch, you can email me at jpd@theunknowntemplar.com. You can also follow me on Twitter @unknown_templar

Further Reading

For those of you who wish to learn more, I recommend the following titles:

Andrew, Christopher, *Defend the Realm – The Authorized History of MI5*, New York: Alfred A. Knopf, 2009

Ackroyd, Peter, *The History of England Volume 1 – Foundation*, London: Macmillan, 2011

Baldwin, David, *Richard III*, Stroud: Amberley Publishing, 2013

Carson, Annette, *Richard III: The Maligned King*, Stroud: The History Press, 2013

Carter, Alicia, *The Women of the Wars of the Roses: Elizabeth Woodville, Margaret Beaufort & Elizabeth of York*, 2013

Castor, Helen, *Blood and Roses, The Paston family and the Wars of the Roses*, London: Faber and Faber, 2005

Gristwood, Sarah, *Blood Sisters: The Women Behind the Wars of the Roses*, London: HarperCollins, 2013

Hancock, Peter. A., *Richard III and the Murder in the Tower*, Stroud: The History Press, 2011

Innes, Arthur D., *England under the Tudors*, London: Methuen, 1905

Jenkins, Simon, *A Short History of England*, London: Profile Books Ltd, 2012

Markham, Clements Robert, *Richard III: His life and character reviewed in the light of recent research*, London: Smith, Elder, and Co, 1906

Mortimer, Ian, *The Fears of Henry IV: The Life of England's Self-Made King*, London: Vintage, 2008

The Perfect King: The Life of Edward III, Father of the English Nation, London: Vintage, 2008

Penn, Thomas, *Winter King – The Dawn of Tudor England*, London and New York: Penguin, 2012

Weir, Alison, *Elizabeth of York*, London: Jonathan Cape, 2013

Lancaster and York: The Wars of the Roses, London: Vintage, 2009

The Princes in the Tower, London: Pimlico, 1993

Printed in Great Britain
by Amazon

46801638R00271